'Miss Catchpole, forward!' boomed Hezekiah. Damn the girl, she looked ready to faint, hunched up like that, with her hands clasped in front of her, and her big eyes like two black raisins in a plum duff. He turned with a professional grimace to the matron: 'Miss Catchpole will see to you, madam.'

There was not much hope of service with this one, the woman thought; the girl looked too seedy to lift a cotton reel, let alone serve material. However, before many minutes were out, Kitty had borne several rolls of cloth to the counter, and one to the door for the advantages of daylight. It was difficult to do too convincing a totter with bales; they were rather heavy for play-acting.

Yes, Miss Catherine Catchpole was in general what Hezekiah would have called an acquisition, had the word been part of his normal vocabulary. Most days, she could sell more yards of dress material than any girl the Skinners had yet housed under their leaky roof. On good days, also, the girl held herself well; she was a pretty creature, with the sort of soft brown hair which made a fellow long to pull out the pins and let it tumble down. And this Kitty had a neck that was really something; it led a man's eyes lower. Hezekiah turned quickly into the large store cupboard, and rearranged a few cardboard boxes.

THE QUALITY

AMY HOLLINS

ARROW BOOKS

Arrow Books Limited
17–21 Conway Street, London W1P 6JD

An imprint of the Hutchinson Publishing Group

London Melbourne Sydney Auckland
Johannesburg and agencies throughout
the world

First published 1985
© Amy Hollins 1985

Set in Baskerville by
D. P. Media Limited, Hitchin, Hertfordshire

Printed and Bound in Great Britain by
Anchor Brendon Limited, Tiptree, Essex

ISBN 0 09 939700 5

THE
QUALITY

SOME of the metal thimbles were so minute it seemed they could fit no finger larger than a toddler's. All were a bright silver outside and a dull gold inside, and they made a thin music when shifted about in their tray. Kitty forced her little finger into one of the smallest; it looked ridiculous, and pinched quite painfully. With her head on one side, she examined the capped finger, and wagged it once or twice; she tried wagging it while keeping the third finger still. A realization that she was being watched made her wrench off the thimble and replace it among the rest; before Mr Skinner could decide to cross the floor, she had resumed the fussy counter-dusting expected of her at 8.45 a.m.

Not that Kitty Catchpole was usually at the Haberdashery end of this counter. Some time ago, she had been promoted to the far end, with its inset edge of brass ruler, and its drawers full of paper patterns. Here, she spent most of her working day, humping down bale after bale from the shelves behind her, so that the exacting ladies of the town might choose their lengths of taffeta, slipper satin, muslin plain or sprigged, and the like. She had become almost as adept as Mr Truscott, that older and more depressed individual at the counter opposite, who, when he was not selling Everything for the Gentleman, would beat out a regular tattoo, winding or unwinding his bales of serge, tweed, curtain velvet and other heavyweights.

On this particular morning, Tish Kelly (Haberdashery and Lingerie) was lying whey-faced on her bed in the attic dormitory. The four beds had been made; she lay partly dressed, with her outdoor coat for top cover, though this was not much use against the winter blast from the open window. A piece of cord, held by rusty wall hooks, stretched across the room; on this, one grey skirt and a white cotton petticoat were swinging in the draught; they smelled strongly of Watson's Matchless Cleanser Soap For All Purposes. Any moment now, Mrs Skinner would be up those stairs, and Tish would be told to put on her things, wet or dry, and get herself behind the shop counter.

It was the Skinners' fault, anyway. If they had laid out a few shillings on stair lino, Tish would never have tripped on that frayed bit at the first tread, and she would have been spared her crash down the entire flight, her sousing from the slop bucket, and the odd twist of a boot that refused to straighten. It was still twisted, with the injured foot inside it; Kitty had undone the laces, but Tish could not bear to have the boot pulled off. Kitty had been kind. When the Skinner was yelling about carelessness and filth, and who was going to get the sack if that mess reached where the carpet began, Kitty had told her a thing or two. Remembering this, Tish managed a smile: 'If she's broken a leg, you'll have some explaining to do,' was the beginning of it, followed by 'We don't all sit on mahogany and blue roses,' and ending with Kitty's expressed wish that the Turkey Axminster would be a write-off. That was as far as she got before Mrs Skinner fetched her a clout that sent her spinning. Kitty was not very big; big or not, she had half carried Tish upstairs, while Eliza and Mary ran for mops and pails in answer to Hezekiah Skinner's bellowing.

That was, in brief, the morning's pre-breakfast drama, which had continued to some extent throughout the meal, for those who were privileged to eat it; only Eliza Heggy and Mary Gibbs were allowed their bread and porridge, washed down with lukewarm tea. Kitty and Tish were left to go hungry, the one for her insolence, the other for not using her eyes. At the time, neither girl had felt she could face food, but now that the shop doors were about to be opened by Mr Skinner, Kitty's naturally healthy appetite was creeping back. She hoped her stomach would rumble loudly enough to be heard by her employer; he prided himself on the good breeding of his lady assistants, knowing in his heart they were no better than his wife, whom he kept as far as possible from the customers. Rumbles of any bodily nature would cause him some concern, but an assistant's stomach rumbles, accompanied by a pinched and hungry-looking face, would hardly improve the Skinners' public reputation. Therefore Kitty was pleased to see a well-fed matron march across the threshold as the doors opened and make her way to the centre island of dress materials.

'Miss Catchpole, forward!' boomed Hezekiah. Damn the girl, she looked ready to faint, hunched up like that, with her hands clasped in front of her, and her big eyes like two black raisins in a plum duff. 'Miss Catchpole!' he repeated, more sharply. That was better; she was moving, if not very smartly. He turned with a professional grimace to the matron: 'Miss Catchpole will see to you, madam.'

There was not much hope of service with this one, the woman thought; the girl looked too seedy to lift a cotton reel, let alone serve material. However, before many minutes were out, Kitty had borne several rolls of cloth to the counter, and one to the door for the advantages of

daylight. It was difficult to do too convincing a totter
with bales; they were rather heavy for play-acting. The
exercise brought colour to her cheeks, and the effort of
selling drove rumbles out of her stomach's mind. Kitty
got on with the job, and with those which succeeded it,
as she always did, and Hezekiah smoothed his sandy
moustache with thumb and second finger, starting
from its middle parting, slowly down and out.

Yes, Miss Katherine Catchpole was in general what
Hezekiah would have called an acquisition, had the
word been part of his normal vocabulary. Most days,
she could sell more yards of dress material than any girl
the Skinners had yet housed under their leaky roof. The
little brass cylinder would be constantly singing along
its overhead wire, impelled at speed by Miss Catchpole's efficient tug, to fill Mrs Skinner's register
inside the glass-walled cash desk. On good days, also,
the girl held herself well; she was a pretty creature, with
the sort of soft brown hair which made a fellow long to
pull out the pins and let it tumble down. She had her
days when she could look pasty, like this morning, but
what woman didn't? There was nothing wrong with
that complexion when it had a bit of glow in it. And
unlike Jinny Skinner, whose thick neck had never been
a strong point, even when Hezekiah first thought he
was in love, this Kitty had a neck that was really
something; it led a man's eyes lower. Hezekiah turned
quickly into the large store cupboard, and rearranged a
few cardboard boxes.

When he emerged, he saw that Kitty was standing in
front of the cash pulpit. Each assistant, except Mr
Truscott, had an appointed time for cocoa in the morning. Mr Truscott never drank the stuff, but when the
wall clock showed 10.30, he would nip into the back
yard, whether he was serving a customer or not, soon to

reappear, patting his lips with a gent's white hem-stitched handkerchief in pure linen (seconds). This routine enraged both Hezekiah and his good wife, but there was not much they could do about it. Over the years, the habit had persisted; it was too late now to stamp it out. Besides, not many men would work for as little as Truscott did and remain honest; and he was always back on the shop floor in half the time it would have taken to drink a hot cup of cocoa. Hezekiah was particularly irritated whenever Truscott left a customer stranded at the counter, for then he himself would have to take over, not to help Truscott, but to keep him at arm's length with a 'See to those shelves, Mr Truscott!' until the man's breath had cleared. With the girls, it was different; each one came quietly to the raised cash desk and stood looking upwards for a sign from – as Tish put it – Lady Muck herself. When Jinny Skinner deigned to notice the submissive figure waiting below, and only after she had jabbed a fair number of receipts on to a bill-spike, or had removed a f. n. of rs. off a b.-s., she would give a regal nod of the head. The lady assistant could then make for the kitchen, there to boil up a drop of water for her mug of cocoa. The modest ration of milk had to be shared with great care. The fourteen-year-old Eliza discovered this to her cost when she once tried to make her drink more palatable.

Of all her functions, cocoa-permission was Jinny Skinner's favourite; afternoon-tea-permission came nowhere near it, because by that hour Jinny was invariably too worn out, too flustered, or too indifferent to give a sound performance. On this occasion, she was about to experience even more gratification than usual; gazing stonily on the uplifted face of that impudent young hussy, Catchpole, she pointed in the direction of Kitty's counter. 'Get back to your work,' she ordered.

The message shot up and over the glass sides. Mr Truscott's cutting scissors stopped in the course of a long run, and jagged as they restarted; the one or two customers turned to stare at Mrs Skinner. Kitty strode back to Haberdashery, to attend to a young woman who dared to ask for sewing needles. Not a word passed Kitty's lips; the brass moneybox tore across the wire, to come to a quivering halt above Mrs Skinner's right ear. The packet of needles was dealt to the customer like a playing card, while some of the returned change rolled about her feet.

This would not do. Hezekiah was deeply alarmed. Jinny had never been endowed with much common sense, but this was going too far. He was not sorry for Kitty Catchpole; he merely wanted her to stay on her feet, and to man two sections until after dinner, when no doubt the Kelly girl would be once more on the job. You did not keep an assistant going by starvation measures, nor could the contempt in Catchpole's face be considered good for business.

He rushed to collect the scattered coins, and to escort the affronted young customer to the door, whipping a card of bodkins from Haberdashery on the way. He took the needles from her, and put them with the bodkins inside a paper bag; this he offered to her, with the compliments of the management and apologies for the little spot of bother – never known before – which would certainly never happen again. Slightly mollified, the customer hoped it never would, and casting a glare back at Kitty, she sailed out of the Bridgemouth Drapery Bazaar, Ladies and Gents a Speciality.

'Miss Catchpole, I will see you in the dining room!' said Hezekiah. 'Dress materials, madam? Mr Truscott, forward!' Her husband marched purposefully past the cash desk, without so much as a glance at Jinny Skinner, who was sitting there like a trapped ferret. He made straight through the archway, and called, 'Miss Heggy, take over for Miss Catchpole when Mr Truscott has seen to his client.' Mary Gibbs was behind a revolving stand of christening robes and matinée jackets. 'Miss Gibbs, attend to Gowns and Millinery *and* Baby Linen.'

There is nothing more exciting to the downtrodden than to see some other poor devil land in the soup, and Kitty was definitely providing the two younger girls with something to tremble over. Not knowing the minute, however, when the tornado might swerve in their own direction, Eliza and Mary replied to their boss's directives with a hasty, 'Yes, sir.' He swept off left to the cramped kitchen, which he had so recently dignified with the title of 'dining room'.

While she had the kitchen to herself, Kitty wasted no time. She opened the upper green cupboard in the fireplace alcove; on its bottom shelf stood the cracked breadboard, with a few chunks of cut bread, left over from breakfast, which were to be served later with the midday dinner. Mrs Jacks, who came daily, and who 'did' everywhere except the shop floor and the girls' top floor – when she was not engaged in cooking the remarkable fare provided – was hard at work in the scullery, peeling potatoes and chopping cabbage. Already there was the familiar smell of butcher's bones as they simmered by the grate-bars, to produce a pale yellow liquid blobbed with grease; under different circumstances this might have become a respectable glue.

Kitty could take only three pieces of bread; indeed, to have taken two might have been wiser, but she risked the extra corner of crust, ramming it all into the pockets of her skirt. Mary had put the tin kettle in the hearth – old Mrs Jacks must have been on the rampage in her

scullery – the milk and cocoa were also on the girls'
dining table. She had just closed the cupboard doors
and picked up the kettle when Mr Skinner appeared in
the doorway. Kitty rocked the kettle gently; it needed
no more water, so she placed it on the trivet and swung
this over the coals, where it soon began to wheeze.

'Yes, well . . .' began Hezekiah with the bluster of
authority.

Standing up from the grate, and wiping her hand on
the knitted kettle holder, the senior lady assistant
directed a cool gaze on him.

'You may have your cocoa this time, Miss Catchpole,' he went on, recovering himself, 'but I must warn
you that any more of your nonsense, and you won't get
off so lightly.'

Kitty raised her eyebrows, and the corners of her
mouth drooped sardonically. She scooped cocoa into
the two enamel mugs on the table.

'Nobody said anything about cocoa for that Miss
Kelly,' he snapped.

'We can't neglect her, can we? We don't want the
doctor in if she gets complications. A cup of cocoa
might just do the trick.' Her eyes flashed at him as she
reached towards the noisy kettle.

But it was the line of her lovely neck that did it.
Hezekiah flung himself three paces forward to get his
hands on her blouse. It was over in seconds. He had let
out a yelp of agony, and was holding on to the mantelpiece, belching heavily. Mrs Skinner was in the doorway.

'And what is going on here, may I ask?' she said
tartly.

Kitty was all concern. 'Mr Skinner was getting the
kettle off for me, ma'am, but it slipped, and I think he
got some of the water.' She tucked the front of her
blouse inside her waistband.

'My leg!' Hezekiah howled, holding the trouser crease away from his shin.

Mrs Skinner fairly snarled at him. 'Put a dab of Vaseline on it,' she said. 'Some of us have to see to the shop.' She raised her voice: 'Mrs Jacks, you are very late this morning with the tea!'

'Ay, well, I'll be bringing it in, if you give us breathing space,' answered that redoubtable female, from the depths of her domain.

Mrs Skinner darted another withering look at Hezekiah. 'You'd better have your tea in here, if it's all that bad.'

'It's easing off,' he said stoically. 'That Vaseline will come off yellow on my trousers.'

'Put your old ones on, and leave your pants off. You'll be sky-blue-pink if you don't get something on that. Mr Skinner's tea and mine, then, Mrs Jacks! And get a move on,' she added, as she went to leave the kitchen. Hideous imprecations rose from the scullery, which she chose to ignore; enough had gone wrong this morning. Before she passed into the shop corridor, however, she did notice Kitty Catchpole was stealing carefully out of the second kitchen door with two full mugs of cocoa in her hands.

'And where do you think you're going with those?' Jinny yelled.

The fact that she was carrying the two drinks saved Kitty from another smack round the head. With a threatening, 'I'll teach you, my girl, before you're much older!' Jinny Skinner hurried back to her post.

Reinstalled, and at last sipping her tea, that scourge of the assistants inspected the shop scene spread before her. Things were never very busy from Monday to

Friday, most of the trade going to Masons' Emporium, that much larger establishment in Cable Street. 'Skinners' Place', as it was known in the neighbourhood, had always been a Saturday shop, because of its proximity to the bustling Saturday market. Jinny looked with distaste into the dark depths of her cup; the tea was stewed. Jacks was another who would go, as soon as a cheaper replacement could be found. It was the Skinners' theory that their daily 'housekeeper' brewed a decent cup of tea for herself, then stood the brown teapot on the hob until she was ready to pour out theirs. Caustic criticism got them nowhere with Mrs Jacks, who was a distinguished product of the Like It or Lump It school.

Jinny sighed. The Bridgemouth Drapery Bazaar had come a long way, mind you, since she first put her hand to it, and that was largely owing to the know-how she had brought with her from the family business, four doors up the street, on the opposite side. Its full legend was spelled out in gold leaf: *Atkinson and Atkinson & Co. / Coachbuilders and Signwriters. / By Appointment*. To speak frankly, there was never any necessity for an appointment, but they considered such a warning obligatory. Her bachelor Uncle Charles had supplied every trade handcart in the locality. Jinny's father, William, had seen to the painting and lettering, with the finest of lining-out and the most elegant of scrollwork – all very eye-catching, as were the cryptic clues like ▬▬, which he was frequently called upon to produce or restore in public places. Her mother, Martha, had ruled both men with unsparing tongue. Jinny's four brothers, in their turn, had entered the firm, enlarging it to a position of solid eminence in Albert Road West.

By contrast – and she sneered openly in the direction of Hezekiah, who at this point was limping across to

greet Mrs Willey, wife of the Mayor-Elect, Councillor
Ernest Willey – by contrast, the Bridgemouth Drapery
Bazaar had been small beer. Old Josiah Skinner and
his wife, Ellen, had risen from their remnants stall in
the market by a process of extreme caution, which
included regular Sunday attendance at the Scotch
Kirk, and the practice of total abstention, to keep
Hezekiah without siblings. With a sockful of savings,
they had moved into no. 15, when Maggie Dooley's
father had been forcibly removed to the Institution.
The premises had reeked of ancient shellfish, unspeak-
able measuring cans and vinegar. But for Atkinson and
Atkinson, this Skinner venture could not have got off
the ground. William, in particular, had such sympathy
for that poor beggar, Josiah, he refused to charge the
going rate for first-class paintwork, inside and out.
Little did he foresee the day when the same old swine
would pay twice the price to a fancy firm from over the
water to clean up no. 17, after knocking the two shops
into one. Right when Jinny and Hezekiah were doing
their courting, too! A fine bust-up it was, followed by a
chill wedding at St James's of all places, with neither
family speaking to the other. She had thought Hezekiah
was different. He had long since owned the business,
and time had long since despatched all four parents,
but Hezekiah had no Christian charity in him; he had
never allowed Uncle Charles over the doorstep, not
even at Christmas, or any one of her brothers, either.
These days, Hezekiah could no longer pay any outside
firm for decoration and repairs; rather than sink his
pride to ask the present Atkinsons for an estimate, he
preferred to wait until the walls caved in.

Meanwhile, that firm could do without the Skinners'
patronage. As Masons' Emporium expanded, so did
their own prospects improve; the condition of the

Drapery Bazaar was the last thing the brothers worried
about, even though it might affect Jinny Atkinson that
was. Appealing to Hezekiah was a waste of Jinny's
breath; he thought customers ignored items like peeling
paintwork and cracked plaster. God knew Jinny had
done everything in her power – totting up accounts
until well past midnight, handling girls who were often
up to no good, adding tone to the shop floor by insisting
on departments, each with its name on a framed board
that dangled from the ceiling. True, Millinery was as
yet only two and a half yards of counter, with a spotted
pier-glass on its wall, and Baby Linen operated from a
baize-covered parlour table and the one rotating stand,
but Rome wasn't built in a day. No one else but Jinny
Skinner could make a go of a shop this size, with four
girls and a dodderer like Truscott. If only she had
married a man like herself! Instead she had to get stuck
with a fellow who could never keep his hands off the
female assistants. Like now, for example, when she had
caught him larking with that faggot . . . Pretty quick
with the excuses, that one – clever with the kettle, too,
but not quite fast enough with the blouse. Or deliberately slow with the blouse? He wasn't able to get far
with the Catchpole, though, not the way he did with her
predecessor, Maude Gates, the senior assistant who
had made his nose bleed. For nothing, he said. Suddenly, for no reason at all, a girl hurls herself at him,
and nearly does for his nose! With a face set with
hatred, Jinny Skinner's arms worked up and down like
a Dutch doll's, to attend to the cash termini. Her husband leaned as majestically as his condition allowed
against Mr Truscott's counter. To his great surprise
and relief, he saw Miss Katherine Catchpole appear at
that instant on the floor, accompanied by her crony,
Miss Laetitia Kelly, who was using one flat foot and

one heel to hobble as far as Haberdashery. Consulting
his silver turnip, Hezekiah checked the shop clock; he
would be glad to close for dinner – an hour and a
quarter to go. His leg was giving him hell; for two pins,
he would take to his bed for the afternoon, and Jacks
could bring his dinner up on a tray. Jinny could see how
she liked that.

When Kitty took the cocoa upstairs to Tish, she found
her in tears. By the time they had drunk some of that
warm, gritty concoction, both were feeling more cheerful. Nobody ever dunked bread at breakfast: Mr and
Mrs Skinner, although they sat apart from the staff at a
collapsible wall-table, maintained a close watch on the
assistants' table manners. Dunking they condemned as
vulgar, nibbling with refinement at their own slices of
bread and butter with their own boiled eggs. At some
breakfasts, the girls' small chunks of bread were so dry
and hard that their teeth squeaked on them. This, too,
was a vulgarity. Young Mary Gibbs, whose chalky
teeth were not her best feature, had broken what Mrs
Skinner termed 'a high tooth' on a piece of this bread,
and had lived in terror of it ever since. It was stale not
merely because it had spent too many days in the
kitchen cupboard; it was stale because it was bought
stale on Saturdays, at Abe Jenkin's on Daisy Street.
Abe and Mrs Jacks had a good laugh about it, once a
week. He swore he never knew anyone as fond of bread
pudding as the Skinners, that being Mrs Skinner's
explanation for the standing order. Had she guessed
that Abe was in full possession of the facts, she would
have fired Mrs Jacks without further hesitation,
replacement or no replacement, and transferred her
custom to Whittle's in Ducie Street. In the privacy of

the attic, the two girls dunked their bread, and sucked it noisily.

Tish's skirts were still swaying gently on the line. They were as wet as ever.

'They might have dried better in the rain,' Kitty said ruefully. 'You'll catch your death if you put them on. Anyway, can you walk?'

Tish got off the bed, and collapsed back on to it, at the first step forward. 'Holy Mary, Mother of God,' she gasped, coming, as she did, from a devout family. 'Would you say it's broke?'

'Could be. It's an awful size; nearly bursting your boot, by the looks. Can you move your toes?'

'Just about. Does that mean it's all right?'

'I don't know.'

With great willpower, Tish got to her feet again, and staggered to the washstand. 'I'll have to get down-stairs,' she said fiercely. 'I'll have to. She'll throw me out.'

'Let her try,' said Kitty, 'that's all.'

'She threw Maudie Gates out, when she sprained her wrist.'

'Only because she sprained it on Skinnybug's nose. You've not kicked anybody. Pity you didn't. By acci-dent, of course, like me with the water.'

'What water? I tipped the bucket.'

'Not that water,' Kitty told her. 'Boiling water.'

Tish was horrified to hear of Hezekiah Skinner's advances in the kitchen, and of the way they were foiled. 'But you might have poured it over yourself!' she exclaimed.

'Well, I didn't.'

'I bet they know you did it on purpose.'

Kitty shrugged. 'She saw enough of my blouse hang-ing out. That's what counts. She didn't really cop him

with Maudie, so he got away with it. You can't put that
wet stuff on – I've told you!'

Tish was feeling the skirts, and glumly coming to the
same conclusion.

'You'll have to wear your best dress,' Kitty suggested.

'I can't put that on; it's got bits of lace.'

'Only round the neck,' Kitty argued.

'But she won't have us in the shop in dresses; you
know she won't.'

'She won't have you there in your drawers, either.'
Kitty pulled out her own best underskirt from their
small chest. She knew that Tish had only one petticoat.
'Lucky this is a taped waist,' she said.

'I'm not as fat as all that!'

'Tell you what, Tish – Eliza has another skirt. Let's
be having it!' And she produced a clean grey topskirt
from the chest shared by Eliza and Mary.

'I daresn't take that!' Tish protested. 'She'll play
Harry. You know Eliza!'

Kitty slipped the white waist petticoat over Tish's
head and tied the tapes. She continued with Eliza's
skirt. The waistband was a tighter fit than expected,
but at least the placket did not bulge open. 'Should
be perfect, if you don't breathe,' she pronounced,
twitching the skirt to fall as it should from the waist.
'Let's go.'

'There'll be blue murder with that Eliza Heggy. You
see if there isn't!' Tish said unhappily, as she descended
the narrow stairs like a war casualty.

Tish was not far wrong. But for the sanctity of the shop
floor, she would have been stripped there and then of
her borrowed skirt by its outraged owner.

'You wait, Tish Kelly! Just you wait! I'm telling Mrs Skinner.'

Hezekiah stopped leaning against Mr Truscott's counter and stood poised to lurch into the fray. Tish held on to the front rack, which displayed dress shields, shoulder pads, buckram interfacings and suspenders.

Kitty fixed her eyes on the gas chandelier and sang some rare incantatory lines under her breath: 'Teller, smeller, pitcher down the cellar . . .'

'Mrs Skinner, ma'am, that Miss Kelly has got my new skirt on!'

Jinny stared down on Eliza with the utmost hostility, which effectively disguised any specific rapport she might have had with the girl. 'Kindly remember you are on duty, Miss Heggy. We are all on duty.'

'Miss Heggy!' roared Hezekiah. 'You are required in Gowns. Forward!'

Kitty waited for Eliza in the back yard before they went in for dinner. It was still raining as she stood on the rough path, her gaberdine cape over her head. As Eliza emerged from the glory-hole, the older girl grabbed her by the scruff of the neck and propelled her towards the kitchen quarters.

'One more word out of you about that damned skirt, Eliza Heggy, and I slit your gizzard. You got that?'

'You're not allowed to swear, Kitty Catchpole,' Eliza choked.

'I'll swear *you*! I'll rub your dirty little snout on the wall till it drops off!' They had reached the house wall by this time. Kitty's cape was lying on the ground, which did not improve Eliza's chances. 'Now I've ruined my cloak, thanks to you!' she blazed, pinching Eliza's neck harder. 'See you remember what I said, or you're for it.'And she released the whimpering Miss Heggy to rescue the soiled cape from the mud.

'It is going to be the rule in future,' announced Mrs Skinner, as the lady assistants unravelled used string after dinner, 'that any young lady – ' she paused to emphasize the designation, 'in our employment has *two* day skirts *as a minimum*. I hope I make myself clear. Naturally, we all know she must have two of everything else, as well, but that has always been a rule at the Drapery Bazaar.'

Eliza Heggy cast a spiteful glance at Tish; like Kitty, she knew Tish had only one underskirt, which was washed and dried regularly during three seasons, but infrequently in the fourth.

'It has come to our notice,' Mrs Skinner went on, her voice becoming increasingly imperious, 'that three of you don't know what it is to have a change of topskirt . . .' She looked in turn at Kitty, Tish and Mary.

That rotten little snitch had been talking, then, thought Kitty.

'Miss Catchpole, do you possess a second skirt?'

'I've a second underskirt.'

'But you've no second topskirt?'

'No.'

'No, *what*?'

'No, ma'am.'

'I should think so. Miss Kelly, I believe you had to borrow the skirt belonging to a newcomer, before you could appear downstairs this morning?'

Tish admitted to the crime.

'And Miss Gibbs – did you bring a second topskirt with you?'

'No, ma'am. I didn't know you had to.'

'You didn't know you had to,' Mrs Skinner repeated.
'Well, you know now. You all know now. Miss Catchpole, you will take a simple skirt pattern from stock,
and cut out three lengths in grey cotton poplin. Make
sure you use no more than two or three pins, and fold
the pattern exactly as you found it before you put it
back. If it needs pressing, use a *cool* iron.'

'Yes, Mrs Skinner.' Good God, was she going to give
them something for nothing?

'You will take one reel of grey sewing thread between
you; two, if necessary; and you will make yourselves an
extra skirt each.' Jinny Skinner paused again, assessing
her effect on the four girls, three looking flushed,
perhaps eager, and one looking sour. 'The cost of materials will be stopped from your wages at one shilling a
week, and there will be no commission on sales until the
skirts are paid for. Miss Catchpole, tell Mr Truscott to
open the shop; Mr Skinner has to rest his leg this
afternoon.'

Miss Heggy's rear expressed the pleasure she felt, as
she waltzed back to Gowns and Millinery. This would
learn them, taking things without asking, and her the
only apprentice, when they were getting proper wages!
Her mum didn't make good clothes for the lowest of the
low to wear; her dad didn't pay out good money for
Eliza to mix with thieves, for that's what it was –
thieving. She'd a good mind to tell her dad to take her
away. Everybody said Skinners' Place wasn't up to
much, anyhow; he should have paid a bit more, and got
her into Masons'.

'No spivs on sales, either,' Tish muttered in despair
to Kitty, as they waited behind their counter. Her ankle
ached abominably, and she felt she would never smile
again. They would be losing a halfpenny for every £1 in
takings, which meant a serious setback.

'She'll be sorry,' Kitty whispered back, moving to her own end of the counter.

Compared with some establishments in and around 1908, the Skinners' Drapery Bazaar had conditions of labour which were no worse than elsewhere; in certain respects, they might have been considered better. After supper, for instance, which was always a cup of Bovril, the lady assistants were free to stay in the kitchen, huddled in the winter months around the hearth. No coal was left by that hour in the gaping iron scuttle, but sprinkles of coal dust, with careful raking of embers, could keep the fire warm until bedtime.

The girls supplied little treats for themselves, such as a handful of windfalls, or 2 ounces of Packer's Chocolate Chewing Nuts. These last were shaken on to the table, and shared out before their coating could smear, which it rarely did in the cold months; any oddments were allocated by heads or tails. Whenever it was Eliza Heggy's turn to buy the sweets, they arrived at the table in an even number. Possibly for this reason, she was for changing to Jap Nuggets, but the others would not hear of it; Jap Nuggets were too big, so that you had too few. In any case, they were twice the price. In the height of summer, the group might go abundance on lemonade powder, preferring a ha'porth of fizz to the slow chew.

One significant effect of the overall decline in Bridgemouth's prosperity was the increasing number of smaller shops which had decided to close on a Wednesday afternoon. For many a proprietor, the savings in fuel and light, and often in wages, made this 'half holiday' an attractive proposition, especially where it might be regarded publicly as a humanitarian gesture. The Bazaar had recently adopted the idea, to save on some overheads, and to give half its staff and both employers a mid-week break. It had become Hezekiah's theory that a broken-winded horse won no races. Accordingly, an assistant had every alternate Wednesday afternoon and evening off, working this rota in twos – two girls on, two girls off. Those girls on duty had to attend to the dressing and inside cleaning of the shop windows. One of the two off duty had a further job to see to, before she was meant to enjoy her freedom. She was to assume the guise of casual shopper, and spy out the land at Masons' Emporium, since that store would be keeping its doors wide open every weekday, until forced in four years' time to toe the early closing line. Since the young lady in question was quickly recognizable as a Skinner spy, the reception was inevitably unfriendly; she would be hounded from one department to another, and bombarded with sneering offers of service from Masons' mobile floorwalkers. If she could spot any goods marked at cheaper prices than the Bazaar's, she was then faced with the extra chore of changing the Bazaar tickets, even those in the windows, on the following day. It was a scheme all set to fail through the natural reluctance of its operators; it was also bound to attract retaliation of a higher order from the Emporium.

Sunday afternoon at Skinners' Place was always free, and any girl who wished to attend evening service at the Scotch Kirk might do so, with special permission. Hezekiah and Jinny never went to evening service, so the assistants' seeming passion for religious observance was not to be wondered at. Very often, they walked the streets of Bridgemouth together. At other times, they would meet young men by prior arrangement; on bitter nights, they were sometimes glad to enter the church to keep warm.

Attendance at the Scotch Kirk's morning service was compulsory if you worked at Skinners' Place; even a member of staff with curious religious affiliations, like Miss Kelly, had to fall in with the rest. When, on her arrival three years ago, Tish had announced that she was a Roman Catholic, Mrs Skinner had told her not to be absurd; she could put cotton wool in her ears, and stand up and sit down with the rest of the congregation; if that proved too much for her convictions, she could pack her bag and go. Tish was too frightened to confess this, either in a church of her own denomination, or in her letters home; her family needed her slender contributions. She was sure God would turn a blind eye, especially of late, when he learned her commission had been axed; he would most certainly be sorry about that, whatever the sin.

A solid phalanx in pew no. 7 was as essential to the Skinners' shaky trade as was the polished florin, which Hezekiah put without exception on the rim of the collection plate. Something like twenty per cent of the leghorns in evidence at the Scotch Kirk had been bought at the Bazaar, and no matter how carefully these were stored during the week in black tissue paper, or refurbished with this year's trimmings from Millinery, Jinny Skinner could date each hat to within a month, either way. That went for suits and costumes, also; many a pinstripe, or herringbone, had been banged loose, smoothed out and cut to length on Mr Truscott's counter. Mrs Bellingham-Smith might have been less delighted to discover a 44-inch corset immediately to hand in Lingerie, had she been aware that for some Sundays past Mrs Skinner was noting her 45½-inch sag.

Therefore, attendance at the Scotch Kirk was to the Drapery Bazaar as Vitamin D is to rickets; it reinforced a threatened structure. And while their employers' presence could be a restriction, nevertheless, in an age of so little cheap entertainment, that morning get-together was better for Kitty and her colleagues than nothing. For certain people, even among the young, it provided the spiritual comfort they needed constantly, so – for one reason or another – morning service was not a penance.

It was well accepted, for instance, that while it might be unusual to see a lonely young sailor at evensong, such a lad would occasionally try his arm, or tip a meaningful wink, in the morning assembly. It could be that he was mindful of his religious upbringing, or desperate to escape from all-male company, but fearful of the lasses who walked the dockland; and so, spruce in blue rig, and bell-bottomed, he would come to this red-brick church. With his gently rolling gait, as if the aisle led to the captain's cabin, he generally made for a middle pew to consider the possibilities. He often expected to excite the attention of several young ladies, if only by the strangeness of his very ordinary face; with luck, he might signal a fancy for one of them during 'Shall we Gather at the River?' In this way, in common with all churches and chapels, the Scotch Kirk performed a function not necessarily anticipated by its founders.

Mary Gibbs had so far put in eighteen months' attendance at this Kirk when, to her gratification and his, a bristle-cropped leading seaman took his seat one Sunday morning, in front of pew no. 7, and made it his business to catch her eye. He sat a bit to one side of the Bazaar contingent, and Mary was nearest to him, as Eliza Heggy was to point out later. He did not appear to be the winking sort, confining himself instead to a grin, under cover of the physical exercises demanded by the service. She, for her part, answered with a half-smile dictated not only by shyness, but also by the gap left by that missing eye-tooth. She decided she would hang back when the service came to an end, to give him a chance to speak to her. But while all the parishioners made their unhurried exit, and Bunny Harris was shuffling close behind Mary, he said nothing. However, when she drew near to the icy porch, she felt an arm around her waist, and the light touch of paper against her gloved hand. She took the proffered missionary leaflet, and read it as she passed the Reverend Andrew Macpherson. GIVE THEM THE WORD, it said. *See you saturday 6 pm at ferry Bunny Harris you got lovly eyes*.

'That's a fat lot of good,' wailed Mary to the others in the bedroom, as they hung their coats in the cupboard, and laid their hats on the beds. 'I suppose he couldn't know I work in a shop. Six on a Saturday night! He must be joking.'

'Stupid, if you ask me,' said Eliza.

'He's got to make a beginning somewhere,' Kitty said encouragingly. 'He writes nicely.'

Mary was not to be encouraged. 'He'll not turn up again.'

'I shouldn't think he will,' Eliza agreed.

'Oh, you shut up, Eliza Heggy,' flared Tish. 'You're only jealous!'

'Me, jealous? With teeth like he's got?'

Tish had not seen the young man's teeth; from the back and side, he had looked quite presentable. She was glad for Mary's sake, but she wished someone would slip a missionary leaflet to her one Sunday.

'There's nothing wrong with his teeth,' lied Kitty, who had taken a good look at the lad. 'Nothing that can't be fixed. Anyhow, they're whiter than some people's round here. You might bump into him this afternoon, Mary.'

Eliza kept her lips tightly closed.

'I might,' said Mary. 'So might pigs fly.'

Sunday dinner at Skinners' Place was always a let-down. At home in Denbighshire, poor though the Catchpoles were, Kitty had known a Sunday roast, even when it was no more than an elderly buck rabbit, poached off the neighbour's land. Nor was Eliza Heggy a stranger to roast meat, with a father employed in the lairage; not that he did dirty work, as she was quick to inform her companions; he had worked his way up to hooking and cleaving. Mary and Tish thought the Bazaar food was deadly, but not much worse than the meals they had always eaten. The chief misery for all four girls, as they returned after church to the Bazaar, was the delicious aroma that seemed to drift from every kitchen en route, reminding them that they were heading for cold, fat brisket, pickled onions and jacket potatoes. The jacket potato was Mrs Skinner's one concession to Sunday cooking, and it was so dependent on the capricious temperament of the coal oven that it could arrive on the plate charred to a near-cinder, or resolutely pale and knife-resistant. Mrs Jacks spent Sunday in her own house, cleaning, washing, ironing, mending and baking; in short, she did on a larger scale what she had to do for her husband and son each evening. Mrs Jacks was responsible for the Bazaar brisket, which she had cooked on the Saturday after-noon, wrapping it in a pudding-cloth and putting it to boil in the copper, before going to Abe Jenkin's for the bread.

They had pudding on Sundays. This could be one of a variety of delights, ranging from a pouring rice pudding, taken with a teaspoon of raspberry and apple jam, to the misnamed Summer Pudding in season. This last would require an even bigger order of stale bread from the bakery, and a Wednesday-afternoon foray by the two free assistants, as far as the cemetery, to gather blackberries. Tish had difficulty in swallowing the Summer Pudding, which she said was no more Summer than Jinny Skinner. She hated its cold wetness and its deep purple dye. If she and Kitty were doing the picking, she would shrink from penetrating the tangle over the most neglected tombstones, where the finest brambles grew. Whenever Tish ate Summer Pudding, she thought she was eating the dead.

At this Sunday meal, Mary Gibbs hardly noticed what she was eating. Eliza, also, was anxious to be off, and cleared her food at a great rate. The other two despatched their dinner quickly enough, exchanging amused glances from time to time. They would not be sorry to be free of the Bazaar for a while, but they recognized more than the younger girls that no amount of hurrying with their dinner would induce the Skinners to do likewise. In fact, the faster the assistants bolted their food, the more deliberately did master and mistress manipulate knife, fork and spoon; the more hastily the girls threw back their weak tea, the more daintily would Mrs Skinner's little finger remain crooked beyond the cup handle. Not until Hezekiah and his wife had patted their lips lightly on their starched table napkins, always a final gesture, did he rise to intone the dismissal grace.

It was a miracle that nothing was smashed. Jinny Skinner's voice shrieked high above the unceremonious clatter of crockery in and around the scullery sink. 'Remember all breakages will be paid for!' she cried, to good effect.

*

Once outside the premises, the two couples divided off, although each pair was making for the Ferry Head. Bridgemouth town lay silent and curiously clean. Since early dawn, a strong breeze from the river had whipped round the street corners, bearing with it Saturday's used tram tickets, the scores of empty Woodbine packets, the crumpled sheets of greasy newspaper – blowing these down narrow jiggers, and into those dead-ends, where the lids sat rakishly on spilling middens. Luckier rubbish frisked along to the park, for a more glorious day of liberty; it bounced and sailed through the park railings on to the grass beyond, up to the nearest clump of laurels; at times, a sheet of the *Bridgemouth Daily Argus* met the railings broadside on, there to corrugate and flap its ends until the wind dropped, or until the spike-man went his rounds on Monday.

Even the market square was blown remarkably clean. Its stalls lay bare, but for the solitary streamer of crêpe paper, waving from a tin-tack, or the occasional tarpaulin lifting and slapping on a superior fruit stall, on one that boasted angled displays.

'Do you think we're getting past it?' Tish queried. The friends had crossed the cobbles gingerly, for neither was forgetting Tish's sprain.

'Past what?'

'You know. Fellows. After all, you and me's eighteen.'

'You do talk drivel,' said Kitty. 'I wish we got out earlier,' she added, turning over a few lightweight boxes, and releasing more shavings and wisps of paper on the air. There was no blemished fruit in any; all had been well picked over long before breakfast. Not a cabbage leaf or stalk was to be seen in the gutter, not one spaded carrot or one soft onion. 'Selfish lot,' she grumbled. 'They might have left us a bit of something. There was that tomato, last week.'

'And it was horrible; all mushy and off.'

'What do you expect? You'd be mushy and off, if someone had split you down the middle.'

'Anyway, it's not ladylike,' said Tish, 'messing about with boxes on a Sunday. The Skinners would have a fit.'

'Ladylike! You wouldn't hold back if we turned up an apple.'

'Give me a pear any day. There's nothing there. Let's go.'

They took the short, steep street down to the ferry. The Sunday trams were few and far between. A 6A was waiting, ready to depart, with no passengers. A no. 12, seedy in its chocolate brown and cream, with the town crest dulled on each side, came grinding noisily down the hill. In spite of the sun, which struggled through the rushing cloud, the driver was feeling cold; he stamped his feet on the open platform, and wished he had brought his muffler. Two ABs, hunched against the weather, clumped down from the top deck, and leapt off before the tram came to a halt.

The lads stood together, lighting up a cigarette, and keeping an eye on Kitty and Tish.

'Not bad, are they?' Tish said.

'Not so dusty,' Kitty allowed. A spare-looking conductor ran round the stationary tramcar, hanging on to its obstinate trolley, which seemed powerful enough to lift him off his feet; it hissed and missed, hissed and missed, before it clicked into place on the line; the man wound the rope round the unwanted driving handle.

The girls were coming nearer to the boys; with a last, searching look at them, the latter – as with one pair of feet – swung on their heels and marched off.

Kitty and Tish stopped short. There was no mistaking the sailors' reaction; they had turned tail as fast as their plain boots would carry them.

'That's what I said, didn't I?' Tish exploded.

'What? What did you say?'

'You never listen, do you? Back there, I said do you think we're getting too old for it? That's what I said.'

'You didn't. You said *getting past it*.'

'Oh, well, if we're going to be funny . . .' And Tish began to walk ahead.

'What's the hurry? Keep your hair on, Tish!'

Tish slowed down for Kitty to catch up.

'Stand still and let's get this straight,' Kitty ordered. 'Look at me. Go on, look at me!' Tish did as she was told. 'What's your real opinion, Tish Kelly? Do I look past it?'

'No, you don't,' Tish answered, examining the vivid face in front of her. 'You look gorgeous, Kitty, honest! You're the prettiest girl in Bridgemouth, and you don't get spots.'

Kitty frowned. 'I do, you know; sometimes.'

'You haven't got none today,' said Tish. 'It must be me,' she declared, a shade tearfully. 'I must be putting them off. You'd do better if you walked by yourself.'

'There's nothing wrong with you, Tish-girl. You could do with your hat a bit more forward.' Kitty gave the brim a firm tug down over Tish's forehead. 'That's it. You've a real nice face, you have; real nice.'

'Freckles. Don't miss out the freckles.'

'Some men like freckles; my dad does, for one. Besides, you've got those curls. I'd give the world for natural curls.'

Tish was relieved to have her worst fears removed. 'Well, then, if it's not me, and it's not you, why did they clear off?'

Kitty had an inspiration. 'I think we're *too* ladylike,'

she stated positively. 'They don't see us rooting around in market boxes. You can bet your bottom dollar it's that: we must look stiff and starchy.'

On that chastening thought, the girls strolled inside the ferry entrance, under cover of its glazed vaulting, and inspected the choice of slot machines in pillar-box red.

'You got a penny?' Tish asked, without hope.

Kitty nodded, with a grin.

'Kitty Catchpole! You didn't put it in the collection, then. I never noticed. It's a wonder Skinnybugs didn't see.'

'I'm waiting for him to see. I'm not putting a bent ha'penny in that plate till we get our spivs back.'

'You're right. Why should we? I must be barmy not thinking that one out. Though it's not God's fault, is it?'

'Of course it is. If he was any good, we'd not be slaving our guts out for no spivs. We'd not be slaving at Skinners' Place at all.'

'Kitty, you know we would,' Tish contradicted. ' "He made us high and lowly" . . .'

'High and lowly, my behind!'

'That's not too ladylike, anyway.'

'All right, all right. Where's that penny gone, for God's sake?' Kitty was searching desperately inside her bag. 'If I've lost it, he'll wait a bit longer before he gets another in that plate. Ah, got it!'

The coin slid narrowly out of sight down the slot. The glass column showed well over a dozen 1d tabs of Nestlé's Milk Chocolate, all begging to be eaten, and Kitty heaved at the metal drawer with a will. It refused to give. She thumped the machine until her hand could take no more. Tish then went at it with her handbag, but the method proved far too kind for the cast iron, and far too severe for the leatherette. How desirable the chocolate was now, lodged in its drawer, within an inch or so of release!

'It's no good, Kitty. That thing's jammed for life. I've nearly put a hole in my bag, look!'

'So you have. You want to use your hand, like me. We can't waste a whole penny! Let's have another go. Both of us get hold of the drawer this time and pull.'

'I can't get a grip. It's too little.'

'You're not trying. I'll count three. On three we pull.'

The drawer remained fast. In her frustration, Kitty lost her temper with Tish, accusing her of pulling on 'two', and was told to do the job herself, if she was so mighty clever.

Over there, some way below the one-man booking office, a snub-nosed ferryboat was nudging in, to land with a thrash-thrash of screw, an apparent chime of tubular bells and, against the frayed mats, a sequence of thuds to send the standing passengers reeling.

Ropes were slung, to protest on the capstans; then came the roll of the rail-gate, and the rattle and slam of the gangway. A few impatient men and boys, eager to exchange deck for promenade, had leapt on to the gangplank before it hit the ground. These energetic types stamped up the exit-slope, to buy their freedom at reluctant turnstiles, where the brass gleamed on one side only.

As Kitty and Tish renewed their assault on the chocolate machine, some folk took note of the struggle and moved on. The echoing commotion created by the ferry trippers lent cover for the clatter the two girls were raising, for in spite of the embarrassment surrounding this unequal encounter, one of them – the owner of the penny – had no intention of giving up.

'Perhaps I could help?'

The girls sprang apart, hot with exertion and flustered by the interruption. The speaker was no boy; this was a full-blown officer, a man from the Mercantile Marine. By the sound of his voice, he hailed from north of the border.

'You won't manage it,' Kitty told him hurriedly, and rather defensively.

'He'll do better than we can,' said Tish, glad to have a chance to nurse her bruised hand.

'We've been working on it for ages,' Kitty said.

'Aha, you have?' he said quietly. Then as if to belie the soft delivery, he dealt the drawer one tremendous punch, followed by a decisive tug. The elusive bar of chocolate shone red and silver on its tray. Now that it was there, each girl was slow to reach out for it, though had they achieved victory earlier, by their own efforts, and with nobody's amused eyes on them, Kitty would certainly have pounced on it.

The young man laughed. 'Come on, don't leave it there,' he said.

His eyes were like the sky on picture postcards; and they had crinkles of merriment at their edges, which made Kitty catch her breath.

'No. Thanks. That was very good of you,' she replied, removing the chocolate, and pushing in the drawer. 'I don't know how you did it.'

It is extraordinary how the faintest hint of flattery will appeal to an otherwise well-balanced male. Henry Bonham was charmed. 'Brute strength,' he admitted with modesty. Taking some small change out of his trouser pocket, he obtained two more Nestlé bars, one for Tish and one for himself. 'Are you walking along the promenade?' he asked.

The girls said they were. They looked up at him, willing the impossible to happen.

'Would you mind if I came with you? Or you may be meeting somebody?'

'We'd love to walk with you,' Tish assured him, and all three left the shelter of the booking entrance for the bracing gale that met them on the promenade.

As a promenade, this Bridgemouth specimen served its purpose; as an aesthetic experience, it scored nil. It did boast the statutory railings, to protect walkers from a precipitous drop on to dark mud, or into murky water – whichever might be waiting there at the time – and the customary flights of grimy steps leading to either. It was peculiarly narrow, so that any chance confrontation between cabs could send strollers scattering for those shore rails, or for the advertising walls of end houses. These walls occurred at regular intervals, where the side streets descended at right angles to the prom, and they blindly extolled the dazzle behind boot polish and the frisk behind liver pills.

What with the grey of the roadway and pavement, the grey sand, the grey water and the dingy brickwork, it was advisable to look steadfastly across the river, until the Tivoli Gardens with their touch of green came into sight. Today, however, no Promenade des Anglais could have appeared more inviting to Kitty and Tish, as they stepped out with their new acquaintance.

Normally, the girls would have peeled back their silver paper, snapped the one slender bar in two, shared its wrappings to protect their fingers, and tackled the chocolate openly. One other drill should be mentioned: while the hand of the 'handbag arm' was holding this chocolate, the other had to be clamped on top of the hat. To let go of a hat in the promenade wind could spell disaster, with the headgear sailing over the pontoons and out to sea. At the least, it could be painful, as the long hatpins took the strain; the resulting wrench at the hair roots could bring tears to the bravest eyes.

The officer had slipped his Nestlé bar inside a pocket of his jacket. His two companions walked forth with him, each holding her own bar intact and unwrapped, between thumb and finger, and each prudently hanging on to her hat.

What pretty girls these were, he thought: one from Wales, and one from Ireland? He was not too far out, of course. For some generations, the male Catchpoles had travelled Cheshire, hiring themselves out as farm labourers and general handymen, but with their marriage, Kitty's parents had crossed the border into North Wales, there to settle permanently, and rear three children. Tish's speech, while it owed more to Laverport than to Ireland, did on occasion reflect the brogue. This branch of the Kelly clan had originally quit that unhappy isle at the time of the potato famine, and had continued hungry ever since. Yes, there was always a trace of the Irish Kelly in Tish's voice, when anything excited her, as now.

'And what would your name be?' she asked Henry.

'Henry.'

'Nothing else?'

He had given his name correctly, almost stiffly, as if unwilling to part with the information.

'You don't have to tell us your full name, if you don't want to,' Kitty said, sensing his hesitation, and feeling her own resentment rising. If they were not good enough for him, he knew what he could do.

'It's Bonham,' he said. 'Henry Bonham.'

'Is that a Scotch name? It doesn't sound very Scotch to me,' she remarked.

'I suppose it's not obviously Scottish, but there are a few of us scattered around Scotland. And what are you called?'

These exchanges over, with some speculation on Henry's part as to the number of Catchpoles to be counted in Wales, he stopped to lean on the promenade rail. Taking the Nestlé bar from his pocket, he stripped off the wrapping and proceeded to eat the contents neatly, piece by piece.

The girls were much encouraged by this human touch, and happily tackled their own chocolate in a less discreet fashion, since they still had to attend to their hats. Kitty decided privately that this labour to eat daintily was too much for her; moreover, she could not bring herself to eat the complete bar. Accordingly, she put a good half inside her bag to give later to Mary Gibbs. Tish had no such compunction, breaking off her pieces with an increased abandon, forgetful – after a while – of the real malevolence of the wind. In one of her unguarded moments, it swept with force under her flapping brim, dashing it upwards against the crown, and lifting hat, hatpins, and one front roll of hair pad off the unlucky wearer's head.

'Good heavens!' exclaimed Henry Bonham, in consternation.

'Oh, no! My best hat!' Tish cried out, her face streaked with chocolate, and one length of hair blowing in her eyes.

Kitty fished in her handbag once again, this time fumbling for a couple of hairpins. There was nothing to be done about the hat; it had risen high, like a triumphant kite, the petersham ribbon streaming out behind, and was now soaring and dipping beyond retrieval, out there in mid-channel.

Tish stood still, as Kitty pinned up the loose curls into a semblance of a roll; the high breeze and lack of hair pad made symmetry impossible. Removing her own faded foulard scarf, and wishing she had been wearing her best Sunday tulle, she draped it securely around Tish's head, tying it in a big bow under the chin; then with her pocket handkerchief, she wiped Tish's cheek clean of smears. 'You look a picture,' she consoled her. 'Doesn't she, Mr Bonham?'

Henry agreed and expressed his sincere regrets to Tish. He was still in heroic mood after the chocolate-machine incident, and would have welcomed a lively dash down the promenade after her hat, if it had chosen that route.

Tish's afternoon was wrecked. She finished her chocolate, and walked along in silence with the other two as far as the Tivoli Gardens. She tried to walk with apparent unconcern, as if it were the most ordinary thing in the world to be hatless and dishevelled on a Sunday, to be attached, yet quite unattached, to a young couple who were deep in talk. She knew Kitty did not really intend to neglect her; what would Tish have done, if the man's eye had been for Tish alone? Besides, she felt so humiliated, it was just as well Kitty was not drawing more attention to her. Tish Kelly shut her ears to the conversation, and concentrated on the dredger, which was making its way upriver; she could not see it too clearly, for her eyes troubled her.

'What a fright I must have looked, with my hair hanging down and my face all mucky!'

The light was out and the four girls were in bed. Eliza and Mary were sound asleep. Kitty and Tish talked in whispers.

'You looked sweet, like I said. He was sorry for you. He told you, didn't he?'

'I'm pretty sure he was dying to laugh.'

'There was nothing to laugh at.'

'What did you talk about?'

'All sorts. They only berthed on Friday. From Valparaiso.'

'Valpa what?'

'Raiso.'

'Where's that?'

Kitty improvised. 'West coast of Africa.'

Tish accepted this; such an area was distant enough to accommodate two Valparaisos, if necessary. 'He wasn't half la-di-da,' she said. 'Lots of big words I couldn't understand.'

'That was only his Edinburgh accent. Words sound la-di-da in Scotch.'

'You were putting it on, as well. Proper Bellingham-Smith, you were.'

Kitty was nettled by the grain of truth in this observation. 'I was *not*. Anyway, you weren't listening; you were gawping at the river.'

'So would you if you'd lost your hat.' Tish changed her tactics. If she wanted to learn more about Henry Bonham, Kitty must be kept even-tempered. 'What did he say about his mam and dad, then? Did you ask him?'

'They're dead. I didn't like to ask what his father was. He didn't call them "mum" and "dad".'

'Why not?'

'Well, it's different in Scotland, isn't it?' Kitty explained lamely; she was sorry she had embarked on this. 'He called them "the mater" and "father".'

Tish had to bury her face in the flock pillow. 'The *mater*!' she gurgled from its depths.

'I told you. It's only Scotch.'

' "Father" isn't Scotch.'

'If you're only going to skit, I'm going to sleep.'

Tish sobered up. 'No, go on,' she said. 'I won't laugh. Cross my heart.'

'He has a brother who's a painter.'

'Like Atkinsons'?'

'A *real* painter. Paints pictures.'

'He'll be on the bone of his backside then. Pity he's not like Atkinsons'.'

'Henry says he's quite famous. He sells his paintings to galleries.'

'*Henry*, is it?'

'He was calling me Katherine. His brother's older than him. I think there was a sister in between who died. They've done a lot of dying. He's very proud of his brother. Stephen, he's called. Henry's going up to Edinburgh to see him at the end of the week. I'm not certain it is Edinburgh; he was on about a new town somewhere. They've got a great big house, with *servants*, all to themselves. And him getting our penny bar out of the machine! And walking along the prom with us two . . . I wish Mary and Eliza could have seen us. Isn't he big? Did you ever see such shoulders? And his hands – real dainty eating chocolate, but they can bash as hard as my dad's! Oh, and all that gold braid! He's reporting back for work on the Monday; says he wants to see me Sunday week. I hope he's got a friend for you, Tish. Sure to have. He said, "When may I see you again, Katherine?" He's the first gentleman I've ever met. Don't you think he's lovely?' Kitty's whisper, by now quite hoarse, came to an end. She waited for Tish's response to her confidences, and was rewarded by a light snore.

How much brighter the Drapery Bazaar appeared to Kitty, on the following day! The sun was slanting through the lofty fanlight, picking out the colours in the shadowy interior; a clean smell of cottons fresh from the mill rose above the beeswax; the letter box and knob on the open doors shone Brasso-bright. Behind her counter, Kitty's feet were walking a dance. She pressed her thumbprints on the red mahogany and watched them slowly fade; with her duster, she rubbed hard at the last traces, as if the entire process had been essential to the counter's finish. Tish was taking in this performance with a mild amusement, not untinged with envy; she could not feel as happy as Kitty, while doing her best to be happy for her. She was coming round to thinking that, curls or no curls, whenever two girls are constantly together, just one of them is likely to get her man, and as this was the prime object of walking-out on Sundays, only by going it alone would she ever do better. This would soon be her lot; either she started her lonely prowl next Sunday, when Henry Bonham would be in Scotland, or from the Sunday after that, and onwards, for as long as he might be at Kitty's side. On no account would Tish accompany them as a third; nor would she join Mary and Eliza, if Mary were to press her. She would go companionless, in her plain 'working' hat, with no Kitty to talk to, even though no head turned in her direction.

She had arrived at this depressing thought on two previous occasions; on each of these, Kitty had attracted a promising young rating, so that Tish had been obliged to fend for herself, which she did badly. When the lads had gone to sea, neither communicated with Kitty, though she did receive one isolated postcard, which almost brought about her dismissal. Mrs Skinner delivered the assistants' mail with her own hands, having read anything immediately accessible, such as a postcard, or anything partly legible through a flimsy envelope. This open message had read: 'I L–U nice to F–U, Cecil XXXXX.' Kitty had seen nothing wrong in Cecil's pleasure at finding her, and was disgusted, as she informed Mrs Skinner, to learn the extent of the latter's vocabulary. She had never heard the word spoken before, leastways not where she came from, and she hoped never to hear it again under the roof of the Bridgemouth Drapery Bazaar. In the end, Hezekiah was begging Kitty to stay on, to give up her threat of an application, with full reasons, for refuge in Masons' Emporium.

If the Skinners had doubted Kitty's word on that occasion, Tish, too, had not known what to believe at first, though she would not have condemned her friend for a life style common to her own poverty-stricken mother and sister; but Kitty had flung off in a fury, to give way upstairs to a storm of weeping. Cecil had obviously written his card under the eye of one or two of the boys, and the consequent show of bravado bore no relation to fact. It was as well that Cecil never found Kitty again, or he might have disappeared over the promenade rail at high tide.

In time, Tish thought, you grew used to sailors and their little ways. You went on hoping that a really decent chap would turn up, one whose romantic nonsense settled into a concrete offer of marriage. This Henry Bonham, now . . . Would he be like the rest? Or would he return to Kitty? He would be a stupid mule, if he didn't. They were all mules, who didn't come back for Kitty Catchpole; she had the love and the laughter that a man needed, and at this very moment she looked good enough to eat.

From a disused pattern drawer, Kitty had taken a lidless cardboard box, which contained used string from yesterday's stock parcels. Unlike the other girls, who with one accord detested the after-dinner chore of unravelling, Kitty enjoyed it, often tying knots where none existed, to untie them later; she found it soothing. When business was slack, she used to fetch more and more string from the store room, until her box was piled to the top, and then her deft fingers would produce countless lengths of usable string for customers' parcels. Hezekiah and Jinny saw no harm in this evidence of thrift; some customers actually noticed and admired it, seeing good training for the young in such employment.

This morning, Kitty skipped across to Tish, with a handful of 'ties', those tidy figures of eight, made by winding string between thumb and little finger. She removed another bunch of tangles from Tish's box. The girls spoke briefly to each other.

Industry with knots was one thing; snatched conversation was another. Kitty Catchpole and Tish Kelly had been pushing their luck of late; and the young Gibbs was getting unmanageable under their influence. Ever since commission had been suspended! Hezekiah had told Jinny how it would be. And now an elderly member of the Scotch Kirk's Sewing Bee had come in, and was rummaging around in Remnants. Hezekiah adopted a Mafeking stance: 'Catchpole!' he commanded. 'Forward!'

Kitty swung round to stare at him. *Catchpole*, indeed! 'Yes, *Skinner*!' she threw back, bearing down on the shrinking old girl at Remnants, as if to add more undesirable shreds to the heaped table.

'It's not as if it's raining,' sighed Tish. 'Not much sun, but it's not raining.'

'You go, for heaven's sake,' Kitty said impatiently. 'I don't want you here, when you could be out, enjoying yourself. You can wear my hat, too, my best one; one of us might as well wear it.'

Tish's face lit up. 'Your *best*? Oh, I couldn't.' She looked sad again. 'I don't specially want to go walking without you. I thought about it all through the service, and the more I thought, the worse it was. It's no fun for me, walking on my own.'

'You'll have to walk on your own next Sunday,' Kitty reminded her. 'Henry will be back.'

'If you don't give cheek to Skinnybugs. Otherwise, you'll be kept in again, and I'll be stuck here talking to you, and Henry will have to go without.'

'He wouldn't. You'd have to go and meet him, and tell him what had happened.'

'Perhaps I would.' Tish quite liked that idea, but when she saw Kitty's dejected face, she added, 'You wouldn't mind if I met him instead of you? I wouldn't stay with him long, unless he asked me to.'

'No, I wouldn't mind,' Kitty fibbed. 'Why should I? Anyway, I'll be there. I'll take damn good care I don't open my trap next week, no matter what Skinnybugs says, or her, either.'

'I had to laugh when she was on about the sales dropping. Inside me, I mean. "And only *one* department showing steady returns – Millinery!" '

'That's a lie, too. Eliza Heggy couldn't sell a bonnet to Red Riding Hood's wolf. Remind me to put some breadcrumbs in one of the hat drawers: the bottom one.'

'Some *what*?'

'Crumbs. If we pull the drawer open a bit, the mice will be in there like a flash.'

'Who says we've got mice? Anyway, you wouldn't!'

'You see if I don't. Tomorrow night, after we shut: I'll pull it out only a little bit, in case a rat gets in.'

'A rat!' Tish looked aghast.

'Yes. That was never a mouse that chewed the back

of the cash-book. It takes more than mice teeth to get right through thick covers overnight. The Skinner thought it was a rat, too, but she wasn't letting on.'

'How d'you know?'

'The way she makes us clear the centre display every night, and put all fabric high on the shelves.'

'She could think it was just a mouse.'

'Whatever it was, it's going to get good nourishment.'

'Eliza will see the drawer's open, of a morning,' said Tish, doubtfully.

'I'll push it to with my leg when I take the mop round, and you can do that on your mop mornings. We'll have to leave it open on Friday and Saturday – take a chance that she won't cotton on.'

'We could ask Mary to see to it on Saturday; that would only leave the Heggy's Friday.'

Kitty shook her head. 'It's safer to keep it to ourselves. Mary's a good lass, but she's not so long out of apprenticeship; she might have some fellow-feeling, you never know. Besides, we might have results before Saturday.'

Tish was full of admiration. 'The way you think of things, Kitty! I wish I had your brain. I didn't know mice climbed.'

Kitty lacked data on this point. 'They ought to manage the rough side of a drawer, if it's open. We could always give them a leg up with Mary's revolving stand. If that's pushed near the drawer, any self-respecting mouse should get in.' She lay back on her bed. 'Why don't you go out? I feel guilty with you here; you didn't cheek Skinnybugs.'

'But you did right, Kitty. Even Eliza Heggy said he ought to apologize for calling you "Catchpole". She said her "father" would take her away like a shot, if anyone called her "Heggy", in front of a shopload of customers.'

'One old woman from the Scotch Kirk.'

'That's as good as a shopload. It's a customer.'

Kitty nodded, though not convinced. 'Go on, Tish. Put your coat on, and my best hat. Never venture . . . You can tell me about all the fellows who chased you when you get back.'

'That'll be the day. Well, maybe I'll go for half an hour, just round the block. Not that I'll enjoy myself.' Tish buttoned her coat deliberately, and took Kitty's natural straw hat from its paper bag. She stroked the wreath of forget-me-nots and straightened the veiling along the brim. Set on her dark red hair, the hat looked beautiful, rather better than it did on Kitty, or so the latter fancied.

'I'd give you that hat for keeps if I knew where the next was coming from. It suits you better than me.'

'It never does. Are you sure you'll be all right?'

Out in the street, Tish was pleased that Kitty had been so insistent. It might have been the borrowed hat that did it; whatever it was, she felt better for being out. Her ankle was stronger, too; all that limping around had done it good. Walking-out alone was not so bad, really. It was time she grew up and learnt to live without Kitty's support. One day, there would be no choice; Kitty would get married, or move away from Skinners'. She might go back to Wales, and then where would Tish be? Friendship was fine while it lasted, but what friends did married people have? No one in Tish's street, back home, had friends. The women might pass the time of day, as they donkey-stoned the front step, or they might call to each other over the back-yard wall, when hanging out the washing, but that was all. Nobody went inside anyone else's house; nobody wasted time and money over a friendly cup of tea; life was too lean for such carryings-on. A fair number of the men used to gather in the pub at night, to share their dirty jokes over a glass of bitter and through a fug of thick twist, but they carried friendship no further. Once a man had staggered back to his own number in the terrace, he shut the wooden door with a slam that lifted the iron knocker, and that was that. Kids, now – kids were different. They'd play all day and night in the street if you'd let them, swinging round the lamp post on their orange-rope, kicking the realleeo can as they raced out of the back jigger. But they never went inside each other's houses, either. They were the cause of rows between mothers, they squabbled among themselves, and they had their gangs and their 'best friends' for street play only; at all other times they, too, retreated behind the closed doors. And when they left school, the street friends drifted apart completely; those who weighed out the potatoes in the corner shop, or worked in the biscuit factory, had nothing to say to one another; courting took them further afield. As for the many who had to leave home to get a job, or take up dubious night work, these were the complete outcasts, to whom the entire street would barely nod.

No, the one friend of her life was Kitty Catchpole, and here she was without her, back at the market place, facing what remained of the collapsed boxes and their possible, mouldy treasures. A barefoot lad ran past her, carrying small pieces of wooden plank under his arm; Tish caught the reminder of slept-in clothes, which she knew so well of old; she continued with a fairly sure foot across the cobbles.

*

Kitty had not changed her position; she lay on her bed, examining the sharp pitch of the ceiling, and its liberal scatter of stains; the latter did nothing for her; she was beyond the age where she might have dwelt on a theme of tropical islands, set in a turquoise sea; these were nasty, non-stop stains – with hard edges. Flakes of blue-wash, long since become brown-wash, hung from them, waiting their turn to fall. Skinners' Place, Skinners' Place, Skinners' Place. Damn Skinners' Place. Damn and blast Skinners' Place. Bugger the place, she added with daring. It was a term she reserved solely for silent monologue, since she was unsure of its literal meaning, though well aware of its respectability-rating. Yes. Bugger it.

She swung off the bed, and crossed the room to the inadequate looking glass on the far wall. Its discoloration and near-diagonal crack made a true reflection impossible, but the girls were used to viewing their faces piecemeal and at curious angles. Kitty scowled into it. Some mirrormirroronthewall, this one . . . It was an insult to be asked to live with it. Stepping back, she took a more comprehensive view of herself, from the hips upwards. If anything, she had what you might call a boy's hips, which did less than justice to her narrow waist. However, she was not exactly flat-chested; nor was she a droopy-tits, like the young Eliza. Twisting for a half-profile, she hoped there was enough on top to make up for the flat hips. Maybe Mr Bonham preferred a boy's hips? But that was expecting too much. Not altogether pleased with herself, she advanced on the glass again, biting her lips hard to give them a better red; the image responded with a deeper orange distortion and a hideous blotch, to ruin the loveliness of the natural object. She shifted her face sideways – transferring the major blemish to her right cheek, in exchange for one darker, but smaller, in the left corner of her mouth. With parted lips, she took to examining her teeth. Making allowances for the overall impression of tartar, she saw that her teeth were still a healthy white, and agreeably regular, though one tooth in the bottom row did tend to lean on its neighbour. She smiled into the glass gently, then wider, and finally she closed her lips, to return a smile of mystery that would have rejoiced Leonardo.

At this moment of mystery, a minute black spot revealed itself by her left nostril; it travelled consistently with her face, up, down and across the glass.

'So I don't get spots!' she said out loud, squeezing forcefully between the two index nails. It was a most determined blackhead for its size. Kitty was dismayed. Had Mr Bonham noticed it? Now that she had seen it herself, she felt sure that for quite some time it must have been obvious to everybody. She would be directing a few remarks to Tish on the subject. She got rid of most of it, by dint of brutality, but the surrounding area was left in an angry state.

Her appetite for self-improvement aroused, she went to work on the few dark hairs that spoiled an otherwise perfect line of eyebrow. With index and thumb nails, she tweaked at these ineffectually. One hair broke off short; others were already too short for an efficient grip. This operation, like the first, was not without pain. Kitty licked the same finger and thumb, and shaped the eyebrows into a reasonably elegant curve; cosmetic surgery was over for the day; she would go downstairs, and stand in the yard; the Skinners could hardly forbid her 'to go to the back'.

Making a brisk clacking with her boots, she went down the stairs; as she left linoleum for carpet, the Skinners' bedroom door opened, and an irate Jinny emerged. Kitty looked at her coldly and proceeded on her way. Jinny Skinner closed her mouth and returned to the room.

Kitty stood in the yard, as far from the wall-midden as possible, and breathed the not too unpleasant air. Several dandelions were pushing ahead in the cracked paving; three golden buds were showing. The Skinners would be waiting in their bedroom for her to go up again. Jinny was probably peering through her lace curtain, to see what Kitty was up to. She knew what they would be up to, the two of them! That was why they got all four lady assistants off the premises, if they could. Many a laugh had to be smothered in the attic on a Sunday night, as calculations were put forward; strangely enough, Eliza Heggy was quite inventive in this respect.

Kitty directed her steps towards the water closet, holding one arm across her stomach. After a decent interval, she pulled the chain and emerged. There was no twitch of the curtain, so she hung around last year's rusted nettles for a while before going indoors. Up the stairs she went, punishing the lino as before.

She would give them a few minutes – time, say, for the removal of a few items of clothing. This she did; the premises were wrapped in silence, a kind of wary silence, as Kitty took to the staircase again, and again made a racket. This time, she was nowhere near the carpet when out flew Jinny Skinner, looking much the same as previously, and certainly wearing the same blouse and skirt.

'What are you doing? Where are you going? I will not have this disturbance!' Jinny rapped out.

Kitty's hand was clutching her middle. 'It must be something I ate for dinner. The potato, or something . . .' Her voice trailed weakly away.

'I see. It can't be something you've eaten. We haven't got it. The others haven't got it.'

'They're out, aren't they? Heaving all over the prom, I wouldn't be surprised.' Kitty tottered down two more stairs, gripping the bannister.

'Well, don't make a song and dance about it when people want a rest. Use the stairs quietly.'

'Yes, ma'am. I'll do my level best, ma'am.'

And it was true; she did do her best to ascend the stairs quietly, so that she did not give offence, yet loudly enough to be heard.

Her third descent was the most tricky: she crept down, avoiding stair creaks by tacking, or by taking two stairs at a time where necessary; her Sunday coat hung about her shoulders, because gastric upsets can bring on the shivers, and her day hat was underneath her skirt, held firmly by the clutching hand. At this attempt, no Mrs Skinner darted from the bedroom, and instead of making for the yard, Kitty tiptoed into the front showroom. There she paused, listening for noises in the room above. The joists bounced and complained under footsteps; a chair seemed to be planted in a different corner. Kitty glanced into the second show-room, the front-only room. Why not begin the mouse campaign right now? She stole to the kitchen for a scrap of bread and returned to sprinkle a crumb or two outside the lowest Millinery drawer. Opening this, she dropped the remaining bread inside, towards the back; one pull at the Baby Linen stand, to bring it closer to the drawer, and a final closing, leaving a small gap for an enquiring rodent, and the job was done.

Kitty went to the first showroom, still on tiptoe. A steady rhythm and squeak of long-suffering mesh came from upstairs. She put on her coat correctly, pinned on her hat before Mr Truscott's cheval-glass, took her black cotton gloves from her pocket, and tripped lightly to the backyard, escaping at last through the solid wooden gate into the side street.

It was going to be a shortish walk, if she wanted to get back before her employers woke up. There was a peculiar ritual associated with Sunday tea, and not one of the girls knew who had been the idiot originally responsible for it. They were not obliged to return to the Bazaar for this meal, if they preferred to go without food, or buy themselves a snack, before evening service at the Scotch Kirk. Jinny Skinner, if no lady assistant had returned for tea, used to come downstairs to prepare a tray for herself and Hezekiah; she then took it up to their sitting room. If, however, some girl or girls had yielded to hunger, the Skinners' tea tray had to be prepared by an assistant, and placed – to the accompaniment of a brief tinkle with the landing handbell – on the table outside the sitting room. It was the unknown originator of this idea, that arrant boot-licker, who regularly earned the curses of the hungry assistant left to carry it out.

For the Skinners, it was an admirable arrangement: either they received their Sunday tea without personal effort, or they saved money. Guided by this latter consideration, they would continue the policy of *laissez-faire*, where evening church attendance was concerned, for they realized that a girl out for enjoyment was less likely to return to the Bazaar for her tea. It was a charade played by employers and staff to everyone's frequent benefit.

This tea time, though, the system would suffer a hitch. One healthy assistant would be indoors, but Jinny would be preparing the Skinners' tray. Kitty aimed to be back about half past three, when she would load a battered black japan tray with her currant bun, her thin slice of seed cake, a Sunday cup and saucer, one pot of tea and a diminutive jug of milk. This she would carry to the attic, and Jinny Skinner could whistle.

She noted the hour of the town hall clock; no seafront stroll was possible; it would have to be a circular tour, ignoring the market square. She was feeling more cheerful. The window frontage of Caradoc Tonks's Funeral Parlour, draped for the most part in black, reflected her slim form; she moved nearer to the glass, as if to examine the domed *immortelles* so tastefully set out in the division of its curtains, but really to tuck in stray wisps of hair. As she walked away, an elderly couple took her place at the window, peering into its depths to consider the three styles of coffin, economy, plain or de luxe. Thoughts of Henry Bonham had been with Kitty before this, and she was able to dismiss the funeral parlour quite easily, and return to livelier concerns.

She went over every word Henry had said to her, and every word he might have said, had he been walking here with her. This great warmth in her chest . . . She supposed that was her heart on fire, a condition she had read about in *Dainty Stories*, and had been exhorted to cultivate, in a different context, at the Scotch Kirk. She had known excitement of a more trivial nature with other young men, in the rougher larks and banter accepted as the done thing, if a girl wanted to 'get off', but never had she felt this mixture of love and admiration for any one of them; admiration – that was it. Henry Bonham was in a breed apart; with him, she was not called upon to be a good sport, with all the boring effort that meant; he was quiet; he treated her with courtesy. If he didn't meet her the next Sunday, Kitty believed she would never trust a man again; nobody on earth was so important, or would remain so important to her; of that she was sure.

She was not so sure when she first recognized the young girl who was hurtling down the street towards her; one moment the approach was entirely empty; the next, there was this distracted figure in a skirt swept up to show the top of her boots – a figure, what was more, wearing a natural straw bonnet, which had slipped to the back of her head, where it bounced up and down with every flying step.

Kitty ran forward. 'Tish! What's up? What's the matter with you?'

Tish was out of breath and not just with running; she was choking like one pulled out of water, and what breath she had was coming in chords.

'Tish-girl!' Kitty's arms were round her. 'Calm down! Whatever is it?'

For answer, Tish tore herself away, rushed to the gutter, and was violently sick. She straightened up, shaking, and Kitty held her again, wiping the loose mouth on a best handkerchief.

'That better?'

Tish shook her head and went on trembling. Kitty was seriously alarmed. There must have been something wrong with that dinner, after all.

The elderly couple, who had observed the scene and were making in the girls' direction, crossed to the opposite side of the street, their faces rigid with distaste.

'Well, it isn't very nice, is it?' Tish got out, with another shudder.

'I hope she spews all over him in bed!' Kitty said clearly. 'As if you could help it! Shall we go back?'

Tish nodded.

'Have you got a stomach ache?' Kitty pursued.

Tish shook her head; she was nearly in tears.

'God, you must be terribly ill, Tish. You look awful. When did it come on?'

'Market Square.'

'You didn't eat something really bad?'

'No. I saw this man.'

'What sort of a man?'

The tears ran down. 'He was half hiding behind Dooley's Whelks,' she wept, 'and he came out with a grin on his face, and, Kitty, he was, he was holding his – ' With a choke, she regained the gutter for a further bout of vomiting, which had now become more noise and retch than anything else.

'He was, was he? I'll get a bobby to him, the stinking hound! Though Lord knows where bobbies get to on a Sunday. I'll go to the square myself. I'll murder him. I'll twist it till it drops off!'

Tish let out a little scream. 'You can't do that! He'll kill you! And you can't go to the police.'

'Who's stopping me?' Kitty had started off.

Tish wiped her eyes on her sleeve. 'Kitty,' she called, 'are you supposed to be out?'

Kitty stopped in her tracks. 'I'd clean forgotten. A good job you reminded me.' She came back to Tish. 'You go to the police; you know where the station is.'

Tish was appalled. 'Not me. I'm not going there. I couldn't tell that to men. I just couldn't.'

'That's what he relies on.'

'I don't care. I'm not going, not on my own. They wouldn't believe me; you know what they are.' Tish had heard plenty of stories from her sister and mother to jaundice her for life against the watchful bobby on the beat. Her sister, especially, regarded the force as a blot on humanity; the only way a girl could earn a fair living was by knowing which palms to grease, and how often. 'He's probably a copper, on his day off,' she added bleakly.

Kitty had to laugh at that. 'Come on, then, if you're not going. Let's be getting back.'

They walked slowly to Skinners' Place. 'You know,' Kitty said, 'I'm not too keen on creeping upstairs in my coat. I can stuff the hat under my skirt again . . . I think I'll leave my coat in the lav. Two of us coming in together, even if I go first — it won't be easy.'

That was what she did. She went quietly up the stairs, once more clutching the hidden hat to her body; no one leapt out of the Skinners' bedroom, and Kitty got to the attic without incident. Tish reached the stairs minutes later and took them carefully; she was still shaken after her frightful outing. She had arrived at the linoleumed top flight when the Skinners' door opened.

To tell the truth, Jinny had come out of that room for one reason only: it was approaching tea time, and if the Catchpole girl had fallen victim to stomach trouble, she would be an unlikely tea-maker, and an undesirable one, for that matter. Hezekiah had been making himself clear: he had no wish to have his food and drink contaminated by that creature: Jinny must prepare and bring up the tray. In this, if in practically nothing else, he was of course quite justified. The girl was still plodding up the stairs. Jinny glanced briefly at the genuinely weak young lady, who was conquering the last few stairs to the top landing. Kitty Catchpole's best Sunday hat hung rakishly at the back of the wearer's head, held by what was left of a small chignon; the back of the head was effectively covered by the large brim.

So that was it! Sneaking out when she thought the coast was clear! 'Miss Catchpole!' cried the incensed Mrs Skinner. 'Where have you been gadding?'

Tish halted, with both feet on one stair. Kitty came

hurrying awkwardly from the girls' bedroom, wearing an agonized expression, and bent slightly forward. 'Did you call me, ma'am?' She spun round to gaze on Tish: 'Anything wrong, Tish? You look bad.'

Tish turned to look at her employer; her cheeks were colourless, and the curls hung in disarray about her ears.

'I've been sick in the street, ma'am,' she said faintly. 'Must have been the dinner.'

Jinny gave a twitch of irritation. 'I hope no one saw you making a spectacle of yourself like that. It's hardly a ladylike thing to do in the street, is it?'

'No, ma'am,' murmured Tish.

'Better than on the carpet,' Kitty suggested helpfully.

'Nonsense!' Jinny declared, conscious of Kitty's eyes on her. 'You won't want any tea, then, either of you. You'd better both lie down.'

'If you don't mind, ma'am,' Kitty put in, as weakly as she knew how, 'I'll make us a bite to eat for later, in case we feel up to it. We don't want to be awake all night, starving hungry, and Monday tomorrow.'

Jinny threw a look of suspicion at her, but there was no doubt that both assistants appeared to be off colour, and Tish Kelly's face was like a sheet. What could have been wrong with that dinner? The brisket? Never. Pickles? They kept for ever with the lid on. She must speak to Jacks. 'Very well,' she agreed unwillingly. 'Don't touch anything for Mr Skinner and me. I'll attend to that.' Her optimism had dwindled; she was starting to feel queasy herself. What if she was about to be stricken by the dinner-bug, and what if the other lady assistants were also disgracing the Drapery Bazaar by a display of public vomiting?

*

'Don't think about it any more,' Kitty advised. 'Put it out of your mind, Tish. I know it's terrible, but it's happening every day somewhere. Don't go to the square next Sunday, that's all. In fact, you'll have to come with me.'

'No, I'll not be doing that. I'll come as far as the Apollo, then I'll cut off on my own.'

'We'll see.'

'We won't *see*. That's what I'll be doing.'

'Have it your own way. Pour out the tea, if you feel up to lifting the pot.'

'It's heavy, all right. How many did you put in?'

'Four spoons, and filled it to the top. That's the best of not having Mary and the Heggy. Eliza would be sure to split if she saw me count to four. The cake's a bit thicker. I wish I could have nicked an extra bun, but you can't have everything.'

Where Mary Gibbs' and Eliza Heggy's immediate health was concerned, there was no cause for Jinny Skinner's fears. Both young ladies were at some distance from the main public thoroughfares. Mary's Scotch Kirk sailor had proved to be a lad who did not give in easily. When Mary, to all intents and purposes, had disregarded his appointment, he had gone to church the following morning to try a second time; a quick exchange on the way out had resolved the problem. At the end of a week's unloading, the young Bunny Harris had been paid off; until he found another berth, their meetings would be as regular as Mary's commitments and his savings allowed. The one fly in the ointment was Eliza, who did not respond readily to hints.

This afternoon, Mr Harris was determined to get rid

of the hanger-on, no matter how much plain speaking might be required. His all-out effort was so plain that these two rivals for Mary's company were soon engaged in a slanging match, which Eliza ended by marching away, in a high old temper, and still shouting. Mrs Skinner would certainly have preferred a discreet throw-up to such a showdown outside the Marine Café (CLOSED FOR RENOVATIONS).

Mary was pleased that Bunny had taken a tough stand, to rid their Sundays of Eliza's presence. She was more pleased, if a little nervous, when he led her behind the disused café, into the hummocks and hollows of a patch of wasteland, where her mother's strap-shoes rapidly shipped sand, so that she was obliged to flop down among the gorse and shake them out.

Eliza Heggy, chock-full of resentment, was led to act out of character: she broke a Skinners' Place rule. In marching off to her parents' house, she ran the double risk of angering the parents, who wanted her apprenticeship to succeed, and the Skinners, whose rules were meant to be obeyed. A local assistant was required to stay away from home, in order not to create unrest among those who came from distant parts, and Eliza understood that she was no more privileged in this respect than any other young lady. As sole apprentice, too, she was expected to keep a reasonably low profile; it would be time enough for experiment when her training was completed.

She strode over the transport bridge, that important link where a water channel had penetrated dockland. Its metal wagon tracks demanded a certain agility – they were such heel-traps for any woman not watching her step. The dockside bristled like a weakened toothbrush, with leaning masts; here and there, the taller funnels showed also, above the boundary wall. Where the wall gave way to high fencing, this leaned more crazily than the masts, and was eked out in places by crude tin sheeting, which in turn was holed by rust and well-aimed kicks, all of which made the KEEP OUT notices largely redundant. Everything looked in need of an overhaul; nothing was likely to get it. On a working day the dirt and dilapidation passed unnoticed, under cover of busy traffic. Today, it lay trafficless and exposed, beyond the formidable cross-hatching of the bridge, and it stank of barnacled hulks, tar, wet rope, oil, dung and river.

Eliza noticed none of it; she would soon be entering the familiar terrain of her childhood, making first for Aitchesons', Newsagents, Sweets and Tobacco, a corner shop which she expected to find open. Aitchesons' stayed open every day, to catch the small trade that was its lifeblood; nothing, short of an Aitcheson demise, could close its door to customers.

She took a morocco purse from her bag and inspected the contents: four pennies, one threepenny bit, one halfpenny and two farthings. She liked to have some cash in hand; if her Bazaar colleagues had apprised the extent of her wealth, they would have been astounded. Her ill temper had cooled off with the proximity of home. Aitchesons' door was indeed wide open, but she did not go in directly. She took her time, surveying the array of temptations that lay behind the somewhat dirty window. It was months since Widow Aitcheson had put a wet chamois to it, or considered the removal of sun-kissed chocolates, et al., from their dusty doyleys. Eliza was not put off; these sadly exposed samples had their fresher counterparts inside the shop. She had the stock of this small establishment by heart;

while others might resort to jumping sheep, Eliza
courted sleep each night with visions of Mackintosh's
Celebrated Toffee, Mother Noblett's Everton Toffee,
Fry's cream bars, Fox's glacier mints, someone else's
fruit bonbons, brown aniseed balls, white acid drops,
pink pear drops, striped pebbles, bull's eyes, sugared
almonds, coconut ice, named rock, fudge, Victory Vs,
creamy whirls, tiger nuts, locusts, Spanish ribbons,
Pontefract cakes, licorice sticks, mint imperials, fon-
dants, dolly mixtures, wine gums, fruit pastilles . . . the
list was endless; it always knocked her out like a light.

This afternoon, she meant to steer clear of the sweets
eaten in the Bazaar kitchen. With even more spare
cash, she would have bought one of those ladling-elf
CDMs (RICH IN CREAM), or one of the more familiar
Peter's – as an extra; milk chocolate bars were never her
first choice. She gazed with regret on the dummy chocolate boxes, all of them faded unevenly, as were the
drooping paper chains and folding paper bells; she
stared at the beige celluloid dolls, which had once been
so rosy, the surface-painted rubber balls, the wooden
pen-holders, balloons for blowing up, windmills for
running against the wind. She could eat none of those;
nor did she think of buying an *Empire News* or a plug of
tobacco for her father. She came out of the shop with
two whipped cream walnuts, which she disposed of at
an impressive speed.

Eliza Heggy faced the family front door, licking her
lips and sucking her teeth clean. Throwing the paper
bag behind the privet, she rattled at the letter box.

Jinny Skinner got short shrift from Hezekiah; the fact
that she, too, was feeling out of sorts was another
instance of an imagination working overtime; she must

pull herself together. There followed some harsh words on the subject of those days Jinny had taken off, for reasons of ill health, since their marriage – two and a half, to be precise, on the occasion of an unmentionable affliction, which had required lancing, and had made sitting at the cash desk impossible. Whereas Hezekiah was quick to take to his bed if his finger ached. Many a time Jinny had been left to cope with shop, lady assistants, old Truscott, Jacks *and* a bedridden Hezekiah, until she was ready to drop. The next time she seemed likely to have a day off was when she was stiff.

Husband and wife both improved after a good cup of tea, laced with whisky from Hezekiah's hip flask. In this more mellow frame of mind, they fell to reviewing the worsening situation of the Bridgemouth Drapery Bazaar.

'You'll have to give in, Jinny. They've got the upper hand and they know it. It would look pretty queer, to be sacking three assistants at once. And they'd use their tongues; that Catchpole would be the worst, once she got started; and Kelly and Gibbs wouldn't take long, following suit. God knows what sort of lies they'd be spreading around; we can't afford that.'

'We can't afford to keep them here, either, the way Catchpole has got them organized; a right trouble-maker, that one, and as crafty as they come. "Better than on the carpet," she says, as smart as you like. I'll smart her, before I've finished with her.'

Hezekiah deemed the moment ripe for soft soap. 'Nobody gets the better of Jinny Skinner in the long run. Make them stump up for the skirts, but put them on commission again, for good behaviour. They won't know where to put their faces when you say "good behaviour". And they'll work a bit harder, if they think you could be letting them off the skirt money.'

'I shan't be doing that.'

'No, I didn't think you would,' Hezekiah allowed smoothly, 'but it won't hurt to look like you might.'

After tea, Kitty and Tish shifted the basin and ewer from the pink marble top of their washhand-stand, and took turns to climb upon it, each standing unnaturally erect, and revolving gradually, as the other made a level pinning of the new skirt hem. The sewing of ankle-length skirts was a time-consuming exercise, when every stitch had to be done by hand. Left to their own devices, the girls would have taken the easy way out, pressing open the long inner seams and oversewing the raw edges, but under Mrs Skinner's constant supervision, standards had to be higher, with flat run-and-fell seams *de rigueur*. Nor would Jinny countenance anything but the smallest of stitches for the final fell. There was nothing to be gained by hurrying the needle so fast that it picked up more than one thread of material, as the luckless sewer would be made to undo her slipshod work, back to the offending stitch, or stitches. In vain did Kitty protest that her mother disliked these seams for topskirts – that in Wales, the women used French seams, for extra neatness. Firmness was everything, came the reply to that. If firmness was so important, the girls grumbled, why had they no access to the Skinner's treadle machine? That humming Singer lay idle for the greater part of Jinny Skinner's year, its weighty head bowed low, inside the walnut table. Since most of Jinny's clothing was made for her by a little woman in Back Ducie Street, at prices to suggest she worked for the love of it, the Singer sewing machine served only two main functions: it stood as a status symbol, particularly fitting to a Drapery Bazaar, in the front window of the first-floor sitting room, and it supported, on a macramé table runner, an oak stand for all to see; this might have been short in the leg, but it was still capacious enough in its brass-bound body to hold a fleshy aspidistra, and one that would not have disgraced the Bridgemouth Botanical Gardens.

'Mean old cow,' said Kitty, as she squared her shoulders to help Tish's task. 'It wouldn't hurt her to put the machine on the landing, where we could all use it.'

'I suppose she feels she paid for it.'

'Dog in the manger,' Kitty asserted, unmindful of the confusion. 'The hours it would save us! And *she* was the one who made all the fuss, that's what gets my goat.'

Tish went into a quiet fit of the giggles. 'We'll have a best skirt; that's something. The two of us'll have to help Mary with hers.' She was giggling and speaking through a number of Newey's plated pins, held between her teeth.

'Don't talk with your mouth full. You'll swallow them. You won't think that's funny.'

Tish picked the pins delicately out of her mouth; she was serious again. 'You can wear this next Sunday, can't you? Eh,' she added, 'I've just remembered. What about your mouse and the crumbs?'

'I did that hours ago, before I went out. How much more is there?' Kitty strained her neck for a glimpse of the hem.

'Stand straight, or we'll never be through,' Tish remonstrated. 'Do you want this fixed, or don't you?'

They worked steadily, pinning, basting and sewing, until their backs ached and their eyes were rubbed sore. The nights were still short, and to sew by flaring fishtail was not the kindest treatment for eyes, however young they might be. Nor was it much fun to be confined to the unheated bedroom, instead of being allowed to crouch over the kitchen fire. When Mrs Skinner had ordered Kitty to stay upstairs, she was inflicting a very heavy penalty. Tish, of course, would not enjoy a fire without Kitty, so they had ended by sitting up in bed, fully clothed but for their boots, to stitch their hems. They had fallen silent. Kitty was lost in thoughts of Henry. What was it like to be sleeping on a boat? How big was his bed? She must ask him what his room was like, then she could imagine him more clearly in it. Did they ever let wives go on board? She could hardly ask him that. How sunburnt he looked, even in winter; and that dark shadow, even though he was clean-shaven . . . Brown hair and dark shadow. She liked dark men, with lots of hair on their chests, like her dad. She couldn't ask Henry that, either. She had loved the way his hair refused to stay completely hidden under his cap; it was too thick not to be unruly. She wished she could speak to him now. Would she ever see him again? She believed she might die if she didn't. Abruptly, she announced to Tish that she was fed up with sewing, and was not going to do another stitch that night.

The girls were now so cold, they could hardly contemplate stripping and getting into their nightdresses.

'Where have those two got to?' Kitty said. 'I'm not bothered about Eliza Heggy, but I wouldn't like Mary to get caught out.'

'They'll be back. They're old enough to look after theirselves,' Tish told her. 'We can't stay like this all night, us two.' Her hands were purple. 'Eliza would tell the Skinners we don't get undressed.'

'You're right. Lay off that chilblain. You're making it worse. By the time I count five, we'll both be out of bed. One . . . two . . . three . . .' Kitty leaped out. 'Come on, Tish! Four . . . five!'

Tish remained in bed, looking pitiful, and with two fingernails poised above the offending knuckle, as if sculpted in that attitude for all time.

'Look, I'll go and make the Bovril,' Kitty offered. 'That should warm us up. I'll put the skirts away. Hand that over.'

So it was that when Eliza Heggy came in after a quarter past nine, the two older girls were once more sitting up in bed, but each was correctly wearing her flannel nightgown, albeit with her day skirt wrapped about her shoulders. Their hands were clasped about their Bovril mugs – second helpings, though Eliza was not to know.

Kitty had run in the pitch dark to the outside lavatory; Tish had availed herself of the chamber pot underneath her bed. Neither girl had washed in the cold ewer-water; neither had thought to clean her teeth. In this, they were no different from Mary and Eliza, and many more; faces, necks and hands would be well-washed in the morning; more comprehensive ablutions were confined to a tepid sponge-down – or rather, flannel-down, while the lady assistant stood in a large zinc washbowl behind the bedroom screen. This 'bath' was a regular Saturday night event; its timing took into account Sunday's clean change of combinations, stockings, drawers and, for girls who possessed two of everything, underskirts; these garments had been dab-washed earlier in the week in that same washbowl.

Only the Skinners' clothing was thoroughly washed each week, by Mrs Jacks. Also on Sunday mornings, each assistant received from Mrs Skinner one huckaback towel and a fresh cotton-twill sheet. The used top-sheet became the new week's under-sheet, in the general practice of topping and tailing. Kitty and Tish had saved hard to buy one uncut Turkish towel, which they shared. Eliza Heggy had brought a thickish hand-towel from home; Mary had to make do with the official issue. Personal towels, like personal clothes, had to be washed by their owners. Only one concession to this was permitted: menstruation cloths, or bandages, which were commonly torn-off pieces of old sheeting – always brought from home, and ink-initialled by the girls – were soaked in cold salt water, in communal buckets, and boiled at the end of the Monday copper wash by Mrs Jacks. These brimming buckets, kept in the outhouse, were not an encouraging sight.

As for oral hygiene, occasionally a girl would rub her teeth with common salt, as good a disinfectant as any, which she applied with a finger, and stole from the block kept in the scullery cupboard; this attention to her teeth usually coincided with the Wednesday or Sunday time off.

'Where do you think you've been?' asked Kitty of Eliza, as the latter came quietly through the door. 'And where's Mary?'

Eliza unpinned her hat with one hand and dropped it on a chair.

'Had a good time, then?' Tish enquired.

Eliza's face darkened.

'She looks as if she's lost a bob and found a tanner,' Kitty commented. 'If that's what going out does for you, I'm glad I stayed in.'

Eliza, ignoring the witticisms, went to her tin trunk, unlocked it awkwardly, again with the one hand, and let fall a net bag inside it.

'Clack-handed, too,' Kitty added.

Eliza's face lit up with spite. She threw on to Kitty's bed what she had been carrying in a tight roll under one arm, something that had not been clearly visible on the off-side, and in the room's poor light.

Kitty's Sunday coat lay, half unrolled now, on the quilt.

'How's that for staying in all day?' Eliza sneered, as she took off her own coat and gloves.

Tish inhaled some of the bread she had been dunking in her Bovril, and the ensuing splutter and coughing lent Kitty a space in which to formulate some defence, though she could have used longer. She was horrified that she had visited the closet, admittedly in the dark, and had forgotten the folded coat, which she had left earlier in a corner, where the rectangular seat met the brick wall. The Heggy must have put a match to the candle-end in there. Kitty was exasperated with Tish, as well, for not reminding her.

'That's what comes of stealing bread,' Eliza remarked heartlessly, as Tish fought for breath.

Kitty thumped her afflicted friend on the back, while struggling herself to put a few words together. When they came, they were not convincing. 'I've had stomach ache; you ask Mrs Skinner. My coat was round me, when I got a bit shivery.'

'Then you folded it up, all neat and tidy, and stood it at the back of the seat!'

'I'm a neat type, aren't I? I wasn't draping it round me sitting *there* – my best coat. Anyway, you mind your own damn business.'

'You sneaked out in it; that's what you did. You don't need your Sunday coat to go to the back. Nobody does.'

Kitty made a noise like a wounded tiger, goaded too far. Eliza bolted for the stairs.

'Any more when she gets back,' Tish forced out, 'and I'll hit her on the head with this mug.'

'Drink up first,' said Kitty. 'You don't want to waste good food. How I could be such a fool! If the Skinners find out, there goes next Sunday!' She began pounding the quilt distractedly with her fist.

Tish drained the mug, as ordered, keeping her mouth on it, with the tip of her nose inside it; her eyes, big with speculation, peered over the top. 'Kitty,' she intoned, sepulchrally.

'What?'

Tish lowered the mug. 'Since when did she have that string bag?'

From where she was, Kitty saw no bag.

Forgetting the cold, Tish got out of bed and crossed the room to Eliza's trunk; a loop of draw-string hung down outside, jammed between lid and base. She raised the lid and lifted out the bag, holding it up for Kitty's inspection. 'Seen it before? I haven't.'

'No. It's new.'

'It's not. It's quite tatty. It smells nice.'

The bag's contents were wrapped in a brown paper bag. Tish scrambled back into bed, bearing her find aloft. A sweet, distinctive smell assailed the two girls.

'Parkin, by God!' Kitty exclaimed.

'She's been home!' Tish crowed. 'We've got her. She's been home!'

In the close community of the attic bedroom at Skinners' Place, successive generations of young assistants had worked out a few rules of their own and, on the whole, a rough time was had by any girl who chose to break these; thus it was that Eliza Heggy often fared badly with Kitty and Tish, and not much better with the younger Mary Gibbs. Loyalty figured at the top of this unwritten list of rules: 'Be loyal to the staff, and to hell with the Skinners!' Eliza was not strong on loyalty, either way. Another important precept concerned food parcels from home. These rare treats were to be shared by all four assistants, even when one of their number, like Tish, received no parcels at any time.

Tonight, this second rule had already been a source of spiritual heartburn to Eliza.

After her parents' initial irritation to see her on the family doorstep, she had devoted the afternoon and evening to a recital of the horrors of the Bridgemouth Drapery Bazaar, dwelling with emphasis on the iniquities of her older colleagues. Her father was so greatly incensed to learn of these and of the vulgarity, in one form or another, obtaining throughout the establishment, that he was for ending her apprenticeship there and then – a response very satisfying to his daughter, who wanted nothing better than to return to the comparative comforts of home. Unfortunately for these hopes, Mrs Heggy proved more worldly-wise than her husband, and it was quickly agreed between the parents that Eliza must get on with it.

To soften this harsh verdict, Mrs Heggy then did a stupid thing; she cut some generous wedges of parkin, to be hidden in Eliza's trunk, which would eke out the starvation diet supplied by the Bazaar. One can only surmise that her husband's thick twist had destroyed her sense of smell. Eliza had no idea when this secret eating would be possible, but such was the excellence of her mother's baking, and her own yearning after it, that she had left the house, carrying the cake in her mother's old net bag. On the way back to Skinners' Place, she had eaten one of the wedges, and broken into another.

Kitty had taken the bag from Tish and was counting how many were left. 'Four and a bit,' she said. 'I bet she demolished a fair amount, coming back.'

'She wouldn't be all that hungry.'

'She'd be guzzling, just the same. It beats me that she's not like a barrel. Four and a bit . . . That's one piece each; we'll let her have the extra bit, since it's mauled. Let's eat ours now, while the going's good.'

'Take Mary's out.'

'Yes, we'd better, in case Eliza hogs it.'

Kitty wrapped Mary's piece in a clean handkerchief. She and Tish ate theirs slowly, savouring every bite. What would Henry say if he could see them now? People like him had breakfast in bed, of course, with thin china on a stand-up tray. But parkin at night before he went to sleep? No. She transferred the cake to her left hand, and licked the parkined fingers clean. No, he would not be doing this in bed. She considered what he might be doing. No, again. He would be too honourable for that. Gentlemen were not like ABs; they had other things to think about, like . . . Parliament and wars and big jobs and hard work. A genuine gentleman didn't play about with girls; he chose one, and he stuck to her – like the vicar at home, and Mr Islwyn Griffith at the Plâs, and Dr Evans. It was a pity those three had such dreary wives: nice women, but you couldn't have a laugh with any of them. Perhaps being a lady meant that – bags of la-di-da and no laughs. In time, she might get her tongue around the la-di-da, but she couldn't go without laughter. Henry's eyes, when they went all wrinkly at the corners, were lit up with fun. *Henry, you've got to marry me*, she rehearsed with urgency – *you've simply got to, if you want to be happy*.

Eliza re-entered the bedroom with Mary for protection; the latter had arrived through the back gate just as Hezekiah had been walking down the yard to lock it. He had sent her indoors with a flea in her ear. There was barely time for her to stir Bovril into cooling water, let alone swallow the brew, before he was in the kitchen, turning out the gaslight, and directing the two assistants upstairs.

Though still apprehensive of Kitty's aggression, Eliza's re-entry was bolder than her recent exit, but any growing confidence suffered a dramatic arrest at the sight which greeted her eyes. She stood there, speechless. Mary, who had followed her in, glanced curiously from Eliza to the two seniors in bed, and back again. Kitty and Tish were finishing their last corners of parkin. Mary herself appeared worn; she sat on her bed and kicked off the bar shoes.

Tish spoke up. 'Have a piece of parkin, Mary. Eliza brought it for us. Wasn't that kind of her?'

'Here's yours,' Kitty said, holding out the handkerchief.

Mary realized there was more in all this than met the eye, but she was too tired to puzzle it out. One fact was plain enough: 'You went home, Eliza?' she said. 'Daring, wasn't it?'

'Give Eliza hers, Tish,' Kitty urged. 'Don't hang on to it. It's in your mum's bag, Eliza. And we left you the extra bit you'd started on.'

Eliza threw her best kid gloves inside the trunk. She took the net bag from Tish, and threw it after the gloves. Letting the lid down with its customary thud, she turned the key in the lock and transferred it to her handbag, which was what she ought to have done with the key in the first place.

'Someone doesn't mind parkined gloves,' Kitty remarked. 'Had a good day, Mary?'

Mary was eating her cake. 'Not bad.'

'Ah, well, hurry up, you two, and get that light out. Some of us need our beauty sleep.' Kitty wriggled down in bed, pulling the sheet over her ear. Tish gleaned the odd cake crumb off her pillow before she did the same.

*

'Remember, Jinny. Give them no cause for offence,' Hezekiah advised.

His wife was sitting at her dressing table, doing up her hair. In the grey light of Monday morning she could do without his nagging. 'You can rely on me,' she replied haughtily. 'You'd do well to remember the assistants have handles to their names.'

As he made for the kitchen fireplace to warm his gentlemanly posterior while scanning the Births, Marriages and Deaths, he reflected that he would not be doing this much longer on these premises, unless Jinny did learn to keep a civil tongue in her head. The dig about handles to their names – that was typical of her; she never could let bygones be bygones; and she must know in her heart that his mistakes slipped out unawares, whereas hers were always deliberate.

Jinny Skinner's brisk ascent up the top staircase meant one thing only – an equally quick descent on the girls' bedroom. They heard her coming, and four pairs of hands flew into operation, dragging covers over beds, pitching articles under beds, folding towels . . . Even so, Mrs Skinner was not over-pleased with the result; she was not so simple as to miss the evidence of haste. Pursing her lips, she wished her young ladies a good morning; the four replies carried overtones of pugnacity, trepidation, foreboding and servility, in that order of seniority. Now she was going to tell them off, as per usual, after deliberately catching them on the hop. Kitty was hoping to keep her own temper in check; she had to play for safety if she wanted to see Henry on Sunday.

Jinny, also, was making an effort, though her voice, when she found it, was more acid than intended, and would not have met with Hezekiah's approval. 'Whose box is that?' she demanded, indicating Eliza's tin trunk.

'It's mine, ma'am,' the owner said, with surprise. What was wrong with the tin trunk? It had been there since Eliza moved in.

'Get it out of here. Miss Gibbs, you will help her with it before you go down to breakfast. The boxroom is the place for trunks.'

Eliza said nothing. Mrs Skinner's nose was wrinkling up.

'What is that smell?'

The assistants looked at each other, wondering what particular smell she referred to, and all prepared to be mightily affronted if Jinny Skinner was being personal.

The woman's face grew tighter, as she sniffed. This was an unmistakable smell of ginger. Ginger cake? But no girl had received a parcel. 'Which of you has brought ginger cake into this bedroom?'

At last, Eliza was brought face to face with Dismay, Despair, Desperation and Doom itself. Her eyes stared, and her mouth began to droop. 'It's me, ma'am,' she said, in a small voice.

'You, Miss Heggy? And where did it come from?'

Eliza had started on the word *from*, when Kitty stepped into the rescue. 'Mrs Heggy sent it for us, ma'am. She met Mary and Eliza on the prom.'

'On the promenade. With ginger cake?'

Tish had taken the cue and was quick to help out. 'It was going to be for Eliza's auntie, really, wasn't it?'

Eliza was too stunned to manage more than a mechanical nod.

'What you never have, you never miss,' Mary chimed in, with courage. 'Besides, your auntie probably had a big plate of parkin on the table, when your mum got there.' This supposition, aimed at Eliza, did succeed in rallying her, and she agreed feelingly that her auntie's tea table was never without a mountain of parkin.

'Where *is* this parkin?' pursued Mrs Skinner, not impressed.

'It's in my trunk, ma'am,' confessed Eliza. 'It's only one slice and a bit.'

'In that box? Whatever for, you stupid girl? See that it's taken out and put in the kitchen, where it ought to be! You know food is not to be kept in the bedroom.'

'Yes, ma'am.' Eliza had never heard that house rule before, but she was not inclined to argue the point.

Believing that she had shown the lady assistants who was boss, Jinny felt she could now reveal the purpose of her visit. When the three debtors heard that their commission on sales was to be restored, they were highly pleased – and not merely because the halfpennies were so precious to them. They saw that they had won a skirmish, that concerted action and loyalty to the assistants' cause could carry the day, even in the Bridgemouth Drapery Bazaar.

'She could have let us off the skirt money,' Mary grumbled, after dinner.

'Oh, I don't know,' said Eliza Heggy, who had fully recovered from the events before breakfast. 'People can't run a business on charity.'

'On charity!' Kitty flared. 'We're not asking for charity! That stuff didn't cost the Skinners two and eleven-three a yard, but we've got to pay full price. If you work at Masons', you get discount on everything.'

'Discount . . . That's different,' Eliza conceded. 'You've got to remember Masons' is bigger. They make more money.'

'They have to pay out more,' Tish argued. 'Think of the rent for a place that size.'

'She could have given us those skirts,' Mary persisted.

'I wish I worked at Masons',' said Eliza.

'Places are all the same. It's the people you work with that count, and you'll get bad 'uns anywhere,' said Kitty, with meaning.

'D'you think Eliza Heggy could ever be nice?' Tish asked Kitty. 'Was she a nice baby, d'you think?'

'Not her. I couldn't see her giving anyone a suck of her bottle.'

The two girls were dressing the principal window, having flicked feather dusters over the limited assortment of leather goods and the bolts of heavy cloth in the other. Eliza and Mary had departed immediately after midday dinner, walking together, yet not together; a well-defined space divided them, testifying to the emotional breach which existed no less markedly. Eliza was expected to return for tea, in view of the showery nature of the weather, and the fact that Mary was to meet Bunny Harris in the region of four o'clock. Even with a pleasant colleague there was little fun to be had in Bridgemouth's streets on a wet Wednesday afternoon. It was Eliza's turn to penetrate enemy territory, as Mary was not slow to remind her, but that young spy had no intention of entering Masons' this afternoon.

'You made up about darning wool two cards for three ha'pence, last time,' she told Mary, which was an indisputable fact.

When next she spoke, Eliza was incapable of keeping off the subject which obsessed her, torn as she was between hatred of Bunny, who had appropriated her walking companion, and envy of Mary, who had acquired a young man. Their time together followed a striped pattern of fiery discontent and black silence. And yet Eliza was determined to stay away from Skinners' Place until tea time; any pleasure she might be extracting from the outing was of a perverse nature, in knowing that her resentment worked on Mary like a nutmeg-grater on skin.

'Her mam was daft, if you like, giving her that parkin,' said Tish, as she unlocked the arms of a breastless window model. A man paused on the pavement, watching as she and Kitty unpinned and drew off frocks and simulated frocks, to leave the dismantled figures bare to the buff.

'Is that him?' Kitty demanded, glowering in the man's direction, '– that foul pig you saw on Sunday?'

'No, that's not him.'

They flung muslin modesty-sheets over the sexless dummies, and turned their own backs on the spectator.

'Go and fetch Skinnybugs, Tish.'

'They're both out.'

There was no need for anybody's help. The man had taken himself off.

Having agreed that Eliza's mother, although a good cook, must be a fool of a woman, they continued their work without talking. Kitty's thoughts turned to home. Her dad and young Georgie would be out in the fields, getting on with the muck-spreading, rain or no rain. Her mum would have banked up the coals, and got the oven ready for the Wednesday bake. What a pity they had to have a boy and two girls! Three lads would have been more use. That Georgie, now, he'd been helping on the land for many a year, at first taking time off school, like other kids, whenever extra hands were needed, and then changing to a half-timer, on his eleventh birthday. Kitty hoped the farm manager would hold to his promise, and make him full-time at the end of the summer; he would be rising thirteen then; one and a half wages in the house and her mum wouldn't know herself! And Rosie hadn't all that long to go, before she would be sent out to service, or to the nearest drapery, like Kitty before her. She would have to do better at her sums if she wanted the drapery; no good being top at writing and bottom at sums; better the other way round, like Tish. A pang of sadness shot through Kitty at the thought of Rosie.

Say she was lucky enough to marry Henry Bonham – she could have Rosie to live with her; not as a servant, of course; but the little girl could help Kitty, and have a bit of money in her pocket, and a nice home. That would save her from the Hezekiahs of this world. Yes, that would be perfect. Her mum and dad could have a week's holiday with them and bring Georgie. No, they couldn't. There was never any holiday on the farm, unless the men wanted to lose a week's wages, or even find themselves with the sack when they got back. It wasn't like Skinners' Place, where you were made to take one week's holiday – on half pay if you were senior assistant. At least, you knew your job was safe, and it taught you to save up.

She wondered how her family would take to anyone as grand as Henry. Worse still, how would he take to them? She felt a quick fear, followed with equal speed by a wave of depression. She was up the shoot; she hardly knew him; ten to one, he'd be like all of them, and she would be dropped like a hot cake. Rosie would be thrown on to a hard world; Kitty and Tish would be dressing windows and standing behind counters for the rest of their natural. She sucked the thumb she had just stabbed on a drawing pin, and looked reflectively at Tish.

It was Tish who spoke up first. 'D'you think they love her, her mam and dad?' she asked.

'Love who? Eliza? Perhaps they do. I suppose if she was your kid, you'd feel different. They've nothing to be proud of, the way she's been brought up. Ruined, she is; a real spoilt brat.'

Tish pointed out that Eliza was a fairly pretty girl. 'If only she'd take that ugly look off her face. Her nose is nice.'

'We can't live with a nose.'

'It's not as if we don't try,' Tish continued. 'But she's always so nasty. She drives Mary potty, and Mary's sweet to us all, really.'

'I don't try much,' said Kitty. 'She gets me down, and that's all there is to it.'

'I know. She gets my rag out. All the same, it's three against one.'

'You going soft in the head, or something? Let me tell you, Tish Kelly, we've never had to work so hard to lick anyone into shape. She'd trample us flat, the same one. Throw over that alpaca.'

With skilled fingers, Kitty draped an attractive blue coat, full of hidden tucks and pinned pleats, on one of the naked ladies. 'If you think I'm going to stop those crumbs, you're mistaken. I don't know what's come over you; you were all for it, before.'

Tish saw that she had to accept this.

While they talked, the two worked with equal speed and efficiency. There was a welcome freedom in the Bazaar air; Hezekiah and Jinny had taken the ferry to Laverport, there to toil uphill, through the sooted office blocks and warehouses, until they reached Nathaniel Dowson's, Wholesale Linens, whose mean trading house was conspicuous only to the initiated. The Skinners dealt with Dowson, because he and they were in a small way, and the same degree of respect could be guaranteed from each side. They took a chance in leaving the shop, closed though it was, in the hands of two lady assistants, but husband and wife did like this monthly trip across the river and, after all, these assistants were senior; the Kelly girl would have been more openly called 'senior' but for the payrise involved.

So it was that Kitty and Tish were 'doing the window' as they wished, without possible instructions and corrections from Jinny Skinner. They were also doing the more interesting job first: they were dressing the window, and leaving the wiping and polishing of the glass to the last, even though it would entail tricky footwork. If their employers could have witnessed this arsy-versy procedure, it is doubtful if the results would have earned any approval. However, with hearts uplifted by the creative aspect of draping dummies, the girls swept their leathers almost gaily over the first pane of glass, and polished it off with scrim until it was so clean, it looked missing. Their polishing had this effect only once a fortnight, when Mrs Jacks had risked life and limb on a pair of steps, to clean the outside windows.

The Bazaar's greyish-white shop blind was still out, having been pulled out by Mr Truscott at nine o'clock that morning, to encourage shoppers to shelter from the rain, and to provide a similar service for the odd shop-window spreers. One of these was profiting by the dry pavement now. It was the man who had previously been there to irritate the window-dressers. Kitty and Tish gathered up the soft brushes and dusters, their faces stony. But the man was smiling at them and pointing at a pink, feathery boa, which was looped gracefully between two rings on the backcloth. 'How much?' he called.

'Heavens! I'd forgotten!' said Kitty, raking through the boot-box. She brought out a price ticket and pinned it by the boa: 9/11¾. He nodded gratefully and walked away.

'We're getting too suspicious by half,' said Kitty.

Among the post delivered to Skinners' Place on Thursday was one letter which defeated Mrs Skinner by the opacity of its envelope. It was addressed in a stylish and unfamiliar hand to Miss Katherine Catchpole.

Inside, the letter was penned with the same distinction; Kitty gasped with pleasure as she read it:

Dear Miss Catchpole, Henry began, though he went on to ask if he might in future start with *Dear Katherine*, or even *Dear Kitty*, since they had so quickly reached the Christian-name stage at their first meeting. He expected to return to Laverport on the Sunday evening. The repairs to his ship were going to take longer than anticipated, and a new freight had therefore been cancelled. With luck, he might have next Tuesday free; if so, he thought he would venture inside the Bridgemouth Drapery Bazaar some time before tea on that day. If there was any article in the shop that she fancied, perhaps she would tell him. He promised not to linger at her counter; his intention was to have a quick word with her, purchase the article and leave the parcel with her. In any case, he would be waiting at the Ferry Head a week on Sunday, around 2 p.m., when he hoped she would pay him the honour of joining him. The letter was signed, *Yours sincerely, H. Bonham*.

For all the joy Kitty felt, she was rather unnerved by Henry's correctness; she guessed that something of the same quality would be required of her, and she was not sure that she was up to it. This writing was so beautiful, for a start – all thick-and-thins. And she could never express herself like this in a letter; it was like reading a book. She had always been on the top row at school, but would that count? Would she be able to disguise her ignorance, or should she back out now, while the going was good? Was there any way she could catch up – maybe by just listening to him? She wished she did speak like Mrs Bellingham-Smith; she wished her mum and dad did; yet whoever heard of farmhands talking like the manor? Her mum and dad were all right as they were; and Henry didn't talk English, anyway. One day, if she worked at it, she might talk Scotch like him.

Tish watched the worry in Kitty's face give way to a softness that she would have termed doolally in anyone else's. She was not sure, herself, whether to be glad or sorry. Kitty passed the letter to her, and she read it with difficulty; the handwriting was impossible – all fancy. She was more at home with script or, better still, with honest-to-God block capitals. The letter was handed back, with no comment.

'What's wrong with it, then?' Kitty demanded.

'Nothing. He goes on a bit about Tuesday. And it's mighty grand, this "H. Bonham", seeing as he wants to call you "Kitty". It's all ever so grand. Well, isn't it? For the likes of us, I mean. I'd be scared of going out with him, myself; but then, I'm not clever, like you.'

'You weren't scared of him when he was getting our chocolate bar.'

Tish reflected on that. 'He was real nice then.'

'I think this letter's real nice,' said Kitty.

Tish did try to make amends for her criticism, but Kitty was not pleased. She knew she would have expressed similar doubts, had the letter been addressed to Tish. But it was not, and Tish's misgivings served only to remove Kitty's. With no further hesitation, as the recipient of this letter she was prepared to yield to its magnetism. If Tish thought it starchy here and there, Kitty was ready to admire the writer for that – the sad truth being that when someone is determined to fall in love, he or she will fashion an ideal mould. No suspicion that the contents may spill over, or fall short of the quantity required, can lessen the ardour.

Whether she wanted to or not, Tish caught some of Kitty's excitement: when in the past Kitty had walked out with a lad, Tish had taken a vicarious pleasure in the affair and had built up a reserve of second-hand experience, which she hoped to use one day on her own behalf. Looking back on these rare events, she assessed them now for what she could see they were – light-hearted concerns, thin on genuine feeling. This new man, by his very standing, was different. Henry Bonham's attraction for Kitty, and the reasons behind it, left Tish uneasy. He represented a fresh kind of threat to Tish: there would be no hope of living in the next street, and still keeping in contact, if Kitty married a chief officer. He would be whisking her off to his new town, wherever it was, and that would be the end of it. To defeat Mr Bonham, Tish would have to wait around invisibly, until the moment came when she could apply for a housemaid's job in his service; that way, she might keep an eye on Kitty. The notion tickled her, but not for long; she had one of her flashbacks to last Sunday's scene in the market square. For Tish, an extra-vile dimension had been added to sex, and she remained greatly distressed by it.

To wake up to a day which promises a meeting with a loved one of consequence, whether that consequence be a lifetime's or nine days', is one reason why many prefer existence to extinction. Kitty was so happy, she was in danger of being utterly selfish; only when she noticed how withdrawn Tish was did some feeling of contrition come over her. 'Cheer up, Tish-love,' she said, under pretext of matching silk thread with a shot-silk taffeta, a task the customer herself could have taken to Tish. 'I'm going to ask him to bring a friend along for you.'

Tish gave a smile, but she appreciated the thought.

Mr and Mrs Skinner were also in a state of exultation; the day's takings were soaring beyond their expectation. This spell of better weather must have affected the good people of Bridgemouth, who for two days had packed the shopping streets and wandered through the Drapery Bazaar with no little effect. So high was the euphoria that Hezekiah did not make his customary advance on the two Emporium spies – one of these none other than the Masons' son and heir, Edgar. What result their presence might have did not enter into his calculations; let Masons come, let Masons go, the Bazaar's prices spoke for themselves.

Never had the assistants worked harder. Jinny made a mental reservation to tell Mary Gibbs not to look so harassed when she was seeing to more than one person. The young Heggy was coming on; she had sold a severe black bonnet to that Myrtle Floyd, whose husband was said to be on his deathbed for the second time. On the first occasion, Myrtle had bought two mourning arm-bands, one for her brown day coat, and the other for her grey Sunday costume. It was almost indecent the way some widows hoped to do a death on the cheap.

But it was Kitty Catchpole who was setting the pace. In spite of Jinny's basic estimate of this lady assistant, she had to allow grudgingly that Miss Catchpole was today's shining light, and no two ways about it. The girl was apparently irresistible; customers who had no real reason for looking at materials were drawn to Fabrics, under the illusion that they might be missing something if they passed it by. The eager queue grew to such a size that Hezekiah had to call upon Mr Truscott to assist Miss Catchpole, while he himself saw to the old man's department. The backwash of Kitty's selling power all but swamped Tish, who had trouble satisfying the demands for sewing threads, pins, needles, hooks and eyes, press studs, braid, buckram, dress shields, petersham bands, buttons, ribbons of all sizes and colours and trimming lace, to name but a few of the more popular items. Their bosses watched this activity with growing approval, and Jinny's ears rang sweetly with the unceasing whizz and crash of travelling cylinders. At this rate, the Drapery Bazaar would be having a fresh dab of paint in the spring.

'Do you think he'll come?' In spite of herself, Kitty sought reassurance from Tish, when the entire morning had gone and Henry had put in no appearance. The two friends were in the kitchen, waiting to be joined by everyone for dinner.

'Of course he'll come!' Tish answered warmly. 'He's got hours yet, till tea time.'

'Who's *he* then?' asked Eliza Heggy, as she came in. 'The cat's father?'

'Ask no questions, you'll be told no lies,' Tish retorted. She and Kitty had not spoken of Henry Bonham to the two younger girls – she, because she was not too happy about him, and Kitty, because she feared Henry would not like it.

'Oh, pardon me for breathing!' Eliza flung back.

Mary arrived, ahead of the well-nigh jovial Skinners. Hezekiah congratulated the four lady assistants on a

good morning's work. Mr Truscott had hurried off to
the Manor Arms, to revive over a half pint of bitter and
a cold beef pie; given another Tuesday like this, he felt
life on the parish might be preferable. Never had he
been so worked off his feet, not since the Diamond
Jubilee, or not since the Christmases you used to get at
Skinners' Place. Not as young as he was, either, and
those two Skinflint bastards expecting him to keep up
with the girls or get out, and not so much as a handshake. He ordered a whole pint; and another.

Thus it was that just before the doors opened for
afternoon business, a most painful scene took place in
the stockroom, where Hezekiah Skinner had bundled
Mr Truscott, there to give him the benefit of a few home
truths. That the man should admit to knocking back
two pints in the middle of a working day was more than
Mr and Mrs Skinner could accept. 'Half a pint, followed by a bad turn' would have stood him in better
stead as a story. The unhappy old fellow battled with
himself to clear a path for words, but they kept piling up
in front of him whenever he made a little space. He tried
to announce that he would be all right in a minute or
two; he knew, and the Skinners knew, that this would
not be so. Fundamentally, he was not one who could
take his drink; he might be partial to it, nevertheless he
was the type of chap who fell over at the smell of the
barman's apron; for such as he, his usual half pint, or
the shortest pull at his little flask of rum, was plenty.

As Mr Truscott negotiated the back door, holding a
full week's pay in lieu, his young colleagues stood to
watch him go. Eliza Heggy looked distinctly frightened; Mary Gibbs and Tish Kelly were weeping into
their house-pinnies, and Kitty Catchpole was swallowing hard. Kitty hesitated at the door as he made
unsteadily for the back gate – his bowler loose on his

head, the overcoat hanging unbuttoned. Where did he live? Where could he work now? Why did they know nothing about Mr Truscott? As he opened the gate, she caught up with him and gave him a kiss. The tears spilled down his cheeks; then with a brief shake of his head, he turned and went down the side street.

Either by the natural law of trade winds, or by the chill that had descended on the assistants, afternoon business reverted to subnormal, and those clients who had missed out on the morning's boom now left the shop resolving not to return to the Bazaar in a hurry; the four girls and their two employers all looked like the man who killed his father; moreover, the place was obviously on the decline; the boss himself was serving customers.

After the morning's freak rush, it would have been surprising if any girl had shown a capacity for more. It would have been especially surprising if Kitty had been able to maintain the high exhilaration which had kept her going throughout those hours. If much of it was on the wane by dinner time, with Henry Bonham's failure to materialize, then the little that remained had been effectively doused by the Truscott affair. In the slack afternoon ahead, she was to have ample time to concentrate on Henry and on his absence, to swing between faint optimism and the bleakest pessimism. She was glad she had not mentioned his existence to Mary and Eliza. Tish would understand, if he let her down; she might be relieved to have him out of the way, but she would never crow.

Kitty moved closer to Tish. 'I don't think he's coming,' she murmured. Tish gave no reply, because Skinnybugs' eye was on her. It was going to be a bit much if the boss stayed in Mr Truscott's place for good; at least they used to see the back of him from time to time, when he went on patrol; but now, Kitty and Tish were going to be landed with him, were they?

The large, mottled face of the wall clock showed three minutes past four. Hezekiah had moved to the right of his counter, deserting Everything For The Gentleman, in favour of Boys' Outfitting. He was sipping his cup of tea. 'Miss Catchpole, you may go for tea.'

Kitty had not bothered to ask for permission, nor had she sneaked out without it. She was not anxious to leave the shopfloor. Tish threw her a glance of compassion as she went to the kitchen. She was back behind the counter in next to no time; the Skinners were staggered.

Kitty believed the first clock got its name from the noise its pendulum made. This shop pendulum was clocking relentlessly to and fro, in its muted fashion. Kitty rubbed her eyes, and fixed her gaze on the counter instead. Perhaps tea time in Scotland was later than Bridgemouth's? The only member of the Mercantile Marine in the shop was a ginger-haired able seaman, whom Kitty at first took to be Bunny Harris until she noted his stockier build, and the girlfriend with him. The girl had taken hold of his arm; they were making for Baby Linen. Kitty hoped the AB's intentions were in every way honourable. She folded the bale of red flannel which lay open on her counter, then climbed the scuffed pair of low steps to return the material to its top shelf. When she regained terra firma, the sailor and his friend were approaching her counter. Kitty's heart sank; she could do without a customer in Fabrics when she was expecting somebody more interesting. In the background, Eliza Heggy stood framed in the archway, staring after the two young people.

'Miss Heggy! Gowns and Millinery, please!' roared Mr Skinner, much to the customers' alarm. As the girlfriend complained, she had jumped out of her skin. As for Eliza, she was blown back to base by the force of Hezekiah's command. He drew himself up to his full five feet ten inches: customers and assistants were not to think that his old role no longer existed, with his adoption of the new.

'Are you Miss Katherine Catchpole?' The sailor's tone was respectful; his companion was studying Kitty in a slightly resentful manner.

Conscious of the many eyes upon her, Kitty said he had the name right.

'I have a letter for you from the chief, ma'am,' he said, handing her another of those quality envelopes, which were manufactured to fox Jinny Skinner.

'Thank you. Thank you very much.' Kitty's smile knocked the lad over; the first mate knew how to pick them. His girl's face darkened and she moved off, leaving him to follow her out of the shop.

The secret was out. Hezekiah and Jinny exchanged looks charged with disbelief. Kitty was not sure that Mary and Eliza would have heard at their end of the shop, but she now wanted everybody to know; never had she felt so proud. To be addressed as *ma'am* in front of the Skinners! Perhaps he should have said *miss*, but *ma'am* was so much better. She touched the envelope inside her pocket. Tish smiled at her. Dear Tish. Oh, how could she wait until this shop closed? The others would grin if she asked permission to leave the room. She would die with the anxiety, the – what was it? – the anticipation, expectation. . . . She pondered on what the realization might be. She prayed to the clock: 'Come on, clock! Oh, come on!'

Shortly before closing time, a shabby man fairly ran into the Bazaar. Again, it was a customer for Fabrics, and again, Kitty groaned inwardly. But then she recognized him; it was the man she and Tish had so misjudged, when dressing the windows.

'I thought you'd be shut,' he panted. 'I couldn't get away from work.'

'We close at a quarter to seven,' Kitty told him gently. 'Seven-thirty on a Saturday.'

'I never remember these things. Can I have it? It's still in the window.'

He wanted the feather boa! Kitty laughed aloud. 'Of course, sir! Just one minute . . .' She would have dismantled the entire display for him, had he asked her to do that.

It was for his wife's birthday. Kitty wrapped the froth of feather with care in white tissue, then ran to stores for a white box. She flew to Tish's section and helped herself to a sprig of yellow daisies at 7½d. This she waved gaily in the direction of the horrified Hezekiah, as she ran back to the boxful of boa. With reverence, she put the daisy-trim inside. 'She'll like that,' she said to the man.

'I'm afraid I've only got a ten-shilling note,' he stammered.

'That's all right, sir. The daisies are with the compliments of the Drapery Bazaar!'

Hezekiah grappled with the knot of his tie like one suffocating. The customer walked beaming out of the shop, his box wrapped in brown paper, and tied with a clear run of Kitty's string. Hezekiah decided that, in view of the chief, a strong warning about those daisies would have to do; he was certain Jinny would see it in that light. After all, a shut fist never caught a bird.

With the shop closed, Mary and Eliza had flung the sheets over their counters in a trice, and were in that bedroom almost as promptly as Kitty and Tish. Kitty had torn roughly at the tough envelope in her eagerness to get it open, and a fine muck-up she had made of it. Mary poured some cold water into the basin she shared with Eliza and began to wash her hands, all with the minimum of noise. Eliza combed her hair with fussy touches, without undoing it; when Mary moved away from the washstand she, also, poured out water and applied soap to her hands.

'Seems to be a lot of washing going on,' Tish commented.

'My mother is surprised we don't have hot water after a day's work,' Eliza stated primly.

'There's lots of things here she'd be surprised at; all the mothers would,' said Tish.

Kitty was reading and re-reading what was only a one-page letter. Her face was radiant.

'You look real moony,' Mary told her, drying her hands.

'It's a nice letter, that's why.' Kitty put it inside its jagged envelope.

'From the chief, I suppose,' said Eliza.

'Yes, from the chief officer.' So Eliza did hear what the AB had said . . .

Mary could see there was to be no more information with Eliza around. Kitty was right to say nothing. She made downstairs for the evening meal of bread, cheese and piccalilli. Eliza hung up her towel and went after her.

Kitty passed the letter to Tish.

'You read it,' said Tish. 'I can't make head nor tail of his writing.'

Kitty read quietly: 'Dear Kitty . . .'

'*Kitty!*' Tish observed.

'Yes . . . Dear Kitty, I am very sorry not to be able to

fulfil my promise to you. I have had to stay on board unexpectedly; a friend has gone sick. By rights, I should have been free today, as you know. Our little arrangement will have to be postponed for a week, when I trust you will let me buy you the present of your choice. Our Sunday appointment remains, and I shall expect to see you that day at the Ferry Head, about 2 p.m. Please forgive me for any disappointment you have suffered today, and I hope you *were* just a little disappointed not to see me! With warmest wishes. Yours sincerely, Henry Bonham.'

Kitty had lingered over the last lines, savouring every delicate stroke of the pen. Naturally, she was disappointed. She was not concerned about his present, but if only he had walked into the Bazaar! She wanted so much to show him off. She wanted the Skinners, the customers, the girls, to be stunned by the sight of him. All the same, a letter was something to have. She would never destroy it as long as she lived.

Tish drew a deep breath. 'It's a lovely letter, that's for certain; nicer than his first.'

'I wouldn't say that. I think they're both lovely.'

'Just as well you do. You're the one who's walking out with him.'

Kitty looked uneasy. 'I'm sorry this other man is ill. I was hoping there'd be a friend for you on Sunday.'

'Never you mind about me. You look after yourself, Kitty-lass. And let's get down there, or there'll be nothing left.'

'By God, you're right. How about washing our hands?'

'Mine aren't dirty, if yours are.'

Kitty was washing her hands vigorously, using Eliza's dirty water, and Eliza's Vinolia.

'She'll know you've used her Stands for Feminine Loveliness,' Tish warned. 'You can smell it a mile off.'

'Mary's very quiet all of a sudden,' Kitty observed, as she adjusted her own best straw on her own pretty head.

'She's been quiet all week,' said Tish, who was not making much noise herself, as she smoothed down her new Sunday skirt, and prepared to face a dull day. 'We didn't help her much with her skirt, you and me. Maybe she's fed up, not having it ready.'

Mary Gibbs and Eliza Heggy had preceded them to the hall, where they were waiting, prayer books in hand, to walk to church. Hezekiah and his wife had joined them, and a high-pitched enquiry soon came floating upstairs: perhaps Miss Catchpole and Miss Kelly would condescend to come down that minute, so that they could all arrive on time for divine service?

'Divine service!' Kitty mimicked, under her breath. 'Hark at the herald angel! Coming, ma'am,' she called downstairs. 'You go ahead, ma'am. We'll catch up.'

'You'll do nothing of the kind!' came the crisp reply – Hezekiah had taken over. 'Downstairs this very second, both of you, or I shall want to know the reason why!'

Tish was already on her way, in the devout hope that Kitty might be a couple of stairs behind her. She was, but halfway down the flight, she gave a cry of alarm. 'Oh, no! I've only got one glove!' And Kitty was haring back up those stairs.

Jinny Skinner had had enough; martialling the three girls and Hezekiah, she led them out of the back gate. 'Leave the gate unlocked, for goodness' sake,' she said crossly to Hezekiah. 'No one's going to run away with the WC.'

As soon as she heard the decisive slam of the back door, Kitty came down the stairs, holding the pair of gloves which had been complete on her way up. She ran to the kitchen for a very small piece of bread; thinking so much about her afternoon meeting with Henry, she had forgotten to take the bread upstairs in her handkerchief, according to her daily custom. A quick sprinkle of crumbs by the millinery drawer, a discreet pull out, since the drawer had been rammed home by someone, and Kitty was ready to leave for church. She shut the back door in Hezekiah style, and closed the gate, also, with force. As she went jauntily along the street, she was humming a song. Had they heard her, the Skinners would have been dismayed; in this, they were not more priggish than the bulk of the population. Sunday observance, even in the homes of non-practising Christians, followed a strict formula of hypocrisy; hymns, only, were picked out on the front-room piano; even pieces in the Star Folio were frowned upon, as being possibly too enjoyable to be played on the Sabbath day; indoor and outdoor games were taboo; the reading of novelettes was out; and most reading was circumscribed. Parents might read the Sunday newspapers, but for those children who were literate, the day's reading was sadly restricted. Few were forced, or would have cared, to study the Bible in the home – that exercise was catered for in the afternoon Sunday school, where most Christians, practising or otherwise, were glad to send their children – so the youngsters who were not taken to church had to languish until, or unless, their street was visited by a Salvation Army contingent. This was the nearest thing to light entertainment that Sunday could offer them.

Little wonder, then, that Miss Katherine Catchpole did not let the words and music of her song penetrate the Sunday streets of Bridgemouth. If she had, the hypocrites would have had a field day, for she sang: 'You are . . . my ping-pong girl . . . You set . . . me in a whirl . . . Every time I see you opposite me . . . with your little kiss-curl . . . And when . . . I see you play . . . You steal . . . my heart away . . . Be my honey love . . . Spend my money, love . . . Sweet little ping-pong girl.'

She was not the last to arrive at the church porch, though she figured among that small number directed to a back pew in the door-draught. Kitty annoyed the sidesman by sweeping past him and taking her place in the Bazaar detachment. She annoyed the Skinners, of course, by her disgracefully late entrance, and Jinny felt sorely tempted, in that house of God, to smite Miss Catchpole across the earhole with *Hymns Ancient and Modern*.

During the service, Tish sank into apathy. When life presented her with one of its more critical problems, she tended to miss the comfort of old routines. Tish was not in the mood to love her neighbour as herself; she found three of her immediate neighbours completely unlovable. She would not pine after the Reverend Andrew Macpherson, either; that sour old devil couldn't hold a candle to Father McManus. She plucked idly at the empty, shiny tips of her black cotton gloves, as she recalled the tubby Father nearer home, a creature of good heart, who had perfected the blind eye, and sometimes, she suspected, the deaf ear. He was able to love sinners and they, in their turn, loved him for his own human weaknesses. Tish's collection-penny dropped with quite a clatter for its size; it had escaped from one of her gloves and had rolled underneath Jinny Skinner's skirts. Apparently, it would have to remain there until the plate came round.

Kitty was seated at the aisle-end of the pew, next to

Eliza. She was raring to go and, like Tish, she had no patience with the preacher, the man who shook hands with the Skinners and ignored their assistants. Her new grey skirt was looking clean and stiff; she wanted Henry to admire it. She must help Mary to get that hem finished. Mary had been working as hard as she could on two hems, finishing a replacement underskirt as well as the topskirt. For some months past, both her underskirts had presented a sorry sight, and one of them was so old that stitches were now refusing to hold. Kitty gave a moment's thought to the half-crown she had lent Mary towards the cost of the white calico. It was something she had no wish to dwell on, for it had obliged her to send less money home, on the pretext that one of her own skirts had gone beyond repair. However, she believed it would not be long before Mary's loan was repaid. Meanwhile, she kept her counsel; for once, she had told Tish nothing. She took a look at Mrs Skinner's profile; its set suggested there was a slating to come, once the service was over and the congregation dispersed. This did not bother her unduly. The Skinners would not go too far until sales maintained the recent improvement. Besides, they had taken in Henry's rank, although this could be no more than a short-term advantage. Henry's effect would wear off.

The sermon had faded into the final blessing, which Macpherson delivered at a gallop. With creaks and a bracing of shoulders, the assembled brethren rose to their feet, to sing lustily, 'Too late, too late shall be the cry, Jesus of Nazareth hath passed by'. Bunny Harris threw a glance at Kitty, and flashed her a wink. The cheeky bounder! Who would have thought it? He was not to imagine that friendship with Mary gave him special privileges with her colleagues. Moreover, she was confident that Henry would never wink at a young lady, without an introduction, or even with one, and particularly in church. Therefore, Kitty rewarded this intrepid seaman with no smile; instead, she raised her chin, gazed ahead at the blue and red patches in the east window, and sang more fervently than before. Bunny Harris was stung; risking a second glance at the uplifted chin, he made a mental reservation: Miss Kitty Thingamy gave herself some mighty fine airs.

When it came to telling that same young lady a thing or two, Mrs Skinner was uncharacteristically not up to the mark; in this instance, she was hoist by her own new policy – that is to say, by hers and Hezekiah's. She was forbidden, by the demands of essential discipline, to overlook Kitty's last-minute scamper into their pew, yet she had to tread more gently than she would have liked, in order to keep this young nuisance moderately sweet, and to impress upon Hezekiah the reality of his wife's good intentions. Then again, she was considerably influenced by the events of the previous day: to have a lady assistant courted by a ship's officer would bring prestige to the Drapery Bazaar. Nor was Kitty Catchpole's sales ability to be sneezed at. Therefore, she decided to speak to the girl coldly, rather than sharply. 'Miss Catchpole,' she said, when the Bazaar group had forged ahead and was clear of all handshakers and insatiable gossips – 'I would be obliged if you would walk into church with the rest of us, next Sunday and every Sunday. You must learn to time yourself, and allow for forgetting things like gloves.'

'Yes, ma'am. I'll do that.' The Skinner was not going to be difficult. Well, she would see that Kitty could play the same line. 'My glove had dropped to the floor, between the chest and my bed,' she volunteered. It was a house rule that Sunday accessories, like Sunday clean underwear, had to be laid out in readiness on the

Saturday night. 'There must be a mouse in our room,' she continued, holding up a gloved thumb, 'because there was a hole chewed in this thumb.'

At the mention of a mouse, Eliza and Mary both gave a little scream.

'Be quiet!' Hezekiah reproved them. 'The idea, screaming like that over a cock-and-bull story!'

'Let me see that hole,' Jinny Skinner ordered. 'We'll soon tell if it's a mouse, or plain wear and tear.'

'I mended it with black cotton, ma'am,' said Kitty meekly. 'That's what made me a bit late.'

Jinny rose to that. 'A *bit* late! You and Miss Kelly were late to start with, if I remember correctly.'

'I'm glad you had the good sense to draw it together,' Hezekiah put in, more reasonably. 'Nothing worse, I always say, than a young lady with a hole in her glove.'

Tish listened with a wry gleam in her eye. That darn had been worked, to her knowledge, two weeks before.

Mary clumped along, as always, in her mother's bar shoes, clenching her toes to the sole, in an effort to minimize the sloppy fit around the heel. Jinny clicked her tongue as she walked behind Mary and Eliza; the latter's neat black boots showed up Mary's ill-fitting hand-me-downs. It would be so much better if the lady assistants all came from decent homes. Class, that was what Jinny Skinner was after, and what she seldom found; sometimes, class was acquired by accident, and not always by those who most deserved it. Kitty Catchpole must be looking forward to her afternoon out. She would be a lucky girl to marry into the merchant service, whatever the rank. But a first mate! Why, that was a cut above Hezekiah! This reflection brought on a twinge of rancour; an old has-been like him, with a struggling Drapery Bazaar, did not compare with a young suitor in navy-blue serge and three stripes up; anyone in Bridgemouth would tell you that.

Trust it to turn out wet, thought Kitty, in disgruntled mood, as she tilted the umbrella to the right to keep the worst of the driving rain off her head and shoulders. Tish had left her at the Apollo theatre, each to go her separate way. By now, Tish ought to be heading back for Skinners' Place, if she had any sense; without Kitty's umbrella she would soon be wet through. Kitty's left boot was shipping water; a tear had developed in the stitching between sole and upper; her foot was uncomfortably cold and wet in its black woollen stocking. She twisted, to assess any damage to her skirt: yes, the back hem had picked up some splashes from the muddy pavement. Straightening up, she shook the drips off her open brolly.

The ferryboat was in mid-channel, riding for Bridgemouth. Kitty might have been up for interview at Masons', she felt so apprehensive; much of her will to succeed was collapsing.

'Just the girl I was expecting!' said the voice of somebody who had all the assurance she herself lacked.

Kitty swung the umbrella to the left, to see a face she had come across once before, but only at a distance.

'I said to myself it was you with your friend, by the Apollo.'

She stared briefly at him; the lad was one of the two who had marched away from Tish and herself that other Sunday. 'Oh, yes?' she commented, looking fixedly towards the boat.

'How about you and me taking a walk, then? There's room for someone as good-looking as me under this.' He had taken hold of the umbrella.

'Do you mind?' Kitty exclaimed angrily, tilting a water-spout down his neck as she pulled the handle away, and knocking his cap awry into the bargain. 'I happen to be waiting for someone.'

'I bet you are.'

God's gift to women, this one, Kitty told herself, as she tried to think of something sufficiently cutting to say. She had to get rid of him. What would Henry think, if he saw her standing there with another fellow? He might have seen this already, if he was on the boat, and how she wanted him to be on it!

'Will you kindly shift yourself?' she said, interposing the brolly between them.

'Ah, come off it, ducks! Who d'you think you're kidding?'

'I don't want to have to call a policeman.'

His laugh was very loud. 'Listen who's talking! *Call a policeman*! You ought to be glad, going a walk with me. It's not every girl gets the chance.'

Kitty went quickly inside the ferry entrance; the boat was edging in, and was taking a terribly long time about it. She closed her umbrella. The sailor was strolling nearer to her; he paused a few feet away to light up a Woodbine. Out of sight to Kitty and others waiting in this area, the boat was repeating its personal moves and alarums.

Henry was the third passenger to reach the turnstile. Once through, he came striding towards Kitty with a hand outstretched to greet her, his face alight with pleasure.

'Good afternoon, Mr Bonham,' said Kitty, her eyes dancing, and all fear gone.

'Good afternoon, Miss Catchpole,' he replied quietly, holding her hand in his. 'We can't tramp around Bridgemouth in this, can we? I suggest we try the hotel for some tea.'

They crossed the road to get to the Pier Hotel, both of them protected by Henry's man-size brolly. The young AB had beaten a retreat; he was boarding a no. 12 tram. Kitty slipped her arm inside Henry's.

The Pier Hotel was a monumental white elephant, kept going by a perennially lugubrious tenant-manager, who was under constant threat of dismissal for poor returns, which were no fault of his. The staff, like the décor, were showing signs of decay. What had once been an ornately gilded interior, with superior carpeting and floor-length brocade curtains, was faded and altogether too shabby to attract custom.

Kitty thought it the most wonderful place she had ever seen. So often, she and Tish had come past this relic of Bridgemouth's earliest days and had longed to step inside, particularly on a winter's evening when the softly lit vestibule seemed more than usually inviting.

She took care not to tread on the polished brass strip, which disguised the join of the old red Wilton with the older pink Brussels of the tea room. Henry had removed her umbrella and had let it fall with his own into the umbrella stand. She hoped the two would be there when they came to reclaim them; left to her own devices, she would never have let go of that precious possession, but Henry seemed to see nothing odd in planting two perfectly good umbrellas in a hotel stand and walking away. How rich did you have to be to trust the whole world and its wife?

She was aware that the elderly waiter was standing behind her; his bony hands fluttered in mid-air, ready to remove her damp three-quarter coat to the coatrack. Blushing, she tried to undo the buttons quickly. He bowed as he laid her coat over his right arm, and extended his left for Henry's. Kitty nervously thumbed her pale shantung blouse into the back of her skirt. She thanked God it was her new grey skirt. For the first time in her experience, she had reason to be grateful to Mrs Skinner. The waiter had given her a smile; she looked a decent young creature, as pretty as a man could wish for. He liked a girl who could blush; he hoped she stayed that way, and didn't grow as hard-boiled as most of the young ladies brought inside the Pier Hotel by ships' officers. Having settled the couple at a table, he offered Kitty the folded menu card.

'Just a cup of tea,' she said in an undertone to Henry, passing the card over; she felt incapable of making a choice.

'A pot of tea for two,' Henry ordered, reading down the items. 'Something a little solid?' he asked Kitty. 'Or perhaps it's too early for that?'

Dear Henry, if only he could guess how eagerly she would have devoured something solid, but not in the tea room of the Pier Hotel. 'Oh, no,' she assured him.

'Perhaps the lady would like some pastries?' the waiter suggested.

'I think that would be a good idea. You could manage a pastry, couldn't you?' Henry said.

'That would be very nice.'

The large, misted mirrors on the wall were little better as looking glasses than the ones she knew at the Bazaar, but these had gilt frames, and reflected the light from more ornamental chandeliers. Only two other tables were occupied, one by a gentleman of stocky build, in brown Harris tweed, whose gaze – when not focused on the buttered teacake in front of him, or on the selection of cakes beside him – rested repeatedly on Kitty; the second was taken by a middle-aged parson and a quietly dressed woman, who was no doubt his wife. They talked earnestly to each other; this man was so obviously in love with the woman that he could spare few glances for Kitty and Henry. Maybe she was not his wife; husbands, as a rule, did not look at wives with so much open admiration, or vice versa.

Kitty surveyed their own plate of cakes: it held a vanilla slice, two fairy cakes, a butterfly cake and one slice of seed cake. She would have liked a vanilla slice but was afraid of tackling it in public. She took the seed cake.

'Are you *sure* you like that?' Henry was not over-partial to seed cake. He took the vanilla slice.

'Yes, really. I love it.' Kitty poured out the tea.

'Tell me what you've been doing with yourself since I last saw you.'

She touched her lips, in Skinner fashion, with the small damask table napkin, before she launched into a résumé of her more recent days at the Drapery Bazaar. She was speaking of an existence totally alien to him; its restrictions and its penalties, though not given in full by Kitty in this low-key recital, fascinated him, while at the same time filling him with horror. It was incredible that a girl could live in such circumstances, and present so fresh an appearance as did the lovely Kitty, now finishing the last crumb of that impossible seed cake.

'Have another,' he invited. She told him she really could eat no more.

'They are rather uninviting,' he admitted. Beckoning the waiter, who hurried across, Henry ordered more interesting cakes than those: he would like a slice or two of tennis cake, and some iced mocha, too, while the man was about it.

Kitty was covered in embarrassment as the old gentleman rushed off to oblige Henry. She studied her hands in her lap. Here she was, a party to sending an elderly man scurrying to the hotel kitchen, for no honest reason at all. In different circumstances she would have tackled any of those so-called pastries with unashamed gusto, but because she had to be finicky, Henry had thrown his weight about. Perhaps he always gave orders in that tone of voice. She was disturbed by it. She knew she would not be able to look that waiter in the face when he returned to their table.

Henry drank his tea slowly. She looked frightened, and very appealing. Funny child – she was worried on the waiter's account; her eyes had followed the old chap right out of the room. She would have to learn that others must give her a correct standard of service, just as she herself had to snap to it at the Bazaar. Naturally, in those clothes, she must feel at a disadvantage. More expensively dressed, Kitty Catchpole would certainly grace any man's table. The chief officer was scrutinizing Kitty's every move, and assessing her every word, from the viewpoint of respectability in his own class. He wanted her to do well when she met his friend Eric. He wanted that desperately. On most issues, he and Eric had always seen eye to eye; where they clashed, they were more or less evenly matched in willpower. In the matter of this girl, Eric must be persuaded somehow to accept her; his approval was essential to Henry.

'There is no need to be scared,' he told her gently.

'I'm not scared,' she whispered back.

'Yes, you are,' he said. 'Ah, here are the cakes. Thank you. These look a little better.'

'Did you get your gamp back?' Tish demanded.

Kitty did. It was drying out in a corner of the bedroom, where Tish had failed to see it in her hurry to join Kitty over the kitchen embers.

'We went and had dinner at the Queen's, after we'd walked and walked.'

'The Queen's? You never! No wonder you can give Bovril a miss.'

The details of every morsel that had passed down Kitty's throat were essential educational material for Tish. When Kitty had finished her account, Tish was able to recite the dinner menu right through, without error; she gained nourishment from it, to the extent of sighing with appreciation at the end of each course.

'What did he do?' she pursued. Kitty was in such a dream, it was hard work to prise anything out of her.

'*Do?*' Kitty's voice was a shade haughty.

'Didn't he kiss you, or anything?'

'He gave me his arm, when we went walking, and he kissed me when I left him. A little kiss on my cheek; very soft.'

Tish said that must have been marvellous, really marvellous. Privately, she wondered if Henry Bonham was a bit of a dull dog; however, Kitty had been fed in hotels and treated to a gentlemanly kiss at the end. She had not been chased in the rain out of the cemetery.

Tish had not continued far beyond the Apollo when she was approached by two ABs, both with their hands rammed inside their pockets, their shoulders hunched and their eyes half shut against the rain. She recognized them easily as the two who had once avoided herself and Kitty. In next to no time, one of the sailors was making his lone way to the Ferry Head.

'I've told you, she's meeting a friend!' Tish called after him. 'He doesn't believe me, does he?' she added indignantly to the other.

She accompanied this Fred Robertson in the direc-

tion of the graveyard. He had an aunt buried in that
hallowed plot, and was given to paying his respects on
wet Sunday afternoons. Tish would have preferred to
make for anywhere other than the Bazaar's bramble
grounds, but perhaps there were tidier sections of the
cemetery to be visited, and less tumbledown monu-
ments to be awed by. And, after all, what places had
Bridgemouth to offer, in the way of peace and quiet?
There was the park, for one, she thought glumly, as the
huge gateway showed up ahead, on their left. It was so
long since she and Kitty had walked there, she had
almost forgotten what the lake and the rockeries looked
like.

'We could always try the park,' she suggested.

'Too crowded.'

'On a day like this? It'll be empty.'

'My auntie isn't buried in the park.'

He had a point there; she understood that. They had
left the shopping area behind, and were passing the
Academy of Art, which was a teaching institution only.

'I wish they had pictures in there like the big one at
Laverport,' she said.

Fred Robertson looked at her in alarm. 'You off your
chump or something? You like pictures?'

'It's somewhere to go, isn't it, when it's raining?
Better than trudging through streets, if you're not going
to the park. I suppose them places close on Sundays,
anyway.'

'There's trees in the cemetery. My Auntie Annie,
she's got a nice big tree. You'll see. Where d'you work,
then?'

Tish was fly to this one. 'I'm in service,' she said.

'You and your friend in the same house?'

'No. Different houses.'

And that was all the information he was given, in

spite of his probing. They plodded on, past the grid of red-bricked terraces on their right, each small retreat bay-windowed and stone-silled, each diminutive garden hedged and railed, each parlour-grate hidden behind an ornamental screen. The whole complex enclosed a small station of the Bridgemouth-Laverport Underground. It was five years since passengers on its trains had not been suffocated by smoke or bespattered with smuts, but three of the Bazaar's young ladies had still to make that journey for the first time.

At the fork in the road, Tish and Fred Robertson bore left, where the more expensive terraces were already encroaching on the Clothes Hill, that breezy drying-acre for the neighbourhood's washing, and where the long greenhouses on the opposite side stretched as far as the stone mason's yard. Soon, those brave seedlings under glass would produce a sizeable and well-ordered forest, dotted with firm fruit, which glowed like red baubles, tasted sharp-sweet, and smelled of mint.

They came to the business yard, which drew its lifeblood from the remains across the way, for this was Cemetery Road, barring the T-junction, and proclaiming to all amateurs of the love-apple that in the midst of life we are in death.

'How far now?' Tish asked half-heartedly.

If she had her suspicions about his defunct aunt, they were not lessened as Fred Robertson led her further and further from the yew-lined main approach, up narrower, overgrown paths beside chipped angels and crippled stones. This was another blackberry territory, far beyond the one known to the four assistants of Skinners' Place. Tish had trouble holding her new skirt clear of the grasses and weeds. However, her companion did eventually come to a halt before a crumbling family memorial, at the foot of a straggling ash. It was inscribed with the names of several generations of Robertsons, and the latest addition read: *Annie Mildred Robertson, sister of the above, d. 4 Mar. 1901, aged 63 years*.

'She wasn't married?' Tish remarked.

He looked at the stone. 'No, that's right. She never got married. She was a good auntie to me.' With that, in the half shelter of the tree, he started to unloop the braided toggles on Tish's Sunday coat.

From her impoverished childhood upwards, although reared on a diet lamentably deficient in every respect, Tish Kelly had exhibited all the muscular ability of a natural athlete; as she had proved in the Market Square encounter, the girl could move. In this present emergency, her weakened ankle had to withstand difficult terrain, as she leapt over unmarked grave mounds, and from slim kerbs to the treacherous hollows between graves; but she did leap, and to some advantage. Young Fred caught up with her when she came into the straight, heading for the main gates. No amount of persuasion had any effect on her. No, she would not go with him on the 12 tram to the little house in Seaton Street – number 5, if she wanted to know. She had not the slightest wish to know; he could go there himself – she was sure his other auntie, or even his dying mother, would be delighted to see him; she was off to church. So saying, Tish walked purposefully towards St Mary and St Modwena's, in Battle Street, with the lad hard-pushed to keep up with her.

'Put this in your pipe and smoke it, Mr Fred Robertson,' she said. 'I never want to clap eyes on you or your precious friend again. Kitty and me thought nothing to you two in the first place.' With that, she entered the blessedly quiet and empty church; kneeling down not far from the altar, she prayed to be directed one day to an honest young man.

When she ventured outside again, Fred Robertson had gone. He had waited a while, like a dog outside a food shop, but he was not the sort of chap to be played up. She might be a cut above the girls he usually took to the Annie Robertson grave, but he wasn't as keen as all that on these superior cuts. It was a foul day; he would take himself to Seaton Street to see if his mate had done better with the other bit of skirt.

Tish now gazed into the remains of the fire; she was revising her opinion of a man who limited himself to a peck on the cheek; better that than the sort who started first on your coat-toggles.

'Poor little Tish,' said Kitty. 'You do collect 'em.' She related her own meeting with Fred Robertson's friend; so much had happened since for Kitty, she could talk about it with unconcern. 'I know what we'll do,' she exclaimed. 'It's not far off the 4th of March – we'll write an *In Memoriam* for the late Annie Robertson, and see what it costs in the *Argus*.'

Tish had her doubts; it would surely cost too much. She picked up Mary's skirt and resumed her work on the hem.

Her pain was long, her joys were few./ *Nobody knows what she went through.* 'That's no good,' Kitty declared. '*Nobody knows what she went through . . .*' She and Tish dissolved into helpless laughter.

'It's not funny, really,' Tish got out.

Kitty agreed it was not, as she almost lost her balance on the kitchen stool. She read further down the *In Memoriam* column of the *Bridgemouth Daily Argus*. She and Tish were transforming back copies of the news-

paper into tight hoops and piling these into a bucket for
Mrs Jacks' firelighting.

Eliza and Mary were supposed to be helping, since
this was a chore the lady assistants undertook at regular intervals, though not as regularly as their unravelling of string. The younger girls were not bestirring
themselves greatly. Eliza was savouring her last chocolate chewing nut, while making some pretence of rolling
up a double page, and Mary was slumped on her chair
with a full day's copy on her lap, and her feet on the
steel D-curb; she was idly studying front page pictures.
They had been told of Tish's escape from the cemetery
and Mary had been all commiseration; Eliza had said it
only went to show you got what you asked for. Neither
girl was much involved in the present goings-on of her
seniors. Mary believed the idea would collapse, for lack
of money; Eliza was of the same opinion, but was rather
more occupied with its possible effect on the sweets
ration. If those two intended squandering their spivs on
a daft newspaper notice, she hoped they didn't expect
Mary and her to keep them in sweets; the notion of the
wealthy subsidising those in want could always be
calculated to rouse Eliza.

'*But O for the touch of a vanish'd hand,/ And the sound of a
voice that is still!* That's more like it!' said Kitty. 'We
needn't have that "sound of a voice" bit. You did give
him what for, didn't you?'

Tish could lay no claim to the brave gesture. 'I did
not! I was too busy getting away.'

'A pity. I like that "touch of a vanish'd hand". Next
time, see you give him a good swipe.'

'There won't be no next time.'

'I should hope not,' chimed in Eliza, righteously.
'Are you two rolling papers or reading them?'

'Whatever we're doing, we seem a sight quicker than

you are!' Kitty rolled up her *In Memoriam* page, and consigned it to the bucket.

The juniors had gone upstairs to bed before the lines were concocted. There were still too many for girls with slender purses.

'We'll say no more about it to those two,' Kitty decided. 'If it goes in, it's paid for by us. How's this, then? *Robertson Annie 4 March 1901* comma *Always remembered by her fond nephew Frederick 5 Seaton Street* comma *Where Grave thy victory* comma, no, question mark. All right?'

It is a fact that plans triggered off by youthful conceptions of a lark, or of revenge, will often misfire. The debagged victim thrown by fellow-bloods into the college fountain, could decide to catch pneumonia; the Dreadnought Hoax might hit the headlines for its ingenuity, but the British Navy and 'Indignant, Basingstoke' would be heaping abuse on the Bloomsbury young. In respect of merry japes, the poor cannot hope to fare better than the rich. Had the *In Memoriam* insertion been left to Tish, it would have died the natural death of its subject; as it was, it could not slip into oblivion; Kitty would raise the required money somehow.

Neither girl had assets; their one small trinket, which they sometimes shared, was a silver name brooch, spelling KATHERINE and decorated in flower relief; it was one of those slight pieces, of no significant weight or value, commonly given by a mistress to a servant who had stayed long enough, and worked hard enough, to merit such reward. This maid-brooch had been presented to Kitty's mother, before marriage, when she was in service, and it had been given to the daughter as an eighteenth birthday present. Nothing could have pleased Kitty more. And now, because she could not bring herself to ask Mary for that half-crown, she was thinking of pledging it.

The pawnshop in Cable Street was another Bridgemouth establishment which had taken to closing on a Wednesday afternoon. There was no obvious way for a Bazaar assistant to get to those three-ball premises on a working day. In any case, the assistant would have to be Kitty; Tish had pawned too many Kelly-bundles in her time not to know the scurvy treatment one's possessions received, and the scorn poured out on the quavering suggestion for a loan.

Never had Mrs Jacks seen such a heap of paper twists for her fires. It filled the spare bucket and one large carton. 'I don't know where you think that lot's going!' she exclaimed.

'That's good, I must say!' said Kitty. 'Here we've been twisting our fingers off, and all you say is, *I don't know where you think that lot's going!*' She lifted the twist containers inside the bottom cupboard. Her mimicry had brought a faint grin to Mrs Jacks' face, but this was soon suppressed.

'Proper famous,' she commented dourly. 'Perhaps you'll tell us where Mr Skinner puts his *Arguses* now?'

'On top. There's bags of room on the bucket if I level it.' Kitty scooped twists from the bucket to add to the overflowing carton.

Mrs Jacks returned to her dolly-pegging; angry steam spouted upwards from the copper; the back of the house reeked of boiling bedsheets and Mrs Jacks' clor-ridiline; this was her standby; she bought it without fail from the chandler, and it says a lot for that gentleman's linguistic ability that he could supply her each week with a pint bottle of chloride of lime. It was the secret of the essential whiteness of twill, which had started out cream, and of the rapid deterioration in the fabric of all sheets and initialled cloths, the latter treated to several dashes of clorridiline, for good measure. If Hezekiah had had his way, these last-named abominations would have been burnt on the fire; this attitude was prompted not by a progressive view on female hygiene, but by a regard for his own sensitive nature: hardly a Bazaar Monday passed without some proof on the line of women's chastity, infertility, or plain good luck, and this invariably drove the delicate Hezekiah to distraction.

Kitty followed Mrs Jacks into the scullery and watched the rhythmic swishing of the wooden dolly in those capable hands. The sweat beaded on the woman's forehead, and spread its dark semi-circles under her arms.

'All right! Out with it! What d'you want?' Minnie Jacks liked to have the narrow work space to herself.

Kitty laughed, but not too confidently; there was no knowing with Mrs J., who could be the toughest nut in Skinners' Place, when she liked; but it was now or never. She plunged into the tale of her dilemma, revised version, under the grim stare of the housekeeper.

Of course, the girl was not telling the truth. That stuck out a mile. The dolly-pegs whirled even more determinedly as Mrs Jacks thought this one out. A fine tarradiddle – wanting to slip out to uncle's so she could pay for an *In Memoriam*! All my eye and Betty Martin, that was.

'Since when did you have family in Bridgemouth? I thought you come from Wales somewhere?'

'It's not *my* auntie,' Kitty emphasized. 'It's Tish's, on her mother's side. It's my brooch.' And she held out the silver brooch for inspection.

The dolly-pegs paused. 'You'll not get much on that.'

'Well, it shouldn't cost much, only a few lines.'

'Them lines mount up, once they start counting.'

'I thought I'd ask for half-a-crown on it.'

'You'll be lucky. I bet you don't get a penny more than two bob on that.'

Kitty was shaken by this expert opinion. She looked quite a child, standing there with her little brooch, her eyes wide with pleading. Mrs Jacks lifted the pegs out of the copper, and set them down with a bang on the floor tiles.

'There's no way you can get there. I'm not sending you for the bread on some trumped-up excuse. You'll be getting me the sack with your antics.' She began lifting out one clinging sheet, holding it aloft in her right hand with a pair of tongs, and then making a bold grab with her left at the end still drooping into the copper; she flicked the whole thing into the stone sink, with a minimal loss of soapy water. Kitty's hopes began to fade.

'Didn't you ought to get back? You've been here long enough to drink a barrel of cocoa.'

This was true; she had been too long away from her counter. Kitty turned slowly on her heel.

'Give it here! I'll take it in myself.' Mrs Jacks extended a red, wash-wrinkled palm for the brooch. 'Ah, get on with you!' she said grumpily, in answer to Kitty's wild hug.

It was as well that Kitty had not attempted to raise the advance herself. Maurice Tapp's was a thriving business, built up, over three decades, on the ignorance and poverty of his customers. He stood now behind his counter, in an ill-lit back room, which did double duty as pledge office and kitchen, and where the vapours rising from clothing bundles and old footwear vied with that from the greasy gas ring.

'How do I get the gas put through? Where does the money come from, if I fall for every yarn I hear over this counter?' He was swinging Kitty's brooch contemptuously by its fragile pin. 'You bring me this stuff – two a penny, these. "KATHERINE"! One and sixpence.'

Mrs Jacks was unperturbed. 'Three and a tanner,' she repeated.

'Three and a – ?' Mr Tapp had to support himself on the counter, such was the blow to his nervous system. The girl waiting behind Mrs Jacks, with a basketful of chipped crocks, saw her mother's chances of one bob recede.

'Two shillin', take it or leave it!' Maurice threw the brooch on the counter.

'Three!' called Mrs Jacks. 'It's real silver.'

'*It's real silver*, she tells me! D'you know what weight there is in this thing? Not above ten penn'orth of silver in any of 'em. Two shillin', and I'm doing you a favour.'

'Half-a-crown!' said Mrs Jacks.

The pawnbroker cast a martyred look to the ceiling, before he went to his cash box. 'Half-a-crown,' he said with disgust, smacking the coin down in front of his unmoved customer. 'No wonder I've one foot in the workhouse.' He reached for his book of diminutive pawn tickets. 'What d'you mean, it's not you?'

'It's not my name, and it's not my brooch.'

'It's going down in your name, whether it's yours or Micky Flaherty's.'

'Is it now? Give us it back, then. I know where I can take it and get a ticket the way I want it.'

Maurice Tapp knew the name was immaterial. 'I wouldn't do this for everybody,' he said. 'Only for old customers, mind. What name was it you said?'

'Catchpole. Miss K. Catchpole.'

The pawnbroker made out his duplicate slip in a well-nigh indecipherable scrawl, to 'Mrs Minnie Jacks 2/6 silver brooch'. Indecipherable or otherwise, she would be unable to read it. Tearing off the bottom half, he pushed a ledger and pencil in front of her. 'Signature,' he demanded.

Mrs Jacks signed as she always did, with a cross.

'One penny,' ordered Mr Tapp.

His customer scooped a few coppers from her apron pocket, selected one halfpenny, and pushed it over the counter. Man and woman stared at each other stonily for some seconds, before he flicked the pawn ticket to her, and tossed the brooch into a cardboard box.

'You can tell Miss Catchpenny to come herself next time.'

'She'll be doing that, for certs.' Minnie picked up her large basket, pushed her way past the queue of sad-eyed folk who had waited behind her, and proceeded to Abe Jenkin's to pick up the Saturday bread.

'I'll lose this, you see if I don't,' said Kitty to Tish. 'It's so small.' She took a safety pin from a graduated bunch on Tish's display and pinned the pledge ticket inside her handbag.

Hezekiah Skinner emerged from the stock-room and looked enquiringly as Kitty slipped her bag inside the string drawer.

She returned an enquiring smile, and he retreated to Suitings. She was recalling what Mrs Jacks had said, as she had slipped her the ticket at tea time. One penny a week interest, even though the charge over the water was only a halfpenny, to Mrs J.'s knowledge. She must redeem that pledge as soon as possible, but how? Meanwhile, Henry should be here, very soon. He had to be with his friend this afternoon, presumably the one who had been so ill. He did say he'd come about five o'clock. Pinning that ticket inside her old handbag had given her an idea. It would be cheaper for Henry, since he insisted on giving her a present, if he bought her one of those beige Dorothy bags at 4/6. They were not *fitted*, of course, being Dorothy bags; there was not much you could do with the inside of a drawstring handbag; but there was one interior pocket, with a tiny mirror, framed in mock tortoiseshell. She would like that. She hoped she was not making a mistake about the cheapness; it was a fortune, moneywise, to her, but it would cost less than the dress length he had mentioned; and she would not have the misery of another tedious sewing job.

She would not allow herself to get as worked up as she had been last Tuesday. If Henry came through the door, that would be lovely. If he couldn't come, she would see him on Sunday; common sense was everything.

She measured out one yard of white cotton cambric for Mrs Bellingham-Smith's housemaid, before sending her over to Tish for the flouncing: the poor girl had to make her own tea apron, although Mrs B.-Smith knew she could find maids' or nannies' uniforms at the end of Lingerie. This young maid had not heard a friendlier tone of voice than the one dispensed by Kitty Catchpole; she concluded that the Skinners must be champion bosses to work for, if their girls could be as happy as that. She smiled back at Kitty, who must have been the sweetest, prettiest girl in all Bridgemouth.

What the little housemaid had not seen was Mr Bonham's entry into the shop; and if she had seen this, its true significance would have been lost on her.

Even Mrs Skinner had to concede that Miss Catchpole conducted herself well at this moment. Kitty was careful to treat Henry as a customer, as a most valued customer. In answer to her question as to what she could do for him, he replied gravely that he wanted a present for a very special young lady.

She led him to an off-centre stand, where handbags of differing shape, size, colour and price were ranged, and recommended the line in Dorothy bags, preferably those in beige, since beige went with everything. They were marked at the competitive price of four shillings and sixpence, which was the week's special offer; the identical article was selling at four and eleven three at a rival store she could mention. Nothing would persuade her that his young lady might prefer something a little more expensive. Henry kept a straight face, but he was vastly entertained by Kitty's sense of economy; he was enjoying the little game immensely. In the end, he gave in to her sales talk and agreed that not only were Dorothy bags the best bargain, but they were also the most tasteful bags on show.

Kitty chose one that 'drew' well.

'I should never have thought of that,' said Henry.

'Your friend would not thank you for a string that draws badly.'

He saw that. He saw, too, that Kitty was not to be sidetracked into choosing a further present. If he was conscious of the attention he attracted from others, he gave no sign of this. Eliza Heggy had crossed and re-crossed the archway for a quiz at him; Mary had advised a grandmother to examine a pram cover in the better light at the door, from which position she had several minutes' and some nine yards' advantage over Eliza. Tish peeped over her customer's shoulder, when she could do so without appearing inattentive.

Hezekiah Skinner felt proud of his senior assistant. He and his wife were the last people to encourage courtships on the shop floor, unless these were managed with the utmost decorum and, better still, could be said to bring distinction with them. In this instance, and in spite of the low profit on Dorothy bags, the Skinners' commercial interests were being well served. It was clear to everybody in the shop that this fine figure of an officer, a gentleman to his fingertips, was more than a mere customer to Miss Catchpole. Without so much as touching the hand that held it, the young man had taken the handbag and was studying it with appreciation, nodding his head to Kitty's explanations of its worth. That was what Hezekiah liked to see – dignity in the young, and a sale brought off.

Jinny Skinner's head, unknown to herself, was likewise nodding in approval, in time with Henry Bonham's. She reached abstractedly overhead for the cash cylinder, which had sauntered to her from Mary's light pull. Twisting it open slowly, she took out the coins and the paper bill, placing these on the desk before her, with the manipulative skill of the blind; she smoothed out the bill, and at a greatly increased speed, stamped it, pronged its carbon copy on the spike, palmed the change into the cylinder, poked the receipt inside, and – her eyes once more fixed on Henry and Kitty – sent the lot singing along the wire to Miss Gibbs.

Here, to Jinny's astonishment, and seemingly to Miss Catchpole's, the gentleman was pointing to yet a different Dorothy bag! Presumably a difficult young man . . . But no! He was buying *two*! Unmindful of the fact that it was ill-bred to show open curiosity, Jinny

Skinner strained awkwardly to catch sight of what was going on. The two were moving across to Miss Catchpole's base. Jinny's head turned to its widest possible extent, pulling a neck muscle; she rocked in the most exquisite pain, her mouth open like a landed cod's, until the tension slackened. Sitting back in her chair, she comforted her neck and ignored the cylinder Tish had just sent along.

Hezekiah and Tish were now the only ones with an uninterrupted view of Kitty's section. Unfortunately for the former, his attention was diverted by the Reverend Andrew Macpherson – a man to be reckoned with, for his influence was as great as his custom was small. In the upheaval which followed, for no fellow ever took longer to select one pair of unclocked black socks than this pillar of the church, Hezekiah was prevented from keeping watch on the daisies; for all he knew, those Dorothy bags might well be stuffed with them, *and* with pink rosebuds, at nearly twice the price. What was infinitely worse, with so much at stake, the minister would drone on about Truscott and the evils of drink. Hezekiah did not need Macpherson to tell him he had done the right thing, and his replies became shorter and shorter, as the man went on and on. This brevity failed in its object; Andrew Macpherson was accustomed to carrying on regardless, with the strategic pause for an automatic response; he was not one to take umbrage, as lesser mortals might. By the time he and his wretched socks were disappearing through the door, Hezekiah had lost his opportunity. Two neat parcels stood on Miss Catchpole's counter; one she put on a low shelf, out of sight. The two young people shook hands, and the officer left, in the wake of the man of God.

Kitty waited until Henry had gone, rather as if she

expected him to give some farewell signal, but he did not look back; once he had made up his mind to go, he went. She lifted the second parcel carefully; it might have contained the most fragile orchid, such was her light handling. Taking it along to Tish, she put it down before her. 'For you,' she said, 'from Mr Bonham.'

That was something to chew over with Jinny! Hezekiah was flabbergasted. One bag for Miss Catchpole, and one for Miss Kelly . . . What was the young fellow playing at?

'Is my change back yet?' The customer was irritated; she had been three times round the floor and had not seen anything else worth buying. She required her change immediately, so that she could move on to Masons' Emporium, where the service and choice were something to write home about.

Much disconcerted, Tish sent an empty cylinder from Fabrics to crash above the cash desk; it went whizzing back, followed by the one on Tish's line with the delayed change. Jinny Skinner was as much flustered as her assistant; she was not given to dozing on the job, but this time she had indeed closed her eyes.

Both Kitty and Tish had been touched by Henry's thoughtfulness – Tish to an overwhelming degree. She was ashamed that she had ever made fun of his *mater*, and the good soul dead, too. She wanted to thank him for her present, but letter-writing was a trial to her. Not wishing to meet him with Kitty, however, she was left with no alternative; she would have to pen him a note. With Kitty's aid, she eventually did this, writing her thanks in script, with some evidence of joins.

'Will it do?' she asked anxiously.

'It's great. He'll be pleased with that,' Kitty told her.

Nobody had been more taken aback than Kitty when Henry had bought the two handbags. Lying in bed that night, listening to the chimes of the town hall clock, she berated herself for the mixed feelings she harboured. The two bags stood open and empty, but for their pocket mirrors, on the chest of drawers. When Tish had scarcely contained her tears for joy, how could she, Kitty, be so mean? Yet, after that first happiness, when she had understood that he would not let her best friend look neglected in public, she had begun to find less delight in her own present. Not that she wanted anything more extravagant for herself – far from it – but her Dorothy bag had dwindled; it was one of two. Perhaps she was one of two? But surely Henry would take Tish out, if that was the way he felt about it? Kitty missed two breaths. Tomorrow might solve it; she could ask him if he would like her to bring Tish along, too. Difficult. It would be tricky to come out with that, and not sound jealous; for she was jealous; that was what it amounted to.

'Kitty!' Tish said in a whisper from her bed.
'Yes?'
'You don't mind about that Dorothy bag, do you?'
'Of course I don't. Why should I?'
'You're so good, Kitty. I'd have minded.'
'Not you, Tish-girl.'
Tish smiled contentedly into the gloom; nowhere in the world could there be a friend so unselfish.

As if to underline that unselfishness, Kitty was up and about long before breakfast. She had the slim remains of a lined writing pad on her knee. This did not excite the attention of Mary or Eliza; it was not unusual for a girl to be writing a few words home. But Kitty was not writing to her family; she would do that later. On this occasion she was making a neat copy of the *In Memoriam* notice, without revealing her own address. She hoped the omission would not deter the *Daily Argus* from accepting the enclosed half-crown, and inserting her lines in the appropriate column on or around the 4th March; at this period in its history, the paper did not carry Births, Marriages and Deaths in every issue.

Tish knew what Kitty was doing, so busied herself with the bedroom chores required of both.

'You can do my bed, while you're at it,' said Eliza.

Tish ignored her. She was thinking about the *Argus* offices, and hoping she would find the right letter box on Sunday afternoon.

Locating the newspaper offices proved easy once Tish had come to Connolly Place, where they rose handsomely from the pavement: the red granite façade owed much to the grander office blocks across the river. Behind half-drawn blinds, men worked in the greenish gas-glare to assemble the morning paper. There was a large letter box in the oak door; she had her envelope under its brass flap when she started to work out the warning above it: *For Births, Marriages, Deaths & Gen. Adverts. Apply Argus Office Back Connolly Place.*

The advertisement office was a shabby, one-storey construction, no bigger than the average back-street shop. No light shone behind these blinds. Tish did eventually let the packet drop through the iron letter box. Back Connolly Place gave on to the railway coalyard, where the linked trucks stood, each packed with shining coal; the longer they stood, the more the loads would glisten, and the less the housewife would get in her hundredweight sack. The acrid smell from the yard set Tish's nostrils twitching; she hurried off, for a breath of polluted river air, which to the valiant folk of Bridgemouth was sweetness itself.

It was the finest box of chocolates Kitty had ever held. It carried a bow of yellow ribbon across one corner, while a portrait of a mutton-sleeved damsel adorned the lid: she held a yellow rose to her chin, buttercup-fashion, and gazed coyly on the chocolate fanciers of this world. Kitty disliked the simper, but it was certainly a splendid box.

'You shouldn't have got this,' she said, exhibiting a more credible brand of shyness.

'You don't seem to care for the portrait,' Henry observed.

'I love it, I really do. It's so beautiful. I don't like her smile much, but the rest is wonderful.'

Henry took her by the shoulders, and gave her a little shake. 'It's an awful thing,' he said, 'so don't pretend it isn't. I was pushed for time. And don't ever pretend to me again, because you're very bad at it.'

'I'm not as a rule,' she retorted. 'I'm the best liar in Skinners' Place. Anyway, I do think it's beautiful.'

Henry gave up. The Dorothy bag incident had led him to suppose that she might have taste. 'Never try lying to me,' he said, 'that's all.'

They were installed in a bedroom in the Queen's Hotel. Henry had made the situation sound quite unexceptional. He had booked in for the weekend, to cut down the time wasted in travelling; his friend had been with him till this morning. Kitty would have been happier downstairs, taking Sunday tea, as they had done at the Pier Hotel.

'We'll go down for tea,' he went on. 'I can see this room puts you off.'

'It's rather a swell room,' she said.

He walked across to the speaking tube: 'Room 24,' he said. 'Don't bring tea up. We shall be taking it in the restaurant.'

'I hope you don't mind.' Kitty's words came lamely.

'Do you want to take your coat and things with you?' he asked.

She put on her hat again, believing this to be proper, and together they descended the wide staircase to the restaurant. Once seated, she remembered that she had Tish's letter inside her Dorothy bag. It was a relief to hand this over; it was something to do, and maybe something to talk about. Henry took the letter and read it with gravity.

'Very neat. I'm glad she liked it.'

'I told her she ought to have given it to you herself.'

'This afternoon?'

Kitty nodded.

Henry Bonham was not annoyed with Kitty. He was amazed at his own stupidity. What had worked, for the most part, with other young ladies, could not be expected to do so with this one. And here it must be stressed that Henry took only the superior type of girl to bed: that way, the encounters could be less sordid. His engagements had always been short-term and, so far, his heart had not been affected. Kitty had looked so pathetic, darting those scared glances at the double bed; he was prepared to wait.

'I amuse you?' She paused, with the milk jug in her hand.

'I like my milk in last, but it doesn't matter.'

'Milk in *last*?'

'Yes, but it's all right. Just don't swamp it.'

'I never swamp it,' she replied warmly. 'Why didn't you mention this last Sunday?'

'There were many things I didn't mention last Sunday. No, I wasn't feeling amused, exactly. Did I tell you about a young filly my grandfather gave me when I was a lad? I had quite a problem calming her down. She used to stand there, when she wasn't rearing, looking perfect and so very nervous. I don't know who was the more frightened, Star or myself. The first time she let me stroke her nose without backing away, I was the proudest lad in Stirling.'

'Not in Edinburgh?'

'No, my father's people lived outside Stirling. You *have* overdone the milk a bit . . .'

'I'm sorry. This horse . . . Star, did you say? You wouldn't be thinking of reaching over to stroke my nose, would you?'

'That was in the back of my mind, but you might spill that hot water over me.'

'I've been known to do that.'

'So he fetched my coat and gloves, and we left the restaurant.'

Tish looked wise. 'He's one of nature's gentlemen. I could see that from the start. And he really liked my letter? You're not just saying that?'

'I told you. He said it was a terrific letter.' The minor exaggeration was exactly what Tish wanted, after her lonely Sunday outing. She was keen to hear, too, what Henry had thought of their *In Memoriam* lark, and was disappointed when Kitty said the subject had not been raised. When all was said and done, that insertion had cost a lot of money and effort; Tish would have thought it worthy of mention some time during the afternoon and evening.

Kitty did not explain that, for her, the thing had become too serious: how was she to raise that half-crown, plus interest, to redeem her brooch? Henry might have thought the whole performance pointless; it was beginning to look feeble in her own eyes. Besides, it would have been dreadful if he had suspected her of cadging. She put the latter possibility to Tish, knowing it would not be contradicted. It was not, though Tish was privately wishing that Henry Bonham had given Kitty the money. Where else was it coming from?

Kitty's chocolates meant over a fortnight's saving all round in staff sweets money. She and Tish put their pennies together; with one or two extra coppers from Kitty's purse, the total came to elevenpence. Kitty had decided against using her leaking boot as a second pretext for sending less money home; these lies to her mother were little better than stealing, and if she felt that way about it, how could she expect Tish to face it?

'I shall have to ask the Skinner for a loan,' she announced finally.

'You'll never get one.'

'If it's for my boot, I might.'

'Never. Anyway, she'll ask to see it.'

'Well, it is split!'

'When it's supposed to be mended, I mean.'

'I'll say I forgot to take it in.' Kitty was trying hard to convince herself.

Tish's argument was relentless. 'Then she'll ask for her money back. Besides, she knows stitching doesn't cost that much.'

But Tish did agree that the money would not be falling out of the sky, and that every avenue would have to be explored. She blamed herself bitterly. If she had not got herself mixed up with Fred Robertson, Kitty would owe no money today; thinking on these lines rendered her so low in spirit that she went down to the shop, looking as sad as Mary Gibbs, whose Bunny Harris had recently sailed away.

'You know perfectly well we don't give advances on staff wages,' Jinny Skinner pronounced severely. 'Mr Skinner and I live within our income, and we expect you to live within yours. In fact, I can't remember when any lady assistant came to me with such a request. Three shillings, indeed!'

She and Tish had that elevenpence put by; Kitty made another attempt: 'Perhaps I could have two shillings, ma'am?'

'Another five minutes and we'll be asking for a shilling.' Jinny pursued her move: 'Which should be quite ample; since when did a few stitches cost three shillings, or even two? It's my belief you are hiding something, Miss Catchpole.'

'Could I have a shilling, then, ma'am?'

'No, you could not, Miss Catchpole.'

Kitty sat down to breakfast and ate in silence. The other girls tried a desultory conversation, but soon gave up. Tish drained her cup to the dregs, surreptitiously emptied the last vestige of liquid into her saucer, and spent some minutes reading the tea leaves. She decided that the coffin, or cradle, was definitely a boat; it was more or less detached from the general mass of black leaf, so it must be sailing away on a long voyage. On the other hand, as it was a trifle up-ended, with the stern still attached to the residue, it could be sinking. Tish paled; neither outlook was promising. Kitty's face was likewise devoid of colour. Her gaze was fixed on the cracked sugar bowl; her thoughts were fixed on Maurice Tapp. Mary ate without appetite, and Eliza ate solidly. Jinny Skinner was very much on her dignity, but she did not allow that to ruin her breakfast. Hezekiah surveyed them all, and dabbed his waxed moustache with his napkin.

Mrs Jacks had not forgotten the breeze with Mrs Skinner, brought about by the Catchpole girl. Although she might despise her employers, she was not one to court dismissal for spending time on other folk's problems. When Minnie Jacks left, she hoped to be following a decision of her own – one that suited her own convenience.

As the week wore on, her surly reception of Kitty, whenever the latter crossed the scullery floor to fill the kettle, declared louder than words that Mrs Jacks was no longer an ally. This lady would not be returning late for a second time from a bread-outing. Even if Kitty were to stumble on a two-shilling piece in the gutter, she would have to get someone else to take what she owed to Tapp's pawnshop. But who? It would have to be either Tish or herself. No, it would have to be herself; only she had the excuse of a split boot; only she could ask permission to slip out of the Bazaar, some fifteen minutes before the shops closed for dinner.

If Eliza had possessed a florin, and if she had inadvertently left her purse lying around, Kitty might have been tempted to borrow it. Then one day, the coin would turn up in a corner of the bedroom, to be returned to Eliza. Stealing with a difference, Kitty told herself, was permissible in desperate circumstances, and she was desperate enough for anything. As it happened, Eliza had no such amount in her purse. When Kitty was driven to ask her outright for a loan, Miss Heggy shook what remained of her week's wealth on to Kitty's bed: two pennies and one farthing. To have steeled herself to beg a loan from Eliza Heggy was torture in a big way; to have achieved nothing from this sacrifice of pride left Kitty utterly mortified; she ought to have known better.

'She's got more than that,' said Tish savagely. 'In her corsets, I bet; or up her knickers.'

'I can't knock her senseless, can I, to find out? We can forget about this week, Tish.'

'Dear God, all that interest piling up.'

Kitty sat on the edge of the bed, considering the boots on her feet. They had done good service, apart from this one split, and a couple of eyelet-holes, which had lately come to grief; she tried to poke their tin rims into position, but the firm lacing held them askew. This summer, she must tell her mother to pick up another pair at St John's jumble sale; as a jumble-sorter, Mrs Catchpole could snap up bargains before they reached the trestle-tables. Meanwhile, this pair must be made to last out. Jinny Skinner was correct, of course; it had never cost Kitty a penny to have her boots stitched, at any time since she had lived in Bridgemouth. On the whole, every lady assistant from Skinners' Place could rely on the cobbler's goodwill; even for Eliza Heggy, he had once hammered a toe-tip into place without charge. And for Kitty Catchpole, Mitchell Caine had the softest of soft spots; Kitty would have nothing to pay.

*

They had no way of learning if their *In Memoriam* notice had appeared in the *Argus*, until Hezekiah Skinner had gathered up his week's papers and thrown them into the kitchen cupboard. This he had not done; having inspected the paper space, and discovered that it was well provided with paper hoops for the fire, he had left the back copies in his sitting room. The girls had to wait some time before he brought down the accumulated supply.

Kitty had no great wish to see it. Outings with Henry, though pleasant, did nothing to lessen her sense of guilt and isolation, for when she was parted from her mother's brooch, she was woefully adrift. The days came, the days went, and the pledge interest mounted.

It was Tish who pounced on the old newspapers before they could be torn up. She removed the back page for the 4th March, on which three inches were actually devoted to one Marriage, two Deaths and one *In Memoriam*, inclusive of Titles. Births had been held over. Under cover of filling the kitchen coal scuttle, the two girls read their insertion in the coal house.

'It's the right day, but it doesn't make sense,' Kitty exclaimed. 'Damn the *Argus*! It's awful!'

'That's a dreadful thing it says,' Tish muttered. '*Whore Grave* . . . That's wicked.'

'It's *Whore, Grave* – not *Whore Grave*. They've put a comma in as well,' said Kitty.

The fine distinction was lost on Tish. 'It's wicked,' she repeated distractedly.

'Whichever way you look at it, it's a terrible mistake,' Kitty admitted. 'It sounds as if we're being nasty about Annie Robertson.'

'The poor dead creature, when she'd nothing to do with it!'

'It's lucky nobody's got our address,' said Kitty.

Then with a sudden suspicion, she rounded on Tish: 'You didn't tell that Fred Robertson where we worked?'

'No. I don't know. I don't think I did.' Tish was too much upset to remember. 'Anyhow, this paper's a while back, the fourth of March.'

'Did you tell him we worked in a shop?' Kitty persisted.

'No, I never. And what difference does it make? He could walk in here any day, whether he's got our address or not. Bridgemouth ain't London.'

'Isn't.'

'*Isn't*, then. I don't care if he does walk in, neither. I'm not afraid of *him*.'

'We'd get Skinnybugs to throw him out.'

'That would be vulgar,' said Tish. 'He'd be real disgusted, would Skinnybugs.'

'Not as vulgar as *Whore, Grave*,' Kitty said soberly.

What both girls missed was the report in a subsequent issue of the *Argus*, concerning a disturbance in Seaton Street, which had amounted to a breach of the peace and had resulted in the arrest of two men – one an Able Seaman by the name of Frederick Robertson, who had needed treatment for cuts and bruises, and the other a dockyard worker, Wilkie Herbert Robertson, both men unrelated. Apparently, a dispute had arisen on account of an insult to W. H. Robertson's late aunt.

What the girls did not miss was the full force of Mrs Skinner's tongue, on the subject of lady assistants who skulked around in the back yard, when their presence was wanted indoors. Miss Kelly would have to take over Baby Linen for a short space that morning until Miss Gibbs recovered.

When Kitty and Tish arrived breathless in the attic, they found Mary sitting on the floor, her head against the wall, and her cheeks as pale as whitewash. They helped her to bed, where she lay as one who might have need of a bowl at any moment; she showed no inclination to talk.

Eliza, while doing nothing practical towards helping Mary, had been full of protest to see yet another colleague fall victim to this kind of distress. 'It'll be me next,' she complained. 'I'm the only one that's not had it. It's something they give us to eat; it must be. My mother says Mrs Jacks shouldn't be boiling brisket and puddings in the copper. We've got a big pan at our house.'

'You like to hear your own voice, you do,' said Kitty scathingly. 'Everybody boils puddings in the copper. Mrs Jacks scours it with salt; you want to see her, on a Monday before she goes.'

'It's Skinners' Disease,' said Tish thoughtfully. 'That's what it is: one by one, we get Skinners' Disease.'

Dear mum and Dad, wrote Eliza, whose Mum was known as *mother* only in the confines of the Drapery Bazaar;

Just a line to let you know Mary Gibs was sick as a dog this morning and I do not feel at all well ether and beleive I shall be the next, You rember I told you Kitty Cachpole and Tish Kelly took ill before I think it must be some thing we eat it is funny how we all keep caching it, Kitty C has desided it is the dranes she just sayd that to Tish K and they both titerd thier heads off, I dont see anything to titer at. I wish I could leave the Drapery Bazaar and work some where respectible like Masons Emporum
your loving Daughter
Eliza   XXXXXXXXX

PS   That KC and TK eat most of my parkin last time please send some more, Eliza

'It wasn't the baked potatoes with Mary Gibbs,' Hezekiah stated. 'You can't blame Jacks for that.'

Jinny knew that was true. She was puzzled and anxious; it only needed tidings to go around that one by one the lady assistants were falling sick for the Skinners to be out of business. She had had her work cut out before, with that Myrtle Floyd, having to fob her off about the Kelly girl being sick in the street. Trust the Floyd to have her spies dotted around the place! 'I'll put a stop to all that sweet-guzzling,' she said. 'You mark my words, that's what it is. Every night alike, stuffing themselves silly. No wonder they're sick! You'd need an inside like a rhinoceros to take it. And that Mrs Heggy, always sending them ginger cake! I never smelt a room like it – reeking of ginger. Imagine going to bed on a stomach burning with that rubbish!'

'We're just getting over the last bother with you and those assistants,' Hezekiah said. 'Leave the sweets alone.'

Jinny followed his advice, not because she thought her diagnosis was wrong, but because Mary Gibbs' recovery was quicker than expected. Though still pale, Mary was back in Baby Linen before dinner.

It was no longer easy for Kitty to hide the split in her left boot. In spite of adopting a careful stance, with her right foot forward, she was nervous, not only of Henry's keen eye, but of the shrewd surveys made of her, when she entered tea rooms and restaurants in his company. She was no slattern and it hurt her to look like one. Yet she had to use this boot repair as a method of getting to Maurice Tapp's, and she could not redeem her brooch, or pay his interest, without money. So the split widened, and the brooch remained with the pawnbroker.

It had been with him far too many weeks when Kitty arrived at her decision – one which had been inevitable from the start: she would have to lie to her mother about the boot repair, and deduct sufficient money from the postal order home for her pledge. Tish could contribute her meagre savings, but the bulk of the money must come from Kitty; there were more mouths to feed in Tish's home, and the silly idea had been Kitty's in the first place.

It was arranged, by gracious permission of Mrs Skinner, that Miss Catchpole should leave her counter on Saturday at 12.10 p.m., in order to have her boot stitched at Mitchell Caine's while she waited. Jinny knew that old Mitchell, who would have been *Michael* had his parents known the pronunciation or the spelling, would oblige the Bazaar by doing a quick job.

All morning, Kitty went through the motions of serving, slight bowing and less scraping. She must remember to transfer the pawn ticket to her purse. She had its number by heart: 37260. It had become as real to her as her mother's often-quoted Co-op number, 47138.

Her weekday cape was hanging on the scullery door hook, underneath Mrs Jacks' black shawl. Shawls were a godsend in sharp weather, especially when they were weighty and folded in two; Kitty would have been glad to wear one over her head to fend off the bitter winds, but no lady assistant could get away with gear of that kind; it was not sufficiently genteel. Mrs Jacks' shawl doubled as a bed-quilt at night and gave off a strong smell of the bedroom, competing with those of paraffin, Sunlight soap, clorridiline, finnan-haddy, beer, camphor balls and other penetrating items recently carried in its folds.

Kitty regretted putting her cape in readiness on that

back door: she should have remembered about the camphor balls, etc. She had five minutes, or thereabouts, before setting out. Tish moved across the counter, to see to the local midwife, who was after a length of unbleached cotton drill for an overall, and was irritated not to be served by the senior lady assistant. As Kitty put away her scissors, pencil and receipt book, however, Nurse Winters – who was 'nurse' by courtesy rather than by professional training – saw that the girl must be going off duty, and Tish's task became more pleasant.

With barely two minutes to go before Kitty's departure, the peace of the shop was disrupted by an exceptionally loud crash coming from beyond the alcove. Jinny Skinner sat transfixed in her cash desk. Hezekiah followed on Kitty's heels towards Baby Linen, where Mary Gibbs lay sprawled across the floor.

Eliza Heggy stood gaping uselessly, as Kitty informed her; one customer, balancing an unpinned, cherry-clustered hat, was bending perilously over Mary's inert form.

Hezekiah could see that the unpaid-for creation would be tumbling to the ground. 'Miss Heggy!' he rapped. 'Attend to madam!'

'Madam' took off the headgear, handing it bemusedly to Eliza, and both continued to hang over Mary. Kitty had the girl's head on her arm and was trying to raise her gently to a sitting position. Hezekiah turned to call for Nurse Winters' assistance, but that lady had already arrived at the scene. Dismissing all helpers, she herself raised Mary and bent the patient's head down. Kitty was sent to fetch a drink of water; the rest were ordered to move off. As Mary revived, she was helped to her feet and on to a chair. Hezekiah reported to Jinny that everything was under control; there was no cause for alarm. He told Miss Catchpole to show Nurse Winters the way to the lady assistants' room, and to render any help necessary to get Miss Gibbs up the stairs. Between them, the midwife and Kitty took Mary to the attic, where she fell thankfully on Tish's bed.

'How long have you been like this?' demanded Maisie Winters, as she opened Mary's blouse and loosened the front lacing of her corset.

'Not long,' came the weak reply.

'You won't be needing me any more?' Kitty was edging out of the room, more from tact than from any unworthy intention to go while the going was good.

'No, I think we'll manage now, thank you. You might see that my order is ready for me down there. I haven't all day to wait, when I've done here.'

Kitty went to the scullery for her cape, where she incurred Mrs Jacks' disapproval as the black shawl fell to the ground; it was restored with quick reverence, but Mrs Jacks' angry face was slow to clear.

Armed with her cape, Kitty hurried into the shop to deliver Nurse Winters' superfluous request to Tish; the parcel of drill was ready to be picked up. To get to the pawnshop now, and to have her boot mended at Mitchell Caine's, was going to leave no time for dinner; no plateful would be put aside for a latecomer. With a discreet nod to Tish, Kitty made to leave.

Hezekiah Skinner stepped forward from the centre of the shop, where he had been waving his arms about as if conducting staff and customers through a difficult score. 'Put that coat, or whatever it is, back!' he commanded fiercely, in a tone meant to be low. 'What can you be thinking of, Miss Catchpole?'

Kitty froze. 'I have permission to get my boot mended, Mr Skinner.'

'Your boot mended? You do realize there's nobody in charge of Baby Linen? I suppose you think we can run a business if you all waltz off! Get back to your work, this minute.'

She returned her cape to the back door, still under the baleful eye of Mrs Jacks, who was dying to ask what was going on, but was hanged if she would speak to the young Catchpole; they'd all know soon what was wrong with Mary Gibbs. In the meantime, if Kitty Catchpole was not getting out to the pawnshop, that was no affair of Minnie's: to hell with these assistants and their hanky-panky!

Which was what she made plain to Mrs Skinner. 'It's no business of mine, ma'am. If your young ladies go and get theirselves in trouble, that's nowt to do with me, is it? So long as she puts her usuals in the bucket, they gets boiled and hung out. I don't go inspecting them things; I'm only paid to wash 'em. And while we're on it, I don't mind telling you that Bessie Coombes up at Masons' never has to soil her hands with the likes of that; not that Mrs Mason lives on the premises, of course, but Bess lands none of it from the assistants, neither: special cotton pads, they got, from the Toiletries, what get burnt. I call that real ladylike.' Mrs Jacks sniffed, and reached for her shawl. 'Don't think I'm grumbling, Mrs Skinner,' she continued inexorably. 'I know we're not all in a position to do like Masons', and I'm sure I've always been very willing to help out. If there's nothing else you have to say, I'll be on my way to Abe Jenkin's, or you'll be getting no bread this Saturday.'

*

The Skinners' fury knew no bounds.

'It's one thing being landed with a loose girl,' Hezekiah raved, 'but to think she has to spread it abroad, passing out in the shop! A fine time she chose, too, with Nurse Winters on the spot! It'll be all over Bridgemouth.'

'If you ask me,' said Jinny with venom, 'that Jacks let us in for it deliberately, kidding on she never noticed. Just as if! And the old buck she gave! She'll go too far one of these days, the same one. She'll find herself going through our back door, same as Truscott.'

'Yes, well, not just yet. Let's get over this little lot first. You watch your step with Jacks.'

'What d'you think I'm watching? Anybody else would have let her have it. You would, for a start.'

As so often happened, their ill temper had switched target, so that they spent a dangerous ten minutes hurling barbed epithets at each other. Jinny passed that night in great discomfort, lying partly on the mesh frame, which the horsehair overlay did little to soften; she had made the error of turning her back on Hezekiah; he had immediately caught his sleep, rolling into the middle of the bed, which area he monopolized till morning.

'I can't go home,' Mary said dully. She was packing her few belongings into a dilapidated Gladstone bag. After the first paroxysm of tears, when she had been given her marching orders by Jinny Skinner, she had calmed down, and to Kitty this calm was worse than the weeping.

She tried a difficult question: 'Where will you go if you don't go home?'

Mary shrugged.

'Have you got Bunny Harris's address? You ought to ask his mum to help you. She might.'

'He never said. Somewhere near Stoke, I think. It wouldn't get me nowhere if I did have it. I don't want his mother. He didn't let on he was sailing, really. He could be in England, for all I know.'

Tish came into the bedroom. Eliza Heggy had stayed in the kitchen, crouched over the fire; she was thinking out a letter to her parents, this time to advise them of the type of girl she had been required to walk out with.

'What train are you catching? There aren't many on Sundays.'

Mary shrugged again, and shook her head.

'She's not going home,' Kitty said.

All three girls fell silent. Mary went on packing her bits and pieces. Kitty and Tish felt their small world was crumbling as they watched her; Kitty's lost silver brooch seemed to count for very little, when she looked at Mary and wondered where the poor girl would be by the same hour the following night.

'You can't walk the streets. You'll have to get a roof over your head, Mary,' Kitty burst out. 'Won't she, Tish?'

'She will, that. Why can't you go home, love? Your mam and dad will be worried sick.'

When she answered that one, Mary's voice was lifeless. 'My dad will throw me out if I go back. I've heard him say what he'd do if a daughter of his got herself in trouble. Besides, they can't feed me. God knows how they'll be fixed without my bit of money.'

'The cops'll take you in if you've no place to go,' Tish warned her. 'They can be awkward.'

Mary said nothing.

Tish plunged on. 'Look, you can try my sister's. It's not much, and you couldn't stay long – she wouldn't want you to stay long.' Mary would soon find out why, and the prospect grieved Tish.

'Where's that?' Mary asked, apathetically. She had no hope that Tish's sister, or anybody else's sister, would give her shelter.

'I'll take you, tomorrow afternoon. It'll be fourpence on the ferry,' Tish added, with a glance at Kitty. 'No, only tuppence for you. Fourpence for me, there and back.'

Kitty smiled. 'That's all right. We've still got that elevenpence.'

Tish felt more miserable. Bang goes the brooch, she thought.

'I've got to go first thing in the morning,' Mary said. 'The Skinners won't have me around.'

'You don't go before breakfast,' Kitty consoled her.

'I do. She was worse than him. She said I wasn't to show my face in the Bazaar after tonight. I wasn't fit to be with clean-living people.'

'I like that! That's rich, when she knows he's the dirtiest thing we've got around here, with his fingers down a girl's blouse and up her skirt, if he thinks the coast's clear. You'll have your breakfast in the morning, Mary, my girl, and let either of them open their cakeholes! They'll be sorry they spoke.'

'I can't face breakfast. I feel too queer then.'

'You can have some tea,' Kitty advised, 'and you can pretend to be eating. You don't have to force any of it down. Just drink the sweet tea; my mum used to.'

There was more to Tish's plan than she was prepared to reveal immediately. She could rely on the generosity of her sister, and she could depend on her know-how; nobody could teach Biddy Kelly anything about unwanted pregnancies.

Eliza Heggy had come to bed, wearing an injured air;

she was much affronted to be sharing a bedroom with a girl who had sinned and been found out. Mary undressed without giving Eliza the chance of a peep; as always, she slipped the nightdress over her clothes, before removing these, one by one, underneath it. This was a fairly simple manoeuvre, for the garment was one her own mother had worn, when expecting Mary's youngest sister, and its tentlike proportions had long been a subject for considerable teasing. Eliza stole the occasional look, but if she hoped to see a great swelling where previously she had detected nothing, she was to be disappointed. Mary would be a trim baby-carrier; but for that unfortunate faint, she might have stayed on longer at the Bazaar before her plight became obvious.

Eliza bounced aggressively into bed, with all the virtuous energy of the stainless virgin. Tonight, she remembered to say a prayer before she fell asleep; she begged God to make her *mother* and *father* move her from Skinners' Place to Masons'.

None of the others had a good night's rest. Mary dozed fitfully and was heard crying quietly some time after midnight. Tish decided not to get out of bed to speak to her; Mary would not be easily comforted, and nobody wished to rouse Eliza. Kitty, also, was listening to Mary; she lay on her back with her eyes closed. A few tears slanted off her cheeks on to the pillow; a fierce hatred for Bunny Harris and his kind raged inside her head; the personal worry concerning her silver brooch surfaced and submerged.

She considered what she might do, if ever she found herself in Mary's boat. Surely her mum and dad would let her return home? On the other hand, would she want to go back? Like Mary's family, there was no money for a non-earning daughter of her age, saddled with a non-earning baby. Kitty dabbed her eyes on the sheet; she was impatient with her wet pillow, and turned it over. She was pretty sure Tish was awake. What a good lass she was, taking Mary to Laverport tomorrow! Tish's sister was no doubt as nice as Tish, but what exactly did she do? How could she cope with Mary? Tish was fairly cagey about her family, and Kitty was not one to ask too many questions. The father was in the second-hand business, so Kitty had once been told, and his wife had worked at something or other, when Tish was a kid. Perhaps they kept a shop? Kitty felt for her hankie under the pillow, and blew her nose as softly as possible. She went on to wonder what Tish's sister looked like. Did she have the same curls? The intense effort to conjure up a picture of someone she had never seen acted like a whiff of chloroform. Kitty was out for the count until the town hall clock woke her at three.

Mary's eyes were wide open and smarting. She was exhausted and wanted to fall asleep, but despair held her like a vice and refused to let go. Tish had been so kind, and Kitty. . . But would Tish's sister take on a stranger, and one in a fix like this? If not, where was she to go? Did you go to ministers for help? She couldn't tell the Reverend Andrew Macpherson! The thought terrified her. He would look at her with the cold eye he always kept for the Bazaar assistants, only this time it would be colder and nastier. He would get her into a home for fallen girls. Mary did not want to be with fallen girls; she wanted to stay clear of such a place. She would have to post that letter home, telling them. More tears welled up. She heard Kitty turn her pillow and moved her own sideways, to find a drier spot. But how would she live? How could she find the money? Where was this home for pregnant girls, anyway? Was it part of the Institution? She dreaded waking up, if ever she got to sleep. And Bunny Harris . . . he was horrible. He tore her open, so that she was stinging for days. Why did she let him? She got nothing out of it, except the sack from the Bazaar, and worse to come.

Kitty was asleep; she was breathing quite heavily, for Kitty. Eliza was on her back, snoring roughly. Tish was turning restlessly in bed. Tish Kelly, on whom everything was to depend, stayed wide awake. In the dark hours of the night, her optimism was evaporating. Did she know Biddy as well as she thought she did? Would Biddy do as much for Mary as she would – say – for her own sister? Tish was racked with sleepless nightmare. She had visions of failure, and a terrible fear for Mary.

Breakfast the next morning was an unpleasant affair. After Hezekiah had overruled his wife in granting Mary a place at the lady assistants' table, Jinny would not address another word to him.

Eliza Heggy's efforts to sit at some distance from Mary were thwarted by the dimensions of the table. She sat, therefore, at a Pisan angle, and spoke only to Kitty, to mention that the tea cosy was missing.

Mary did not fancy the tea; she drank very little, and ate nothing. She was to take her bag as far as the Ferry Head; there she would sit on a bench until Tish and Kitty would come to collect her. It was going to be a long wait, for church and dinner would have to be attended by her two friends. They proposed to save a good portion of brisket and baked potato. Kitty would take out their plates to the scullery – this would offer no problem, with a junior as lazy as Eliza – and there she would transfer the untouched food into a couple of sheets of ruled notepaper, wrapping the whole inside a clean handkerchief, or inside two, if necessary. Unlike

her more accustomed attitude to awkward commitments, she could work up no enthusiasm for this one;
the job would be done, and Mary would have a bite of
cold dinner to eat, with no pudding. The hankie-parcel
was to hide inside one of Mrs Jacks' cooking pots, to be
retrieved when Eliza and the Skinners had made themselves scarce.

Kitty was in an altogether dogged mood. She meant
to accompany Tish as far as the ferry, and to see her and
Mary disappear down the passageway to the boat, that
same ferryboat which would be bringing in Henry, for
he had given up his weekend room at the Queen's
Hotel. Her mind was so completely preoccupied with
Mary's problem that she had omitted Sunday's ritual
of the mouse bread. It was unlikely that she would ever
repeat this again; trying to score off Eliza Heggy held
no further interest for her. Life had assumed a more
forbidding aspect, in which not only Mary Gibbs and
Bunny Harris loomed large, but also Kitty Catchpole
and Henry Bonham. If Mary could be caught out, so
might Kitty. She half comforted herself with the
thought that Henry was different; he respected her. As
Tish kept pointing out, he was a gentleman.

'You don't go to that Macpherson fellow. If he was the
last priest on God's earth, you're not asking him for any
help.' Tish pulled up short at the landing-stage barrier,
where she dumped Mary's bag thankfully on the
ground. 'You got the cash register in this?'

'It's the bag itself weighs heavy,' Mary said. 'Real
leather, that is. It fell off the back of a cab, my dad said.'

'I bet it did, too. I don't know how you carried it all
that way.'

'I've been carting it around best part of the morning.'

Mary opened the brisket-and-potato packet, and tackled some of the meat.

'What for?'

Mary chewed hard on a piece of gristle. 'You know how it is, if you're sitting: chaps come by, giving you the once-over, and they try sitting down next to you.'

'They make you puke,' said Tish, rather forgetting that under different circumstances, these male overtures would have been welcome to a lady assistant on her free day.

'They make you puke, all right,' Mary agreed grimly, as she tackled the cold potato.

'Steady on! You're going at that like you'd been on bread and water.'

'I get starving about now. You are angels, you and Kitty, saving me this. Would you like some?'

'Of course not. You get it down you. By the way, if you're dying to see Macpherson, don't let me stop you; it's just that I wouldn't touch him with a barge-pole, myself.'

'Neither would I.'

'It's a pity you're not of the Faith. Father McManus would be your man; there's a priest who knows how to listen.'

Mary flushed. She had no wish to hurt Tish's feelings, but she had to get this straight: 'I'm sorry, Tish. I wouldn't want that, either; and nuns give me the creeps.'

Tish frowned. 'You shouldn't be put off by the gear; under all the flap and shuffle, nuns are the same as us. It's food and keep, isn't it?'

'I thought you had to have a special call.'

'You do, but you don't make a bad nun if your first call comes from your stomach. God's not as fussy as that. He believes in feeding his lambs, doesn't he?

That's how my Auntie Marj saw it: Sister Theresa Augusta she is now, and no more vocation than that seagull to start with.'

Mary finished her potato, watching the hovering rise and dip of the unholy seagull. She hoped Tish's sister Biddy would not be trying to bundle her into the arms of Father McWhatsit, or lead her to the forbidding doors of Auntie Marj's convent.

Storm clouds threatened the far bank of the River Mease. Mary's dinner was eaten; she gave Tish the two handkerchiefs, and deposited the two screws of notepaper in a wire basket. 'The hankies are ruined,' she apologized.

'It'll come out.'

'I'm glad I managed to eat it before the boat got in.'

'Ay. Let's be ladies to the last. I can see Henry Bonham standing there on top.'

'You can't! I'm going over to those other people.'

'Don't be so daft. You know he can't cross to our side; he's got to stick with the Exit lot. We'll turn our backs, and take no notice. Anyway, it's not Henry. It's too fat for him.'

Henry was, in fact, on the top deck, but positioned to starboard and not visible from the Bridgemouth barrier.

'Is anything wrong?' Henry glanced down at the hand he was holding in his right palm, before he covered it with his left. It was a protective gesture, affirming both the smallness of Kitty's hand and the disturbing shabbiness of her glove.

She forced a smile. That second correct kiss, though welcome, had not lightened her mood. 'Yes,' she said. 'There's plenty wrong. And Mary has left today, so that doesn't make Tish and me jump for joy, exactly.'

'I saw Tish with another girl, standing at the barrier.'

'That was Mary. Didn't you see her and Eliza, when you came to the shop?'

'I was looking for just one young lady. I shouldn't have seen Tish if she had not been working near you.'

Her hand had been guided to rest on his sleeve. Arm in arm, they walked away from the ferry. 'You know how to flatter, Mr Bonham,' she remarked, a shade automatically.

'But I mean it. Why is Mary leaving?'

'She's got a job in Laverport. She's going to stay with Tish's sister till she gets a room of her own.'

He was not greatly interested in the fortunes of this girl, Mary, but they were something to talk about. 'What sort of job?' he asked.

Kitty was not enjoying this. 'Like the Bazaar, only more money,' she said.

Henry looked down at the solemn face under this dreadful straw hat. He would have to replace the hat as soon as possible. But what a rare mouth! Almost mutinous, at the moment; very Pre-Raphaelite. He was pleased to observe that the disfiguring little blackhead had disappeared. 'That girl with Tish,' he said, 'certainly didn't look old enough to live on her own in Laverport. What do her parents think of it?'

'She's very independent.' Kitty was not prepared to discuss Mary's private affairs with Henry; she blamed all men for Mary's predicament, for the fact that they would never be brought as low as that. God made one law for women, and one for men, because God was a man.

'You look remarkably vexed about something. What have I done?'

'Nothing. Why isn't God a woman?'

It was a full minute before he controlled his mirth.

'I'm not being funny. Why isn't he?'

'My dear Kitty, you can't play about with the basic structure of Christianity – God the Father. . . .'

'God the Son, and God the Holy Ghost, I know, I know. . . .' Kitty finished heatedly. 'An all-male cast, like this week at the Apollo.'

'You have the Virgin Mary as a mother-figure.'

'Thank you very much. A life of suffering she got, for having a holy terror, if you ask me. *Wist ye not that I must be about my father's business?* – when she'd been worried to death, wondering where he'd got to. A good hiding would have improved him.'

Henry coughed. 'We have to see it in perspective. We've to take into account the role of women in that period. Are you listening? You are. Well, the scriptures are not to be swallowed, hook, line and sinker. It's one beautiful declaration, a lovely myth, if you like; and if it makes the world a better place to live in, then it's a fine thing.'

'It doesn't, though, does it?' she returned. They had reached the steps of the Pier Hotel. 'I don't feel like going in here.'

'Very well. It's not compulsory. Where would you rather go?'

She gave a shrug.

'Perhaps you would prefer to go home?' He spoke a little curtly.

She shook her head.

He became contrite. 'You do look pale. Have you a headache?'

'I didn't sleep much last night.'

'Ah, I see. You were upset about Mary.'

Kitty wanted to shout yes, she was upset about Mary, and about a silver brooch, at present in the clutches of a Mr Tapp in Cable Street. She nodded.

'Poor, soft-hearted Kitty. One day, you'll tell me the whole story about her.'

Kitty looked away. Was she never to pull the wool successfully over this man's eyes?

'How about crossing the river ourselves? The blow would do you good.'

The suggestion appealed to her, though she hesitated.

'Tish and Mary have had a good head start,' he said.

'You read everything I'm thinking. They were going straight to Biddy's place. We shouldn't bump into them.'

Henry was cheered to see one of her real smiles. 'Back to the ferry, then, and a lobster tea in Laverport.'

'A *what*?'

'Come on, don't dawdle. We should catch the next boat. You mean you wouldn't know a lobster if you fell over one?'

'Yes, I would, only – '

'They don't grab you from the plate. Besides, I'm getting tired of tea and pastries. We can have a later dinner.'

'We shan't need your later dinner, even if we had time for it.'

'Both depend on what we do in between.'

Kitty let the matter drop.

The number of trips she had made on a ferryboat could be counted on one hand; she was not as blasé as most passengers. And the gangplank was not as still as she would have liked; it lifted and sank, and generally slithered about. Henry was mildly tickled that she had stepped so cautiously over a ferry gangway.

From the engine room an overpowering smell of

machine oil offended her; it was crude and hot, and it came in a slipstream, as if the men below deck were in training for Hell. If such fumes had greeted Mary, Kitty hoped they had not bowled her out.

The behaviour of the gangplank could be forgiven, in view of the pitch and roll of the boat. Henry guided her to the open stairway; on the second step, she was flung sideways against the handrail. Henry's arm went round her waist, and the rest of the flight was taken in good style. He released her when they had gained the upper deck; here, the wind proved quite penetrating.

'It's windier when we get out there, isn't it?' Kitty was already hanging on to her hat.

Henry did not favour the idea of a hatless Kitty. He undid the knot of her best blue scarf, and removed it carefully from her neck.

'I'll be cold.'

With equal care, he draped the tulle across the crown of the hat, and tied it firmly under her chin. He thought the scarf went well with the forget-me-knots, while it toned down the garish colour of the rest. He then raised her coat-collar high about her neck, and fastened the top button. 'You should always button up on board ship,' he told her.

She rubbed her arm.

'Is that hurting badly?'

'Horribly.'

As he stroked comfort into the bruised flesh, she decided that God could stay a man, for all she cared; he was not as important as all that to Kitty Catchpole. The one figure who meant something to her was standing here, smiling down at her, dressed in navy blue with gold braid. The boat eased away from the landing stage. Kitty looked over the rail at the churning water. 'It's just like beer,' she said.

'A poisonous river,' Henry commented. 'When I see swimmers in it upstream I want to order them out. Imagine swallowing a gulp of that!'

'It's no worse than most, I should think.'

'I could take you to clean rivers where we could bathe in safety.'

'I can't swim.'

'I would soon teach you.'

'I'm not sure I want to learn.'

Henry was shocked by this. 'Of course you do! Everybody ought to know how to swim.'

'Everybody hasn't got a bathing suit.'

'The rivers I am talking about are so remote, you don't need a bathing suit.'

'Henry Bonham! I'm not that sort of a girl.'

'And what sort would that be? I'm merely suggesting a bathe in a quiet, little river. How about a turn on deck?'

At the second time round, Kitty was beginning to get the hang of it. She stepped out with his rhythm which he took naturally from the deck's; so the two of them continued to walk, when lesser performers had settled for the wooden slats. Bridgemouth's dead cranes were left behind, their tall necks nicely defined against the dull sky; the ferryboat ploughed continuously across the paths of dredgers and tugs, making for Laverport. Kitty was enchanted by the important Cunard liner, which was waiting at the stage for its transatlantic passengers.

'Is your boat as beautiful as that one?' she asked Henry.

'I think she is; she's nothing like that for size, but she's a fine ship.'

'We can't see it from here?'

'Heavens, no! We don't use that berth.'

'I think I'll sit down.'

'Certainly. Are you all right? Don't tell me you feel bad on a ferryboat!'

'No, I don't.' But she did feel bad, if not with the roll of the boat. When you let yourself love a sailor, he then left, even if he did intend to return; the leaving was always with you, to ruin the hours you spent together. Did it mean nothing to Henry? He had spoken in such a matter-of-fact way, it had set her shivering.

'Are you cold, Kitty? Would you like my coat?'

'No, I'm not as cold as all that.'

'I shall be sad when I have to sail,' he said quietly, 'but don't cry now, *please*. There's a woman over there, with her eyes glued on us. She'll be thinking this is a sailor's farewell.'

She blinked and looked upriver. 'I'm sorry. I ought to have more sense. It's not your fault that you have to go away.'

They sat without speaking, as the vast landing stage drew nearer, with its mighty pontoons, and its mean cluster of green wooden huts, which housed a minute fraction of its day-to-day management.

In spite of her overall dumpiness, their boat turned gracefully to sidle in, with a stopping and starting of engines, and a renewal of gongs and paddle-thrashing.

'I don't see Tish with anybody, do you?' said Henry.

To Kitty's relief, there was no sign of her two friends, so they would not be thinking she was tailing them. She was reluctant to leave the landing stage immediately. It was thronged with Sunday trippers – and strollers, for many were content to promenade slowly up and down the stage, pausing at times to examine the lesser boats moored there, or to gaze up the large floating bridge, so oddly free today of its lumbering drays, though it still gave off that unmistakable suggestion of the stable, which not even the high wind off the Mease could defeat.

'Let's walk as far as the liner,' Kitty suggested.

'The liner? Whatever for?'

'It's a lot bigger than the ferryboat.'

'You can't get very close; the railing cuts you off.'

Kitty declared she would like to go as far as the railing.

'If you must,' Henry said, with more resignation than indulgence. He was not overkeen on pushing his way against this crowd in order to stare vacantly through iron fencing at a ship, the like of which he could see any day of the week, with much less trouble. However, Kitty was on her way, weaving swiftly and efficiently through the crush, and it was all he could do to keep up with her.

'You move better on dry land,' he remarked, as they broke free, some ten yards from the fencing.

'I wouldn't call it that. This stage is going up and down.'

'I told you we aren't allowed past the railing.'

'That man is going through.'

'He has a pass. The constable will stop him for a check, you'll see.'

'So he has. But isn't it a beauty? Did you ever see such a boat, Henry? There's a man in a white coat, look, high up, in that doorway.'

'A steward.'

Kitty held on to the rails with both hands. If only she could go on a boat like that to America – Henry and Kitty together on a big liner . . . .

Henry had turned his back on the ship, and was surveying the Laverportians with disfavour, as they still milled about in their hundreds. What enjoyment could they find in such a celebration? Yet they laughed and talked, many of them at the top of their voices, the women all bust, behind and brolly, the men cloth-capped, bowlered, or in some cases actually straw-cadied in anticipation of a jaunty summer. Nearly all seemed to be burdened with children, who would have been better left unborn. It struck him that these people might be avoided by walking up the floating bridge.

'But that's where the horse-drays go! You can see it's all dirty,' she objected, when he put his alternative route to Kitty. Henry informed her that a horse between shafts was unlikely to soil the extreme sides of the bridge. Leading a handful of like-minded pedestrians, he took her through the less orthodox exit into Laverport's own Ferry Head.

Tish was uneasy to be paying out so many coppers on fares. Mary had asked to pay their travelling expenses, but Kitty had insisted that Mary's wages should be kept as far as possible intact. All the same, to be parting with so much was worrying to Tish.

Just to be making the journey disturbed Mary. In spite of Tish's encouragement on the noisy, rocking tram, she was in a sorry state of nerves when they had stepped off it, and felt even worse when they had covered the short distance to Biddy's lodgings.

The sight of that decaying terrace helped in no way to boost Mary's flagging morale. One or two children fought in the street; they were poorly clad, and unwashed. The cobbles were littered with unswept rubbish; a number of doorways stood open, significant of constant traffic, of an indifferent sense of property. Private houses, which had once been the pride of flourishing traders, had become public; and with the opening of their doors, vermin, too, had moved in. Mary and Tish stopped at no. 9, Temple Gardens.

A man in his shirtsleeves was sitting on the doorstep of no. 7; he sized up the two girls, as they gained the worn steps of the house next door; they were a sight for sore eyes, they were. Tish had called once before at no. 9, but he did not recognize her; he thought the other young lady, with the frightened look on her face, might be Biddy Kelly's sister; there was something about the mouth and chin, and the way she held herself.

'That brown door at the end of the passage,' Tish said, steering Mary forward, on the first-floor landing. She was doing her utmost to brave it out; this house was no worse than her parents' home, but she might have felt ashamed of that, too, had she been introducing Mary to it. It was a shame tinged with defiance and fear; she wanted her sister to be appreciated.

Mary was put off by the size of the place, and by the all-too-familiar dilapidation. She came from cottage property that had not gone down in the world, since it could go no lower; her terrace, also, was damp, verminous, and not one hundred per cent respectable.

Tish knocked on the blistered and scaling door. It opened to reveal Biddy Kelly in satin négligée, of a flamboyant oriental design. Her assisted-Titian hair fell in corkscrew curls over her forehead, and escaped from loose pins at the back; her eyelashes stuck out in Cherry Blossom triangles, and her complexion owed much to the flour bag. Mary was mesmerized by the scarlet expanse of mouth and the red-smeared teeth.

'What you standing there for?' said Biddy. 'Come along in.'

*

With the departure of Mary, Eliza Heggy was left without a walking-companion. Until another lady assistant could be appointed, she would remain in this high and dry situation, and the outlook did not please her. She had stayed behind, after the departure of Kitty, Tish and Mary, in order to complete a strong letter to her parents. There had been such a scramble and tension in the bedroom that morning, she had not been able to collect her thoughts.

Dear mum and Dad [it ran]

Just a line to tell you bad news which you may know becose bad news travels fast This morning Mary Gibbs is gone she was saked by Mr Skinner, she is a lose woman feinting in the shop and gave the show away. As luck would have it nurse Winters was nice and handy in Fabrics so there was no getting away from it, She was found out having a baby if you please. she is the girl I had to walk out with and Mrs Skinner is sorry a respectible girl like me got to mix with such rif raf but she was a quite one nobdy woud have guest I coud have told them. He was a AB Bunny Harras by name and Bunny by nachure She use to leave me and go off in the sandhills of a Sunday, Now he as bolted and left her to it I think you orght to take me from this place of sin and put me to Masons,

your loving Daughter
Eliza Heggy XXXX

Having finished writing, Eliza searched in her black leather handbag for a penny stamp, but no amount of poking about could expose one. Positive that she did, in fact, have a penny stamp – for hadn't she bought two from Mrs Skinner not a week ago? – she scattered the bag's contents over her quilt, and rummaged among the hairpins, the safety pin in case a button fell off her knickers, the sterling silver thimble inscribed E.H., this letter from her mother, warning her against slipping home or moaning about life at the Bazaar, and unique treasures like the pink-pearl leaflet of *papier poudre* presented free some months earlier with *Woman's Chat*.

It was obvious, Eliza concluded, one of The Three had pinched it. She went to the chest shared by Kitty and Tish, to ransack that; it held nothing remotely resembling a purse or wallet, in which she might have hoped to discover stolen goods. Mary Gibbs probably took it from Eliza's bag; a girl like her would stoop to anything. Vastly put out, Eliza pinned on her green velvet hat, trimmed with counterfeit kingfisher, donned her coat of blue melton cloth, and went with Kitty-Catchpole stealth down the stairs; once again the Skinners were not to be disturbed.

The half-glazed door to the cash office was unlocked; it was Hezekiah's habit to remove cash every night, and bills, ledgers and cash every Saturday night. There were two drawers in the desk, and Eliza knew which one held the supply of stamps. She tugged at this left-hand drawer, but it resisted; disconsolately, she tried the other. This gave, to disclose two piles of used envelopes, one thick, one slender; all the envelopes were for re-use, but the smaller pile bore unscathed postage stamps. Eliza helped herself to a buff envelope, whose stamp was not only unfranked, but barely attached. She transferred this to her own letter, and bore the envelope to the kitchen fire.

'It's an untidy operation,' said Kitty, dipping her fingers in the finger bowl.

She had come a long way from the unsure girl who had first taken tea with him at the Pier Hotel; it was

good to see her dealing so ably with her first lobster
. . . . 'I hope it's worth the struggle,' he replied.

'Oh, it is – it is!'

They had taken a cab to this new hotel, which stood
resplendent in its white stone, a mock-Palladian refuge
for the truly well-to-do. On entering the luxurious hall,
Kitty had held her head proudly, as befitted a lady
escorted by a chief officer, and wearing his recent gift of
elegant kid gloves. The split boot, however, and the
shabby gentility of her best coat and hat, had not
escaped the eye of the floor-manager, who had ushered
the couple with wary suavity to a far corner of the
restaurant. Henry had then made a sterner resolution
to remedy some of the defects in Kitty's wardrobe; he
disliked a café seclusion not of his own choosing. As it
turned out, with Kitty's initiation into the tackling of
lobster salad, the siting of their table had not been a
disadvantage, and it had allowed private conversation.

'How long is it before you go away?' she asked him,
when the waitress had left them to their sherry trifle.

'I have some weeks still, the way things are going.'

'Weeks? How many weeks?' Her spoon flicked lightly
at the piped twirls of cream, the tiny silver balls and the
glacé cherries.

'Five . . . even six. It's exceptional, you understand.
A ship can't afford lengthy repair work every time she
comes into port.'

Henry could have added that he himself was
sufficiently in funds to miss the next sailing, if the fancy
took him. It was always possible for him to sign on
later, as first mate under a new skipper, or he could bide
his time further, until a vacancy arose for a captain. It
would be gratifying to have a command before his
thirtieth birthday, and he stood well with the company.
However, he was fond of the Old Man, and would not

say no to a few more trips with him. And it would be sensible to put some distance fairly soon between himself and Kitty. He was not a man to be hustled; in the past, he had come to value separation as a standard test for any romantic attachment. . . . He was tempted to return this sherry trifle to source; there was little or no sherry in it. Unfortunately, Kitty would not know where to put herself, if he did. She had just said something which he had not caught. He gave her a questioning look . . .

'How long will you be gone for?' she repeated.

'I shall be signing on for six months' articles.'

'What does that mean?'

'Precisely what it says! About six months; not long at all.'

'Where will you go?' she asked.

'I don't know yet. We could have a light cargo for Singapore; then we might go on to Rangoon, say, to pick up rice, and then back home.'

'Rangoon?' Kitty remembered her Valparaiso, on the west coast of Africa. 'Where's that? Africa?'

There was a note of exasperation in Henry's laugh. 'My dear girl,' he said, 'Rangoon is in Burma. Where's your geography?'

She blushed. 'I'm afraid I don't know much. How long were you away last time?'

His voice was testy. '*Much longer*, but do we have to spoil a meal with this catechism? You said this afternoon that you would have to accept all that. Sailors go away, Kitty – friends, lovers, husbands, what have you? – we leave our womenfolk. It's a way of life one gets used to.'

'What are you, then? A friend, lover, or a husband? You could be all three if you were married.'

'And what if I were just two, and not married?'

'Rubbish,' she said. But was there some friend, lover or wife, tucked away elsewhere, waiting for Henry? What had he done for a girl-friend on previous leaves in Laverport?

'If that upsets you, put it out of your mind. Get on with your trifle, Miss Catchpole; that is, if you like trifle.'

'I do like it a lot.'

'But you haven't had it before?'

'I have, as a matter of fact. Once.'

'At home?'

'No. I haven't been sitting around all my life, waiting for Henry Bonham to give me trifle.'

'No,' he said in his turn. 'I don't suppose you have.'

They were reduced to eating for several minutes without talk. Kitty was annoyed, because Henry's past was to remain a closed book, while Henry was pained to learn that the girl he had believed inexperienced, whose education was to be his sole privilege and pleasure, was in all likelihood not so naive as he had assumed.

Although there was good reason for Kitty to want some filling-in on Henry's love life, or at least an assurance that she was now the one participant in it, there was far less reason for her invention of a man-friend who had laid sherry trifle at her feet, so to speak. The most she had ever been given was a half-share in a bottle of cream soda, and that was more years ago than she cared to remember. Out of spleen, Kitty had denied Henry his due as trifle-introducer; moreover, she should have recognized that a man might have as many women in as many categories as he chose, without incurring great censure, whereas a young lady assistant would do well to keep even the most uneventful relationship to herself.

There was going to be no more enlightenment from

Kitty on this thorny subject. Henry asked himself why he should expect more from her than from other girls thrown on to a hard world to earn a living. If he wished to play for safety, he could wait until he returned home, perhaps for good; there he could take his pick among the young ladies known to his family, whose lives were supervised by watchful mamas – young ladies versed in the social arts, and invariably delivered as green as grass to the marital bed. Was he prepared to wait? He was not. Looking across at Kitty, as she ate that ridiculous trifle, his vexation melted.

'I'm afraid I crushed your brim, rather, with that scarf.' His expression of regret lacked sincerity. She would be more likely to welcome a new hat, if this monstrosity were wrecked beyond recall.

Both her hands had flown up to the brim to assess the damage.

'Silly girl! Now you have a streak of cream on it! You should have put your spoon down. Lean over . . .' He removed the cream with his table napkin.

'Does it show?' she asked him nervously.

'Not really. It looks a bit darker, but it ought to dry out.'

'But is the brim all crooked? Badly?' Her fingers were trying to straighten it. She would go across to the ladies' cloakroom to use the looking glass, if only people didn't stare at her.

'It's not too bad. I'm sorry I mentioned it, but since I did the tying, I owe you an apology.'

'You did it with the best of intentions. If it's not really skew-whiff, you can do it again, when we go back.'

'May I? And if it ends up well and truly bent, I must buy you another.'

Kitty looked at him in dismay. 'I'm sorry, I couldn't allow that. I mean, I don't want another.'

Having presented her with a first-class reason for abandoning the thing, Henry saw no logic in the refusal. He had bought her other items to wear; and she could have had two hats, like the natural straw she was wearing, for the price of those gloves, but perhaps she did not realize that. 'You let me give you things before,' he countered.

How could she explain to him the difference, as she saw it, between small accessories and personal clothing? He would be offering to buy her a coat next! He was not her husband. 'I'm sorry,' she repeated. 'This one will do me for quite a time yet.'

She was telling him, in effect, that she was not to be bought. He would not be allowed to replace her shocking boots, either. 'I see,' he said. 'Perhaps I shall earn the right to buy you a hat, one day.'

They walked at a leisurely pace up the hill beyond the hotel, as far as the elegant Georgian squares which housed the still-comfortable merchants of Laverport. It was in one of those squares, each enclosing its private garden for residents, that Henry had his lodging. There was a similar quarter in Bridgemouth, on a more limited scale; the assistants had often speculated on the kind of person who owned a key to one of these horticultural oases; well screened with plain and variegated laurel, with holly, dark privet and the white-flowered rhododendron, you could sit for hours on a wrought iron seat, stroking the ears of your King Charles's spaniel: if you had a spaniel.

'Damp places,' Henry declared, 'overgrown with moss and old ladies. I never go into ours.'

His landlady was one of these old ladies – a widow, who let only one room; she was a creature of such refinement that Henry felt obliged to her for the favour. It was a house he had patronized over a number of years, on the personal recommendation of a previous ship's captain, and he would not be taking a young lady into it.

'It's down there,' he told Kitty, waving an arm in the direction of his square.

'A house like these here?'

'I've just the one room in it,' he reminded her, 'and the use of the dining room, of course.'

'I wouldn't mind half a room in such a house. No, I don't mean sharing, or anything like that.' She was momentarily covered in confusion.

'It's not the sort of house for anything like that. I do sometimes feel I ought to move, if only to have a sitting room; I can't easily invite men-friends round; there's only one easy chair in my room.'

'Have you got men-friends, then?'

'Of course I have! I work with men, don't I?'

'You don't talk about them.'

Henry explained that he was too busy, talking about Kitty, to bother mentioning his men-friends. She asked him if he was too busy, talking to his men-friends, to write to her on Tuesdays.

Henry's face was expressionless. 'I generally spend the day with my closest friend. He has been ill lately.'

'You did his duty for him. You told me.'

'That was the second mate. My friend Eric often goes to sea, but only as a passenger.'

'Then what does your Eric Whatshisname *do*?'

'Eric Cannon-Budge. He writes these days, for the most part. He's making a survey of fifteenth-century *putti*.'

Kitty fell silent. She wanted to ask when she could meet this invisible friend, for she always had Tish's interests at heart, but Henry's tone of voice was not helpful. She would have liked to know what made fifteenth-century putty so interesting, but that, too, would have to wait.

They moved away from the high-class squares into streets where the property was still good, if on a more modest scale.

'I'm inclined to think I pay out too much in rent,' Henry began, 'with nothing to show for it in the long run. It might be wiser to buy a smallish place, since I come here fairly frequently.'

She could hardly believe her ears; never before had she met anyone who talked of buying bricks and mortar. 'You don't mean a house of your own? You can't!'

'Why not?'

'You must earn a bright penny, that's all I can say.'

'I certainly don't. It would be a pretty poor house out of my earnings. I'm sure you'll strain your eyes if you don't blink. That's better. I was afraid they'd be fixed that way.'

'Maybe the Skinners own the Bazaar . . .'

'I imagine they do. My house would not be quite the size of the Bazaar! We can start looking for one now.'

She pointed out that it was Sunday. Henry maintained that houses for sale could be spotted on Sundays, even viewed on Sundays, if one had the key. Kitty speculated a moment or two on this: it might not take long; he had only to come across a house full of moss and old ladies for the search to be off.

'If I can change my day, will you be free on Wednesday?' he asked.

This was a new departure. 'No. Mary and Eliza – I mean, Eliza Heggy has this Wednesday afternoon off.'

'I may do some scouting around on Tuesday, in that

case, and you can help me, perhaps, next Sunday. That is, if it interests you.'

It did interest Kitty. They had arrived at the sooted Botanical Gardens, where they eventually joined sauntering families, and couples like themselves with nowhere else to go, inside the conservatories. Squatter-sparrows darted between manic climbers. The intense steam-heat in the middle section hampered breathing, and brought out a glisten of sweat on noses. Coats were flung open, and rubber dress shields added their own especial overkill to the dankness of the lily basin; but the floating blooms enchanted Kitty, as much as she, in her pleasure, enchanted Henry. Her animated face was most attractive under that wavy brim; the wave was an improvement. Taking a moment's cover among the fronds of a medium palm, Henry Bonham kissed Kitty Catchpole as she had never been kissed before.

'How did they get on?' Kitty asked Tish.

'Not so bad. Biddy did most of the talking, but she always does. Mary was real scared – more frightened than she was here, somehow. I think she was ready to run for it when we got to the house; and she started crying, when I was going.'

'That's not like Mary.'

'I know. I started crying, as well. It was all so unfair. And then, blow me if our Biddy didn't start crying her eyes out, so that made three of us.'

'Yes.' Kitty paused. 'Your Biddy sounds a grand girl. Mary is staying with her, then?'

'Yes and no. It's awkward, you see, with just the one room.'

'That's what Henry said.'

'He what?'

'Nothing. Go on. She's only got one room, your Biddy.'

'That's right. There's a sink and a gas ring in a sort of cupboard, so it's better than some, but I don't know how they'll manage. Mary can take turns with the bed, and she can walk round Laverport in the day . . .' Tish was groping for words to explain the situation, and finding none. She rushed on: 'There may be a room going soon, upstairs. There's a girl might move out.'

'In the same house? What will Mary do for rent?'

'She could go on the parish if she had to, couldn't she? But she says they'll put her in a home, and she won't have that. She's keeping the baby.'

'She's not! What for? She must be mad!'

'That's what our Biddy told her, but she wouldn't shift. She's determined to keep it.'

'You mean have it, and then keep it? She'll never get taken on with a kid. I thought – well, I thought she might be getting rid of it.'

'You don't have to yell at me. We all thought that.'

The girls sat side by side on Kitty's bed, staring at their cracked washbowl.

'Before I scrape the Bazaar dust off my feet, I'll smash that blasted bowl. Oh, God! She's keeping it, and she's not going into a home. So who's keeping her when this week's money disappears?'

'Biddy is.'

Kitty had turned to look at Tish. 'How can she do that?'

'She doesn't have much, but she gets by. She says Mary can pay her back some time.'

Kitty drew a long breath. 'Then she's a saint, your Biddy.'

'I think she is; others mightn't.'

Kitty waited for more elaboration, but Tish had finished; she left Kitty's bed, and went over to hers, where she threw back the covers, and extracted her nightgown. She undid the buttons of her Sunday dress with studied care. If Mary had been scared to be alone with Biddy, Tish was now uncomfortable to be with Kitty, to be left with a lot of explaining to do. But where else could she have taken Mary? Kitty, for once, had come up with no bright ideas. Only two buttons to go. Would a nice girl like Kitty accept Tish's sister, or Tish's mother? The dress was undone. Tish's face was flushed; she was disgusted with herself:

'If you must know, Kitty, and you've a right to know, our Biddy earns her living on the streets, giving men what they want. My mam did it, when she had to, and I'm proud of the two of them. Biddy took over the lot of us once, when mam went ill, and the rags wasn't bringing in much. When dad got on a bit, Biddy said she'd pay for me to be apprenticed, like, so's I'd get a better deal than her. That's about it. And that's what frightened Mary as much as anything. She's not thick; she must have tumbled to the set-up. And if she didn't, she has by now; Biddy will have told her. It's awful, having one room. You can't do a job like Biddy's if you've got a *respectable* girl sharing.' The bitterness in Tish's voice brought it to breaking point.

Before Kitty could speak, the bedroom door flew open to admit Eliza, who skirted round the room to her corner. Tish continued to undress; Kitty stood looking in Eliza's direction, over the flat and empty bed that had been Mary's, her eyes seeing nothing. Tish, too, was more or less impervious to Eliza's presence, so that any icy tarring-with-the-one-brush was wasted on the seniors.

As Tish now struggled to fasten the linen buttons on

her nightdress, with fingers that were unaccountably all thumbs, Kitty smiled. 'It's what I said, Tish-girl. Your Biddy's a saint,' she told her.

'It's like there's been a death,' Tish said, 'with Mary gone.'

Eliza responded with a snort, as her pearl-handled buttonhook slotted and twisted its way up the side of her boot.

'You were in late enough last night, Miss Eliza,' Kitty remarked drily. 'Late for a young girl walking alone, that is.'

'There's nothing against walking alone,' Eliza retorted. 'I can come and go as I want, without asking your permission. I wasn't late anyway.'

'Late enough, I said. What you do is your own business, but the streets aren't all that safe for a girl on her own.'

'If you ask me, they're as safe as the sandhills of an afternoon.'

'Will you shut your mouth, for Pete's sake?' Kitty warned.

That morning, the Skinners cold-shouldered their customers, as far as this was practicable; most of these people, in Jinny's estimation, had come in for a penn'orth of hat elastic, merely to stroll with it into Baby Linen, there to confirm that the flustered junior from Gowns and Millinery was holding the fort, and making her usual bungle of it. For at least two hours, that area of the floor had overflowed with standing clients, and no more than the sale of one baby's comforter to show for them. With reluctance, Hezekiah transferred Miss Kelly beyond the archway, where tougher challenging – as to what they might be requiring –

helped to disperse many of the non-customers. He brought Miss Heggy into Haberdashery, to assist Miss Catchpole in the rush on elastic; he had been surprised to see the Catchpole girl show signs of wear under a couple of hours' pressure; she was the last to lose her head, as a rule. Her agitation became clearer to him when he heard what his wife had to say to her at cocoa-time.

Jinny Skinner was so greatly provoked by the outcome of Nurse Winters' scandalmongering that she proved stone-deaf to Kitty's appeal. Miss Catchpole would not be visiting the cobbler's today, nor on any foreseeable day in the near future; she would have to ask again, when a new lady assistant had been appointed. Jinny could always relax her standards concerning a down-at-heel appearance when it suited her. Lowering her voice, she advised the senior assistant to pull her skirt down; a decently covered ankle would not come amiss; it might distract attention from the boot.

Kitty had been prepared for this. Using the elastic-scissors, which Eliza was now privately cursing, since they would not cut butter, she had hacked away at the tear in her boot, enlarging it formidably. As Mrs Skinner raised her head for the regal cocoa-nod, Miss Catchpole raised her left boot high, for all to see; she exposed not only an unseemly depth of ankle, but also a bulge of the late Grandma Catchpole's fawn stocking, where it escaped between sole and upper. 'It's the only pair I've got ma'am. I can't go another week like this!'

'As God's my witness,' Jinny seethed, hanging on to her Singer table, and breathing fire and brimstone over the aspidistra, 'I tell you straight, as God's my witness, I'll lay hold on her tonight and sling her out! I'm not putting up with one more week of that one – *not one more week*, d'you hear me?'

His wife's hysteria had reached a degree where reasoning could have no effect. Hezekiah supplied the one antidote he knew; it was guaranteed to work as well as a jug of cold water, and it required no mopping up. Raising his voice to Minotaur volume, he shouted her down. 'She stays,' he bellowed. 'You don't sack a girl when she begs in front of customers to go to Mitchell Caine's. Do you want me to close the doors tonight for good? Use your loaf, woman!'

Jinny Skinner sat down, her feet on the unyielding treadle, and howled into her off-duty pinafore. Her husband quitted the room; she would get over it faster without him.

In twelve minutes, the shop would open for the afternoon. Hezekiah trusted the Catchpole would appear by then. He had not thought she would miss her dinner; there had been time for her to have a boot mended twice over, and get herself back to eat her tripe and onions. This reminded him to inform Minnie Jacks not to let the seam go to the assistants' table in future; she should know without telling that honeycomb was not meant for her employers' plates. Indeed, he was sure she did know; a rage equal to Jinny's finest swelled in his chest and reduced his eyes to a dead man's squint; now there was someone he could enjoy throwing out – Jacks and her bedshawl.

The Catchpole had met her la-di-da sailor boy, that was it! The sneaky little bitch! Hezekiah's neck grew redder. Not back yet, and candidates for Baby Linen knocking on the back door all morning! Four to see this afternoon . . . Jinny was right; he'd like to screw the Catchpole's neck, himself. More than that. Hezekiah stood glaring at the grandfather clock on the landing, his face a dangerous shade.

The Skinners were not alone in their desire for Kitty's return. Tish, in her less selfish way, was also on edge. She stood at the attic window, willing Kitty to open the gate and walk into the yard.

'What's the time?' she asked Eliza.

The junior glanced up from a heel she was drawing together. 'Couldn't say. My clock's stopped. You won't bring her back, goggling through the window. I bet you tuppence she's off on a joy ride with Our Henry. Goodness knows what he sees in a girl with busted boots.' Growing suddenly bored with her mending, she stuffed wooden mushroom, stocking and crewel needle into her top drawer. 'The bell's not far off. Looks like you and me's going to be slaving hell for leather, Mr Skinner busy with the job-girls, and all.'

Tish made no comment. Left to herself, she stayed by the window, her lips moving instinctively in prayer. Apart from the suspicion, a near certainty, that Kitty had lost her brooch for ever to Maurice Tapp, there was that recollection of the vile man in the market place. Today was Monday. Surely no fellow like him would be lurking about on a weekday? She fell to praying again, rather as others might bite their nails; halfway through a Hail Mary, she slipped unawares into a prayer addressed to Kitty, beseeching her in the name of the Blessed Mother of God to come home.

After the first shock of stepping out in a boot more critically ripped than before, Kitty became accustomed to the keener impact of cold, and the bite of the upper, as its wide crease met her foot. The faster she went, the less discomfort she seemed to notice. Her first port of call was to be the pawnshop, and she made this in fair time; the sight of those three balls suspended Damocletianlike at the corner of Cable Street had increased her final speed; the quicker she arrived, the sooner she could leave them behind.

She stood under them, and for a moment her sore foot asserted itself. Of greater concern, however, was the closed shop door, and the dim interior behind it. Kitty tried the handle. Tapp's was shut for dinner.

With internal screaming, which, like internal bleeding, does the sufferer no good, she ran round the corner and found the pledge door. She was on the correct side of it just as Maurice Tapp came into the narrow lobby with his keys. Could she tell the time? He closed for dinner at a quarter past, and everybody knew it. There was a notice telling her that in both windows. He ought to send her packing, he ought; what was it she wanted?

As the pawnbroker bolted his side door against further invasion, Kitty produced the pledge ticket from her purse. The disdain on the man's face, when she described her brooch, told her what she had refused to believe: there was no room for sentiment in trade.

Mr Tapp held the scrap of paper at arm's length, scrutinizing it with incredulity, as if he could not credit the evidence of his long-sighted eyes. Was she Mrs Minnie Jacks? She was not. What did she call herself then? How did he know she was Miss Katherine Catchpole, whoever that might be? How was he to know she hadn't picked this ticket up in the street?

Kitty had not thought to ask why Mrs Jacks' name came to be on the ticket; she had not realized this would matter, and, legally, it did not, as Mr Tapp had known before. Nor had the latter forgotten the circumstances of the pledge. Convinced that Minnie Jacks would not be coming to redeem it, since she herself never left an article in pawn for more than one week, he had decided the brooch was forfeited.

'But I thought I could leave it for six months!' Kitty pleaded. She was wrong; by law, she could have left it for twelve months.

'One month in this establishment,' said Maurice Tapp, smacking the ticket down under his fleshy hand. The brooch was no longer in his possession; it had been disposed of the previous week. And now he would like his dinner, if she had no objection. Striding back to the door, he ushered Kitty off the premises; the iron bolt shot into position behind her, as she stood shaking on the pavement.

Blindly, she took to her heels once more, hurrying with her oddly limping gait through the confusion of small streets which led to the cobbler's; at one wider junction, she was the cause of a burst of swearing, with a clanging of footbell, and a shower of sparks, as steel ground to a halt on steel. She sped on, until she virtually stumbled upon an open door marked *Quality Leather, Lowest Prices*. Here, she flopped on to a rickety chair and wept.

Old Mitchell Caine patted her cheeks dry, as best he could, with a yellow finishing duster; this was not an office which came his way often, and the dabs tended to be wild.

When Kitty could speak, and when she had produced her handkerchief, she told him haltingly that her mother was ill, and that she, Kitty, had been bottling it up all morning. Clicking his tongue, and shaking his head until the wisps of dry, white hair fell over his sheepdog eyes, Mitchell pulled the split boot off her foot and looked it over. He was mystified by the extent and character of the damage; about half a dozen torn stitches were badly soiled and worn flat, but the rest were upstanding and clean enough to suggest a more recent accident.

'However did it get like this?' he said, half to himself.

'It's been like that for weeks.'

'But this part wasn't done weeks ago,' he pointed out.

'Oh, that bit? I caught it on the bootscraper coming in from the yard.' Kitty's voice was subdued.

'You could have hurt your foot, doing that.' Old Mitchell's hands, those clumsy tear-moppers, had the stitching done in quick time; he asked for the other boot, and gave each a new heel tip.

Sitting in her stockinged feet in this lopsided shack, which was all that Mitchell Caine had ever known for a workshop, Kitty felt a sorrow that was so weighty it threatened to push her and the chair into the ground: with Mary gone, and the silver brooch sacrificed, she felt her heart – or whatever it was that pulled at the bottom of every breath – could never recover. Before long, she must write home, confessing the loss of her brooch; no matter what story she thought up, it was bound to upset her mother.

The stitched boot pinched the side of her foot, but no longer caught it across the top.

'That's better, isn't it?' Mitchell prompted.

She rewarded him with a faint smile. 'It's lovely, Mr Caine, thank you.'

The cobbler refused payment, but he reminded Kitty that boots must be treated with kindness. 'Remember, leather needs feeding,' he said.

She walked to the door, trying not to hobble.

'It will stretch as you go,' he told her. 'I hope you

soon have good news of your mother.' As she hurried away, he called after her, 'And give that bootscraper a miss!' He dropped the catch on his door and turned the swinging card to OPEN.

With under three minutes to go, Hezekiah Skinner had the brass bell in one hand, with its clapper muted in the other. He heard several slams as someone shut the back gate, then a scamper of light feet, as Kitty Catchpole passed him to take the stairs two at a time.

'Where have you been till this hour?' he shouted. A strangled retort, which sounded remarkably like, 'Where do you think?' was the sole excuse to be had from Kitty as she made for the bedroom.

Hezekiah rang the bell with a ferocious violence, slapping it down so hard on the hall shelf that it retaliated with a loud *wah-wah* . . . He threw open the shop doors to admit four frightened young ladies and two customers. With no ceremony, he directed the applicants to the first-floor landing, there to stand outside the sitting room, until he was ready to deal with them. They were clearly in for a rough ride; they were about to receive the brunt of the hectoring meant for the senior assistant, and they would be expected to take it with due humility.

As Kitty took her place at the counter, he detected an angry line to her mouth, and a glint in her eye. Tish Kelly was hovering irresolutely by the centre display; she looked like death warmed up, he thought, and was adding nothing to the sales appeal of the shop floor. 'Miss Kelly!' he commanded, with a gesture towards the archway. Tish obeyed, but with an air that increased his displeasure. Dammit, that girl was getting more like the Catchpole every day. He sighed. He would have given his right arm not to have those interviews this afternoon; but with a wife who always went for money and no looks . . . ! Thanks to her, they now had Eliza Heggy. Incidentally, where was that lairage product? He had started towards the kitchen when Eliza showed up; she was swallowing hard, after a secret toffee session. Before the boss could thunder his, 'Haberdashery!' Miss Heggy was homing for her new station as fast as any spider for its skirting board.

Hezekiah resolved to say no more to Kitty Catchpole, but to tell Jinny that he had given that young woman a strong warning. Fortified with this decision, he was able to greet his wife with a look that could have passed for kindly as she approached the steps to her cash office. On a further impulse, he moved across to her: 'Shall we halve it? I'll see two, and you can see two.'

'I went to Tapp's; he'd got rid of my brooch. I went to Mitchell Caine's; he mended my boot.'

The brevity of Kitty's account made Tish all the more desolate; its starkness led her to fill in the blanks herself, so that she finished up with a true story, padded with many a fictive detail. Her guilt oppressed her; Kitty's own share in the loss of her brooch no longer figured in Tish's reckoning. It needed more than the Father's mild words to absolve this: it wanted a miracle-worker, somebody who could walk up to Kitty and put the brooch in her hand.

'And it's all my fault; it's all my fault,' she murmured aloud.

'What is?' Eliza Heggy was in the attic doorway. 'What's all your fault?'

Kitty and Tish stood up in mutual accord, and walked out of the room. Eliza followed them downstairs.

'I suppose you two know who got the job,' she went on. 'But why is it all your fault?' she asked Tish again.

'Do I have to tell you to get to bed?' Kitty demanded.

'I'll go to bed when it suits me, not when you say.'

'You'll go to bed now!' Kitty and Tish made one concerted grab at Eliza; they bundled her out of the kitchen and pushed her resisting form with difficulty up the stairs. The victim's non-co-operation was loud and unrestricted; by the time the three were on the top stair of the first flight, the result was predictable.

Jinny Skinner, at the end of her endurance after an acrimonious debate with Hezekiah on the handicap of flat chests and ravaged complexions, was actively hopping with temper on her black chenille doormat. She demanded a reason for the disgraceful uproar.

Kitty made no bones about it. 'We can't get rid of Miss Heggy, ma'am; it's as simple as that. And a young girl shouldn't be listening to everything the seniors say; there are some things not meant for young ears.'

Jinny was not slow to grasp this. While she liked to think senior conversation might generally be fit for junior ears, nevertheless in principle she believed juniors were better off with their own age group.

'There will be a second apprentice assistant from tomorrow,' she informed them, 'so Miss Heggy will have a companion, and one, this time, who comes from an excellent family.' Dismissing Eliza to the bedroom, she told Kitty and Tish to go quietly, if they knew how, to the kitchen.

They went very quietly.

'Which one is it? I didn't take much notice of them.'

'I didn't. They seemed a scraggy bunch, poor things. You must be feeling scraggy, with no dinner inside you.'

'Don't remind me,' returned Kitty. 'I was a fool to waste bread on mice; I could have saved it in my boot-box for emergencies.' She took a peep at the break-fast bread in the cupboard. 'Mrs Jacks has put Mary's bread out still. That's nice of her; or forgetful.'

'What will you tell your mam, Kitty? No, I'll just have that edge. You eat it.'

Kitty broke off the bread and handed it to Tish. 'What about?' she asked, deliberately obtuse.

'Your brooch.'

'I'll tell her the pin must have snapped when I was wearing it.'

'But that's a lie,' Tish said gratuitously.

'It's a lie,' Kitty allowed. 'I spend my days telling them; some are better than others.'

'You don't tell as many as me, come to that; but it's not so bad for me because I can go to confession.'

'I thought you didn't go any more?'

Tish looked away. 'I don't, but I could, if things really got me down.'

Kitty shrugged in despair. 'Don't start on that tack, or we'll get nowhere. A lie's a lie, whoever tells it, whoever confesses it. Unless you take it back, it's still there.'

On the Tuesday morning, the new assistant called at the Bazaar to be introduced to her colleagues. Contrary to the Skinners' expectations, she was not to begin work there until Wednesday; her mother needed at least one day to gather Cecilia's belongings together.

'Where does she think it's all going?' Kitty remarked. 'Has no one shown her the bedroom yet?'

Tish and Kitty tried to concentrate on the new-comer's fine eyes, when they spoke to her; they were more embarrassed by the pock-marked complexion than they cared to admit. With regard to dress, Cecilia more than passed muster, quite putting the other members of staff in the shade; even Eliza Heggy looked dowdy in comparison. Only Mrs Skinner could be said to rival Miss Bingle in elegance of costume.

The girl stayed only a short time before leaving with her mother, who had come to take her home, and was the recipient of an amount of kowtowing rarely accorded by the Skinners to an assistant's parent.

'They should have tied gloves on her hands, like my cousin Ernie had. She's been left to scratch her face to pieces,' Eliza declared. 'I don't fancy walking out with a girl who looks like that.'

'She can't help it,' Tish remonstrated. 'She's well turned out; you could go out with worse.'

'With Mary Gibbs, for one.' Eliza let out a scream as Tish boxed her ear. 'You keep your big hands to yourself, Tish Kelly. I'll tell Mrs Skinner on you.' And she fled to knock on the sitting-room door.

As Hezekiah emerged bleary-eyed from his after-dinner nap, his cold pipe in one hand and a box of Bryant and Mays in the other, Tish leaned over the bannister to check on Eliza's wailing report. Kitty came beside her for moral support.

Eliza need not have bothered; she found herself, as Kitty said later, up a gum tree, for it was as much as Mr Skinner could do to refrain from boxing the other ear.

'Miss Bingle is in every way suitable for you to walk out with,' he told her angrily. 'I would remind you, Miss Heggy, that Councillor Austin Bingle and his lady wife are important members of Bridgemouth society. It's a privilege for you to have their daughter as a companion.' With his waistcoat buttons strained to bursting point, he added, 'And she chose to come to the Bazaar, rather than go to Masons', I might tell you.'

As Eliza flounced up the stairs, past her satisfied seniors, and into the attic once more, she muttered, 'With a skin like that, it would take more than Councillor Bingle to get her into Masons'.'

'Someone should have put her wise to that Eliza,' Kitty remarked. 'She'd have done better at the Emporium.'

'So would we,' said Tish.

Dear mum and Dad,
    I am sick and tied of this Bazaar, Now we have got a new junior assistant Cecelia Bingle Cissy for short, That makes too juniors me and one more and no proper pay for me as how I am the senor junior asistant, Now I have to walk out with a girl that had small pox and no gloves to keep her nails of it like Ernie Heggy You never saw a face like it all holes like she been picked over with a skewar, I am ashamd to be seen out with such She starts work tomorow Wenesday one thing Mr Skinner brags her father is Counseller Bingle a pity he did not buy her a pair of cotton gloves at the right time I say, She his only at our place becose Masons turnd her down I am sure they would not turn me down with my complection,
                    your Loving Daughter
                    ElizaXXXXXXXXXX

The above effort brought a reply by return from Eliza's mother, congratulating her on her good fortune in working with the Bingles' only child,

a girl going to be worth a mint, when anything happens, Councillor Bingle you must mind your spelling Eliza is a big man in Waterhead and Smith Meat Purveyers and well known as such to everybody in the lairage your father included, Count your blessings
                    your loving mother
                    Adeline Heggy XX

*

Hezekiah admitted for once, if only to himself, that his wife had made a sound choice. From a handful of applicants, none of whom would have stood an earthly chance in days gone by, she had picked a winner. Of course, he had not been fooled by Mrs Bingle's big talk about Masons'; that establishment was under no obligation to Mrs Councillor Bingle, or any other Bingle. If her daughter had been offered a job there, it must have been behind the scenes in their Repairs and Renovations, 24-hour Service.

All the same, despite her unattractive face, this junior assistant was pulling in the customers. It was not that Cissy Bingle had flair; at the moment, she showed little: the quiet Mary Gibbs could have made rings round her. *Quiet*? But who would have guessed? He had missed something there. No, it was not a question of Miss Bingle's sales ability, but of the circle she had moved in – would still move in. She brought with her a sizeable group of friendly customers; Jinny had been sharp to take credit for this and to rub it in at every turn; he had to give her her due, but he must remind her soon that she had foreseen none of it.

In a town as small as Bridgemouth, the religious affiliations of its dignitaries will be common knowledge to the townsfolk. In the case of the Bingles, Hezekiah and Jinny had assigned both the Councillor and Mrs Bingle to the Church of England, and they had not anticipated a volume of new trade from that loose-knit section of the faithful. They deduced, therefore, that the extra clients attracted by Cissy Bingle's appointment must be coming from the family's business and social contacts. In this they were largely mistaken; they had not counted on the long-standing divergence in the Bingles' habits of worship: Councillor Austin Bingle might be a bastion of the C. of E., but his wife, née

Gwyneth Wynn-Williams, had never faltered in her loyalty to the Bethesda of her childhood. Nowadays, she was a substantial member of its Bridgemouth equivalent – of that rosy Welsh chapel tucked away behind the park, where every Sabbath the expatriate Welsh found uplift in the *hwyl*, and solace in their native language. It was this close band of worshippers, formerly part of the dribs-and-drabs custom at Skinners' Place, who were now lending their support to the young Cissy Bingle. These were the animated talkers, who were ousting the hat-elastic harpies; these were the shrewd examiners of dress material between finger and thumb, the quibblers over weaving flaws, the quoters, wherever possible, of Masons' cheaper prices. They kept Hezekiah on his toes, but he was in no doubt about the quick returns.

'Not doing so badly, Jinny, are we?' he chuckled, rubbing his hands at the end of Cissy's half-week. 'What with the Scotch and the Welsh, things are coming on. I told you that young lady would be a draw.'

There was no hand-rubbing session for Kitty and Tish; neither felt the week had brought more than routine work of an exhausting kind. Tish was happy to be back in Haberdashery; on the other hand, Jinny Skinner had decided to upgrade Handbags to a more inclusive Leathergoods Department, comprising three tables. These carried a display of trunks, suitcases, gladstone and other bags, silver-bottled vanity cases and steel-rodded portfolios; it gave rise to more congestion, particularly where goods spread over the floor. It also provided more harassment for Miss Kelly, who was delegated to run it, when not supplying tape measures at half the price of Masons' to a new customer. After two days with this new department, Tish was not looking forward to the holiday season.

With this increase in custom, and in the price decisions he constantly had to make, Hezekiah had reverted to his role of boss-shopwalker, with the result that Kitty's scissors were as often as not ploughing through men's suiting, when they were not gliding through white dimity.

Nor had there been sweets to eat in the evenings; the two older girls were still opting out of the communal scheme, and neither would accept offerings from Cissy Bingle, who had arrived on the job with half a pound of Buttered Brazil Nuts and a quarter of white marshmallows. She and Eliza had made short work of these by Saturday night.

Mary had sent a postcard to say she would wait in for Tish this Sunday afternoon. Mrs Skinner had been torn between an urge to forbid Tish to go, and a hesitation to reveal that she read other people's correspondence.

'I shan't go again,' Tish said to Kitty, 'if she has settled happily with Biddy.'

'Or vice versa.'

'What?'

'Biddy might not be settling with Mary.' Kitty frowned. She was unsure of 'vice versa'.

'Biddy will make do as long as she has to. It's Mary I'm not easy about; she was always one to keep to herself. I'm worried to death about Mary.'

Kitty was, too. 'You go and see,' she said.

They were standing once more at the ferry. Impulsively, the girls kissed each other, to the diversion of a group of shipyard lads. Accompanied by their catcalls,

Tish made for the turnstile, but not before she had exclaimed hotly, 'I hate men!'

'She hates men!' crowed the lads in chorus. 'Oh, Mabel! I'm a rosebud!'

Kitty strode off with a back like a ramrod. If Henry had to wait for her return, it was no fault of hers; she was not going to be the butt of those fellows until he showed up.

'What kept you?' he asked.

Kitty bridled. 'You were nowhere in sight when I got here.'

'So?'

'You're never here, are you? This is the first time I haven't been cooling my heels waiting for you.'

'My dear Kitty, you know the boat I always take.'

'And you know the sort of fellows who hang about the ferry, making my life a misery!'

The fellows had moved away and were nowhere to be seen.

'You can always cross the water, if you like.' Henry's eyes were as unfeeling as slate. 'We can meet on the other side.'

This took the wind out of Kitty's sails. Henry had made the remark unguardedly, and with no true conception of the state of her purse.

As she turned from him, the colour mounting in her cheeks, he saw his mistake, and was filled with compunction. He changed the subject: 'Did I see your friend Tish, waiting to sail off again?'

'At the Ferry Head? You know you did.'

'So I do,' he returned equably. 'Has she gone to visit your friend, Mary Gibson?'

'Gibbs.'

'Mary Gibbs. I beg her pardon.'

'Yes, Tish has gone to her sister's place. It's some-where to go. She's rather lonely now that I meet you.'

'She must be.'

'You don't know anybody she could be introduced to?' There! She had said it.

This had no interest for Henry; he had not come to Bridgemouth to discuss Tish Kelly's problems. 'I don't. I can think of nobody.' With less indifference, he continued, 'You remember I told you I was thinking of buying a house? I have found one.'

'That's quick.'

He had been put on to it by his landlady, a friend of the late owner. The executors were selling it lock, stock and barrel, but for a few bits and pieces of sentimental value, to be dispersed among relatives.

'But there could be some things there of genuine value,' Kitty suggested.

'The same relatives will have called round with a cab for those.'

Henry thought she might like to see the property. Kitty had nothing against this; presuming he had the key, she repeated that it would be somewhere to go.

'You don't sound very enthusiastic! I hoped you would be pleased.'

'About the house? I am pleased for you, Henry. I hope you get it.'

'No question about that. They have my deposit.'

No. 28 Hampden Square was a house to dream about on bleak nights at Skinners' Place. Kitty's depression lifted several degrees.

'Not big, is it?' Henry smiled ruefully.

'It's a dream,' she replied softly. 'How much bigger do you want it?'

'I suppose it will be that much easier to clean.' He supposed equally vaguely that there would be a cleaning woman available; the neighbours would be sure to know of one.

Kitty ran her finger along the mahogany sideboard; it came off comparatively dust-free. 'It has been done through quite recently,' she observed. 'Somebody must have loved it.'

'Perhaps somebody will love it again, therefore it doesn't have to feel unhappy.'

'Will you love it enough?' she demanded.

He laughed. 'That is most unlikely. I don't fall passionately in love with – ' he paused ' – things like this.'

'Inanimate objects,' she supplied, to his discomfiture. 'Well, I do. I think they can have a life of their own if you love them enough.'

He shook his head in wonder. 'You odd girl! Go ahead, get yourself acquainted! Allow me to introduce one upright Monington and Weston, in figured walnut, with green silk panel and twin brass candlesticks.' He swung one candlestick to and fro on its bracket. 'Do you play, by the way?'

Kitty did not play the piano, or any other instrument; at her request, Henry sat down at the keyboard and coaxed a cascade of notes from the yellowing ivories. Kitty had never heard the music before; it fascinated her.

'Don't stop,' she said, when he gave up.

Shutting the lid decisively, he declared, 'It needs tuning. I must find a man.'

In turn they tried out the plush-covered armchairs in the sitting room.

'You haven't found one that is *just right*?'

'You haven't made me any porridge, either,' she remarked.

'It's the wrong house for porridge.'

'It can't be, Henry. I thought you came from Scotland?'

He waved a weak hand from the depths of the biggest chair. 'If you love me, Miss Catchpole, never, but *never*, give me porridge, haggis, Arbroath smokies, oatcake or black bun!'

'They all sound delicious to me. What makes you think I love you, Mr Bonham?'

'Because I ask you so nicely.'

'I thought these things were always mutual? Is that the right word, *mutual*?'

'Perfectly correct. One can use it in phrases like, "a mutual love of inanimate objects".'

She laughed at that.

They sat at the circular mahogany table and pulled out the shallow drawers; inside one, Henry found an old Bible. 'That goes out,' he decided, consigning it to the grate. 'I have at least five.'

'But it's gold-edged, and you can bend this leather; it's too good to throw out,' Kitty said, as she retrieved it. 'And look, it has family names and birthdays in the front, like ours at home.'

Henry glanced over the list. 'Family deaths, too,' he commented, 'Keep it, by all means, if you want to.'

'I'll give it to Tish. She doesn't seem to have one.'

'I thought she was a practising Catholic?'

'She's a bit out of practice. She still hankers after her Father MacSomething. There's no Bible in her drawer, anyway, so she can have this one, if you are really throwing it away.'

'Of course, of course. But it's not the Douai, you know.' He had opened the glazed alcove cupboard, and was inspecting the half shelf of books it contained. '*Can You Forgive Her?* in two volumes,' he read out.

Kitty was thinking how worn the 'Persian' carpet was, especially near the fireplace, where the hearthrug had been too small, to judge from the protected area now revealed. What had been the value of the hearthrug? 'Can you forgive her in two volumes?' she echoed. 'What's that?'

'*Can You Forgive Her?* Volumes One and Two, my precious idiot! Chapman and Hall,' he added, musing. '1865.'

'Chapman and Hall? Did they write a volume each?'

'You know damn well they didn't.'

'What else did they write? I've never heard of them, honest, I haven't.'

'They published the book. Trollope wrote it. Not that I've ever read it.' he allowed.

'That will be something you can do, to improve your education. I do like these marbled covers and the leather corners.'

'Yes, they are good; and the spine, too; it's a handsome edition. I'm surprised these have been left behind. The rest seem run-of-the-mill rubbish: *The Encyclopaedia of Household Management*, Mrs Theodora Stock . . . Here, take that home for yourself and study it.'

'Why should I want to study it?'

'To improve *your* education. After all, it's only one volume. I have to read two.'

'Mine is twice as thick as your two!' she argued.

'Nonsense.' Henry measured the books, side by side, on the table. 'Nothing in it. Besides, yours is a mass of illustrations.'

'You've got pictures in yours!'

'Not a *mass*, my dear – just a sprinkle, to spur me on.'

The dining room was plainly furnished in oak, with a gateleg table and three leather-seated dining chairs.

'One missing,' Henry remarked.

They were to discover the missing chair later in the guest bedroom.

And so the exploration continued, through kitchen, scullery, outhouse and back garden, then upstairs, through six bedrooms on two floors, ending with an inspection of the bathroom and lavatory.

'Blue paeonies!' breathed Kitty.

Henry was overcome with mirth. He ran downstairs to the yard, to turn on the water. He was lying on the large bed in the master bedroom when she joined him.

She was rather troubled. 'Should we be turning on the water and using someone else's house?' she asked.

'It is my house. It's our house, if you will. I left enough money with that agent to let us take a bath in it, if need be. This bed is not too good. I fear it has a nasty sag in the middle.'

If Henry's technique in house purchase had prevailed with the estate agent, he now proved equally businesslike, once he was sure that Kitty was available to him. To reach that degree of confidence, since he had not forgotten her reluctance in the Pier Hotel, he put out an inviting hand for her to sit on the bed. She responded to this, knowing exactly what he had in mind. For a short space, and almost in the approved manner, they looked into each other's eyes; his were a little calculating, a little mocking – gauging his chances; hers reflected fear, love and an engaging hint of capitulation.

For Kitty, the assumption that he was a gentleman had touched off a stage-mist to envelop both of them; she began to feel irrationally safe inside it.

Once she had indicated her willingness, Henry

wasted no time. She had reckoned on more magic, on something more in keeping with those paper serials strung up by Mrs Skinner in the back closet; but there were to be no breathtaking preliminaries in this bedroom, no impassioned running of privileged fingers through her luxuriant tresses, no tender sighs or avowals of undying love. True, she was soon to find her breath taken away — first, by his tremendous weight, and second, by the penetration. A few hairpins gave trouble, too, as they dug relentlessly into her head and neck. She was startled by his greed; for he was greedy, plain greedy.

And yet she was not Henry's first virgin. He had not forgotten the cries which had wrecked that earlier occasion for both participants; it was an experience he wished never to repeat. Today, in spite of what Kitty might be thinking and feeling, his approach had improved. He had no comprehension of the amount of pain which he still inflicted, nor would he have credited the complete dearth of ecstasy, that lay behind Kitty's gasping.

'It won't hurt when you get used to it,' he promised her, with an unconcerned kiss, before he rolled back on the bed.

'I hope not,' she answered huskily. Starting to shiver because the room was so chilly, she pulled part of the eiderdown over her breasts and stomach; it slipped away from her thighs, leaving legs and feet exposed. Henry's eyes were shut; he lay spreadeagled across most of the bed. It might sound mean to ask him to move over; she began to feel very mean. 'Henry!' she said tentatively.

He turned towards her with the lightest of grunts, and the full impact of his left arm flung over her chest. Her one scrap of eiderdown had disappeared. This time there could be no retrieval; it was pinned lower down, under the bend of his elbow.

So they lay together, Henry in his sleep of satisfaction, and Kitty very much awake, a prey to her reflections and the temperature. The former began to warm up, as she moved her head to look at his, which rested half on her pillow. With her free hand, she stroked the dark brush of hair that showed its customary unruliness, in spite of a recent regulation cut. She ran a finger along the imprisoning arm, ruffling the black, silkier hairs, and watching them arch slowly back. She was lying here with this man, because he had left the choice to her. But he had left the choice to her before. She began again. She was lying here with Henry Bonham because she had decided to trust him, because he was already making provision to house the two of them. Surely he must be serious? She knew her mother had married Dan Catchpole as soon as a tied cottage had shown up. In the Catchpole's limited circle, a man who provided a roof had nailed his colours to the chimney. Kitty wondered what her mother's first night had been like. She returned abruptly to her own situation. She had wanted so much to please Henry, to make this Henry–Kitty affair stronger – too strong to be broken. She was out to catch him? Well, yes, she was. She had no wish to trap him, but she would like to catch him. She would like him to remain caught; and if this first gift had to be part of the contract, then she had given it freely.

The bed did sag; he was right. They would have to buy a new mesh. It was really very exciting to be on any bed with a man like Henry. She was just a bit dashed that he could be sleeping so soundly.

Meanwhile, his arm was growing heavier by the minute, and her shallow breathing had become intolerable. With difficulty, she took several deep breaths, and felt an immediate need for more. She rubbed one numb foot on one frozen shin.

'Henry!' she said with decision, pushing his arm away.

Only when she had cleaned up with ice-cold water, and had dressed, did a worse cold clutch her. Maybe she was a fool, and no better than young Mary – she, who prided herself on having common sense. Henry's assurance that she would have no baby . . . Bunny Harris must have told that tale. 'It's our house, if you will.' That was not the same as, 'It's our marriage, if you will.' Outside the bedroom, the possibility of failure seemed all too substantial. She went to the kitchen and sat in the rocking-chair. She stood up, undid the taped back cushion and put it on the seat; with that addition, sitting was still acutely uncomfortable; she wondered how long that raw burn would last.

Kitty was touching her blouse at the throat, where the brooch used to be, when Henry came bounding downstairs, as fully clothed as herself. He was astounded to find her in the kitchen.

'I like the kitchen,' she said defensively.

'You'll have me die of frostbite. Let's go out for tea, shall we?'

She pinned on her hat, catching the scalp with one of those lethal weapons when his hands came round from behind to undo her coat. She pulled away to refasten the buttons.

'If you will permit me,' he said, with a little bow, and fastened the coat for her.

They left the house, looking like any other young couple, who had just been inspecting a desirable property.

*

'How could I tell him about my brooch?'

'I think you should have,' Tish said. 'What's a friend for, if you can't tell him things?'

'I can, but not about brooches in pawn.'

'Something his family wouldn't stoop to, I suppose.'

'Look, there's no call to bring his family into it.'

'Is that so? Well, if you do get round to telling him, don't forget to say it was on account of me.'

'I'll not be saying that, either,' said Kitty, less crossly. 'How did you find Mary?'

Tish shook her head. 'You could have knocked me down with a feather. I still can't get over it.'

'Is she happy?'

'I wouldn't think so. She's gone different, all of a sudden, and it's not fair to say it's our Biddy's fault, though I know she's behind it. She's got to be behind it, or Mary will go to the wall, that's what.'

'God!' Kitty shuddered. 'It's awful, at sixteen.'

Tish went on steadily. 'Mary's fighting the only way she can, and somehow it's making her go hard. Biddy's never gone hard; all these years, and she's still a proper pushover.'

'Perhaps Mary put it on because you were there. I think I might turn hard, faced with that.'

'I don't see you going cool and unfriendly,' said Tish.

'No, I don't, and that's a fact.'

'Mary's not unfriendly. She'd made her mind up she wasn't going to cry. Is she well, d'you think?'

'She says the sickness isn't so bad; she doesn't work mornings, anyway. You couldn't tell, like; looking at her, I mean. You can't see her face for war-paint; much thicker than our Biddy's, and that's saying something.'

Kitty gave a quick sigh. 'She won't be able to work many months, don't forget. She's got to get the money while she can.'

'Holy saints, what can I be thinking of?' Tish went quickly to their wardrobe and came back to Kitty with a half-crown in her hand. 'It's for you. She said she was sorry she'd taken such an age, but you'd understand.' There was an undisguised question in Tish's voice.

'She should have kept it.' Kitty's eyes had filled with tears. 'She had to find that new underskirt from somewhere.' She paused for control. 'I'll send this home to mum,' she continued, more evenly. 'Did you see Biddy, then?'

'No, she was out.'

Neither girl could think of anything more to say, either on Mary, or on half-crowns. Tish roused herself to ask if Kitty had had a good time at the house; she wished regretfully that she could have been there.

'I wish you had been,' said Kitty.

Both girls were fast asleep when the two younger assistants came to bed.

Although Mrs Jacks had kept herself to herself, Kitty's recent efforts to get to the pawnbroker's had not escaped her notice. She did not have to be told where Miss C. had been that dinner hour, and why she had looked like a corpse when she got back. Day in, day out, Minnie had kept an eye open for the reappearance of the silver brooch on the senior assistant's blouse; when this failed to materialize, she knew for sure that the pledge had been forfeited, and in spite of maintaining the dour exterior, she felt sorry for the girl. She ought to have warned her that Tapp was likely to foreclose if he could get away with it. 'Foreclose' was one of the few semi-legal terms known to the Minnie Jacks of this locality, and it was used with dread. If that Jinny Skinner hadn't turned shirty, of course, Minnie would have volunteered to take the interest along. The more she dwelt on the subject, the more decided she grew. Before she left the Bazaar on Saturday, with the bread-basket on her arm, she marched into the kitchen, where the lady assistants were busy with their string.

'You've lost your brooch, then, have you?' she threw at Kitty.

Startled by this change in the Jacks' policy, and aware of the juniors' inquisitive eyes, Kitty gave a shaky reply: 'Seems I have, yes.'

'I thought as much,' said Minnie ominously, and she made off.

'You get out of my shop!' shouted Mr Tapp, at bay against his pledge shelves. 'Go on, clear off!'

Mrs Jacks ignored the interruption; if anything, her broad superstructure leaned further across the counter, on which she continued her menacing beats with one of Abe Jenkin's rock-hard oven-bottoms. 'Everyone standing here knows what you are, Maurice Tapp. You're nothing more'an a bloody louse, living off the backs of the poor, and squaring it up with God on Sundays.'

She turned to address the bundle holders, who crowded the office to capacity. 'And if you had a ha'porth of sense, you'd be off to Harry Chadwick's, the lot of yous,' she informed them. 'You don't want telling what this one is. If I wasn't a lady, I'd blind him. He'd sell his own father for a threepenny joey.'

The customers, one tiny lad and three women, shifted uncertainly. They considered their bundles, the floor, the shelves – or Mr Tapp, who was quickly regaining his nerve, as Minnie Jacks headed for the door.

'We'll thank you not to show your face here again,' he blustered. 'You can take your tin brooches somewhere else, you and your friends. We don't need your kind in a shop of class.'

Mrs Jacks pushed her way past the ignominious customers. 'No spunk, some people,' she said, giving each an unceremonious prod with her basket – 'no sodding spunk.'

'What's to do?' asked a fourth woman, newly arrived on the doorstep.

'It's to do with a silver brooch, that's what! And this bugger's gone and got rid of it, when she come a couple of weeks late.'

'When who come?' The woman went into the street with Minnie.

'Now, son, what do you want for nothing?' demanded the pawnbroker, resuming business. 'And let's hope you're over twelve.'

'I wouldn't trust Tapp as far as I could chuck him,' said the last woman. 'Too much damn psalm-singing, there.' She lowered her voice. 'And that's not all, from the tales going round. Bible in one hand, and you-know-what in the other, so I've heard. I only live at the back, or you wouldn't catch me using him.'

'Ay, well,' Minnie replied shortly, 'I'll be dragging myself to Chadwick's after this. I wouldn't give Tapp another brass farthing, not if his head hung with diamonds.'

'What more is there to say, Tish? A house is a house.' Kitty's tone was resigned.

Having been deprived of information, Tish had worked up an immoderate curiosity. Something had happened in connection with that house, otherwise why should Kitty be so unwilling to talk? 'Will it lie empty when he goes away?' she tried.

'I imagine so. I didn't ask.'

'You didn't care for it, did you?'

'What makes you think that? It's a nice house. I said so. It's very nice.'

'Anything wrong with the furniture, then?'

Kitty spoke with exasperation. 'There's nothing wrong with the furniture, Tish.'

'Well, there's *something* wrong with the place,' Tish said obstinately.

'Why don't you ask him to take you round it, if you're that keen?'

'I'd be more interested in it than you are, for a start. I wouldn't be going round with my face like a fiddle.'

'I don't find much to laugh about these days.'

They fell into another of those difficult silences, which for the last few days had punctuated most of their conversation. They were on window duty, and the work, like the verbal exchange, was dragging badly.

Tish tried again. 'I expect the house is for you to live in. Didn't he say?'

Kitty pulled the well-draped length of slub cotton off her dummy, and began to re-drape, with elaborate attention to each fold and pin.

'Didn't he, then?'

'Didn't he what?' asked Kitty, frowning over a waist pleat.

'Didn't he say nothing about you living in it?'

'*Anything*. Not exactly. He was rambling on a bit. I didn't take it very seriously.'

Tish sat back on her heels. 'I don't understand you, Kitty Catchpole. It's the most serious thing in the world if a man asks you to marry him.'

'I'm sure it would be.' Kitty stuck several pins at

random into the dummy's receptive backside. 'Need we say any more?'

Tish rubbed her nose on the back of her hand. 'No,' she said. She sat up, and renewed her sorting out of price tickets. But she was unable to let the matter drop for long: 'He will ask you one day. It could be he's frightened you'd refuse.'

Kitty smiled sceptically. 'Lead me to the man who's frightened of being refused. You've been reading too many pages in the lav.'

'I'd be scared you'd refuse, if I was a man,' Tish volunteered under her breath.

'He'll be soon on the high seas, or the low seas, or some other seas, him and his passenger – Eric. If he wants to pluck up courage, he'll have to put a move on. I shan't be doing a grass-widow act for him.'

'You will, Kitty.'

'Will you give it a rest, Tish Kelly!' Kitty scrambled out of the window, and stood for a while gazing at Baby Linen.

If Henry Bonham dared to hurt Kitty, Tish would hate him to the death. She would hate him with a venom that would send the Father's absolutions up in smoke. She righted the glove stand, which Kitty's exit had sent flying; she replaced the handbag on the dummy's bent arm. 'Henry Bonham!' she burst out, punishing the floor severely with a handbrush. 'Bad cess to him!' She remained kneeling with her back to the window. She stroked the back of the brush, neither thinking nor seeing; she felt drained.

A smart rap on the window made her jump to her feet and turn round. 'Mary, Mother of God!' she exclaimed involuntarily, for there on the pavement outside, rather as if she were a latter-day Aladdin, stood Mr Bonham himself.

Tish raised her arms ineffectually, indicative of the helplessness she felt. How much had he watched or heard? Had she known it, Henry had approached the shop at his usual brisk pace; he had been mystified to some extent by the demonstration with the handbrush, but had concluded that Tish might be slaughtering a murmuration of moths. He had heard no remark and had actually let her kneel motionless for a while before knocking on the pane.

He had not realized how ridiculous it could be to talk through a thick plate-glass window. He and Tish made enough hand-signals to greet a flotilla, when in fact each could hear what the other was saying quite adequately. Under her instructions, he went round to the back gate, where she let him into the yard.

'You'll have to wait here,' she told him. 'The Skinners are in their rooms, and Mrs Jacks is doing the first-floor windows. I'll fetch Kitty.'

'Where is she?'

'She had to go upstairs for a minute,' said Tish primly. Kitty had overheard Tish's conversation, had ascertained through the window-door that Henry was outside, and had fled, incomprehensibly, to the attic.

'I see.'

When Kitty appeared, her manner led him to believe that she and Tish had been having a row. That had been no slaughter of moths; it had been an exhibition of sheer bad temper.

'I can't talk to you here,' she said, almost distractedly. 'I'm supposed to be dressing the window.'

'I shan't keep you more than a minute,' he said firmly.

'I can't. You'll have to go!'

'Miss Catchpole!' The raucous yell came from the Skinners' bedroom window.

'I told you!' Kitty whispered furiously.

'Miss Catchpole!' Jinny raised her sash window higher, and leaned out further.

'Yes, ma'am?'

'We do not keep visitors standing in the back yard. Show the gentleman into the dining room!'

'Yes, ma'am.'

The gentleman lifted his cap a fraction, and acknowledged Mrs Skinner with one of his slight bows, before he went indoors with Kitty.

'Why have you come?' she asked him, once they were in the kitchen. 'Why did you change your free day?'

'What has been aggravating you?'

'Nothing. Why have you come?'

'I came to tell you I'll be spending a few days with Eric at his parents' place; they live in the Cotswolds,' Henry said.

Kitty looked at him without a word.

'Eric will be staying on, but I shall travel back on Sunday. I shall do what I can to get home early, but Sunday trains are not good, as you know. How mournful you look! May I kiss you in the dining room?'

'No.'

'Surely we don't keep visitors sitting without a kiss?'

'We do in this dining room.'

'I must consult Mrs Skinner. I suspect you are straightening the rules, Miss Catchpole.'

'You were saying Sunday trains were not good.'

'That's right.' He handed her a black key, with label attached. 'I ought to take the label off; perhaps you will do that, in case the key gets lost.'

'I'm not in the habit of losing keys.'

Henry rose to take the key from her; he tore the label off. 'And I'm not fond of risks. Here it is, and get yourself to the house on Sunday. You do remember where it is?'

She nodded, still not knowing what to say.

'I thought you would like to have your friend Tish with you for company, in case I'm late.'

She nodded again.

Henry took out his wallet. 'I can't expect you to pay for my entertainment of Miss Kelly. Could you see that she has tea, if I'm delayed?' He was holding out two pound notes.

'I can't take that. It's too much. We don't need tea. In fact, we mightn't get there.'

'I wish you to have it, Kitty, please, just in case you do get there. Or don't you want Tish to see the house?'

'I would like to take her, but that's too much money; you know it is. One pound would leave us with change.'

'Keep it; you never know when a few shillings could be useful.'

'*I* never know? God!' she said bitterly, crushing the notes in her hand. 'Two pounds in my hand, just like that! Oh, but you wouldn't understand . . .'

'I do feel somewhat in the dark,' he said dryly. 'You are not going to weep, I hope?'

'I can't help it.'

Henry groaned. 'Have my shoulder, then, if you must, and get it over.'

'I don't want your shoulder.'

'Yes, you do. Everyone tells me it's a wonderful help.'

He ruffled her hair, while she came out with the story of her lost brooch. Distraught though she was, she did not disclose the true reason behind the money-raising.

The recital left him alarmed. 'But why didn't you ask *me*? Really, Kitty, this is ludicrous. Why do you have to pawn anything for a paltry half-crown?'

She informed him fiercely that people pawned stuff for much less than that. Now that she had told him about it, she began to recover.

'That may be so, but you don't have to. In any case that man has cheated you. No pledge could possibly be forfeited in such a short time. I shall report him to the police.'

She went to the window and looked at the back gate. Henry would be walking through that, free as a bird. 'I like to do things my own way,' she said.

'And a mad way that turns out to be. We shall have to find another brooch like it, that's all.'

'It's too old. I'll never find one like it.' She came back to him. 'I think you ought to go now. You won't take this money?'

'No. Be a good girl until Sunday.'

'I shall be good on Sunday as well.'

'I'm afraid you might be.' He kissed her till she panicked and broke away from him.

A slow tread had announced Mrs Jacks' imminent descent from the upper regions. Henry left by the back door, watched by Jinny Skinner, who was seated this time behind her Nottingham lace.

Henry's visit to Chard proved more fleeting than anticipated. Eric was already installed when he got there, but had every intention of leaving the next morning.

'I cannot listen to those two for another day,' he told Henry plaintively, ' – the pater prosing on about Jaffna, and Cynthia still moaning about the stretch marks I gave her. I feel positively in a state of shock, dear boy. I shall borrow the automobile, and we can spend a week, just moving around. It will be Paradise enow, you'll see.'

'It will not, and I shan't,' said Henry grimly. 'You can drive me back to Laverport. I must have been a fool to come, when I have better things to do.'

Eric's eyes were wide with dismay. 'What better things? Henry, you haven't fallen for another of your ghastly females? I can't bear it! It's becoming monotonous.'

'I have fallen for a house, in point of fact, though it's true I have met a young lady, who pleases me, too.'

Eric's pout hardened to a straight line. He would show interest in the house and ignore the existence of the woman.

They set off in the Coventry Humber before the Cannon-Budge parents were astir. Eric's resolution of the night before went by the board within the first hour of the journey home. Henry's prospective house intrigued him, but it posed no threat. The young woman, however, seemed to have an exceptional grip on the man so close to his own heart; she must be dealt with promptly.

'She will be like your other shopgirls,' he said, ' – useful for a while, but impossible in the long run.'

'She is not like my other shopgirls, as you so elegantly put it. Miss Catchpole is a young lady of considerable character.'

'Oh, *character*! I am sure that must be of great advantage in trade. It will not satisfy you for any length of time, nor your family. The Bonhams look for a touch of distinction.'

'She has that, also.'

'My dear, you are lying! Young ladies of distinction do not serve behind counters, and you know it. Sooner or later, you will grow tired of picking up the dropped aitches.'

'Kitty does not happen to drop her aitches,' said Henry.

'You amaze me. In that case, she will make an excellent captain's wife.' And Eric broke into song, with a liberal dash of malice: '*Est-ce dans la Baltique,/ Dans la mer Pacifique,/ Dans l'île de Java?/ Ou bien est-ce Norvège,/ Cueillir la fleur de neige,/ Ou la fleur d'Angsoka?/ Dites, dites, la jeune belle,/ Dites, où voulez-vous aller?*'

Henry gazed out of the side-flap window, privately cursing him, for the way he could pinpoint everything so diabolically. No, Kitty had a lot of leeway to make up, before she could take her place as a skipper's wife. Yet where was she going to find the experience? Perhaps he ought to arrange some, while the ship was in dock? Only the captain, the chief steward and himself were on board, and the Old Man would not jib at the presence of a pretty young thing, for a weekend, or even for a week. A weekend would be enough; it would save disclosing the generous free time Henry now had. But he must fix this quickly.

'She knows her Berlioz, of course?'

Henry looked through the windscreen. 'What?' he asked.

'I said, she knows her Berlioz, I trust.'

'She is fond of music. She has some acquaintance with Schumann.'

Eric was annoyed. This paragon was going to be tougher to dislodge than her predecessors. How had she come across Schumann? He glanced at Henry, but that impassive face was giving nothing away. 'What is there to talk about with a girl of that – from that milieu?' he went on. 'I presume she doesn't ride, and she doesn't read? If you pretend she does either, I shall never believe a word you say again.'

'She must ride. She comes of farming stock. And at

the moment she is keen on Trollope. She would rather have him than Mrs Theodora Stock, I might tell you.'

'Who the devil is Mrs Theodora Spock?'

'Stock. There you are! You fancy yourself as a reader, and you are ignorant of Theodora.'

'I am panting to be enlightened.'

'You will be,' Henry assured him, 'when we arrive at no. 28.'

By the time they had dined well, and locked the Cannon-Budge Humber in its Laverport stable, near Henry's former lodgings, they were too weary to do more than open the door of no. 28, and grope their way to bed. Henry could not lay his hands on any candles; nor could he be bothered with the one oil lamp. He must get to the gas offices in the morning.

'Tomorrow, we have to light a fire, somehow,' he announced, as they lay in the unlit bedroom.

'Oh, God, you have the most frightful ideas! I'd rather freeze to death.'

'Well, at least you must decide on the rooms you want.'

'Simple. Just the best you have. When is that horrid Kitty Polecat coming?'

'If you don't stop being beastly about Kitty, I shall throw you out now, into the street. She comes Sunday afternoon.'

'Sunday. She comes Sunday. Eric and Henry get out.'

'We get out Sunday morning. Sleep on board Sunday night.' Henry was growing as drowsy as Eric.

'Lovely warm ship. Roll on Sunday.' Eric slept the light sleep of a child, punctuated every so often with tremulous breathing.

*

Tish had not enjoyed a day like this since her last Sunday-school treat, when with the connivance of a street pal, she had tagged on to the St Aidan's C. of E. outing.

Her appreciation of Henry's house knew no bounds. She was like a child let loose in a toyshop. Kitty stood by, watching her touch the kitchen walls in a kind of ritual dance, one after the other.

'No bumps or cracks,' she enthused, 'and the tiles are perfect!'

'Not all of them. You'll find some cracks round the back of the oven.'

Tish dismissed such inevitable flaws with contempt. Seating herself at the deal table, with Henry's Saturday newspaper, a rag and what remained in a Brasso tin, she set to work on the scales.

'Don't forget the sitting-room fire irons, while you're in the mood,' Kitty teased, 'and the fender; then there's this steel one.'

'Right you are!' Tish agreed happily. If only life could go on this way, with Kitty and herself in this perfect house! And Mary could come here, if she wanted, with the baby . . . Tish cleaned a 2-ounce weight thoughtfully. Mary might never be the same again. It was certain that Biddy would never come to live here – it was too far from the seafront – but if she just came to tea one day, that would be something. One snag remained; there was no room in Tish's fantasies for Henry Bonham.

Kitty had removed some of the newspaper and was laying a fire in the kitchen grate, with screws of the financial news, which she considered dry enough, some criss-crossed sticks from the oven top, and bright pieces of coal still left in the coal house. The mantelpiece Pilots were so damp, she broke four without achieving a light.

'Try the bars,' Tish advised.

The sixth match responded to the grate-bar with a feeble spurt of flame. Kitty shielded it with her hand, begging it not to die. The financial news looked like burning out before the sticks had caught. Up went the long steel poker against the grate, to support a double page; with a roar, the draught sucked the Lord Mayor's Banquet and the Seamen's Orphanage perilously inwards, towards the flames. The brown scorches spread larger; the smell of hot newsprint became more ominous; the paper's title and date grew blacker and bolder. Neither girl had paid heed to the date.

'Watch it!' Tish shrieked.

Kitty had been ready with the shovel; she smacked the burning pages into the fire and up the chimney. 'We'll soon know if it's swept,' she remarked coolly.

There was no tea in the caddy, and no shop open. Kitty suggested they should bank up their fire with coal dust, and go out for a bite. Tish had no experience of eating or drinking out; she launched another attack with the Brasso rag, and would have gone on to those sitting-room fire irons but for Kitty's restraining hand. 'He won't thank you for it,' Kitty told her. 'In fact, I doubt if he sees things like that.'

'I wasn't doing it for Henry.'

Like most people used to stringent economies, the two young women were most at ease when keeping within them. The Victoria Teashop was a place to relax in, to stir a teacup noisily, to eat with your fingers, without attracting covert glances; it was a place where they gave you heavy change out of a ten-shilling note – where they looked at a pound note as if they had not seen one of those before.

'I'll send mum all the money I kept back, and we'll still have a nest egg, you and me.'

'It's your money, Kitty, not mine.'

'We go on sharing, like we've always done.'

By force of habit, Tish peered at the marooned leaves in her cup. 'Looks like a load of old tea leaves to me,' she said, putting the cup down. 'I can't help thinking how terrible it is, all this money in your purse, instead of when you were desperate.'

'Henry said we must find another brooch, but we never will.'

'So you've told him at last! But not the bit about Fred Robertson?'

'Not that bit. I did tell him the rest – about Tapp, and all that. He was ever so angry; with me.'

'I suppose he would be.' Tish withheld her private opinion, recollecting that Kitty had no use for it. 'Has he got a key?'

'For no. 28? He said you and me were to have tea out, so he must have one.'

On their return, Kitty sat by the fire, with Volume I of *Can You Forgive Her?* on her lap. One or two particulars had puzzled her today. She had the impression that someone had been using the house since her last visit with Henry. He might have been here, before he went away, but was he free to sleep here during the week? That bed was not as she had left it; it had been slept in, and then made up roughly. And there had been an attempt at a fire in this kitchen grate; the grate and its hearth had been clean and unused last Sunday. She decided not to speak of these matters to Tish, who was going through the cutlery drawer, sorting and arranging everything into its own bed of green baize.

The Trollope proved rather more difficult than

Dainty Stories. Kitty understood the words, or most of them; she was not too sure of *insolvent*, and had certainly never heard of a *comitatus* of relatives, but then, who had? However, she made a good shot at the definitions, and was relieved to see that conversation would open up on page eight. She was indignant to find that the book was not sprinkled with illustrations – it was positively plastered with them. She deserted the text for the pictures: they were most attractive. *Dear Greenhow! dear Husband!* read one. *So you've come back, have you? – said the Squire*, ran another. She thought she would try to read both books when Henry had finished with them.

'I wish we didn't have to go back,' Tish sighed. 'I wish we could go to bed here.'

Kitty rose to her feet. 'Let's go. He won't come now.'

They had been counting the hours by the local church clock, for the hall timepiece had stopped. As they shut the front door behind them, they heard the three-quarters' chime.

'A quarter to eight,' Kitty observed. 'Nobody could have waited longer for him. He's missed every train in the book.'

'What book?'

'Bradshaw's.'

'You talk in riddles, half your time,' Tish said crossly. 'What a lovely, lovely day, though,' she added, more happily. 'Pity you threw so much money about.'

'How long is it since Eliza Heggy was in bed before us?' Tish pondered aloud, scratching at the top sheet with her toenails.

'You'll put a hole in that sheet before long. I don't know. She certainly stays out with Cissy-girl till the last minute.'

'What it is to be young! I'd like to know where they get to, all the same. D'you think they sneak off to Eliza's place for parkin?'

'I can't see young Cissy Bingle doing that, somehow.' Kitty closed her eyes.

Both girls were dozing when the two juniors burst in. Eliza Heggy turned the fish-tail full on, to Kitty's annoyance. 'Turn that down, will you?' she commanded.

Cissy lowered the flame at once. There followed a deal of unaccustomed banter between the younger assistants, who were seemingly on the best of terms; at last, Eliza had a compatible workmate, pock-marked or not.

'Where you been, you two?' queried Tish, muzzily.

'Church,' Eliza informed her, with an air of Christian triumph.

'*Church?*' Tish was fully awake. 'Till this hour?'

'Not quite all the time,' said Eliza, with a grin in Cissy's direction. 'We went to the Bethesda Band of Youth afterwards.'

'To the what?' It was Kitty's turn to sound incredulous.

Cissy spoke up. 'I always go on to Band of Youth after chapel on Sundays.'

'You mean Band of Hope?' Kitty suggested.

'No, Band of Youth. We have a bit of fun, and a cup of soup for a penny. You can have a bun for a halfpenny, if you're hungry.'

'Crikey!' said Tish. 'That sounds interesting.'

'You'd be welcome to come, any time.'

'That's very kind of you, Cissy. We'll bear that in mind, won't we, Tish?'

'Too dear for us,' Tish decided.

'You're too old, anyhow,' said Eliza bluntly.

Cissy hastened to correct her. 'They're not, Eliza. Some of those boys are a lot older than us.'

'Don't worry, Eliza; we shan't come poaching,' Kitty assured her. 'Put the light out, one of you; it shows up the ceiling.'

'We're not undressed yet. Take no notice of her, Cissy!' Eliza was peeling off her clothes at a tremendous rate, all the time talking her head off; and there was Cissy Bingle, bouncing on Mary's bed and laughing fit to kill. You would have said they'd downed more than a penny cup of soup, to hear the carry-on. Like Tish, Kitty wondered at the ways of the young.

Cissy, at last, turned out the light. 'Listen,' she exclaimed, as she climbed into bed, 'who's that?'

A chorus of men's voices had risen in the street outside.

'Drunks,' Eliza pronounced, with a splutter.

'That's not drunks,' Tish said. 'Leastways, not drunk drunks. That's the Park Cricket Club on its way home. You've heard them many a time.'

'I never have. I've never heard sober drunks in my life.'

'Well, you're hearing them now, Eliza, if you'll keep quiet,' said Kitty.

'If we'll all keep quiet,' Tish put in.

The four lady assistants listened in their darkened room to singing that was more than usually fine from an untrained choir. Tish was right; this was the cricket club; these men sang, in season or out, game or no game, any night of the week. As a first-rate excuse to escape from the wife and family, the Park Club would have been hard to beat. Tonight, as the Bridgemouth moon obliged fitfully in a clouded sky, the lead tenor sailed into his discreetly backed solo: *Shine, bright moon,/ While I dance with Dinah dear./ Shine, bright moon,/ Whisper while there's no one near./ Someone calls,/ Hark, it is the overseer!/ Steal away, and say/ Goodnight . . . goodnight . . . goodnight.*

The music, like the lyric, was unremarkable, but it came so true on the night air, it could not have affected our listeners more. The distancing of the singers, as they made down the street, added a poignancy to those three 'goodnights'. Spontaneously, though not loud enough to be heard by the departing men, the girls lent their voices to the end of the song; lying in their comfortless beds, they were moved by a nostalgia they did not fully understand.

A familiar bawl cut short the reveries. 'Who is that, singing upstairs?'

Nobody spoke up.

'If I hear any more of it, I'll be up there to see who's responsible! Put that light out, and get to sleep.'

'It's out,' Kitty shouted back.

'Then you keep it out!' thundered Hezekiah, as he marched back to his sitting room. The very idea – Bazaar assistants joining song with that beer-swilling crew from the Park! All the same if he and Jinnie had been in bed, trying to catch their sleep!

The four waited warily. Their silence was broken by a convulsive snort of merriment from Eliza, followed by another from Cissy.

'Sh!' Tish warned.

A quavering, 'Goodnight . . . goodnight . . .' came from Eliza's bed.

'Shut up!' hissed Kitty.

'I'm only singing goodnight to Skinnybugs,' Eliza claimed. She and Cissy Bingle stuffed their faces into their pillows to smother a renewed attack of the giggles.

Tish and Kitty were smiling to themselves. It had been a good day, Kitty reflected. It would have been better had she seen Henry. Just to have kissed him once before leaving Hampden Square would have set the seal on the day for her; though it would have spoilt Tish's enjoyment; Kitty nursed no illusions on that score.

Tish was not milling over the fun in Hampden Square; that would come to her later, as a pleasant pathway into sleep. Meanwhile, she was considering the extraordinary change in Eliza Heggy; never, before tonight, had this junior talked of 'Skinnybugs'. Under the influence of that dark horse, Cissy Bingle, Eliza was coming out. For the first time, there was a warmth in their bedroom, and it had taken the tragedy of Mary to make this possible.

Arriving after lunch, Wednesday. Hope to meet you 2 p.m. at Bridgemouth Ferry./ Yours,/ H.B.

The card had been posted on Friday, in some place called Stackleby. Kitty examined every word on it, including the Chard address, to see if any hint of an apology lay hidden there.

'I think that's cool, to say the least,' Tish said, 'but that's what we have to put up with. When a man calls, the girl is meant to come running. And you'll run, like all of us. You'll be at the ferry on Wednesday.'

'That's what you think.'

'Ah,' Tish mocked, 'pull the other one.'

'Eric gets bored so soon with his parents. We slipped away on Friday.' Henry would not be admitting that they slipped all the way to Laverport.

Kitty wanted to condemn Eric for his filial disloyalty, but she remembered how bored she was at home, after that first joy of seeing her own parents. If she had Eric's funds, would she spend the whole of her precious holiday week with hers?

Henry described Stackleby – the first halt – to her. He extolled its fistful of stone-built houses grouped around the oversized church, the low walls in place of hedges, the small inn, and the leisurely pace of village life. But for the low walls, it sounded like a grey-stone version of Kitty's home village. She herself would have wanted a more exciting place for a holiday – somewhere with lots of yellow sand, high cliffs and a pier with pierrots.

'His people get terribly bored with Eric,' he went on, 'and I have no illusions as to their opinion of me. They could hardly conceal their relief when we said we'd be going.'

That struck Kitty as really odd. 'Yet they know he's been ill? What rum folk they are! Is it a huge family?'

'He's the only child.'

'Sounds a funny set-up to me. Do you mind if we don't go to the house this afternoon?'

Henry was nonplussed. 'I was expecting to check the inventory,' he said. 'I had it by post this morning.'

'Tish and me went over the place with a fine-tooth comb. We could check that list for you from memory in a couple of evenings. Tish is better at it than me, if it comes to that; she's got a better memory. She was counting everything in the kitchen drawers, down to the last saltspoon. She just loves that sort of thing.'

'And you don't?'

'I have to be in the mood.'

'Say no more. I can attend to the matter later. Eric will help me. I expect him in Laverport for a few days.'

'Bully for Eric!' Kitty commented. Had Eric already slept upstairs?

Since it was generally held among young women of Kitty's age and experience that no baby would result from a first intercourse, she had about ten days left in which to test the infallibility of the theory. Meanwhile, she was not anxious to lie for a second time on Henry's bed. The soreness had healed; she believed she loved him; but did he love her? The example of Mary's catastrophe was always before her; if she could avoid the intimate situation, she would.

They exchanged few words, as they went along the uninspiring promenade. Henry whistled almost inaudibly; he was recalling that drive home to Laverport, and Eric's caustic comments on Kitty's interests. Had she indeed ridden anything lighter than a carthorse? Should he ask her? Should he launch into some talk on opera? He was not overeager to prove Eric right. Besides, the thing to do was to educate the girl first, and have the discussions later. Eric would be moping at this moment in his cabin, or in Henry's. He was friendly enough with the Old Man, but the chief steward had taken against him some years back; ship food was there to be eaten, not criticized. So Eric would be lying in a bunk, with a book and a fit of the sulks; as with the ship food, he would never countenance Henry's forebearance with Kitty, nor would he have the grace to try. Moreover, the animosity was mutual, as Kitty would say. *Bully for Eric*, indeed!

The afternoon's frustration was no less acute for Kitty. It was something of a strain to walk by the side of a man she wanted, and did not want – who could be generosity itself, yet take too much for nothing – who treated her with more respect than other men had shown, but still with less than she required.

'You played that on the piano. What is it?'
'Did I?'

When his eyes lit up like that, she was more than ever glad to be walking along a promenade. She tried to hum the snatch he had been whistling, but the notes were too fast for accuracy.

He had not consciously chosen his tune, nor had he really believed she would remember it. 'It's the opening of Schumann's Piano Concerto. You look most delectable when you wear that frown.'

'You mean like a mountain?'

Henry liked that. This girl would never cease to astound him. Could she have read a book, in fact? 'Where did you hit upon the Delectable Mountains?' he asked her.

'I forget. Are they in the Bible?'

'No, they are not.'

'Then it must have been in some sermon. I was frowning because we were both a bit out of tune.'

He was discouraged. 'Remind me to have that instrument put right,' he said, 'or we shall all be out of tune. I must get it done before I leave.'

'Who will play it?'

His face clouded. 'Eric is a possibility. He's not quite back on his feet. He thinks he is, but he should have more rest.'

'He won't be joining the boat as a passenger, then?'

'I can't see him well enough to travel. He might move into Hampden Square. I did mention it. It's up to him.'

'I'm sorry he's not well,' Kitty said formally, though the sorrow she had for this particular invalid was of a most perfunctory nature. The sorrow she felt about his possible tenancy went much deeper. 'What's wrong with him, by the way?'

Henry gave a non-committal reply: 'Nothing that a less hectic life won't cure.'

'It would be better if you stayed in one place, too,' she remarked bitterly.

'You can't mean that seriously,' he said. 'The sea is my life.'

She did mean it; she wanted to be his life; she had no desire to share possession with the sea; nor did she want to share him with Eric. 'What's his surname?'

'Eric's? I told you before. Cannon-Budge.'

'Eric Budge?'

'No, Eric Cannon-Budge.'

'Ah, that makes all the difference.'

Henry was tired of talking about his friend Eric. They came to a halt by the Tivoli Gardens, where he judged the moment ripe to take a small box from his pocket. It opened to show a slender gold ring, set with a medium opal of good fire. It was a pretty object, and it had cost more than twenty silver brooches.

She could not speak, and he would not. She bit hard on her lip, turned, and ran from Henry and his ring.

She had not counted on his speed, nor he on hers; they were both out of breath, when he caught her.

'Don't do that again!' he said furiously. 'If you dislike a thing, say so; but don't set up a sprinting match.'

'In public,' she managed.

'In public, or anywhere else.'

'You simply don't understand.'

'You keep saying that,' he retorted. 'A gold ring is like a hat, I suppose. I mustn't presume to buy you either.'

'It's nothing to do with that!'

'For God's sake, Kitty, don't start crying here.' Henry looked frantically around him; taking her arm, he steered her firmly into the pea-green promenade shelter ahead of them, whose sole occupants were one elderly woman and her off-white terrier.

Henry sat with clasped hands, looking across the roadway to the two strips of sand and river.

Kitty stared at the dog; it lay slumped on the shelter floor. Like Tish, she was always running away from something or somebody. Henry buys a ring, and she dashes away from that, or from him. Which finger did he intend it for? Would he say anything when he put it on?

She held out her hand. Henry took the box from his pocket and placed it on her palm. The woman watched them closely, as the ring was gently persuaded from its velvet slot, and tried for size on the third finger of Kitty's left hand; it was so loose, it fell off, into her lap. She tried it on the second finger, where it proved a safer fit.

Henry looked down at her hand; the opal flashed against the fresh whiteness of Kitty's skin. He was glad he had chosen this opal. It reminded him of Kitty herself – not ostentatious, so delicately pale, yet capable of colour; it went with her innocence, her lack of sophistication. He must watch out for an opal brooch, to go with it, or a bracelet, perhaps. Turning the ring a fraction, he centred the stone exactly on her finger; its beauty cried out against the shoddiness of her outfit, and he was momentarily unmanned by a surge of tenderness for this pathetic young creature. She was like a stray kitten.

'It doesn't fit on this other finger,' she said hesitatingly.

'I think it looks well on that one,' he replied.

The old woman got up in disgust. Of late, she had grown increasingly hard of hearing, and though she could see what was going on, nevertheless these two were talking in such a mumble, she had missed every word of it. She leaned forward on her stick, in the hope that her feet would oblige. The dog rose cautiously, its four legs splayed like a wooden stool's; after attempting a shake it swung off broadly, on the heels of its mistress, with lowered head.

Kitty studied her ring. 'Thank you,' she said dutifully. 'I've never had a ring like it.'

'But you would prefer your silver brooch.'

'Yes.'

'Would you mind if we left this hideous shelter?'

'You're no lover of sitting in public, either.'

'Are you? It's years since this place saw a paintbrush.'

They stood up almost as slowly as the woman and her dog.

Henry smiled at her. 'You go in front,' he recommended. 'I'll come after you, looking thoughtful.'

'But an engagement ring so soon!' Tish was wearing Kitty's opal, twisting it to catch the vestige of light in the backyard.

'There was no talk of an engagement,' Kitty told her calmly.

'You can have it squeezed smaller at a jeweller's, so it fits your third finger.'

'Yes. Remind me to take it round to Tapp's, some time.'

'Witty, aren't we? I can't see what's biting you, Kitty Catchpole. It wasn't Henry's fault it turned out too big.'

'I'm sorry – I can't imagine any man buying an *engagement* ring without taking the girl with him.'

'But I thought you loved him because he was different. You want it both ways.' Tish removed the ring with reverence and handed it back. 'It's a gorgeous stone. I'd be raving happy if someone give me one.'

'Gave,' said Kitty absently.

'*Gave*,' Tish repeated crossly. 'You make mistakes, yourself.' She led the way indoors. 'Anyway, why are you back so early?'

It was impossible to explain to Tish why she had returned to Skinners' Place at this hour – how suddenly, in Bridgemouth, it had seemed there was nowhere to go after tea, unless they moved on to another restaurant, and toyed with another meal. She and Henry had been at conflict with each other; she had shown it by her laconic answers to his studied remarks. When he had consulted his watch and suggested that they might part, since he had a 'wealth of papers' to sort out, she had promptly agreed. Accompanying her as far as the Bazaar corner, he had kissed her correctly, before they went their opposite ways.

Smouldering with discontent, Kitty had entered the yard, where Tish was taking the air, after a solitary walk round the park and a Bazaar tea. Tish had been at such a loose end that, before going on to the park, she had passed the time of day with the old beanpole, Mrs Floyd, and had actually entered Masons' Emporium in her company, there to infuriate its floorwalkers by circumnavigating the displays under Myrtle's protection. On her return, she had immediately changed window-prices on brown winsey and the Amazona Bodice for the Fuller Figure, dropping one farthing per yard on the one, and adding threepence to the other. These alterations had not been made without vociferous argument from Eliza and Cissy, who had just completed the window-dressing, and who thought she might have had the decency to wait until the following morning before she made a right shambles of it with her big feet – size four or no size four. Their wails had been tolerably good-humoured, however, and they were soon prattling on about girlish matters known only to themselves. Tish had begun to feel distinctly old.

The juniors had made an indifferent job of the windows, thereby incurring a reprimand from Jinny Skinner, but neither had taken this to heart.

Kitty pulled up at the scullery door. 'Tish,' she called quietly. Tish retraced her steps from the hall. 'Tish, get your coat. We must be barmy, when we've got money; let's go to Joe's Fried Eels.'

'We're not sitting down.'

'No, we'll take out. Nobody can see us much in the dark.'

What does a young lady do with an elegant ring which she would like to wear on her engagement finger, but which has no rightful, or even comfortable, place there? In this instance, does she put up with its looseness, and gratify her employers by letting it dazzle the customers' eyes from time to time? Does she allow it to remain with the stone palmwards, giving the impression that she is married? Perhaps she ought to put it on the middle finger, and proclaim Henry's reticence to the world? This last form of publicity would puzzle her colleagues and the Skinners, but it would hardly affect Henry, one way or the other. 'You're a lovely thing,' Kitty told her ring dejectedly, as she touched the filigree setting, 'but your fires are cold.'

Cissy and Eliza had not seen the ring, nor had they been informed about it, therefore they were not seized with the curiosity which Tish was finding unbearable. Kitty had been wearing that opal on her third finger when they had left the Bazaar together on Sunday afternoon. She had returned in the evening without it.

The two seniors were improving on the juniors' faulty window-work, which had rendered their own task more complicated.

'You might tell me,' Tish broke out, 'instead of keeping it dark!'

'What dark?'

'Oh, don't try that dodge on me! *What dark?*' she railed. 'I never kept secrets from you.'

'Didn't you? What about Biddy?' That was unwarranted, and Kitty knew it. 'I shouldn't have said that, Tish. You were saying?'

'Nothing. Forget it.'

Each continued with her work.

'If you're asking about my ring,' Kitty remarked finally, 'why don't you say so?'

'All right, then – what have you done with it?'

'I've lost it.'

'Kitty Catchpole . . .' Tish's mind seized up. 'You never. . . . You couldn't have.'

'I tell you. I lost it, and that's an end of it,' Kitty stated shortly.

'Where?'

'In the river.'

Tish was never to know how the ring came to be lost that Sunday afternoon. There were certain features to do with her own carelessness, excusable or otherwise, that Kitty was not prepared to divulge. That particular day illustrated what was to be the ritual for Kitty and Henry. There were only two alternatives, she reflected, as they once more boarded the ferry; either you walked up and down Bridgemouth promenade, until a dissatisfied Henry departed, or you went with him to Hampden Square, where he made love to you. The second was more comfortable, and had become more enjoyable; she was beginning to enjoy, also, the sense of intimacy born of a shared secret.

Eric had taken the Humber back to Chard, so not much of the inventory had been checked.

'You didn't spend long on it,' Kitty declared, on learning how many pages remained to be done.

'I don't know,' Henry answered. 'One can only do a certain amount at a time. It's very boring.'

Kitty knew all about boring work; she did it every day. 'Men have no staying power,' she said.

'Really? You have statistics on this, or do you speak from mere prejudice?' He was laughing at her; he liked to see the heightened colour in her cheeks, which was not caused solely by the breeze in mid-river.

'I've watched men at work. If they can slip out of it, they will.'

'Well, of course I don't have your vast experience, but to judge from the few men I have observed, I would say you are talking through your hat, Miss Catchpole. Allow me to tie it down for you, before it takes off.' And he tied the hat, in his masterly fashion, with her scarf. 'This is quite a regular performance, isn't it? In future, I must do it before we step on board, so that we don't give the passengers a treat.'

'It also does my brim no good,' she said.

'Not to mention the veil, or whatever you call it. I reckon one more trip will put paid to this hat, then you will have to let me buy you a new one.'

'There's plenty of life in this for months to come. A wavy brim is neither here nor there.'

'Very aptly put, if I may say so. Did I tell you I've had the piano tuned?'

Her eyes sparkled. 'Then you'll play for me?'

'If you wish. I see you are wearing your ring.' She was carrying her left glove. Henry felt she must be proud of the opal.

'Yes, my glove snags on it; the stone sticks up a bit.'

'It hasn't ripped it?'

'No. The leather holds, but it's a tight fit over the ring, and it's not good for the opal; it could work loose.'

He did notice that the ring was on her engagement finger, but he made no comment.

As Kitty had predicted, the man had no staying power. At the house, he ticked off one page of the inventory before packing the work in. She moved into the sitting room to check more pages, while he played her some of the Schumann, and Chopin's 'Berçeuse'.

'I like its second bit even better.'

'The second bit was Chopin. They are both romantic.'

'You played them perfectly.'

'Far from it. I must get that chap back to see to the action. If he can't do it, I shall have to find a firm that can.'

'They went up and down all right,' she said, glancing at the pedals.

With a delighted laugh, since Eric was far from his mind, he came across to the chesterfield, where she was sitting. 'You say the most incredible things, Kitty!'

Papers fell in a wide scatter on the carpet. Impatiently, he hurled the loose cushions after them. In cramped conditions, which were totally unnecessary, he made love to her, to his own quick satisfaction, but not to hers.

'Was that good?' he asked.

'Yes, yes.' Any reference to his lack of consideration could have triggered off a breach, or so she feared. 'The water will be like ice.'

'I don't mind. The gas is turned on, you know. You can boil a kettle now.'

'And make up a fire while I'm at it,' she said, apathetically.

'I saw you and Tish had done that,' he called back, as he reached the stairs. 'You must teach me. I can never get a fire to go.'

You say the most incredible things, Kitty! . . . You do them, as well, she told herself ruefully. You're a damn fool, Kitty Catchpole, and if Tish knew, she would pass out.

'So that's why you smell like attar of roses,' she said, when she rejoined him in the sitting room. 'Bubbles soap!'

'You're fond of it? Take it with you.'

'A used tablet? What would the girls think? I bet Eliza's nose will be wrinkling, anyway; it doesn't miss much. There was a shindy not so long ago when I borrowed her Vinolia.'

'What is your own soap? I could put one in the bathroom for you.'

She did not tell him that he already had a plentiful supply of it in the scullery. 'Cold cream,' she invented, 'any white cold cream soap.'

Henry was in jolly mood; for a time his talk at the restaurant table ranged happily between compliment and banter. Then he fell silent, eyeing her as she ate, taking in every move she made to retrieve crumbs discreetly from her plate, and smiling as she missed with her pastry fork. She could stand it no longer. Laying down the fork, she looked steadily at him: 'I can't eat, when you are watching every mouthful,' she said.

'Have you ever been to Venice?' he asked, disregarding the reproach.

'Venice? In Germany?' she tried.

'No, not Vienna, in *Austria*,' he corrected, with a despairing shake of the head. 'Venice, in Italy.'

'No. How could I go to one of them places? Those places,' she replied, with discomfiture. Tish was right; she made mistakes herself, and when they mattered most, like now.

'We must take tea one day in Florian's. It's a stone's throw from St Mark's, and you can listen to the orchestra and the slap of waves against the gondolas. You would like that.' He was aware that no ears in the south of the Piazza could hope to catch this wave-slapping by the Piazzetta, but the discrepancy did not bother him unduly.

Kitty's mood had improved at the mention of a gondola, which until today she had stressed like 'pianola'. 'Have you ever been in a gondola?' she asked him, with care.

'Of course I have, you goose! And in a steamboat. How else would I get around Venice?'

'Couldn't you walk?'

'Nobody walks far in Venice. In fact, you can't walk everywhere. You would love St Mark's – it glitters inside with gold mosaics.'

Kitty resumed her eating. 'St Mark's, you said? In Italy? That would be Roman Catholic, then?'

'Why, yes,' Henry answered. 'They have excellent ice cream at Florian's,' he added, a shade ironically.

Her fork rested on an empty plate. Henry summoned the waiter. His request was received with an ill-disguised lack of sympathy.

'I don't think we have a paper bag, sir.'

Henry picked up his crumpled damask napkin and let it drop back on the table with a dismissive spread of his fingers. 'Bring a clean piece of paper,' he ordered frostily.

A white paper bag was produced without further delay. With superlative finesse, the two vanilla slices were removed from the pastry plate and introduced into the bag.

'You will have to hold these level,' he advised Kitty. 'The filling is oozing out.'

So he had taken in that earlier manoeuvre, some time previously, when Kitty had slipped a maid of honour inside her Dorothy bag for Tish . . . She shrugged him off now, as he tickled her neck, under cover of adjusting her coat collar.

With the pastries carried steadily on Kitty's glove-less hand, they left the bowing waiter to his distribution of crumbs from table to floor, under the slap of his serviette, and to his pocketing of Henry's florin.

'You leave too big a tip,' she said, when they were outside the hotel.

'He came close to getting nothing,' Henry replied bluntly. 'However, he may be entitled to think his duties have to do with plates, not paper bags.'

'And he's got evening dinners to serve yet. I don't suppose he arrives home till all hours.'

'When he's probably too tired to do anything but sleep, poor man,' said Henry.

'His wife might thank him for that.'

'That is a very caustic remark, Miss Catchpole. How do you know his wife is not this very minute beating her breast *in public*, up and down the street, because he'll be home late?'

'She's more likely beating her breast, or whatever, in private, because he can eat the customers' leftovers, while her and the kids go hungry.'

'Ah, she and the children go hungry. You expect them to have children? That's the trouble with the poor, I agree. They've never done spawning infants.'

'I can't see why there should be one law for the poor, and one for you.'

'As far as I'm aware, Kitty, I have no howling offspring anywhere.'

'Haven't you, now? And no wife?'

'Why should I have a wife?' He thought that one over, before he continued. 'After your spirited defence of the poor, I'm surprised you considered my tip too generous.'

'I was wrong,' she said hotly. 'It should have been twice as much.'

No children and no wife, she reflected, standing near the rail on the leaning top deck. And no fiancée tucked away anywhere? Her knees hurt against the perimeter seating; the spare glove was inside her bag which swung on its cord from her right arm; with her right hand, she held on to her hat; for some reason, Henry had not thought to tie it down for her, either before or after stepping on board. Her left hand still balanced the paper bag, with its vanilla slices; the hat-clutching was making her arm ache.

The river churned in the wake of the ferry, and then lunged on towards the open sea – to the limb of that sea which possessed Henry. If this was his life, how could she hope to break in? She was not the heroic type, to fight on indefinitely for him, when the chips were loaded against her. What chips, anyway? Perhaps they were granite chips, the sort on graves. If Henry loved the sea more than he loved Kitty, the sea could have him. She lowered the pastries to the wooden seat, and let her numb right arm fall to her side. The sly wind took its chance, lifting her hat on the pins. She was too quick for it; her left hand flew upwards to secure the crown, and in so doing, shed the loose ring off her third finger into the waves below.

The girl had a talent for losing jewellery; that was clear. Henry thanked his stars that he had resisted the salesman's blandishments, and had not bought the larger opal, set in an oval of small diamonds. He was feeling out of patience, for all that. 'It was the wrong finger to wear it on; you knew the ring was too loose for it; you told me so yourself.'

'It was the wrong finger,' she granted. 'I should have had more sense.' She felt curiously lighter without his ring; a pretence had been cast upon the waters, and she was in no mood to weep for it.

For his part, he was resolved not to make good the loss for a while. He might not be stuck for money, but neither did he pick it up in the street; his next gift to Kitty would cost less.

He remembered the man's name, Maurice Tapps. Or was it Matthew? No – Maurice. He imagined the shop would not be far from the Bridgemouth Drapery Bazaar, though Kitty, of course, was capable of a smart sprint.

It was galling to take the ferry on a weekday without the remotest chance of seeing her. The affair of the ring was already fading in importance. Her desirability had precedence over her foolishness, but not enough to tempt him inside the Bazaar again, if he could help it. He could not abide that loud-mouthed harridan, Mrs Skinner, nor was he one to enjoy being the cynosure of neighbouring eyes. He must ask Kitty if she read poetry. Highly unlikely, if she read no prose. But this infernal pawnshop, now – surely it must be hereabouts?

The police station supplied Henry with directions, after some heavy humour from both constables; that, too, was maddening. Did he look the type to need a pawnbroker? And their inane emphasis on *Tapp! Tapp* or *Tapps*, as if that had any bearing on the question!

He arrived at the shop, and scanned its front window for brooches. Mr Tapp's overall presentation was haphazard; second-hand articles in gold were isolated from those in silver, but that was as far as it went. There were trays of jumbled rings containing the odd locket, or of lockets with bracelets, or of odd bracelets thrown among necklaces. More care was lavished on those pieces which commanded stiffer prices; they were individually mounted on dingy white card, and held at a slant by metal clips, along taut wires for easy viewing: two diamond rings with claw settings gleamed here, next to a slim gold brooch, that bore two swallows in flight, their wings set with microscopic seed pearls. Henry's eye ran idly over these window wires; the effect was hypnotic. He blinked and started again, concentrating on the trays of silver jumble and working his way round, into the shop porch. Here, in the porch window, he was spurred on by the sight of an outsize tray with lacklustre crucifixes, tie pins, links, fobs and – to his real excitement – name brooches. These last were three in number, one half submerged, and two upside down. The first read, MOTH and could be discounted; the first upside-downer spelt, ELSIE and was equally useless; the third brooch, which was not so quickly ddeciphered, because of its worn condition and discolouration, eventually yielded up CHARLOTTE. Henry breathed deeply and ran a finger inside his stiff collar; the errand looked hopeless.

The bell on the shop door did not ping and end at that; it shook in a tinkling fever, to bring Maurice Tapp at a run from his pledge office; his expression was vaguely accusing, as if he suspected stealing, even where tough glass cases denied access.

The pawnbroker unlocked the door of his side window to lift out the big tray. 'There you are, sir,' he said, with scant courtesy in the wave of his hand, or behind the ironic *sir*. Everything on this tray was cheap; he was not going to devote much energy to the transaction.

Henry's attention wandered momentarily to the items housed inside the glass-topped counter. It held a collection of old gold and silver watches, many with appropriate alberts.

'You'd like to see a watch?' Mr Tapp said more eagerly. 'We can do you a very reliable hunter.'

Henry smiled: when a man was in business on his own account, it was invariably *we* who could, or could not, oblige the customer; whereas the employee in a bigger establishment more often used the first person singular; he must ask Kitty what she said. 'No,' he replied. 'I have several watches. I came in about the *Mother* brooch.' Henry Bonham was no mean tactician; he planned to reach any goal in a series of shrewd moves.

In spite of himself, Mr Tapp launched into his sales patter. Henry had to realize that this *Mother* brooch was the best of its kind that money could buy; he was to take note of the silver balls around the edge – they added extra weight, they did, to a very stylish arrangement. Henry was lucky to have found a jeweller who would let him have this unusual piece for a song. At this point, the pawnbroker scrutinized the hieroglyphics on its price tag: CGH/JL/205, which, being deciphered, read, *Clearance Granny Hesketh's/Job Lot/February 1905.* 'Twenty-seven and six!' he announced imperturbably.

'But it's second-hand, isn't it?'

Maurice Tapp looked at him. Naturally, it was

second-hand; where did he expect to find a *Mother* brooch of quality, at a give-away price, and brand new?

'I know maids' brooches sell for half a guinea,' Henry stated, picking up his gloves from the counter.

Maids' brooches! Mr Tapp was under the impression he'd asked for a *Mother* brooch. Maids' brooches – that was a different kettle of fish, now, wasn't it? We could let him have a nice one at fifteen and a tanner, and not a break in it.

'Why the difference in price?' Henry enquired, putting his gloves down again.

Why the difference? You only had to handle one; if you didn't watch out, your maid's brooch would snap like a carrot.

Maurice Tapp let *Elsie* skitter along the glass top; it went as lightly as a smooth shilling, but Henry was fairly positive that *Mother* weighed little more. He lifted the latter from the tray and turned it over.

'I see the pin has been mended.'

'The pin?' Tapp took the brooch from him, and, with a theatrical side-screw of his face, inspected it through his pawnbroker's eyeglass. 'It's been *reinforced* at one time, yes. That won't break in a hurry. You can have it for a guinea, and that's giving it away.'

'You haven't a *Kitty*, by any chance?'

Tapp looked inattentive. '*Kitty*? We haven't a *Kitty* in stock.' Then he remembered. 'Half a minute . . . now I think on . . .' He went through to the pledge room, where he tossed a short remark to the queue, returning quickly with another brooch in his hand. '*Katherine*,' he said, in a voice big with victory. 'How's that for *Kitty*?'

'I have an idea she spells it with a *C*,' Henry demurred, wickedly.

'Some Kitty with a *C*! Look, I've a shopful of customers waiting in the back. Thirty-five bob the two, and you've got yourself a bargain, *C* or no *C*.'

To clinch the business, Henry would have been happy to smash Mr Tapp's teeth in. Instead, he reached for his wallet. 'I'll take them,' he said.

'I thought you might send this one to your mother – from yourself, I mean; if you think she would like it.'

'I'm sure she would, Henry; it's so pretty. But I shouldn't be taking the praise, when you've bought it.'

'I've not been introduced to your mother.'

'No.'

Her parents were still ignorant of Henry's existence. Her thoughts ran back to that speculative fuss when she had first walked out with an AB, and to the many irksome questions in her mother's letters after he had disappeared. She could only guess now at her mother's private despair when letters from Kitty continued to reveal no friend other than Tish. And that was how it was going to be, as far as Kitty was concerned. When Henry was ready to be announced to her family, he could say so.

They were lying on top of the bed. She fingered the *Katherine* brooch at her throat. Its pin had taken up too much blouse; it was also askew, but must stay that way. He had been all thumbs, pinning it on, and so anxious to be told it was right; that was a little-boy moment she had not seen before. She asked him if Eric was back in Laverport.

He was not, but a few lines had come from him, indicating that he would like to move into no. 28, before Henry went away.

'Have you agreed on the rent?'

The idea seemed novel to Henry. He plumped up his

pillow to a more comfortable depth, then lay propped on his elbow for a better view of her. 'Eric has no head for minor considerations like rent. Your ears are so delicious, they destroy me, but I suppose you realize that.'

'Who pays Eric's rent when he doesn't live with you?'

Henry prevaricated. 'Someone always bails him out – his father, his uncle, someone.'

'You do, Henry.'

He laughed. 'I have been known to, but it's not as unequal as you may think. Eric can be counted on for the most exciting food: I've known butchers' wives actually cook for him; everybody takes pity on Eric when he looks helpless; he's very good at looking helpless.'

She moved to make more space between them. 'Which room will he have?'

'Which rooms will he take? You'll find he has unerring taste in all things. He will choose the best rooms in the house.' Indeed, he had already chosen them, thought Henry to himself.

'Rooms? You can't mean he'll have the sitting room?' she said with indignation.

'Don't get worked up.' He leaned over to kiss her on the nose. 'I believe he'll take this room and the one next door, because he hates the ground floor anywhere. Eric is sensitive to draughts.'

'He's not sensitive to double beds, by any chance?'

'A most unworthy remark! Besides, we have a three-quarter bed in the back room, and you know there's another double in the front, upstairs.'

'What would he want with the bed next door?'

'That single could go in the back attic, out of the way. He needs a sitting room, not an extra bedroom.'

'Does he light fires better than you?'

'Heavens, no! Remind me to look out for a woman.'

'You wanted reminding about the action.'

'Action? Oh, the piano!' He lay back on the counterpane, again overcome with laughter.

'She does it on purpose, I tell you!' Hezekiah fumed. 'I go down to the yard to check the coal, and I guarantee she's out there in five seconds, hanging out the flags!'

'You imagine it,' Jinny retorted. 'It's a fine day; where else do you want them? Better outside than dripping round our ears in the scullery.'

'It's the way she does it, with that look on her face.'

'Why don't you see how the coal's doing on a Tuesday, if you're so particular?'

Mrs Jacks had nearly finished pegging the white squares on the line. It was a good day for a blow, and the sheets were already folded, ready for the iron. She hung the squares according to their initials; only two lots this week: C.B. and K.C. It was a few days early, she thought, for K.C.; all that worry about the brooch, most like. Minnie had foolproof diagnoses to hand, to cover any physical discrepancy which might arise. That was funny about the brooch, though. Who'd have expected anyone to spot it at an auction? He'd got his wits about him, that officer chap – or the luck of the damned.

Tish was the only one to learn how Henry had rescued the Katherine brooch; and the version, as retailed by Kitty, gave no more than a bare outline of the affair, since Henry himself had played it down in the telling.

It was Henry who had arrived at the auction idea to be presented to Mrs Jacks. Kitty was interested to observe that he could think up a convenient untruth, when it suited both of them. One pitfall could not be overlooked: what if Mrs Jacks went to the pawnbroker's to blast that gentleman sky-high, and referred to the mythical auction? Kitty had not forgotten Minnie's fierce face when she heard the silver brooch was lost.

If they had been informed of the lady housekeeper's last visit to Tapp's, they could have relished the knowledge that he had already been blasted – that being a woman of strong principle, Minnie would never again step inside the Cable Street pawnshop.

Eliza Heggy had presented no problem. Her curiosity about the missing brooch had cooled when she learned the pin was broken. Since then, the reformed Eliza had more pleasurable concerns to occupy her waking hours. She and her new friend, Cissy, were walking out with two junior clerks from the London North Western Railway, when all four were not drinking soup and munching buns at the Bethesda Band of Youth.

Kitty and Tish were tidying the juniors' beds before breakfast.

'Juniors aren't what they were when I was a girl,' said Kitty.

'I prayed for the return of your brooch,' Tish announced shyly, but with a determination to have credit given, where credit was due. 'I prayed to St Jude.'

'When was that?'

'One Sunday, on my own. I bought a candle.'

'Out of our money? You've a cheek! It's a good thing we've inherited a fortune lately.'

'I'd like to give thanks,' Tish went on, obstinately.

'Another candle? How much?'

Tish plunged ahead. 'It would be better if I put it in the *Argus*. That brings comfort to others who are praying for something.'

'Proper waste of money, if you ask me. You don't get me pushing thanks to St Jude through the letter box.'

'Nobody's asking you to do it. It won't cost as much as the *In Memoriam*, and you have got your brooch back.'

Kitty had to allow that. 'I have, and I'm an ungrateful heathen.'

'It doesn't have to be long. "Grateful thanks to St Jude for favours received," that's what people generally put; signed "L.A.K. and K.C."'

'*Favour*, surely? Did I hear you say, "L.*A*.K."? Who's that?'

Tish's temper rose. 'I was baptized "Laetitia Anne",' she retorted.

'Pardon my ignorance. But no, Tish, come off it! One more candle, if you're desperate, and that's the lot.'

It would be a few days before Tish recovered her good humour, and then only because she had decided to stop the money in minute amounts out of the remittance home, until she could pay without Kitty's knowledge for the insertion. St Jude would surely intercede for such a sin.

It is doubtful if Tish could have reached that decision had she not been left on her own. Her faith gained in strength with Kitty's prolonged absence – prolonged, that is to say, for three days: Friday, Saturday and Sunday. Tish had a stint of praying to do on Kitty's behalf, to ask that her friend be forgiven and not detected in falsehood. What if Skinnybugs wrote to Kitty's mother, to check if that lady was really ill? She comforted herself with the knowledge that he was too mean to waste a stamp, and that he would be docking the three days, anyhow, off Kitty's summer holiday.

At least she was not cold. In fact, the cabin was overheated. She felt stifled by the lack of air, and longed for the stiff gales which tore through Skinners' Place. With every heave of the ship, as it rocked romantically through the night, the timbers creaked fit to split. It hung at the top of one creak, before it pitched to the lowest rasp of the next, taking Kitty's stomach with it. She had spent some time leaning over Henry's steel washbowl to no effect.

He was sleeping soundly. Although he had pulled the bunk out from the wall to make it larger, he was peacefully oblivious of the change, and had taken over the middle of it.

Another night of this did not bear thinking of. Two more days of it . . . These terrible meals. The food was good; that Eric had no reason to grumble about it; but having to make conversation about a man on Lesko, which turned out to be music – that was frightening. The captain had been wiping tears off his face, he had laughed so much. Henry had laughed, as well, but she could see that he was ashamed because she didn't know where Lesko was. This was not fair; nobody ought to expect her to know places like sailors did. She would have to ask him to buy her a book of maps or something. That would be better than a new hat.

She twisted the thin gold band on her third finger. Henry had told her she could keep it; the Old Man, he said, required young ladies to wear one, even if it was only a curtain ring. How often had this happened before? God, she felt awful. She had not wanted to come; her idea of a thrill was not that ordeal of sitting at a captain's table. She wanted to be an ordinary passenger, nowhere near an Old Man, on a big liner. Did big liners toss around like this? It was a nice boat – no, ship – but Henry could have it for keeps. All he could think of was taking her quickly, before he slept, and tomorrow's bacon and eggs in the saloon. She moved to the bowl. No good. Such a treat, bacon and eggs, hardly ever seen when the ABs were on board, never seen at Skinners' Place. She should be more grateful. But two more days and a whole night! If only she could swap places with Eric Budge, who was fast asleep, no doubt, at no. 28. And in their bedroom. Or swap with Tish – dear, kind Tish, who now knew what she must have guessed before. Poor Tish had been given a lot to pray about. She would be asking to burn more candles.

Kitty lay down, exhausted, on the edge of the bunk, and was cradled into a queasy sleep.

'One day,' Tish mused, over a fragment of Fry's Chocolate Cream.

'One day what?' said Kitty.

'One day, some little boy will empty a pail round his sand castle, and there he'll see a ring floating in the moat.'

'One day,' Kitty half sang, 'a fishergirl will be gutting a herring, and – lo and behold – she'll pull out a shining opal.'

'A slimy opal.'

'What are you two on about?' Eliza wanted to know. 'Opals and rings? You must be well away.'

'You don't know your fairy tales, Miss Heggy, that's your trouble,' Kitty reproved her, 'or these things wouldn't surprise you.'

Eliza looked across the table, where Cissy Bingle was smoothing out the silver paper for her Bible. 'I told you these two were off their rockers half the time.'

Cissy grinned. 'Anybody lost a ring?' she enquired.

'Everybody has lost a ring,' Kitty replied sadly. 'The whole sea is filled with rings we throw away each week; every time life fails to measure up, we lose another ring.'

'Barmy,' said Eliza. 'My Percy and me, we were looking at rings only last Wednesday.'

'No!' exclaimed Cissy, delightedly. 'Were you really?'

'Small ones,' Eliza confessed. 'None of your fairy-tale opals or anything. He says he's saving up to buy me a gold mizpah.'

'That's lovely, Eliza,' said Tish. 'You and Cissy will be married before we know where we are.'

'Arthur hasn't gone as far as a ring,' Cissy sighed, with a smile. 'To mention it, or anything.'

'He will,' Eliza declared. 'You only have to walk him down the right street. Harry Chadwick has a real nice selection in the window. We always go that way to the prom. And we come back same way without fail. That shop never shuts till eight, any night.'

'It never shuts Wednesdays?' Tish's voice was hoarse with disbelief.

'No. Well, there's the pawnshop round the side, isn't there? Percy says Chadwick's stays open Saturdays till gone eleven. Gone eleven! You think of that! It's all for the pawns.'

'For the pawns,' Kitty repeated weakly. 'Good God!' She and Tish stared at each other, dumbfounded. Why had they never heard about Harry Chadwick's hours? Why hadn't Mrs Jacks told Kitty? Surely she must have known?

Indeed, if she had been pressed, Minnie Jacks would

certainly have remembered Chadwick's long business hours. Unfortunately, she was a creature of habit; she had gone to Maurice Tapp's for the best part of a lifetime, and it had not crossed her one-track mind to refer Kitty to the other pawnbroker. It had taken that row with Mr Tapp to send Minnie tramping the greater distance to his rival – to remind her of the flexibility in the latter's opening hours. The guilt she felt with regard to her omission could be measured by the secrecy she had maintained on the subject.

It was one of those mornings when Kitty and Tish woke up in an unaccountably good mood. Together, they tore the bedclothes off the shrieking juniors. Jinny Skinner flew on to the landing, beating her fists in the air like a pantomime dame. To confirm the image, Hezekiah came on the scene, to drag her backwards off the stage. The resistance and yells from the top floor persisted for some uproarious minutes.

Hezekiah's rebuke at breakfast was delivered with restraint. His wife was pained to remark the devilment in the assistants' eyes. It was a revelation to see Miss Heggy so clearly hand in glove with her seniors; nor had Jinny anticipated this corruption of Miss Bingle's good manners. Over the years, her regime of divide and rule had worked well; unlike Hezekiah, she saw no great advantage in a united staff.

Apart from the threat imposed by Eric's installation in Hampden Square, Kitty was not too downhearted. Henry had proved in many ways that he loved her, even though his wedding ring had to hide in her Dorothy bag; she was not pregnant, and this gave her confidence in him. Secure in the attentions of a good and cautious man, surely she could withstand competition from both

Mr Cannon-Budge and the sea? She tapped out a daring dance on Mitchell Caine's steel tips, and beamed across at Tish in Haberdashery. Tish smiled back, but with less assurance. Whenever Henry Bonham sailed away, poor Kitty was likely to be heartbroken; then it would be Tish's turn to comfort her, to walk out with her as she used to do, to be the prop Kitty must have. Tish Kelly, one of the most deserving subjects ever to direct a prayer skywards, begged the saints in general to make her worthy of this important task; the fervour of her silent request was matched only by the joy with which she contemplated Henry's departure.

Eliza minced across the shop floor, waggling her backside and drooping her fingers, in a recognizable impersonation of Mrs Skinner's progress towards the cash office. As she drew near to Millinery, a cough from Cissy alerted her to Hezekiah's presence at the alcove.

It was hard to credit that the young Heggy would be playing the fool, but – whatever she was doing – she was not yet behind her counter. 'When you are ready, Miss Heggy!' he boomed, with a jangle of shop keys.

'One moment, sir!' Eliza stuttered, opening each millinery drawer a little way, as if this were an essential preliminary to her day's work, rather than a gambit to avoid facing the boss.

He darted a perfunctory glance at Baby Linen. Miss Bingle was at her post behind christening veils and baby bonnets, looking every inch a lady in her tailored blouse and skirt. As he strode off to open the doors, Cissy's flat bosom rose and fell in a dangerous spasm of suppressed giggling.

Eliza blew her nose more than thoroughly. Cissy was now seized with a smothered coughing into her handkerchief, which obliged her to turn towards bootees and buttoned gaiters.

From their position, Kitty and Tish could see nothing that was happening beyond the alcove, but they gathered enough from the noises-off to convince them that the junior lady assistants were not straight-faced.

'They're off!' whispered Kitty.

Tish grinned and nodded. Were she and Kitty ever such a pair of gigglers? From what she could remember, there had not been much to giggle about. Perhaps if they'd had more pennies to play around with, their days might have been one long laugh, too.

From her crow's nest, Jinny Skinner had heard as much as the older lady assistants, and it had not sweetened her temper. Trust Hezekiah to open the doors before he had perfect discipline on the floor! One new client, a Welshman, was over the threshold in a trice. Miss Catchpole had slipped across to attend to him. Jinny breathed more evenly; the man was being shown celluloid collars; the morning was off to some sort of a start.

In most towns, and we know Bridgemouth to be no exception, there will be districts populated by what the Skinners would term a better class of person. This curious class contains within its ranks an amorphous female section, which stays reasonably dispersed about its various neighbourhoods. At two distinct points in the day, however, these females will converge in knots – viz. at eleven o'clock in the morning, and at three-thirty in the afternoon. At such hours, they can be seen in their droves, entering the local coffee parlours in the morning, and the local tea rooms, if these are not indeed the self-same places, in the afternoon. What they have to talk about is anybody's guess; where they find the money is another, since not every better class of purse is bulging; and how these good women can spare the time, for not all will be elderly widows or retired spinsters, is again a matter of conjecture, and one that is generally kept hidden from the better class of husband.

Jinny was thinking about this. The Skinners had heard on the Scotch Kirk grapevine that Masons' top floor was housing not only their restaurant with soda fountain, but also a separate lounge that did duty for morning coffee or afternoon *thé dansant*.

A flash of annoyance convulsed her. It was true that the Kelly girl had recently changed a couple of window tickets – Tish had not omitted to report this – but just how often did the four assistants really explore Masons'? It was about time Hezekiah put his foot down. She returned to the notion of running a restaurant, which did not appeal to her. On the other hand, the provision of tea and coffee, scones and pastries, or even soft drinks and ices, definitely did. The Bazaar's lady assistants took up too much room; if they could be lodged elsewhere on the premises, it would leave their long attic and the broom cupboard for conversion. Two door plates reading PRIVATE would be needed for the Skinners' first-floor rooms, and a third to say WC on the same landing. Mrs Skinner nodded and stretched a smile in Myrtle Floyd's direction: that meant the Millinery Department upside-down for an hour, and Mrs Floyd with no more intention of buying another black bonnet than Mother Murphy's cat. It was just a question of where to put those assistants: the outhouse was doing nothing; it was wasted as coal house and toolshed; she would have to swallow her pride and ask Atkinsons to build a large coal bunker and a small wooden shed for the tools. The interior walls of the outhouse would be all right with a coat of whitewash; a thin concrete skim would fix the broken floor, and the attic lino could go on top of that. The four attic curtains could be joined up, to hang at the one longer window; there was life still in that pink cretonne, one of the better rags inherited from the firm's founders. Gas would have to be put through, of course; that would be an unfortunate expense, but there would be no need for a ceiling. Those wooden beams were quite charming in themselves, and a touch of brown paint was all they wanted. The place should be very comfortable in every respect, and it was so much nearer the back lavatory. *And so much nearer the back gate!* With great agitation, Jinny attended to the queue of cash tubes, which had gathered overhead during her deliberations.

She thanked God she had remembered the back gate. It would be bad enough to have those young women out of earshot, but to have them close to a gate! It had a strong lock and was high, but she had visions of chairs and stepladders being dragged towards it . . . chairs being dropped on ropes of unravelled string to the pavement outside. . . . Jinny Skinner rested her head in her hands while she thought this one out: barbed wire along the gate top . . . splintered glass along the wall. . . .

If an earthquake had struck the Drapery Bazaar, no greater chaos could have followed. Men were shouting; women were screaming; there was a temporary jam at the entrance, as too many screamers rushed to get out. Hezekiah exhorted his customers to stand still and keep calm; his stentorian commands acted more quickly than smelling-salts on Mrs Floyd, who regained her senses sufficiently to grab her shabby black straw from the Millinery counter and to stagger moaning into the street, still wearing the lace-edged bonnet she had been trying on for size. Other ladies, rooted to the ground, found that their legs would shift after all; they, too, made a dash for the door.

'It's gone through your store room, somewhere. Not a sign of it,' declared Kitty's Welshman to Hezekiah, throwing down the blind-pole. 'I'll help you with the young lady, shall I?'

'Get down off the counter, Miss Heggy!' Hezekiah barked, before he joined this considerate customer. Together, they approached Cissy Bingle, where she lay among the scattered pushchairs and bassinets, and carried her light form with some strain to the kitchen; there, they laid her gently on the hearthrug. Blood streaked her cheek from an ugly gash across the temple. Miss Kelly was summoned to sit by the unconscious girl. Miss Catchpole was sent to fetch Dr Hicks.

Standing by the Millinery drawers, Jinny Skinner was beside herself with distress and anger. Eliza was sobbing loudly. The shop was empty of all customers.

'Look at it, girl! Take a look at it!' Jinny stormed.

The distraught junior tried to obey, though the bottom hat drawer was the last thing she wanted to look at.

'You have not tidied that drawer for months, Miss Heggy.'

In vain did Eliza begin a tearful explanation; Mrs Skinner refused to listen. 'I don't care how many black bonnets you have in the drawer above! You know your duty as well as I do. No hats are left unattended for a rat to make a nest like that. Now you can just start clearing it out.'

With a cry, the terrified Eliza backed away, 'I can't, ma'am! I can't touch that! There might be another.'

'Rubbish! Hand me that pole.'

Standing well back herself, the intrepid Jinny broke up the masterpiece of a nest. No further vermin were to be seen. 'No wonder!' she exclaimed. 'There's a way gnawed through at the back. Months they've been at it. Months! Will you stop that abominable noise, Miss

Heggy, and do something useful! If you can't bring yourself to see to the drawer, then get that pram section to rights and tidy up Leather Goods. Ah, Dr Hicks! So good of you to come. It's just a faint, you know. Lady assistants have no stamina these days.'

As she led the doctor to the kitchen, she turned with dignity towards Kitty and Eliza, who were both working flat out to restore order to the shop floor: 'All morning cocoa is cancelled,' she informed them.

Hezekiah came down from the sitting room, where he had been recovering, and locked the shop doors one and a half hours before dinner.

'Not young Cissy!' Kitty said frantically. 'How *could* I do it? I never meant to hurt anybody!'

'I bet it's nothing to do with you,' Tish declared. 'What about the Skinner's cash book, gnawed to bits before you thought of crumbs?'

Kitty shuddered. 'What if Cissy dies? I'll be a murderer. I'll have to own up. I can't go round feeling like this.'

Tish's reaction was fierce. 'You can forget about owning up,' she said, 'or we'll both be in the cart. I'm as much in it as you are.'

'You never dropped a single crumb, not one. You'd be let off with a caution.'

'Who wants that? What sort of life would I have, if you were hung?'

'Hanged.'

'Who says it's *hanged*? Hung.'

'Oh, *Tish*!'

Tish rocked Kitty in her arms. 'There, there! Don't carry on so. She'll be all right, you'll see.'

Eliza joined them in the attic; she, too, looked ashen.

'Mrs Skinner is crying her eyes out on the landing.'

The seniors were stunned.

'Cissy?' Tish managed, her voice rising in an incongruous squeak.

Eliza shook her head. 'She's not dead; she's not come round, neither. Mr Skinner's back from the hospital. He said something about Councillor Bingle and compensation, and then *she* burst out crying. . . . It's all my fault,' Eliza added brokenly. 'If I'd done my job, it wouldn't have happened. If Cissy dies, I've killed her.' The young junior stood there, grief-stricken and staring, like one possessed.

'No, Eliza!' Kitty had leapt off her bed. 'You've not! You're not to think that, ever!'

'Or say it,' Tish warned. 'Nobody here has tried to kill anyone. Cissy's had an accident, that's all. I'm going to see Mrs Skinner.'

'Yes, you go and see Mrs Skinner,' Kitty repeated dully.

Tish threw her a worried glance. 'And remember, you two, nobody made Cissy bang her head on a bassinet.'

'What can she want with Mrs Skinner?' Eliza asked quietly. 'She won't have stopped her crying yet.'

'God knows.'

Eliza was right. Jinny was still having a good weep in her bedroom. It was her husband who answered Tish's timid knock on the sitting-room door, and he was in no mood to listen to a lady assistant; he had had a bellyful of assistants for one day.

'I should like to go out, sir,' Tish quavered.

'You'd like to *what*?'

'Go out, sir. I'd like to go to church.'

He spoke more civilly. 'And what church is open at this time?'

'St Mary and St Modwena's, sir.'

Of course, the girl was a pape; he had forgotten that for the moment. His brow knitted: 'You can't leave the premises, you know that. You can get to your church any Sunday afternoon or evening, or in your own time on a Wednesday, if you have to.'

That might be too late. Tish stuck to her guns, afraid though she was; it was debatable which was upsetting her more — the seeking after permission, or the unavoidably frantic rush to Battle Street if this were granted. 'I want to pray, and I know I must get there soon,' she submitted.

A suspicion crossed his mind; but no – the Kelly girl was not one to try it on; apart from her unfortunate attachment to Kitty Catchpole, Miss Kelly was not to be faulted. He looked down at her earnest face. By gad, she was pretty, too! When he spoke, his voice was quite kindly: 'Well, now, I think most of us want to be praying, but we can't all be running off to church, can we? I suggest you go to your bedroom and kneel down there. You'll find God can hear us wherever we are.' He had amazed himself. Andrew Macpherson could not have done better.

Tish turned away, defeated; the attic was not enough. She wanted an altar for genuflection, an image to gaze upon, dark shadows around her and a few bright flames, leaning and leaping in the draught, to light the track of her prayer. She went slowly up the stairs, and re-entered the cheerless room. Kitty was sitting on a chair, looking into space. By the end cot, Eliza was kneeling, deep in whatever Protestants said when they prayed. Tish went to her own bedside and knelt down.

Kitty blinked, and stood up to see what the others were doing; she was unable to copy their example.

Lying back on her bed, she covered her face with her hands: 'God! God! God!' she prayed, 'If you let her die, I shall hate you forever.' She turned over to let the warm tears spill through her fingers, instead of into her ears and down her neck.

When she woke up, the room was empty. Leaping off the bed, she ran down to the kitchen, to find Tish and Eliza huddled over the low fire.

Mrs Jacks poked her head round the scullery door with a cup in her hand. 'There's cocoa in here, for any that likes it,' she said.

After the first non-Bank Holiday closure since its inception, the Drapery Bazaar was ready to open as usual on Saturday morning. Apart from the disquieting fact that the invader rat had not been traced – and who would be telling the customers that? – and apart from the sickening anxiety about Cissy Bingle, which weighed heavily upon everybody concerned, the establishment was presenting a brave and tidy face to the public.

During that painful afternoon, when the lady assistants had been restoring order and polish to the shop floor, Hezekiah had cleaned out the offending drawer and had carried it across to Atkinsons' – not without mortification – for an emergency repair. This morning, Eliza took her place nervously beyond the alcove. There was no Cissy to giggle with; there was that nasty gap in the drawer stack, through which she was expecting a troop of rats to come nosing. If one, just one, showed as much as a whisker, she knew she would scream and scream again; nor had she any faith in those other hat drawers, although the Skinners had sworn that all were in good shape. Indeed, Eliza had decided to tell hat-hunters that any article not on view was out of stock.

Jinny Skinner was thankful to be perched so high above the floor; even so, she had given her cash office a wary inspection before stepping inside. Hezekiah had refused to send for a catcher, in case word got round that Skinners' Place was rat-ridden from top to bottom. He himself had laid down poison bait at the back of the drawer space, and was awaiting developments. Jinny could see the force of his argument, while remaining not entirely happy with it.

Kitty and Tish were similarly unconvinced; neither believed she could be heroic if any livestock scampered behind her counter.

Hezekiah, to his credit, was not afraid; he feared customer-reaction far more than rat-infestation: the former was the more difficult to kill stone-dead. One dispute with his wife still rankled: he did not accept that his splendid notice, BUSINESS AS USUAL, ought to be omitted from the larger front window. Jinny had been vehemently against it on the grounds that it would underline the reason for yesterday's shut-down, and perhaps it would. On the other hand, it might put the clients' fears to rest, for how could business be as usual, if a rat kept roaming the premises? His notice could bring comfort to the hat-elastic brigade, to name but one crowd; he was sure that lot would be back. He thought grimly that scrawled crosses would not come amiss, to mark where two assistants, so far, had crashed to the ground.

As the morning wore on, staff and employers dwelt less on this matter for anxiety and more on the fate of Cissy Bingle, each in his or her own way despatching messages to heaven, to plead for her recovery. Only two people came into the shop; one was Mrs Macpherson, who was authorized to collect the Scotch Kirk Missionary Box and to replace it with an empty one; she came

and went swiftly, hardly returning the nod from Jinny
Skinner; the second, who arrived shortly before dinner-
time, was none other than old Uncle Charles Atkinson,
who had the effrontery not only to step across the
threshold, where he had never been admitted before,
but to trundle a small handcart in front of him, bearing
the missing drawer.

It was an excellent repair. Hezekiah admitted that.
And it had been quick. It had been worth an ounce of
pride down the chute to get the drawer back into place
as soon as possible. He would wait until the bill came
before he passed final judgement; meanwhile, he would
send Mrs Jacks with a strong note to Atkinson and
Atkinson, informing them that the Bridgemouth Drapery Bazaar had a back entrance for deliveries.

'It's a bad day for the Bazaar, sir,' said that lady, as
she took the envelope from him.

'What do you mean, *a bad day*?'

'Them rats,' she returned, wrapping the shawl over
her broad chest.

'Rats? *One* rat, Mrs Jacks. *One stray rat!*'

She sniffed. 'That's as maybe. Rumour's going
round you're snooing with 'em.'

Hezekiah fought for the upper hand. 'I've asked you
to take that note across the road before you serve dinner.'

'I'm off now,' she told him. 'Seems like you'll be
serving your own dinner, you and the missis, before
long.'

'*The missis!*' Jinny screeched. 'That's it! She's out!'

Hezekiah wished he hadn't opened his mouth. 'For
goodness' sake, let her serve dinner first.'

'To blazes with the dinner! The assistants can serve

it. They've done nothing but twiddle their thumbs all morning, when they weren't drinking cocoa.'

No narrator, intent on discretion, could give a verbatim report of that encounter in the scullery, during the course of which a cup slipped of its own volition from Minnie Jacks' nerveless fingers. They sprang to life, as Mrs Skinner took back one of the three florins on the deal table, to deduct from it the cost of one cup replacement.

Minnie whipped the other two coins into the pocket of her sack apron before she started her final onslaught, both verbal and physical: 'Keep the bleedin' change!' she cried, 'It'll pay for the rest of this bleedin' lot, which you bought for bleedin' tuppence!' A shower of crockery, augmented with two blocks of Monkey Brand, fell in fragments about Jinny Skinner's feet – some pieces landing perilously close; and with one higher sweep of Minnie's arm, every earthenware pot and jug took off; they hit the tiles with a crump like grape shot. Upon which, Minnie Jacks flipped her shawl off the door hook and picked her way out of Skinners' Place, never to return.

Hezekiah had not been too craven; he had rushed to Jinny's assistance and had directed some pithy commands at Mrs Jacks, but his stand, like that of his wife, was hampered by the hail of missiles. He had therefore been reduced to dithering beyond range, advancing and retreating without foot-change, like a child entering French skipping.

Complete silence followed Minnie's departure. Jinny continued to stand there, curiously stiff, and as red as a forgotten poker.

'Well, come on!' Hezekiah ordered. 'Is this mess to be cleared so that Mrs Skinner can move?'

The lady assistants came from the kitchen to obey.

'Get upstairs, all of you!' Jinny rapped. 'Off!'

'But, ma'am . . .' Kitty began.

'Nobody can walk over this pile,' Hezekiah said impatiently. 'It's got to be brushed up. Miss Heggy, fetch the big brush and shovel from upstairs.'

'And stay there!' Jinny shouted. 'And you two, do as you're told – get yourselves upstairs, after her; and don't come down till I call you.'

Perplexed, the girls turned to go, but not before the telltale trickle had wound its way through the broken crocks towards their exit.

'I'm sorry for her,' said Tish.

'So am I,' Kitty agreed. 'Almost in public, too.'

'That's laughing at her,' Tish reproved.

'Not really. I don't like to see anyone shamed like that; not even a Skinner.'

'She was in a funk, when Mrs Jacks was throwing things at her. I'm sure I'd have passed out,' said Eliza.

'We all would. It was horrible,' Kitty declared. 'Not that I blame Mrs Jacks for smashing every pot in the place, but she'd no right to aim them straight at Jinny Skinner.'

'She wasn't hit, was she?' asked Tish. 'It wasn't *straight* at her.'

'Near enough,' Eliza said. 'I wonder how we'll eat our dinner with no plates?'

'I bet we'll find some big bits we can use,' Kitty speculated. 'Could be one or two whole plates just chipped at the edges.'

They could hear the clatter Hezekiah was making, as he brushed up those items broken beyond recall and sorted out the more possible pieces.

'I've a mind to go down and help him,' Tish said. 'Dinner's going to be late.'

'Don't do that,' Kitty put in quickly. 'It makes things worse for her if we don't keep out of the way.'

It was a very subdued Mrs Skinner, in a clean change of clothing, who at last called the lady assistants down to their meal. She herself had washed and dried the salvaged crockery, and this was sufficient to see them through until a new service could be bought. Which may be never, she thought to herself. She stole a furtive glance at the girls as they sat eating at their table, and her spirits improved; not one of them showed signs of having witnessed anything untoward; where she had feared smirks, she found none.

The shop-window spreers and the hat-elastic buyers were nowhere to be seen; nor was there a hint of a genuine customer.

'You'd think we had the plague,' Kitty muttered to Tish, putting two cups of tea on a polished oak tray for the Skinners. She had just returned with the basketful of bread, and had been subjected to lively probing on the related questions of Mrs Jacks' dismissal and rat-runs.

Tish walked out of the scullery, carrying the Skinners' tray with care, yet slopping the tea into the saucers. 'I reckon we must have,' she said. 'Lift that brisket out, Kitty; it smells done.'

The dearth of trade that afternoon had resulted in a smooth takeover of Mrs Jacks' duties by the assistants; but long before closing time, there were many domestic women knocking on the back door, begging for employment; rats or no rats, these workers could not afford to be squeamish. One of them was appointed to start on the Monday.

*

The first thing Hezekiah did after Sunday breakfast was to take a brisk walk to the hospital. He was not allowed near the ward, of course, but was advised, after a wait, that Miss Cecilia Bingle had recovered consciousness during the previous afternoon and was as well as could be expected.

The girls were overjoyed. 'We'll get some flowers,' Kitty suggested.

'Flowers on a Sunday?' Eliza queried.

Kitty told her there was always a chap who sold flowers outside the cemetery.

Tish shivered. 'Don't talk about the cemetery.'

'It makes no difference to the flowers where you get them,' Kitty stressed. 'We'll buy them, and leave them with the porter, or someone.'

'They might let us take them up,' said Eliza, rather fearfully. 'Tish and I could see her.'

The idea pleased Tish. 'We wouldn't stay long, because of her mam and dad, and people.'

Kitty was looking miserable.

'I thought you wouldn't be able to come,' Eliza said to her. 'It would be nicer for Cissy if you were with us.'

'I think she'll be too poorly to see so many of us. I will come, though, just in case I can have a second with her.'

'What about Henry?' Tish asked.

'He'll have to wait, won't he?'

'I don't know how much longer you slowcoaches are going to take,' called Hezekiah. He was so relieved to hear of Miss Bingle's improved condition that he sounded relatively benevolent. 'We've something to offer thanks for this morning, if ever we had,' he observed, as the girls joined him and his wife for the walk to church.

'I'm surprised,' said Jinny to him, as they led the

way, 'that the Bingles didn't have the decency to let us
know last night. They don't seem to care about other
people's peace of mind.'

'Well, we know now,' Hezekiah said heartily. 'The
good Lord has answered our prayers, and Councillor
Bingle hasn't a leg to stand on.'

'I wouldn't say that,' she replied. 'We're not out of
the wood yet – not by a long chalk. That girl will never
have to get a headache as long as she lives, if he's not
going to sue.'

The assistants kept at a distance behind them.

'I wish I could go to Bethesda,' said Eliza, very
quietly.

'I wish I could go to St Mary and St Modwena's,'
Tish said.

'The Scotch Kirk will do for me,' Kitty declared. 'All
I have to say is, *God, I don't hate you, after all*. That should
tickle him to death.'

Tish was horrified. 'Kitty Catchpole, you could be
struck dead, saying things like that! It's no laughing
matter!'

'You won't let God and me be human, Tish. That's
your trouble.'

'But God the Father isn't human,' Eliza put in. 'Tish
is right.'

'Ah, you both take church too seriously,' Kitty said.
'And that reminds me, Tish Kelly: none of your nonsense about St Jude, this time! Remember, Eliza and
yours truly had a hand in it.'

Tish's voice shook. 'I wish you'd shut up on a Sunday. You've got all the other days of the week for that
kind of talk, and Cissy isn't better yet.'

No further exchange took place before the Bazaar
group reached the Kirk. They walked down the aisle,
with the Skinners receiving no answering nods or

smiles from those already seated. Indeed, Mrs Floyd's chin crumpled, as if she were about to burst into tears, when in reality it was nothing more than a facial twitch of terror, in case Mrs Skinner recognized the new silk bonnet she was sporting. Jinny did, but how could she prove it, when Masons' stocked the same model, and neither she nor Hezekiah had held a post-mortem on the remains? She was deeply sorry that she could not blame her husband for this, as she recalled how she had urged him to throw the rat evidence quickly on the kitchen fire.

The Skinners and their contingent took their places, looking no more to right or left; as far as they were concerned, this was a congregation of profiles. They made their responses, they sang the hymns, and they listened stiff-backed to Macpherson's third-rate sermon, which had been sent to him by post, for a modest expenditure, together with nine more. Had they been the only worshippers present, the segregation could not have been more effective. Tish and Eliza were on edge; Kitty was ready to whistle the hymns; Hezekiah and Jinny were filled with apprehension and wrath, in equal proportion.

It was a new experience for Hezekiah and Jinny to be favoured with a cool farewell from the minister, and a handshake that slid away too fast towards the parishioner who came behind their lady assistants. It had taken today's personal affront to open their eyes to the one served each Sabbath to their staff.

They stood outside Ward 14 on the third floor of the Bridgemouth General Hospital with other early visitors, all concentrating on the half-glazed doors, through which they caught the occasional glimpse of a nurse, as she hurried meaningfully across the ward. Was she rushing to attend to Cissie?

Eliza held the small irises and early daffodils in a screw of white paper. The young trio stood close together and talked in an undertone.

'Miss Heggy?' The middle-aged man spoke in surprise.

Eliza turned in confusion. 'Councillor Bingle,' she said, hesitantly, 'these are the senior lady assistants, Miss Catchpole and Miss Kelly.'

Councillor Bingle was more courteous to the young ladies than he might be subsequently to their employers. He would speak to the nurse when the doors were opened. He was sure his daughter's three friends would be allowed to go in, but only for a few minutes. Mrs Bingle was resting down the corridor until it was time to go in. Cissy's church friends had been asked not to visit for some days yet.

Thus it was that they stood by the iron bed, halfway along the ward, looking down at the bandaged head and drawn face of its occupant. Cissy's complexion appeared smoother, with its absence of colour. She smiled up at them, as Eliza handed her the flowers: 'Wasn't I silly?' she said.

He was not at the Ferry Head. He was nowhere on the promenade.

'I'll wait outside,' said Tish when they reached the Pier Hotel.

Kitty investigated the tea room, but no Henry was there. 'It's hopeless,' she said, as she joined Tish again. 'There's no point in trailing along to the Queen's. He's probably in Hampden Square by now. He might have waited!'

'I don't see why,' said Tish. 'Look at the time by that clock. Maybe he went to Skinners' Place?'

'No, I shouldn't think so. I'm not crossing the water; it's too late. You and I can have tea in there, and then we'll go home. I can write him a letter.'

'We keep spending your money. It isn't elastic.'

'One pot of tea for two, and pastries, please,' Kitty ordered, with something like the authority of a Henry Bonham.

The old waiter wondered what had happened to the chief officer. Had he set sail? She was a quiet young lady, and her friend seemed a nice type, too. He hoped they were not touting, so that he wouldn't be told to get shut of them – to request them to leave.

Henry had not approached the Bazaar; he had kept strictly within the area of the promenade and Ferry Head, growing more and more testy as no Kitty hove in sight. He reminded himself that this was the second time he had been kept waiting. As she arrived at the ferry, he was mid-stream, heading for Laverport. After tea and a stimulating game of chess with Eric, he wrote a lukewarm note to Kitty, asking her to meet him, if she could manage to be prompt, on the Wednesday following, at the usual hour and place.

Henry had done well to give the Bazaar a miss; his arrival might have coincided with that of the Bingle parents, who had made directly for that establishment after visiting their daughter in hospital. Far from taking their Sunday ease in bed, the Skinners were on their feet, dealing with two adversaries who put even Minnie Jacks in the shade, since what the former wanted in brute force, they made up for in a cold acumen unknown to that valiant creature.

The doctor's report on Cissy had been favourable; she was expected to recover quickly, given rest and good after-care at home, but she would not be discharged from hospital for some days to come. Councillor Bingle demanded the return in full of the apprentice fee paid on her behalf, plus the same amount again as compensation for the disfigurement of stitches, and the suffering endured, in consequence of rat-infestation. If the Skinners preferred to settle in court, he would instruct his solicitors to act accordingly, with the compensation set at a higher sum. While this ultimatum was being delivered, primarily to Hezekiah Skinner, the two wives were engaged in their own set-to, in which Mrs Bingle, like her husband, proved the superior. Shouting got the Skinners nowhere. Apprentice fees were not returnable, Hezekiah yelled. Councillor Bingle only had to read the agreement he had signed to find that out. As for assessment of injuries, and their compensation value, Hezekiah would be taking expert advice.

The Skinners could do as they pleased, the councillor announced, as he and his wife prepared to depart. This matter of infestation was already being bandied about from one end of Bridgemouth to the other; if the Skinners would like it to hit the press, they could go ahead.

'I'll see you in hell first!' Hezekiah thundered as he slammed the front doors to, after his visitors.

Councillor and Mrs Bingle trod carefully to their gig, as if every few inches of gutter might be hiding a Bazaar rat.

Mrs Skinner's new 'housekeeper' turned out to be the antithesis of her predecessor: small and frail, where

Minnie had been large and brawny, quiet-spoken, where Minnie had been loud, she fitted Jinny Skinner's bill to a T. At least, Mrs Ethel Mellors would not break into violence like that ugly brute, Jacks.

The lady assistants were shocked to see such a tiny individual at work on the Monday, and were astonished at the results of the little woman's labours.

'She's as good as Mrs Jacks,' Tish observed. 'I don't know how she does it.'

'She'll fall in the copper before the day's out,' Eliza prophesied.

Ethel Mellors knew all about the Bazaar; she lived in the same street as Minnie Jacks. Minnie had told her to stick out for six bob a week, but Mr Skinner had cut it down to five, and glad she was to get it, with four mouths to feed, and a husband taken bad with the consumption. She reckoned she was lucky, or so she told Kitty, in a burst of confidence. It was Mrs Mellors who let on, also, that Minnie had gone straight to Masons' to ask for a job, but there was nothing doing. Fortunately for her, she then bumped into Mrs Bellingham-Smith, who immediately offered her two days a week at two shillings; two more jobs like that and Minnie would be in clover, taking home her six bob by Saturday night. Whether more work would crop up was another affair.

Mr and Mrs Skinner had not got over the Bingles' Sunday call; the memory of everything said remained with them, and the threat of court action oppressed both of them cruelly.

'It's that Jacks!' vowed Jinny. 'She's spreading her damned lies about, you see if she isn't!'

'It's never her,' Hezekiah replied morosely. 'People won't take much notice of Minnie Jacks and her tales. It's the Bingles that have emptied the shop.'

The two were sitting by the kitchen fire, taking their mid-morning refreshment; like others recently, it was an event without precedent at the Drapery Bazaar. Miss Kelly had instructions to let Mrs Skinner know if her presence was required at the cash desk; Miss Catchpole was in charge of the floor. Miss Heggy, had the Skinners seen her, was occupying a customer's chair; she had positioned herself reasonably out of sight while she scribbled a letter to her parents.

Dear mum and Dad,
    You will have heard the terble story about my freind Cissy Bingle and the rat, Me and Tish we never stop praying she woud come round and Saturday she did, Yesterday Sunday the 3 of us went to hospital with flowers she looks very white and all bandiges, Then there is Mrs Jacks, who through ever dish and plate in the scullry at Mrs Skinner, She must have nine livs and no mistake not that us lady assistants blame Mrs Jacks she was as you migt say goded and Kitty says she is not a bad woman at hart, she got the sack We have a Mrs Mellers We are still very unhappy about Cissy she is the ony freind I ever had, I am glad you never put me to Masons

Your Loving Daughter
Eliza XXXXXXXXXX

PS I am corting a nice boy in the railway ofice, Eliza

This letter was not to be posted. Soon after she had sealed its envelope, Eliza was obliged to stand up quickly, as some customer came into the shop; or rather, she thought it must be a customer until she heard the unmistakable tones of her own mother, in discord with those of Mr Skinner. As Eliza slipped her notepad under the layers of white flannel petticoats (Infants), Mrs Skinner's boots came tap-tapping from the kitchen, and her voice was involved before long in

the verbal free-for-all. Nothing would induce Mrs
Heggy to move upstairs to the sitting room; what she
had to say was common knowledge, and needed no
hushing-up. Besides, the shop was empty, wasn't it? –
and likely to stay that way. She was ashamed to have a
daughter working in such filth; the neighbours were
asking what she was thinking about – putting down
good money for a girl to catch typhus. Mrs Heggy had
come to remove Eliza, and get the fees back.

'Now see here, Mrs Heggy . . .' began Hezekiah, as
his wife made a bee-line through the alcove to push the
reluctant apprentice into the open.

There followed a most harrowing ten minutes or
more for Eliza, in which the long list of her shortcom-
ings was laid before her open-mouthed parent. The
unfortunate child had nothing to offer in self-defence;
she stood there, sobbing and nodding her head in
admission as she was accused of every transgression
under the Bazaar sun, including that of having encouraged, by her disgraceful laziness, one rat to live in
luxury at the expense of God knew how many trimmed
bonnets. But for Mrs Heggy's slut of a daughter, Jinny
raged, the Bazaar would never have seen a rat, and this
spotlessly clean shop would be packed to the doors with
customers, as it always had been.

'Oh, no! That's not true!' Kitty could bear no more.
'It was nothing to do with Eliza.' She faced the angry
Skinners and Mrs Heggy, determined to tell all.

For the first time in his business career, Hezekiah
laid hands on a lady assistant in front of his wife, and
with no adulterous design. Kitty found herself pushed
forcibly out of the shop.

'I did it! I put crumbs down! I did it! It's nothing to
do with . . .' she screamed. 'You let go of me! You're
hurting!'

Hezekiah marched her upstairs, getting himself badly kicked in the process. 'I'll deal with you when they've gone,' he wheezed, as his breath threatened to give out. 'One more word, and you follow Minnie Jacks! And your pal, Kelly! The pair of you can pack your bags. I hope that's plain.' He tottered downstairs, leaving Kitty slumped on the top landing.

Jinny Skinner snorted. 'We can take no notice of that,' she said. 'Loyalty among thieves, they call it.'

Mrs Heggy was listening to no more. Her daughter had been labelled, among other things, a slut and a thief; defamation of character, that was. Mrs Skinner could look out.

Hezekiah reappeared at the moment where Jinny realized she had gone too far. Mrs Heggy ordered Eliza to get her things together at once; they were leaving. Mr and Mrs Skinner would be hearing further from Mr and Mrs Heggy.

Eliza ran upstairs to cry in Kitty's arms. 'I don't want to leave,' she wept. 'I don't want to.'

Kitty helped her to carry her trunk from the boxroom and to throw her possessions into it. The cabbie carried it down the stairs and out of the shop.

As Eliza and her mother were reunited at the shop door, Hezekiah shouted after his junior assistant, 'Don't bother writing for a reference! You'll be getting none from me.'

It was then that Mrs Heggy played her trump card. 'Mr Mason doesn't want references from Skinners' Place; they wouldn't be worth the paper they were written on, he says. Eliza starts there Wednesday morning.' With that, she steered her dumbstruck daughter into the waiting cab.

Hezekiah and Jinny gaped blankly at each other; they were shattered. He was the first to regain his wits.

Addressing Miss Kelly, who, since the start of the Heggy drama, had been transfixed in Haberdashery, he demanded a bit of action: 'You can tell your hysterical friend to come down and take charge of this side of the shop. Then you can take yourself through the alcove.'

'Yes, sir,' Tish answered, glad to escape from the battlefield for a few minutes.

'You put your foot in it, fair and square!' he hissed at Jinny. 'Did I hear her say you called her daughter a *thief*? You must be demented! We'll be lucky to get away with the full fees to shut that woman up. God help us, if Bert Heggy comes here after work; he could arrive with a cleaver.'

Jinny turned on her heel and stamped up the steps to her cash office.

A thin face peered fearfully inside the shop at the domestic quarters' end.

'Well?' Hezekiah bawled. 'What's wrong with *you*?'

Mrs Mellors swallowed hard; she had overheard more than she had bargained for, this first morning: 'Please, sir,' she stammered, 'there's two girls at the back, wants to know about a job going. Something about a Miss Bengal, they said it was.'

'Was it now?' He made with awful strides past the shrinking Ethel, almost flattening her against the wall as he went. 'There's no assistant's job here,' he stormed, as he rushed through the scullery. 'And when there is, it'll be advertised in the front window and will be for young *ladies* only.'

The two girls fled as if the devil himself were after them.

Mrs Heggy's bombshell was sufficiently near to the truth for her to use it. Eliza had a short interview at 9 a.m. the next day, when she was indeed told to report for work on the Wednesday, in Masons' Household Goods basement. The job was non-residential, and no training premium was needed, but it was imperative that Mrs Heggy should get that refund from the Skinners. Eliza could do with new clothes, and her tram fares would be mounting up.

Promotion prospects in Masons' new department were held by her parents to be more interesting than working in Gowns and Millinery at the dying Drapery Bazaar. The miserable Eliza felt that pots and pans were something of a comedown. However, she was cheered by the possibility of meeting her young man most evenings, and of taking him home to meet her father and mother.

After work on Wednesday, she made straight for the hospital, armed with Cissy's favourite sweets – half a pound of pink and white Turkish Delight. She had shaken most of the loose icing sugar out of the bag under the hospital bushes, so that it would not spill over Cissy's bed. That was the worst of old Mrs Aitcheson: you could count on one ounce of icing sugar to every half-pound of Delight; she apparently saved it up for certain customers. Next time, Eliza would pluck up courage to tell her about it; or she would get her mother to go in for it.

Councillor Bingle was detained at a meeting, and Eliza had Cissy all to herself for a quarter of an hour, until Mrs Bingle arrived.

The patient seemed little better than before. Eliza could not tell her that, of course, and she was worried to find her so dispirited.

'I'm going home on Friday,' Cissy said.

'You'll love that!'

'Yes. It's earlier than I'd thought.' Cissy turned her head away on the pillow. 'Will you come and see me?'

'Of course I will. I expect Arthur will be there every night!'

'He hasn't been here once.'

'Arthur was put off coming!' Eliza explained. 'Your dad told the Band of Youth you were too ill for visitors.'

Cissy had turned back, in the twinkling of an eye, towards Eliza. 'Did he?' she said. 'I wish dad wouldn't always decide what's best for me.' But her face had brightened. She searched around in her locker and produced a slim packet of correspondence, tied with purple ribbon. From it, she extracted a sepia picture postcard, depicting the Laverport Central Station.

'Cissy, what a spiffing card! And he says he hopes to see you soon, *Love, Arthur* . . .'

'All the same, there's more in life than Arthur.' Cissy looked depressed once more, in spite of Eliza's emphatic disagreement with that theory. 'I wanted to come back to the Bazaar,' she went on, 'and now I can't. My dad told me, Monday night. I didn't want them to go there, mum and him. It wasn't the rat's fault that I cut my head, and we didn't see rats all over the place, did we? I told him that, but he won't let me go back.'

'I've got something to tell you,' said Eliza. 'I've left.'

'You've left the Bazaar? Eliza! Whatever for?'

'It was awful. You never heard such things as they said about me. They said I was bone-lazy, and then Jinny Skinny told my mum I was a slut and a thief.'

Cissy was galvanized into real signs of life. She sat up in bed and took hold of her friend's hand. 'That's a sinful thing to say about you! It's a wicked, wicked lie.'

'It was because Kitty was sticking up for me.' Eliza wiped her eyes angrily with her lace-edged handkerchief. ' "Loyalty among thieves," Jinny Skinner said, so that was making out me and Kitty were thieves. My mum was there, Monday, like your mum and dad – was

it Sunday? She'd come to take me away, on account of
the typhus.'

'Who's caught typhus?'

'No one that I know of; but she told them I was
leaving the Bazaar, so I left, and I'm at Masons'.'

Cissy flopped back on her pillows. 'I suppose you're
upstairs in Millinery, or in their Gowns? Or have they
put you on the ground floor in Baby Linen?'

'No, I'm living at home. I'm working in the basement, in Household Goods,' Eliza replied in embarrassment. 'I'm Hardware, really; pots and pans. I wish
I was China. It's nothing to laugh at, Cissy,' she added,
on the defensive. 'Someone has got to sell them.'

'I know they have,' Cissy said comfortingly. 'And
there's one thing – you'll see the customers. They
wouldn't have me, last time I tried there – before I went
to the Bazaar, that was. They wouldn't have me behind
the counter, but they said I could try again later, for
their Mail and Despatch, when the basement got
going.'

Eliza flung her arms round Cissy and fairly lifted her
off the pillows. A passing nurse skidded to a halt, and
remonstrated with both patient and visitor, restoring
order to the bedcovers with ungentle tugs and tucking
in. Eliza sat back on her chair, suitably circumspect.
When the woman had moved on, both girls dissolved,
after their old habit, in muffled giggles.

'We must shut up, Eliza,' said Cissy, trying to set the
example. 'My mum will be here soon from Mothers'
Union.'

'Right,' Eliza said, with an effort. 'Now, listen,
Cissy . . .'

'No, you listen . . .'

'You're giggling again! *Listen*! You've got to apply to
Masons' *at once*, before someone else grabs that job.'

'I've got it. My dad reminded Mr Mason, and I've got it. Look out! She's coming back.'

Sitting bolt upright, under the disapproving glare of the same staff nurse, who had paused at her table in the middle of the ward, Eliza said properly, 'And when do you take up your employment, Miss Bingle?'

'As soon as the doctor says I can, Miss Heggy; by the end of the month, perhaps.'

Eliza's back relaxed. 'We'll be able to go out every evening, you, me, Arthur and Percy, if we want to. And I don't care about the pots and pans, really. They haven't to be *tried on*, that's one thing.'

'And someone's got to wrap things up for the carter,' said Cissy. 'Here's my mother. Mum, Eliza has a job at Masons'; isn't that lovely?'

Mrs Bingle kissed the young girl who meant so much to her daughter, and Eliza left the ward, walking on disinfected air.

'D'you think they'll be getting two more assistants?' Tish wanted to know.

'No, I don't,' said Kitty flatly. 'They won't get one, let alone two. How much have we taken since Monday? Five bob, all told – if that.'

'It might improve, come Christmas.'

'That's months off. I don't want to scare the lights out of you, Tish, but if you hear of anything going, you'd better take a snatch at it.'

'And leave you? Kitty, I couldn't do that! You wouldn't leave me, would you?'

'One of us may have to go first. We can't both sit around waiting to be fired; that's all I'm saying. If we found ourselves two jobs in Bridgemouth, at least we could see each other.'

'By all that's holy, how can you talk of such things?' Tish whispered.

'Christ Almighty,' returned Kitty, heatedly, 'how can you duck your head and pretend you're safe? Skinners' Place is going to close, Tish-girl,' she spelt out deliberately. 'The stock will be sold off cheap, the shop will stand empty, the two of them will retire on what they've salted down.'

Tish could scarcely trust herself to speak. 'Should we try for Masons'?' she got out.

'Why not? Why don't we try all the shops in town? Every girl in Bridgemouth goes for Masons'. I bet we don't stand a dog's chance at the Emporium.'

'Isn't it a bit mean to be trying before they've sacked us?'

'Don't start on about rats.'

'I wasn't. I was on about us.'

Kitty groaned. 'Never mind. The only thing you've got to remember is that the Skinners don't have your kind heart. They'd put us both in the street tomorrow and never bat an eyelid. We'll write our applications when I get back tonight.'

Tish saw the wisdom in this. 'I'll get going on the windows,' she said.

'And no killing yourself on those. From now on, we give them the odd flick, and dress one dummy, see? I'll have to dash. If I'm late again, he'll begin to think it's a habit.'

A new rota for window-dressing had come into force, with only one girl on duty. Tish was not looking forward to this arrangement. Kitty had argued for a fortnightly stint, with both lady assistants on duty together, but Hezekiah and Jinny had remained adamant, with their high-falutin' palaver on 'standards' and so forth. In the end, as Kitty said to Tish, the effect of ca'canny tactics would persuade them that the ruling was a failure.

Tish waited at the back door to watch Kitty go. Before passing through the gate, Kitty called back, 'Be thinking about our letters!'

'What letters would they be?' asked Jinny Skinner, dropping the lace curtain.

'What are you talking about now?'

'The Catchpole girl, shouting back to the Kelly, *Be thinking about our letters*.'

'Good God, woman, how should I know? Love letters, most likely,' Hezekiah growled from the bed. 'Remind me afterwards to write to Nat Dowson; no point in piling up cottons we can't sell.'

Although Henry was on his dignity as he came to the ferry exit, the sight of Kitty was more touching than he had calculated. His face, which was meant to look composed, or even aloof, lit up with pleasure, and his kiss was far from dutiful. 'What a little waif you look!' he exclaimed, holding her at arm's length for better scrutiny. 'You haven't been ill, have you?'

'No. I don't know where to start – there's so much to tell.'

'Try the beginning.'

He listened closely, as they crossed the water, to everything Kitty had to say, and this included her apologies for visiting Cissy Bingle when she was supposed to be with him.

'And you say no rat-catcher has been called in?' he said with anger. 'It's high time we had legislation on vermin! I call it criminal to do nothing about infested premises.'

'Mr Skinner has put bait down somewhere; there was only one rat, you know.'

'They'll be sidestepping his bait; and one rat didn't have those silk bonnets all to itself. No, they'll be doing a spot of resettling, still in the Bazaar, I fancy. But what a chapter of accidents! Eliza fired, and Cissy not coming back – what will they do now for jobs?'

Kitty had no knowledge of that, nor could she speak of her supporting role in the rat drama, and of how near she had come to making a clean breast of it. 'The shop's empty these days,' she said. 'The Welsh, the Scotch, the lot – they're all giving it the go-by. Skinners' Place was fighting Masons', anyway, but this has put the top hat on it.'

'If that is so, what will Kitty and Tish do for work?'

Henry approved of their plan to apply at once to Masons'; he appreciated a little foresight in women; but what was wrong with Laverport? It struck him that they would have a wider choice in a big city, and it would be more convenient to have Kitty closer to Hampden Square.

'There are still more people after the jobs in big cities,' Kitty said, 'so it can work out the same. You need a good reference. Tish has her Father MacManus, but she got nowhere in Laverport before. She was glad to take Bridgemouth, like me.'

'Who was your referee, then?'

'Our vicar at home. He doesn't carry much weight, either, unless you want domestic service. A vicar in the town would be better.'

'I thought you went to the Scotch Kirk on a Sunday morning?'

'I've told you about him before.'

'You have never mentioned him.'

When Henry had been given a detailed run-down on

the Reverend Andrew Macpherson, he had to agree that a testimonial from him would do less than justice to a Bazaar assistant.

They were at the corner of Hampden Square, and Henry had other things to think about. 'Eric is looking forward to meeting you,' he said.

Kitty's face fell. 'Oh. Is he there?'

'Well, of course he's there, you softy! He lives there, doesn't he?'

'I don't like *him*,' Kitty announced decisively. 'He can budge off.'

'What's wrong with him?' laughed Tish.

'You won't laugh, if you ever meet him. He's just horrible. Henry shouldn't have asked me what I thought of him.'

'Of Eric?'

'Yes. He says I'm never to tell lies, then when I tell him Eric Budge is stuck-up he doesn't like it. He wants me grovelling in adoration, like himself.'

'Not *adoration*, Kitty. A man doesn't adore another man.'

Kitty gave Tish an odd look. 'Doesn't he?'

'He can't, can he? I mean, how could he?' Tish was flustered. 'He can like him a lot, I suppose, and admire him.'

Kitty gave up.

Her visit to no. 28 had been a disturbing experience. It could have been good, without Eric, though Kitty could not shake off the feeling that to keep Henry, she would have to accept this friend of his. He was leaning against the bannister at the head of the stairs as Henry and Kitty entered the narrow hall. Gazing down on them, he said something like, *Milady Kitty, I presume*, which Henry found amusing.

Eric looked as thin as Kitty herself; his face seemed all eyes; wearing a green silk smoking-jacket, handsomely embroidered, he should have been carrying an elegant cigarette holder to complete the picture. Instead, he held a porcelain pomander on a black cord, which swung like a censer as he came down the staircase.

Kitty's reply that she was *very well, thank you* to his *how d'you do?* had him convulsed, yet she could see nothing hilarious in that. The colour of those heavily shadowed eyes unnerved her: they were a beautiful green, like a cat's, and they blinked slowly. Kitty wondered if his eyes changed colour with his jackets.

Eric allowed Henry to remove Kitty's coat and hat, watching the procedure closely. She had the impression that Eric was stripping her, layer by layer – that he knew of the armpit-split in her camisole, and the missing hook on her underbodice.

Henry was childishly happy to be introducing them to each other. Eric, for his part, had been unable to contain his impatience, he said, until Kitty's arrival. His fire upstairs had gone out while he was taking a breather in Hampden Square gardens, and he was an utter ass with fires, just like dear Henry, whereas she was a natural with them, or so he had been told. It must be quite marvellous to have these things at one's fingertips, in a manner of speaking. She wouldn't like to live there, would she, and see to his fire, and so on? She wouldn't? Then perhaps she would be a good girl and see to it now?

Kitty looked at Henry for support and found none. She went, not too meekly, to scrape out cinders and ash, to bring sticks, paper and matches, to set Eric's fire once more ablaze.

Henry said he was proud of her; she was a very clever girl – and a perfectionist, too, he was pleased to see, as she brushed the hearth and wiped it clean with a floor cloth. Meanwhile he and Eric had busied themselves quite commendably with the tea, which was now on the dining-room table. Eric expected them to take tea in the house; he had gone to endless trouble the day before, toddling around his favourite suppliers to buy the food.

Kitty made her way, in a rebellious frame of mind, to the bathroom. As she came to what was now Eric's bedroom, her resentment increased. The door was half open; pushing it wider, she looked inside. What she saw was hard to take in; the bed was unmade, and every available surface was strewn with ebony-backed hair-brushes, cravats, shoes, slippers, day and nightshirts, socks and much more besides. Did Eric always have two sets of pillows, and sleep on both? Was there a girlfriend, who borrowed one of his nightshirts? She grew afraid and retreated, to remove the coal dirt off her hands in the bathroom basin.

After tea, Henry leaned back in his dining chair, and declared he did not know how Eric did it. Kitty remarked that she did, having seen the disgusting state of the kitchen. Eric thought that very droll, very droll indeed. His charwoman would clear it on Friday, if Kitty felt unable to cope. Friday seemed a long way off, Kitty thought as she went to the kitchen. It was not just the tea things, of course; no real washing-up had taken place since the unlucky charlady last came. She was obviously not coming daily; cups and plates were being held under a tap as required. If Kitty tidied up, there was no guarantee that the same muddle would not pile up again by Friday. That poor woman! Having

searched for an apron and found none, Kitty once more
rolled up her sleeves and set to work.

She was drying the milk pan when Henry finally
appeared in the doorway. All the crockery was now
clean and stacked away. Henry wondered aloud at her
efficiency; only a woman who loved doing it could work
like that. When she told him that she hated washing
dishes, she hated lighting fires, she hated . . . he
whisked her off, to silence the protests on their sitting-
room rug.

'When Henry and me went upstairs,' Kitty continued to Tish, 'Eric's fire was nearly out again. He was
sitting almost on top of it, with a face like thunder.'

'Where had you been?'

'In *our* sitting room. There's no conversation for us
two when he's around; he takes over and cuts me dead.
I might not exist.'

'Henry shouldn't let him do that.'

'I'm the outsider, that's why.'

'You won't always be; then you can cut Eric dead.'

'That'll be the day,' said Kitty. 'Let's get on with
those letters.'

Henry could tell that in spite of Kitty's sorry performance at his table, the Old Man had not taken
against her; on the contrary, he had spoken of her since
with some warmth, though it was still tinged with
amusement.

It did not require much persuasion, therefore, to get
two of the briefest of references from him; they testified
to the probity, efficiency, willingness and God-fearing
ways of a couple of shop assistants, one of whom he had
not even set eyes on. The captain could trust Henry not
to promise too much to either of them. Washing his

hands in mime, he calculated with relief that his ship would soon be ready for the new freight and a newly signed-on crew to see to it. In next to no time, the chief mate would be rescued from the young women of Laverport and district.

On Friday morning, three letters lay on the door mat for the lady assistants – two for Kitty and one for Tish.

Tish opened hers first. It brought a terse rejection from Edgar T. Mason, Staff and Dry Goods. Rising nineteen, Edgar was a spiky chip of the old block.

'What does yours say?' Tish asked Kitty, dismally.

Kitty was in the act of opening Henry's envelope. 'What's that? Not from Masons'?' She read Tish's letter rapidly and put down the one from Henry, to tear open hers. 'Same. *All vacancies are advertised.* The liars! *Nothing residential to offer for some time ahead.* Thank you very much, Mr Edgar T. Mason. I hope you get rats in your soup.'

They looked at each other. The thought of rejection, though ever present, had not felt so leaden until now.

'Good thing the Skinners were late down,' Tish remarked.

Kitty examined the outsize **M** and the small *asons for Merchandise* rubber-stamped on the back of the envelope and nodded. Masons' seemed to have dropped 'Emporium' from their title.

Mrs Skinner had her narrow eye on Kitty Catchpole. The girl's head was lowered at table, and most definitely not in prayer. 'Miss Catchpole!' Jinny warned.

Kitty put away Henry's letter and attacked her watery porridge with renewed hope.

Hezekiah shifted his eyes from the folded *Argus* by his

side plate. He and Jinny had talked long into the night, and now he was suffering from their late rising. He had read enough of that throat-slitting case to make his curiosity a torment; it would be a pleasure to get rid of this place so that he could enjoy his paper at table in comfort.

Jinny asked herself if they were doing the right thing, and if anybody would be likely to bite. Nobody local would offer a price for the Bazaar as it stood; their only chance of selling the goodwill lay in catching some innocent buyer from further away. And the shop was not as spick and span as it used to be. She must speak to that skinny Mrs Mellors, who would have to help out more with the shop cleaning – not that those two over there were exactly killing themselves these days. She must draft them, one at a time, into more polishing during shop hours; they could help Mellors with all the window-cleaning, too, inside and out, to advance that job a bit; the shop windows, in particular, had never been more dingy: a fine front the Bazaar was showing to the world!

When Hezekiah had thanked God for what all four had received, and had escaped with the *Argus*, Jinny Skinner came over to the assistants' table.

'Wait for it!' breathed Kitty into the new milk jug.

'Miss Kelly,' Jinny began, 'what exactly did you *do* in the shop windows on Wednesday? Put the jug down, Miss Catchpole. I have something to say to both of you.'

She lost that round. Tish was not called upon to fight, for Kitty took over and knocked Mrs Skinner's arguments out of the ring. Window-dressing, if the Skinners wanted the job done properly, was in future to be worked by the two lady assistants one week, and by their two employers the next.

'So we'll be free next Wednesday for any interviews in Laverport,' Kitty said to Tish, in the safety of their attic.

'If they give them on a Wednesday.'

'They've got to, if they want people with experience like us.' Kitty was glowing, after the verbal exercise. She handed over the captain's written tribute to the astonished Miss Laetitia Kelly.

'*To whom it may concern*,' Kitty sang, '*one* for *you*, and *one* for *me*!' She went on more quietly: 'Henry says we're to try Maxwell Dilk's. *I am calling in there on your behalf*, he says. Yes, well, you and me will get writing to Maxwell Dilk's tonight.'

'Maxwell Dilk's!' Tish repeated with rapture, hugging her testimonial. 'That's where the quality go!'

'Like Eric. He must get his jackets there, *and* his nightshirts.'

'What do you know about his nightshirts?'

'One was on his bedroom floor, and the door was open,' Kitty fibbed. 'Soft white cotton, with a green E on the pocket.'

'Embroidered? Glory be!'

'He favours green. The first meal I ever serve him starts off with beetroot soup, then an underdone steak with tomatoes and red cabbage, and ends up with stewed rhubarb.'

'When will that be?' Tish enquired.

'When I'm married,' Kitty returned, airily. 'We mustn't forget to send Cissy a postcard this week.'

Jinny Skinner was too much exhausted to create one of her scenes. 'You can shut the doors,' she said bitterly. 'Two of us can't man the shop. The sly, mealy-mouthed bitches! Slipping off for an interview while we slave our soulcases out, dressing windows! I don't know how I kept my hands off that Catchpole!'

'Maxwell Dilk's . . .' Hezekiah was stupefied; he spoke like one coming out of ether. 'Why wasn't I written to for references?'

'Because everyone knows we're finished, that's why. All Laverport knows, never mind Bridgemouth.'

'We shan't get a penny for the goodwill if we do close down.'

Jinny plucked a dead leaf off the aspidistra. 'Ethel Mellors can have one of my coats to come to work in, the one dyed black for your mother's funeral. She can be lady housekeeper-assistant; we'll step up her money.'

Hezekiah looked doubtful. 'Nine shillings?'

'You must be out of your mind. Seven. We'll be doing the bulk, don't forget. No cash desk. I'll have a cash box with me, behind the counter, if it's needed.' Jinny bit savagely on her Phul Nana cachou, trapping a piece of inner cheek between her false molars. The consequent pain promised to bring her contribution to an abrupt end.

This was too much of a break with tradition for Hezekiah. At all costs, his wife must be kept in that cash desk, to give tone to what was left of the establishment, and to protect what might remain of the clientèle.

'The Drapery Bazaar has always had you in the cash desk,' he said.

'Not always.'

'As near as makes no matter. You might as well take the admiral off his bridge.'

Jinny could see that.

It would be hard to say who was the next to speak. As with one voice, they both came out with the solution: 'Truscott!'

'Not a penny more than eight shillings, mind!' Jinny warned. 'And he's lucky to get that.'

'We've still got a week before those two can go,' Hezekiah went on, ' – if they want their wages, that is. They don't get a penny for this week if they don't work out their notice.'

'I'd give them it,' Jinny said with difficulty, 'to see the back of them.'

'Then you'd be stupid, as usual. We could get a buyer round here next week. They look better than your Ethel Mellors.'

Thus it was decided to check Truscott's address in the staff book, and to despatch Ethel Mellors with a written command that he should report for work the following week. It did not occur to them that their former employee might ignore the message, nor did it occur to him to do so. He was delighted to have a couple of shillings again for food.

When she returned from her successful mission, Mrs Mellors was informed of her upgrading. Delirious with her good fortune, the little woman fell to singing 'Sweet Genevieve' in the scullery and had to be called to order by Hezekiah.

It was decided, also, to maintain a working relationship with the two lady assistants throughout their last week, in case that hypothetical buyer should arrive to inspect the business. This arrangement was waived on the final Saturday, as the girls' boxes were carried out of Skinners' Place. Hezekiah and Jinny then let fly remarks that neither girl deigned to answer. When young ladies are leaving by cab, it adds to their stature, and more so, perhaps, when the first mate has insisted on a truly decent tip for the driver.

The last-mentioned was scratching his head vigorously. 'She's got a mouth on her, that one!' he observed, as Mrs Skinner slammed the back gate behind them.

Kitty grinned. 'Common, isn't she?' she said.

Mr Truscott resumed his place in Everything for the Gentleman as if he had never been away from it. He had boiled his handkerchief the night before in his milk pan, and ironed it with his little flatiron, so that its corner could triangle whitely, as of old, above his breast-pocket.

On arrival, he had had the grace to look sheepish, but the presence on the shop floor of the wilting lady housekeeper-assistant had restored his self-esteem. He now took action with the counter duster, before banging a bolt of Harris tweed into submission.

Hezekiah stroked his moustache; Jinny sent the empty cylinders whizzing back in readiness to their stations; Mrs Mellors stood midway between Baby Linen and Millinery, trembling with beginner's palsy. Mrs Mellors' hands were none too clean, after her early morning rush with fires and door-brasses.

Mr Truscott's pocket flask featured no more in his daily regime; it had lain empty for too many weeks, and would not be filled again on a wage of eight shillings. He would have to try for a cup of tea, if this quaking woman and Jinny Skinner were agreeable; he might be somewhat cowed, but he had not sunk low enough to drink Bazaar cocoa. He missed the four young girls, especially his dear Kitty Catchpole. It grieved him to see that waster, Skinner, in Fabrics. But where were the customers, for God's sake? He unrolled some heavyweight kersey, and measured out four and three-quarter yards. These he concertinaed swiftly to one side, together with his open scissors, to give full attention to the first client of the day – for many a day, if he had known it.

Word of Truscott's reinstatement must have travelled via Jacks and Mrs Bellingham-Smith. Who had told Jacks? Jinny shot a nasty look through the cash window at the skinny Mellors. Nevertheless, the Reverend Macpherson was uncommonly welcome; after him, what queue might not follow from the Scotch Kirk?

Mr Truscott had every sock in the shop spread out for examination, including the preacher's unclocked favourites.

'There is nothing rejoices the good Lord more than the return of a sinner to the fold,' Macpherson trumpeted.

Mr Truscott said he was glad to be back, himself, and he could recommend the wearing quality of these double-knit heels. No, he did not fancy the chief role of repenter at this week's Temperance Fellowship, though grateful, of course, to be invited.

It transpired that Mr Truscott had nothing for the reverend gentleman, who was distressed to meet with so little Christian humility, and such unappealing socks.

It was the last time Macpherson was to enter the Drapery Bazaar, and he was the last client ever to approach Mr Truscott's counter.

But for Kitty's presence and support, Tish would have been in a sad way during that first week. From being big fish in a third-rate establishment, each girl was reduced to a mere minnow in this first-class haberdashers and clothiers; each had to adjust to working with a substantial number of equals and several superiors. Fortunately, the standard of the new assistants' work was beyond reproach, a fact soon recognized with grudging approval by their seniors, and with watchfulness by the rest.

After submitting resignedly to apple-pie beds and other dormitory indignities, Tish and Kitty were allowed to live in peace among their twenty new associates, and could begin to count a few blessings. They had been allocated two end cots, side by side, in that long gallery of a bedroom. At the opposite end, there was an indoor lavatory and a separate cubicle, which contained six washbasins with running cold water. Tall cans stood on the floor for hot water to be brought from the kitchens, whenever wanted; beyond this washplace, there was yet another door, leading to a cast-iron bath, its white paint mottled with brown under the one cold-water tap; it was a luxury the girls had not dared to hope for. They had accepted the jobs without being shown the living accommodation, since no assistant had been available to take them upstairs. They would have accepted them, if they had been expected to sleep on the roof.

'Two shillings a week extra, and a bath,' Tish murmured. 'Not so dusty, is it?'

'And a bob for me . . . It's wonderful. We're in work; we can see Mary, and I can see Henry,' said Kitty. 'For close on two weeks,' she amended, less steadily. Then rallying, she exclaimed, 'Hell, I forgot to smash that bowl!'

'What bowl?'

'Ours, under the jug, at Skinners' Place.'

'Oh, *that*!' Tish said with a shrug.

'You must have this key back,' Henry said. 'You can use any part of the house whenever you wish, except Eric's two rooms, of course.'

'Keep it. I shan't want to come here. You ought to have the key.'

'I would like you to have this one, Kitty. You know I have a spare, so you're not taking mine.'

'Would you let Tish come?'

Henry hesitated only a fraction, but Kitty noticed. 'Yes, by all means,' he replied. 'I am sure neither of you would disturb Eric, if she did come.'

'Oh, we'd have a real get-together, me and Tish and a good half of Maxwell Dilk's, swarming all over the house! Dear Eric would be driven distracted by the vulgarity.'

Henry's mouth was set. 'You know perfectly well, Kitty . . .'

'You sound exactly like the Skinner! I always knew perfectly well for her.'

'Perhaps you did,' he commented. 'You are not always on your best behaviour, are you?'

'And what does that mean? When have I behaved badly, Mr Bonham, according to you?'

'Quite often, where Eric is concerned,' he answered stonily.

There were things that rose to her tongue but could not be said. 'Have you once considered his behaviour towards me?' she asked.

'I have, and I have not found him lacking in courtesy. I don't expect him to like a young lady who goes out of her way to be rude to him, as you do.'

Kitty considered this for a second or two. 'You keep the key,' she told him, and turned into Maxwell Dilk's side entrance; she took the twisting stone steps at a tremendous pace as far as the fourth floor. Taking out her own key, she found the keyhole blurred, and her legs aching intolerably.

*

Henry was glad of that last-minute pressure of work which always preceded the ship's departure. It kept his mind more or less off Kitty. When he had a break, he allowed himself to dwell on Eric, though he was forced to admit that his recent spells with this other glorious creature had not been conspicuously restful. Henry was growing weary of his personal position as buffer-state. Loyalty to either side achieved little, and he could see that he would soon have to make a difficult decision.

He would have agreed, also, that he was not as courageous as he might be. When with Kitty, he tended to stress Eric's case too far, without giving her much of a say in her own defence; and he took the same equivocal stand with Eric. He was unwilling to admit to either that she, or he, might have a point, and this lack of resolution oppressed him.

Why, for instance, had he disallowed last night that Eric could be abominably insolent – when he himself had been a witness to this and found himself secretly repelled by it?

Perhaps because he had invested so many hopes in that earliest meeting of his two friends, the memory of it refused to leave him. Why did Kitty, at the very first introduction to Eric, have to return that ridiculous, 'I'm very well, thank you'? It was such a howling error, and one that played right into Eric's hands. Henry had felt obliged to laugh with Eric in an effort to cover it up as one of Kitty's merrier little idiosyncrasies, but the gaffe had irritated him. And all that unreadiness on her part, to see to Eric's fire, when the poor boy had been slaving for hours preparing their superb meal! As the only woman present, who else could have been asked to do it? Similarly with the washing-up, Kitty had looked absolutely savage – but surely she had not expected men to roll up their shirtsleeves and tackle that? She did the jobs so well, too; they clearly gave her no trouble at all. He blamed himself for not appointing a woman cleaner to come in every day. Before long, there would have to be a better arrangement, for Eric's sake – that is, if he stayed on at no. 28.

He could hear Eric's scathing voice now: 'At least, I am unlikely to disgrace you at the captain's table!' How true that was! How many years would it take to teach Kitty an equal competence? *Man on Lesko*, for God's sake! His eyes closed in horror, as he switched from Eric to the captain's saloon, and recalled the howlers perpetrated in that bower of rosewood.

It was a nuisance about the wedding ring – one of the skipper's more peculiar rulings – when Henry had taken scrupulous care not to buy an engagement ring. But, apparently, she had got the message; the wedding ring was no longer in evidence. All the same, rings or no rings, he had the impression of being committed, with no easy escape route, and that – he realized – was a measure of her worth; this was not a young lady to be dispensed with on an impulse, and without a qualm. He cursed his own naïveté in buying a house, and in believing that Eric and Kitty would share the use of it.

'Drop her off in Edinburgh, dear boy,' Eric had advised. 'Stephen will immortalize her, I feel sure, with her scissors poised over a roll of red flannel: "Counter-girl of Character".' That time, he had narrowly missed a punch aimed at his head. Ducking so swiftly had brought on another attack of coughing, so that Henry had been racked with remorse.

That mention of Stephen had struck home more accurately than Henry's wild fist. Eric knew that the astute Stephen Bonham would censure any perma-nent liaison with a drapery assistant. As an established artist, he did not want for women; but if ever he decided to marry, the lady would come from his own class, or above it. Henry was not unaware of this. He would have to teach Kitty some introduction technique, at least, before he took her anywhere near his brother. There was this about Stephen – he would not turn out to be as insanely jealous as Eric. On the other hand, he might want Kitty for himself, as a model. Once again the idea left Henry agitated.

It would be a relief to sail away from these complications. Not for the first time, he wondered how a man could survive without the solace of the sea. Taking a stout envelope from his cabin chest, he slipped the Hampden Square key inside it, with no accompanying line, and addressed it to Miss Kitty Catchpole, c/o Maxwell Dilk and Co., Bridge Street, Laverport.

'It will be somewhere to go,' Tish declared. 'When it rains, it'll be better than tramping the streets, won't it?'

Kitty turned the key over and over on her palm. 'Yes, and no. I don't really know. In one way, I wish he hadn't sent it!'

'Don't you go losing it in the river,' Tish said apprehensively. 'In fact, we ought to have another one made, for safety.'

'I'll think about it.'

Kitty was heavy-hearted these days. Henry was right, she did behave badly sometimes – though not with that Eric. He was wrong there; he deliberately closed his eyes and ears to Eric's rudeness. But she had behaved badly to Henry on that last night together; not even to kiss him goodbye. . . .

'Don't cry, Kitty,' said Tish.

'Who's crying?' she returned furiously. After a pause, she had arrived at a decision: 'I'll give this key to one of the van men. There's lots of small shops round about the stables; he may know of a locksmith's.'

When Tish next went to Henry Bonham's house, she was disheartened to see the change wrought by Eric. The home she had fallen in love with, on her first visit with Kitty, was no more. Eric was everywhere; he might have only two rooms, but his presence overflowed into all the others. Even the top floor offered no escape from him; the scent of his Turkish cigarettes came floating through the doors and floorboards. She detested the man; in Tish, Kitty had the perfect ally.

Eric had tried the helpless fire-restorer act on Tish, but she had been forewarned. Neither Tish nor Kitty would lift a finger to rescue his fire; he could perish.

The girls cleared and washed any dishes they themselves had used; the results of Eric's kitchen excursions were now left by the sink for the charlady's attention. As he ate in his own room, she had that post-prandial wreckage, also, to attend to. Each Monday morning, she found neat screws of newspaper piled in the hearth of the downstairs sitting room, and a dry bundle of firewood; as she untied the wire round the small sticks, she released a brown envelope, which always contained a silver sixpence and the message: *With many thanks from Kitty and Tish*. Every Sunday afternoon, they found a clean hearth and a fire ready to burn at the touch of a match.

Every Sunday afternoon except this one. St Christopher's C. of E. nave had been chilly that morning. The subsequent meal of cold roast beef, with turnips and mashed potatoes, had been adequate but not stimulating; the prunes had been diminutive and tight-wrinkled, and the custard a near-green better suited to a canary. Food at the elegant emporium of Maxwell Dilk was no great improvement on the Drapery Bazaar's. As a result, the girls were looking forward to toasting their own bread at their own open fire, and drinking their own tea from the warm depths of their armchairs.

The hearth was clean, but for the odd scattering of ash and one grey cinder; the dirty grate held the dead remains of a fire.

'She set it. The paper and sticks have gone,' Kitty ruminated. 'The room hasn't been used, though.'

With one voice, they said, 'That Eric!'

Kitty rapped on his door and was inside his sitting room almost before his languid invitation to enter. 'How dare you light our fire?' she said with unnatural calm.

He twisted half-round from the good fire blazing in front of him and picked up his cigarette. After a long draw, he leaned back again in his chair, a slim book dangling from his right hand, to address the mantelpiece: 'My dear girl, if I care to entertain my friends in Henry's sitting room, that is certainly no business of yours. I happen to be reading. Would you mind removing yourself?' He restored the book to his lap; the long, black eyelashes swept down.

'You are a stranger to the truth, Mr Cannon-Budge.'

He laughed immoderately at that, flicking the tip of his cigarette against the head of a Buddha in green onyx. 'Nicely put, Milady Kitty. I didn't know you were capable of these neater turns of phrase.'

'I am capable of more than you think, Mr Budge,' she answered, watching his face darken at the foreshortened name. 'You and your friends have not used that room; the cushions are not crushed, the furniture is undisturbed, the magazines on the table are the way we left them, and the ashtray is clean.'

'My godfathers!' He was completely taken aback. 'Now you really impress me, my dear Watson! However, do go, will you? You are creating the most frightful draught, standing in my doorway.'

'And that's another thing: you would never use a sitting room on the ground floor, according to Henry; you are so very sensitive to draughts.' His green eyes were fixed on her; the book slipped from his lap as he fingered the large gold cross on his chest; its thick chain was long enough to strangle two girls at once. She was not afraid of him, and he was beginning to see this. 'If we have any more nonsense from you,' she went on, 'I shall report it to Henry. He wanted me and Miss Kelly to use this house as often as we liked; he didn't expect interference from his lodger.'

'What did he say?' Tish had cleared out the grate and had nearly set the fire.

Kitty helped with the top coals. 'Not much. He couldn't deny it. I don't think he'll try it on again. I don't think he'll give me fancy names again, either, after I called him Mr Budge. He didn't care for that.'

'What names does he call you? Rude ones?'

'They sound rude, the way he says them, with a sneer, like *Milady Kitty* – that's one he's always trotting out. He had a new one today, *Watkins*, or something. Lord knows what he was getting at.'

'Cheeky devil! Was he still wearing his green?'

'He wasn't, as a matter of fact. He had a black jacket on, and a sort of creamy shirt, and a huge gold cross on a big chain. Pass the box.' Kitty put a match to the fire. 'That's going to be a beauty, Tish.'

'A gold cross . . .' said Tish. 'If Eric Budge is one of us, I'll quit the Faith.'

*

They were not to be troubled any more by Eric. For some weeks, he had kept strictly out of their path when they were in the house. They had heard his distinct moves upstairs, but had never seen him. Then on their first free Wednesday afternoon, which was still a rare treat at the high and mighty Maxwell Dilk's, they arrived to find that he had gone – that he was not just missing for a short holiday. He must have left some time between the Sunday and that Wednesday; there was no untidiness in the house. The charwoman had obviously been asked to come in; if she had been dismissed, she had done a magnificent job before she went. The doors of his two rooms were unlocked, and the bed had been stripped of its dirty linen; this had been washed and ironed; it now lay folded on the ottoman at the foot of the bed. Kitty opened the wardrobe. A few clothes which she recognized as Henry's, such as his heavy dressing gown and his brown alpaca jacket, were hanging there, together with an insidious perfume that was undeniably Eric's. The knick-knacks had disappeared. No Buddha sat impassively offering its head to the brand, no ebonized brushes waited to be dropped on the floor, no pomander spread its spiced fragrance from the whatnot, and no silver-mounted manicure-set graced the chest of drawers. Every drawer in both rooms was empty; every visible sign of E. Cannon-Budge had vanished.

'The buzzard has flown!' Kitty announced.

'Do they fly back in the winter?' Tish asked.

Kitty thought it a possibility; meanwhile, they both ran up and down the stairs, dashing in and out of rooms, laughing and singing loud enough to fill the Albert Hippodrome, until Kitty collapsed on the bed Eric had usurped too long.

'You all right?' Tish stood, looking down at her.

'I'm not as young as I was,' Kitty said, breathing hard. 'Haven't got your stamina.'

'Isn't it lovely all over again, without the Budge?' Tish almost crooned, as she sank on the bed beside Kitty. If that fellow and Henry would fly off permanently, it would be just the ticket.

'We shall have to do something about Mary.'

'I know. She can't have been earning for quite a time.' Tish put the last domino into its coffin.

Kitty slid the lid across and slammed the box on the table. 'When I think of *Mary* doing that, I could die.'

'When I think of *Biddy*,' said Tish.

'Hell, yes.' Kitty sat staring at the table-top.

One of the advantages of their new situation lay in the common room for the lady assistants and the few apprentices, with its worthless collection of chairs and tables. This did provide corners where friends could sit in comparative freedom, engaged in their own conversation against the general hubbub.

'That's why she's given up her top room; she must be more in the way for Biddy than ever. She said she spends most of the night walking around the streets. Imagine it, tonight.' Tish lifted a corner of the curtain. 'Hailstones,' she murmured. 'And the risk, no matter what weather, this night of our Lord.'

'Henry's well on his way, by now,' Kitty said thoughtfully.

'Where to?'

'Morlta, or somewhere.'

'Morlta? Where would that be? There's some place called Mollta, isn't there?'

Kitty pursed her lips. 'This one's Morlta. Not as far as Valparaiso. He's back in September, he said.'

Tish digested this for a moment. 'I call it wicked,' she said, 'to leave a good house empty, doing nothing.'

'You're right there. I'd have to tell him, but there's no harm in getting Mary in there now. She'd have a week or so before he could get a letter back to me; and if he says no, then I'll have finished with him. He can take his choice.'

'He might think of the neighbours.'

'I expect he will, but he'll have to think again, won't he? I'll send her the second key, then she doesn't have to wait till Sunday.'

If Henry had suspected Mary's condition from the outset, he had restrained his curiosity remarkably well; unless, of course, he regarded these common occurrences with indifference.

Kitty's letter brought with it no enchantment. He had put it aside for some days, but even now his annoyance hampered any attempt at a civil reply.

Why did she always indulge in this petty deceit? What other lies had she been spinning? Between them, she and her friend had driven Eric out of the house at a time when he was in need of complete rest. Eric might do better in Cassis, and he might not. The fact remained that no one should have compelled him to seek refuge there. And this girl, Mary? What class of young woman was she? How had she been living until now? What was all the mystery about Tish's sister?

Henry's heart sank; the nib scratched on the rim of his inkwell. What kind of house would the Hampden Square people think he was keeping? Would anyone pass the time of day with him again? The notion of returning to no. 28 was unattractive. And yet, if this Mary Gibson was destitute and well advanced in pregnancy, one could hardly refuse her a room: an uncomfortable analogy presented itself.

The nib, charged with the blackest of ink, touched down. He wrote without sentiment, pulling no punches. Mary might live in the house until her baby was born; after that, she and the child must obtain different accommodation. On no account was any other pregnant woman to be given shelter in his home.

'He's not exactly over the moon about it, but who's to worry on that score? Mary can stay on there,' Kitty reported.

'Please God, she'll be safely through it before he comes back,' Tish said.

'That's the next headache. Where does she go from there? What happens to the baby? Let's face it, they'd both have to be with Biddy when Henry's on leave.'

'I'm not facing it,' Tish confessed. 'I can't. I'm kidding myself it won't happen.'

'We ought to have plans, Tish.'

'How can anybody have plans without the tin?' Tish burst out. 'The bit we've saved from our raise should have gone home; all right, it's for Mary, it's got to be. What she's put by won't take her far, and when it runs out, she'll be on the parish, with that baby given away, you see if it isn't.'

'What future has it got, one way or the other?'

Tish shook her head, which did not ease the turmoil affecting it. She was being less than honest with Kitty; there was one further aspect of this situation which Kitty did not know, and which Tish was in no hurry to reveal. If Mary and her baby had to find shelter again in Temple Gardens, it would be with a very reluctant Biddy; no doubt the two would be accommodated somehow, but the older girl had not minced matters in this regard. She could ill afford a loss of earnings through another period of room-sharing; worse still, she was afraid in case Mary fell back on full-time prostitution. With the best will and the kindest heart in the business, Biddy had to protect her own pitch; she had no wish to lose clients, as she had done that first time, to a newcomer.

'She's a real nice kid, but she'll have to branch out for herself, that's all,' Biddy had told Tish. 'It's not just me that's lost out to Mary. There's other girls in the house, and I might tell you some of them's got pretty nasty.'

Tish had assured her sister that Mary would never return, but Biddy had been sceptical.

'A lot's said that before now. Anyway, don't tell her, unless you've got to. If it doesn't come to the crunch, like, there'll be no need to hurt her feelings.'

'It's got no future,' said Kitty, rousing Tish from her private reflections, 'and nobody knows this better than Mary.'

Tish felt defeated. 'I can't work that one out,' she answered, 'no more'n you can. Let's go.'

They went down, with the rest of the girls, to tackle their greasy breakfast sausage in the basement dining room.

Before midday, Kitty was feeling more herself and was able to resume her place in Fabrics. At the long dinner table, she ate her plateful of tepid cottage pie with a real hunger, after which she did justice to the Dilk jam brick, an individual tart as tough as any Abe Jenkin crust she might have tackled in former days.

'It was that awful sausage,' she confided to Tish. 'The grease . . . Just to think about it turns me over.'

For what was left of the working week, she ate abstemiously at breakfast, passing over her bacon, fried bread or fried egg to Tish, under the disapproving eye of a senior lady assistant who sat opposite. On the third morning, this young woman, who was a mere two months older than Kitty, called her to one side as they left the room.

'We don't want to see Bridgemouth table manners here, Miss Catchpole,' she said cuttingly. 'If you find Maxwell Dilk's portions too generous, you've only to tell the servers.'

'Yes, miss,' said Kitty. 'I'll remember that, miss.'

The senior looked at her sharply and moved on.

Deep breaths were her one salvation. By leaning on the counter and breathing slowly but deeply, she could just about fight it down; this routine was thrown agley if she happened to have a customer.

She would have to tell Tish now, if Tish needed telling. Kitty was leaning over a handbasin before Sunday church. 'Obvious, isn't it?' she gasped, mopping her eyes.

'The others are talking about it,' Tish replied unhappily. 'They're not a very kind lot. One of them asked me if we weren't used to good food. Good food! I could have wiped that snigger off her face.'

'I'll have to get on with it,' said Kitty, blowing her nose, 'so long as I don't faint, like our Mary. We want the money.'

'But surely you'll let him know?'

'Yes, I'll let him know. We have to remember that Mary is the last pregnant woman he'll allow in the house.'

'Holy saints, he can't be saying that, and it's his own! Watch out, let's get our coats.'

They moved out of the washplace, running a small gauntlet of hostile faces, to the locker room.

'Pleasant, aren't they?' Tish said, when they were out of hearing.

'Pure, you see. That gives them the right to look superior. It beats me why you don't look the same.'

'They'll not attain the heavenly grace,' declared Tish with conviction, 'unless they confess their pride. And neither will Henry Bonham, unless he takes care of you and his child, and marries you.'

Kitty pulled on her gloves. 'He may not believe it's his.'

'What are you talking about? It's no one else's.'

'I knew I was being a fool, Tish. If you give in to one, he starts thinking you might be easy – any other man could be having the same ... What's more, Henry never has babies. He didn't forget to tell me that.'

'He didn't, did he? Don't you love him, Kitty?'

'There are times I love him so much. . . . At the moment, I've other things to think of.'

They joined the Maxwell Dilk's queue of young ladies to walk to St Christopher's.

'That reminds me,' Tish began again. 'You know Eileen Cogan, the one with the really dark hair? Yes, you do, Kitty – in Hosiery. Well, she's not here for St Christopher's, is she? D'you know why? It's because she's at St Anne's Cathedral Church, that's why. They let you go to your own church; they trust you to go. I think that's very nice, don't you?'

'Yes.'

Tish was immediately contrite. 'But I won't, Kitty; I don't have to. I could go to St Aloysius' tonight, if I was that keen. I wouldn't leave you on your own with this bunch.'

'Maybe I'll tell Maxwell Dilk's I'm an atheist, and see how they take that.'

'But you're not, Kitty.'

'I am, you know, as near as makes no odds.'

The longish crocodile wound its correct way to the top of Bridge Street, past the roller-shuttered window of Chas. Ridler, Watchmaker and Jeweller to the Queen, whose elegantly inscribed brass would still be announcing that through some reigns to come. Kettle's, Confectioners and Pastrycooks, presented an uninspired front, its shelves neatly covered with tissue paper, and with nothing more than three-tiered wedding cakes inside its glazed cupboards. L. F. Lumley's, Pharmacist and Perfumier, like its tobacconist neighbour, Jas. Heseltine's, had a thick beige window blind, which shielded everything from view except, in the one instance, an escaped vial of Carter's Little Liver Pills – at one shilling and three-halfpence for forty – and in the other, a hint of briar stems.

The young ladies chatted in Sabbath key with one another until they reached the island monument to the late Victoria which, after only a handful of years, stood unevenly blackened with soot, where it was not bleached with pigeon-lime. A squealing tram edged around this fairly restricted roundabout, before it drove off down Queen Street. The crocodile followed the same route.

This was banking and shipping territory, where the granite-faced offices, so assiduously copied in small-scale Bridgemouth, reared sufficiently high to block out much of a day's sunshine, and to give grounded Laverportians the conviction that New York had a lot to learn. An overall air of cleanliness distinguished the flights of stone steps, and reached as far as the well-swept pavements and gutters. Laverport's business face on a Sunday was both dignified and wholesome, giving no indication of the high-powered jiggery-pokery that lay behind it for the rest of the week.

Even the hot air fanning out from the Queen Street Underground smelt sweeter this morning. The leading senior assistants turned sharp right after the station, taking their charges along the less popular road towards the port's parish church. They advanced with sure tread, and with nearly every heart eager for whatever salvation that house of God might have to offer.

Mary's gratitude to Kitty, for making sure of her comfort, was as sincere as it was quiet. These afternoons, when Kitty and Tish arrived home, as they called it, a splendid fire awaited them in the sitting room and another glowed in the kitchen. It was becoming difficult to prevent Mary from doing too much.

'We don't want waiting on hand and foot,' Kitty told her, today. 'You've done the fires, so Tish and I will make the tea. You sit down, and when we're eating, I'll tell you a story.'

'And it's not a fairy story, either,' said Tish.

Mary had loved Kitty and Tish for many a long day. The three girls sat over their kitchen fire, united by the common disaster of their poverty, and the predicament of pregnancy which burdened two of them.

To say that Mary was surprised by Kitty's news would be putting it too mildly. She was greatly shaken by it, and found it impossible to keep the disapproval out of her voice. By now, she had come to terms with her own folly, but to be told that Kitty Catchpole was just as simple as herself – this took some swallowing.

'I don't see how you could be so daft,' was her first reaction.

That, at least, raised a small laugh.

As Kitty toasted her face, fingers and bread, she filled in some of the details for Mary, without exonerating herself at all.

'I'm sorry I've disappointed you and Tish,' she said, 'though I didn't ask you to put me on a pedestal, did I? I've got to write home and tell them. They'll be disappointed, too. And I don't think Henry's going to be delighted, either. I'm one big let-down to everybody.'

'That you're not,' said Tish, staunchly.

'No, you're not,' Mary said, rallying. 'And you've been so good to me. I've no right to be making you feel low, specially as Henry's sure to marry you. He's not like that Bunny Harris. Your Henry's a proper gentleman – anybody could tell that.' Her words trailed away, unconvincingly.

'That's what I keep saying,' said Tish, 'but she won't listen. What will you do, Mary, when you've got the baby?' There – she had finally got round to putting the question which not one of them could answer satisfactorily.

'Well, like I told you, I don't want to go back to that life,' Mary said firmly. 'I had to be someone else, or I couldn't have gone on with it. That's what Biddy is – she's two people all the time; I don't know how she keeps on. She's a wonder. And there's another thing – some of the girls in the house got at Biddy, on account of me taking their regulars. I heard them going on about it, and Biddy sticking up for me like blazes. I could have pinched a few of hers for all I know. If you work the same beat, that's what happens, till you get wise to who's who. So even if I wanted, I wouldn't go back there. I suppose I'd like to go back to the Drapery, but nobody will ever take me, not with a child. If I could find a man who'd marry me, I'd say yes, like a shot, to get a home. I wouldn't be looking for love – just a home for me and the baby; but men don't pick up fallen women for their wives, if they can help it.'

'No, but we have to take any old handrag for a husband, and no questions asked,' said Tish ferociously. She was relieved, however, that Mary had not proved deaf to the irritation brewing at no. 9. That let Tish out of having to do the explaining, while at the same time it solved nothing.

Dear Kitty,

I need hardly say how horrified I was to read your news. However, I suppose I must accept it as true.

You yourself will judge how long you can work at Maxwell Dilk's. I shall do my best to come to Laverport at the end of this trip, if there is no emergency in Provence. Eric's recovery is still taking its time.

You will, of course, move into no. 28 when you wish. I hope you will disregard my previous strictures on pregnant women. Perhaps, when the child is born, we could come to some arrangement about its welfare. In the meantime, you will be receiving a regular allowance of £10 per calendar month through my bankers, so that you will be able to pay for extra clothing, food and medical attention.

I trust you will take care of yourself, and that all goes well with your friends, Miss Gibson and Miss Kelly.

> Yours,
> Henry.

Reading over his letter, Henry was satisfied it covered all he had to say. He had hesitated at the penultimate line, not wanting a *Love* to be misconstrued; he felt no especial ardour for a girl who claimed to be pregnant by him. He settled for the simpler *Yours*: its ambiguity could convey either the coolness in his heart, or the possessiveness in hers.

No. 28 Hampden Square was irrevocably lost to him. He might have to visit it once, to see how Kitty fared, but it could be dismissed as a dwelling house for himself and Eric. He was not an entirely callous man and had not altogether forgotten Kitty's undoubted charms, but Eric was never wrong. Miss Catchpole would have required grooming, in every sense of the word, to qualify for that seat at a skipper's table; and with the company she kept, she would be a handicap no ambitious officer could afford to take on.

'For two pins I'd tell him where he could put his ten pounds!' said Kitty into the towel as she patted her eyes dry. 'Do they look red?'

'Not too bad,' Tish lied.

Kitty moved over to the looking glass. 'Christ, they're all puffy! I can't go down like this.'

'Talk through your nose, and keep using your hankie,' Tish urged. 'They'll think you've got a cold. Hurry *up*! They'll have started eating.'

The two girls slipped into their places as grace was about to be said. Kitty managed a passable sneeze in the middle of it. She toyed with her porridge and declined the second course, blowing her nose with not too much ostentation.

'You seem to have a heavy cold, Miss Catchpole,' the senior assistant observed. 'You should try eating your breakfast. Feed a cold, starve a fever.'

Kitty dabbed her dry eyes, and attempted a smile. 'Goodness knows where I caught it, miss,' she said.

She kept up the nose-blowing so convincingly, as she leaned on her counter, that the floor-walker ordered her upstairs as a preventive measure; a lady assistant so visibly afflicted with the snuffles was no ornament in Fabrics; the girl looked ready to pass out. She was a good-looker and a good worker, but if she was a weakling she would have to go.

Kitty heated a little water on the gas ring in the staff cubby-hole; the smell of the gas made her feel worse, but the cup of hot water did prove helpful. She lay on her bed, and let the nausea take its slow course. It was the most comfortable morning she had known for some days; she wished she could have a bad cold for the rest of the week.

She was able, also, to reflect with more self-command on the letter that had been the cause of her red eyes. She would not dwell on the tender things Henry used to say; she would not let herself think of the twinkle in his eye, and the teasing in his voice: these had been wiped out. This was the blunt answer of the quality, as Tish called them. Where the Bunny Harrises pulled up their trousers and ran off, the Henry Bonhams wrote a letter to the bank, before doing the same. She might never see him again; she would probably never see his money. How was she to believe in promises? Her friends meant so little to him, he was still referring to Miss Gibson. . . . If he had any real interest in his child's welfare, he would give it a father. He seemed cocksure that she would go ahead with the pregnancy. He was right: she would. If the sickness wore off, she ought to be able to work a further four to five months at Maxwell Dilk's; the accepted use of sanitary pads in this dormitory would help her greatly. The regular £10, if ever it came, would cover Mary's bills. Kitty would send her mother some of it; she would break eggs with a big stick; however, if they all watched their step, she argued, they should get by. Thinking of her mother's constant need for money reminded her painfully that she had yet to announce this pregnancy to her parents. She had been putting it off for two understandable reasons: she was afraid to tell them, and she had been hoping the shock might be tempered by an announcement of marriage.

Sitting up gingerly, she moved her legs over the edge of the bed. She felt much better, if a little dizzy after the lying down. This was as good an opportunity as any to get that letter written. She took pencil and notepad from her bedside locker, and set down the bald truth for her mum and dad to read. Once she had started, the words flowed more easily than expected and her fear evaporated; they had always loved her so much, why should she doubt them now? The feint lines took to dissolving as she wrote her sad apology for disappointing them; she hoped they would believe it was a mistake she would never repeat again. She would be sending her postal order after she left Dilk's, and it should be bigger than before if all went according to plan. She sent kisses to all at home, and remained their ever-loving daughter, Kitty. It was done and she was left in better spirits, for having got it off her chest.

Mary was told she was one of the lucky ones; she had a normal delivery, twenty-seven hours of it, and six stitches. Olive Mary Gibbs had given notice of arrival around six o'clock on the Monday morning. Mary had taken herself round to the midwife's cottage to advise her that things were moving, and had been unable to get back to no. 28; the baby had been delivered in hospital the following day, on the dot of 9.15 a.m. Kitty and Tish found the midwife's note to this effect waiting at home for them on the Wednesday, and were delighted to see Mary that afternoon; no babies were on view in the ward.

'She's an ugly little thing', Mary said. 'She doesn't look like anybody I know. I've got to stay the fortnight here, worse luck.'

She was not an ugly little thing; as babies go, she was prettier than most. Tish doted on her, and Kitty was not totally averse to her.

'I wish I didn't think of Bunny Harris, and that wink of his, every time I look at her,' Kitty confessed to Tish, when Mary was upstairs in the bath.

'But she's nothing like him,' Tish protested.

'Wait till she gets his teeth.'

'Kitty Catchpole, that's not fair. It's not little Olive's fault! Besides, she's not going to have his teeth, is she, the little sweetie girl, then?'

'Lord love a duck,' Kitty sighed. 'Why don't you have one yourself and make it a day?'

'I tell you what – next week, we'll have her photo taken.'

'We're not in Bridgemouth still. You can't count on our Wednesdays. Besides, we might drag all that way for nothing if the photographer gives himself a half day.'

'Is he likely, in a big town like Laverport? Well, maybe Mary can get it done.'

'Not yet awhile. Wait till she's stronger, and Olive Mary looks a bit more human, before you get going on photographs.'

Miss Catchpole's new job as housekeeper-nanny to Mrs Gibbs of 28 Hampden Square was a subject for speculation, envy, or barely concealed derision among her ex-colleagues at Maxwell Dilk's. They had not forgotten Kitty's two months of bad turns and poor appetite for breakfast, and their gimlet eyes had noted the rounder breasts, which had popped more fasteners off her underbodice, and the thicker waist, which had her skirt-placket bulging.

'Kind of put on weight lately, hasn't she?' one of these young ladies remarked.

Tish was having a hard time of it, batting on her own. 'Kitty was always the stocky type at the Drapery Bazaar,' she invented.

'She went into a decline just before you came, like?'

'If I had my way, I'd shoot the lot of them,' Tish fumed, pacing the kitchen, 'only shooting's too good for them.'

She and Kitty had returned to the Henry Bonham house, having accompanied Mary and baby Olive to Tish's family home. There was no room available there, but such was the Kelly freemasonry that for one week the few pillows in the house could be laid at night on the parlour floor as a bed for Mary and her child. It was a draughty arrangement, but they were safe.

'Take no notice of the Dilk's crowd, Tish,' said Kitty. 'Empty vessels, that's what they are. We ought to remember the day we got those jobs, and how we skipped all the way back to Skinners' Place.'

That seemed years ago to Tish; so much had happened since. 'I must go,' she said abruptly. 'I mustn't be here when he arrives.'

Kitty hugged her goodbye. 'Wish I could miss him,' she said.

In point of fact, Henry did not reach Hampden

Square until quite late the following evening. The evidence of Kitty's pregnancy was all too apparent to him, for his memory had preserved so slim an image of her. It acted as an efficient brake on any immediate compassion which might have influenced him.

She offered her hand in greeting, and retreated from the kiss he was considering. 'I have made up your double bed,' she told him politely. 'I sleep in the back room.'

'You always use that room?'

'Always. I like a single bed.' Tish had helped with the removal of Kitty's scanty possessions into Mary's back bedroom to leave the double bed free for Henry.

'I thought we might go out for dinner,' he said, 'before we get down to business.'

'You do as you please. I shall have mine here.'

'You used to like eating out.'

She used to like a lot of things. 'I prefer to eat at home, but don't let me stop you from dining elsewhere.'

He shrugged. 'I'm sure your food will be excellent. I was trying to put off the discussion until later.'

'That was obvious.' She went about her work, setting the table for their evening meal. 'Did you have a nice trip?'

'Very good.' He was feeling awkward, faced by her off-putting coolness, and could think of no topic to keep the talk going. 'Are you keeping well?'

'Nothing to complain of.'

'Good.' He stood with his back to the kitchen fire; he might have been Hezekiah Skinner. 'Do you usually eat in here?'

'Oh, I'm sorry. I haven't lit the fire in the dining room, but I can do.'

He begged her not to bother. 'The room will be chilly. Tomorrow night, perhaps.'

Tomorrow night. And the next, and the next. . . . Surely he didn't have to stay the whole week? 'When are you going back?' she enquired.

He laughed. 'Ten minutes after I arrive, and she asks when I am going back!'

There was enough suggestion of the old teasing in his voice to make her move quickly away.

'I shall go as soon as my affairs are settled,' he told her.

That was what he always said.

The vegetable soup had been good; the cold meats and salad were first class.

'You can have a hot meal tomorrow,' Kitty offered, as he dealt with his apple pie and cream, 'but you must let me know what time you will need it.'

'Thank you. You seem to manage splendidly on the money. This food is delicious.'

'It's special because you are here, and it kept all right because we've had a cold weekend. I thought you might be coming yesterday.'

He took his coffee in the sitting room. It was the first time Kitty had made coffee; the hand-grinder had been heavy going, and the result was paler than Henry would have liked, but no doubt she would improve. He could look forward to a better cup tomorrow night; with luck, he should be on his way by mid-week to fit in one damnably brief interval in Cassis. Why in God's name did Eric have to choose a place that meant hours of travel, and did nothing for his health? Unless that artists' colony was still going strong, of course; that could be keeping him merry and bright.

Kitty saw to the dishes, and tidied the kitchen, alone. He heard her go upstairs. As she came out of her bedroom, he pushed her back towards the bed, and in spite of her resistance, pinned her down, kneeling above her.

'You'll hurt the baby!' she cried out frantically, and for that same reason she kept still, to avoid further damage.

I will not cry, she told herself, on the way to the bathroom; he was not to be given that satisfaction. *Easy Kitty – easy for a ride – I've called for the rent!* How was she to rejoin him, for pity's sake, and talk to him?

While he lay on his back on the single bed, Henry idly opened the shallow drawer of the chamber-stand. One pair of brown leather gloves, one phial of Purple Orchis, one blue satin sachet of lavender. . . . The gloves were not nearly as elegant as those he had bought for her, though they were quite good. What had happened to the other pair? She was indeed doing well on the money. At the back of the drawer, he saw a small grey card. He pulled it out and read the pencilled inscription: *513 (2)*, and on the line below, *Olive Mary Gibbs/ age 12 weeks*. He turned the pasteboard over to examine the mounted portrait, with its flowing gold embellishment: *Parisian Studios / 12 Hanover Street / Laverport*. So this was the Gibson baby. No, the Gibbs baby. A fat child. And these were Mary's belongings, of course, in what was still Mary's room. On the other hand, Mary might have given the photograph to Kitty: and that cheap bottle of scent could have been Kitty's; she had never shown much taste in soap, for instance. He joined her eventually in the kitchen.

'I want no more of that,' she informed him icily. 'I shan't be staying here, if it means that sort of payment.'

'I apologize,' he said stiffly. 'If I'm still in Laverport tomorrow, I shall sleep in an hotel.'

'You have a right to your own room in your own house. I am just asking you to leave me alone.'

He bowed his head a moment and examined his fingernails. 'I can say all there is to say quite shortly; we don't need to meet after tonight.' The finality of this shook her control. It could have been that her own principles were not as strong as she thought, or perhaps she had wanted the prerogative in coldness, while hoping he would summon up warmth enough to propose marriage. To her shame, her eyes had filled with tears; tears were the last thing he liked.

'You don't know what you've done, do you?' she said.

'How do you mean, *done*?'

'I thought it was love. I thought you were a gentleman.' She wiped her eyes angrily on her cuff.

'Life isn't a romantic novel,' he said flatly, 'and gentlemen don't come as a separate species. I have no recollection of giving any promises. Now, if you will just let me explain the agreement. . . .'

It was to be a legal settlement, and she would receive her copy of it in due course from his lawyers. Kitty and her child could live rent-free for life in this house, and he would continue to pay for heat and light, within reason. On the death of both, the vacant possession reverted to Henry, or to his heirs. She would continue to receive £10 per calendar month, also for life. After the birth, she would be paid one extra pound per week, until the child reached school age, when a reserve fund of £40 per annum would be available to cover school fees, uniform, books and other expenses, either at St Joseph's Convent, or at St Bede's School for Boys. All this was reeled off to her mechanically. Henry had mulled over it with such thoroughness, he had it by heart.

Kitty jibbed at his last requirement. 'No child of mine goes to a Catholic school,' she said.

Henry had anticipated this. 'You may choose any school you please,' he said. 'The extra money applies only if the child goes to St Joseph's or St Bede's.'

'But you're no Catholic,' she argued, 'and neither am I! It doesn't make sense.'

'Those schools give a sounder education than most. I would like the child to be well disciplined from the start.'

'How do you know about their sounder education, as you call it? I suppose this is the famous Eric's idea?'

'Not at all. As far as I know, Eric has no interest in child education.'

'But he's a Roman Catholic, with that big gold cross of his.'

Henry smiled wearily. 'Eric has a few Russian icons, too. They don't make him a member of the Orthodox Church. I would remind you that you are the one with the Roman Catholic friend. But we shouldn't lose our tempers about schooling when the child is not yet born. You have some years before you decide what to do.'

He had the same number of years in which to change his mind. Kitty looked with bewilderment at the man she would never fathom.

As the months passed, Mary was growing increasingly morose. Her savings were at an end, and every attempt to find work had drawn a blank. Unlike Kitty and Tish, she had no impressive reference to wave around. As a last resort she thought of throwing herself on the mercy of Mr and Mrs Skinner. She had no hope of being taken back at the Bridgemouth Drapery Bazaar, but she would beg for a testimonial on the grounds that she had done a good job in Baby Linen, could be trusted not to steal and was at all times a well-mannered lady assistant. Surely having a baby without a husband didn't wipe out everything?

She was more than earning her keep at Hampden Square, as Kitty was at pains to emphasize; and when Kitty's time came, Mary was sure to prove invaluable. However, she was determined to bring money into the house; to be sharing Kitty's monthly £10 was a worry to her; it was a way of life she had to remedy somehow, without taking to those awful streets again.

Accordingly, shod in a pair of shoes sufficiently good to impress Jinny Skinner, and wearing a close-fitting navy costume, to bring a light to the appreciative eye of Hezekiah, she left Olive Mary in the care of Kitty, and made her way across the water to Bridgemouth.

It was a journey bound to be overloaded with traumatic recollections, not unmixed with the same terror she had felt when travelling away from the Bazaar. In spite of what experience had taught her since then, she was still unable to contemplate this interview without a tremor. She tried to take her mind off it by concentrating on another of those hovering seagulls, and on Tish's Auntie Marj, who was beginning to figure in Mary's estimation, too, as a woman of sound common sense.

'Don't I know you?' A middle-aged man, immaculately dressed, was smiling down at her.

'You do not,' Mary replied with disquiet and went to sit inside the passenger saloon, where the atmosphere was stuffy but safer.

Walking up Ferry Hill, she bent her steps towards those old streets which led to the market square. More and more nervous with every minute, she passed by Dooley's Whelks into the longer street, where Tish had once indulged in public vomiting. Turning the last corner into Albert Road West, she saw the side alley, nearly opposite Atkinson and Atkinson Ltd, that led to the Drapery Bazaar's back door. A wave of faintness swept over her, obliging her to stand still. As her head cleared, she was amazed to see how much shabbier the road seemed, after the impressive shopping walks of Laverport. And how *small* these shops were! Even the flourishing Atkinsons' would have counted for nothing in the city. As for the Bazaar, whatever had happened to it? She crossed the road to reach the establishment, walking with firmer step to its first window. Looking through the dirty glass, she took in the broken partition, the bare shelves, the floor pale with dust, the mahogany hall door now aslant on one hinge, the hall floor carpetless, the wallpaper torn here and there and hanging like tired battle-flags. Skinners' Place was no more.

The three girls sat drinking tea in no. 28's sitting room. All three faces were glum, but since that abortive journey to Bridgemouth, Mary had been the most seriously depressed. For her, the Skinners' disappearance off the trading map had proved a blow almost equal to any rejection of her services, for the former had not been anticipated.

That disappearance, while more or less expected by Kitty and Tish, had in fact affected these two more than either would have thought possible. It revived memories of an existence which, though rigorous enough, had often broken down to let the sunlight through. It reminded them of a united foursome unfamiliar to Mary.

'I wonder how Cissy and Eliza are doing?' Tish said quietly. 'Seems ages since we nipped into Masons' that Wednesday and said goodbye.'

'Funny, I was just going to say that. We only saw Eliza, anyway.' Kitty glanced across at Mary, who had flushed. 'We know you'd plenty of reason to hate Eliza,' she said to her. 'Tish and me used to loathe her as much as you did, but she improved. She was a changed character.'

'That she was,' Tish added.

'I suppose Cissy Whatyoum'callit suited her better than me,' said Mary, heavily.

This was so manifestly right, her companions had trouble concocting a straight reply.

'They both came from Bridgemouth,' said Kitty. 'That gave Cissy a pull over the rest of us.'

'You'd have liked Cissy,' Tish put in.

'She wouldn't have liked me.'

Kitty thought this one over for a space. 'You're wrong there. Cissy Bingle was a proper baby sometimes, with all that giggling, but in many ways she was old for her age – rather wise, I'd say.'

'She was. You'd have liked Cissy,' Tish repeated.

'Then why don't you ask them round? Why don't you let them give me and Olive Mary the once-over? They must have talked about me often enough, the pair of them.' Her teacup had smacked down on the low table, tilted in its saucer, and Mary was at the door before Tish stopped her.

'Nobody's asking them round here,' said Tish, 'so come and sit down.'

Kitty was sorry she and Tish had spoken. 'You don't think I want them to see me like this? Or afterwards, either? You know how it is – I don't care, and yet I do. All the time it's at the back of your mind that you've been a fool, and the proof is there for everyone to see.'

'Yes, I know how it is.' Mary came back to her chair.

'It's cowardly, but I'd rather those two remembered me as I was. Pathetic, aren't I?'

'No, you're not pathetic,' said Mary. 'You're just another who's been left in the cart.'

'Cups! Come on!' Tish demanded briskly. 'Let's forget about carts.' She took the few crocks out to the scullery. 'Can you tell me why we waste time yattering about girls we'll never see again?' she called back. 'Eliza and Cissy, they've got their life; we've got ours; and the river's in between. Whoever heard of visiting friends across the water?'

'Leave those pots, will you?' Kitty returned. 'You spend your life washing up.' She raised her voice to compete with the high pressure of tap water. 'This house may be here to be used, but you're not to wear out that sink.'

Tish came as far as the sitting-room doorway, holding the dishcloth.

'That's it!' Kitty cried, smacking her own forehead hard, and jumping up in excitement. 'Of course! It's here to be used! I'll write and ask him.'

'You'll ask who what?' said Tish, looking alarmed.

'Henry kept a lodger, didn't he, even if Budge never paid up? Why can't we? Mary can be resident as a member of staff. We'll fill the empty rooms with officers like him, so he won't complain, and we'll get one advert into the *Courier* and one in Saturday's *Express*. When things are fixed, you can give Dilk's the go-by, Tish. That's if you want to?'

For once, Tish was not carried away by Kitty's inspiration. These marvellous schemes had a nasty habit of going wrong; this one was so very wonderful, how could it come to anything? The kibosh would be worse than ever when it came; it would be cruel; but if the idea worked . . . if it did. . . . She looked across at Mary, whose face had lit up with hope.

'Well?' Kitty demanded, a shade put out.

'It would be heaven,' Mary said, 'just heaven.'

'You wouldn't want to leave Dilk's, then?' Kitty said to Tish.

Tish flung most of her misgivings overboard; her eyes were as brightly open as a wax doll's. 'I want to, all right,' she replied, 'but will Henry Bonham stand for that?'

'He'll stand for it,' Kitty said, regaining her good humour. 'He's got no choice. There's nothing in the paper I signed that's against it. Leastways, I don't think there is. Would you get rid of that dishcloth? You look on the warpath.'

Kitty fetched her copy of the signed settlement; nowhere did it stipulate that she must not use the premises for business purposes; and there was already one other house in Hampden Square where lodgers with pretensions to 'class' were taken. Between them, the three girls drew up the advertisement copies for Mary to take to town on the Monday.

There are some days that have no intention of going right. Kitty had been kept waiting a while for this letter from home. Now that it was waiting for her in the wire letter-catcher on the door, with her father's laboured handwriting uppermost, she made no move to retrieve it. Instead, she opened the door and put the covered milk jug on the step. Straightening up, she stood gazing across at the suggestion of a garden in the centre of the square, with its sparse trees, its step-over railing and the well-trodden grass. Not for the first time, she wished Hampden Square had a real garden, one that required a real key.

Shivering a little, she moved back, closing the door

slowly. Her father wrote so rarely; this was why the sight of his writing, rather than her mother's, was disturbing. She pulled the letter quickly from its cage and tore it open.

The message left her dazed. Maybe she had expected it? Yet not so long ago she had thought differently, when rating her own mum and dad at a higher level than Mary's. This letter went to show that where it was a question of loss of face, the Catchpole parents were no better than the Gibbs.

Dan Catchpole's contemptuous dismissal of his daughter was in proportion to the inordinate love he had always professed for her. Her mother shared his opinion, he wrote – after all they had done for her – and neither wished to set eyes on Kitty again. (That went deep; she and her mother had been so close.) Nor was she to send any more postal orders; they could do without her tainted money. They would be glad if she did not try writing to her young brother and sister who, they prayed, would not turn out a disgrace to the family. With Rosie all set to get taken on next year at the Plâs, and Georgie promised full time, no scandal was wanted to ruin their chances in the village: *yours truly*, he signed off, *Daniel George Catchpole*.

'Oh, no!' breathed Kitty. 'No, not that on top of it!' The miserable ache, which had been dogging her since the small hours, had decided to change character. She held on to the doorknob for a while, then she walked heavily upstairs to hand her letter without comment to Mary, to take her wedding ring out of the Dorothy bag, and to struggle quickly into her nightdress.

But for Mary's calm efficiency on the day of Kitty's extremity, the first two gentlemen-residents would have had a thin time of it. Neither, as it happened, was a merchant officer; one was a retired widower, profession as yet undisclosed, who occupied the back bedroom in what seemed to be an apologetic manner; the second was a youngish man, working in accounts, it was thought, at the new University College. He lived and slept in what had been Eric Cannon-Budge's sitting room. Kitty, Mary and Olive Mary slept on the top floor: it was like old times, to be once more in the attics.

Mary always maintained that if Kitty had not lugged that bed single-handed down to Eric's room, instead of waiting until Mary had returned from the greengrocer's, things would never have gone wrong. This had probably nothing to do with it.

Out of respect for their lodgers' comfort, should they be indoors, and out of an odd pride that forbade groaning aloud, Kitty rolled in silent agony on Henry's double bed. Mary had sensibly bundled her into that room for the emergency. The doctor said he would come back later. The midwife rushed home to put on her Irish stew, which she left in charge of a nine-year-old daughter; this child was fortunately off school with a septic heel and could be trusted to feed the other two when they came home.

Kitty lost count of time, and looked forward to its end.

'I was yelling the place down,' said Mary in admiration. 'I don't know how you can keep so quiet; and I had long waits in between – not like this.'

The midwife and doctor had words. The doctor told her to keep her place; he would attend to the medical side. His wife had invited friends to dinner; he would come back when something was happening.

A man walked past the house, whistling. Kitty heard him, and one low murmur of hatred escaped her. 'Death! Death! Oh, Death!' she prayed wildly. 'Death! Oh, Christ, I can't, I can't.'

The midwife said what she'd do to men, if she had her way, and she was going round to that doctor's, if he never gave her a case again.

It was cold in the room; the gas mantle roared in its yellow globe. Kitty lay motionless in bed. The doctor said how fortunate she was to have got through it so quickly – a mere ten hours; and she was possibly better off without a baby – *eh, Mrs Catchpole*?

Kitty heard the click of the front door, and Mary's hurried step to the back of the house. She would be giving the midwife a cup of tea, if that poor woman had time to drink it. Kitty was not interested in tea; she was not interested in anything. What a God-forsaken day. What a hell-fire, God-forsaken day. Bully for gentleman Henry! Mrs Catchpole removed the wedding ring from her finger and let it drop to the floor. It rolled in an aimless curve, before settling for a generous crack in the floorboards.

Tish had become frantic with self-recrimination. 'I should have left Dilk's earlier,' she wept, 'and been here with you.'

'Nobody could have done more than Mary,' Kitty said, struggling to say something, in spite of a crushing despondency.

'Mary shouldn't have had all that to do, and look after the men and Baby Olive. It was too much for her.'

'No, it wasn't,' said Mary touchily, coming into the bedroom. 'We managed all right.'

'You being here or at Dilk's made not a blind bit of

difference,' Kitty said in a tired voice from the bed. 'My baby would have been dead, anyway. It's no good fretting, Tish. Besides, we all agreed you were staying on at Dilk's till I had the baby.'

'We did an' all,' said Tish, wiping her running nose. 'And now there's no Baby Catchpole for me to see to, what d'you tell Henry Bonham about me living here?'

'We'll tell him nothing,' Mary told her crisply. 'Not until we have to.'

'That's right,' said Kitty, with a listless attempt at normal energy. 'Not a word to the vicar. You get your notice in at Dilk's, Tish-girl. Soon as I'm up, we'll advertise for more lodgers.'

'But what if he *asks*?' Tish persisted.

'Well, you'll be looking after Olive Mary, on top of doing everything else.' Kitty turned over on her side, as if going to sleep.

'Why Olive Mary? He won't swallow that!' Tish glanced at Mary, who shrugged her shoulders.

'Look, I'm done to the wide,' Kitty pleaded. 'There's a letter from my dad somewhere. Have a read of it, Tish.'

Her two friends tucked her in and left her to rest. No doubt she was wandering about Olive Mary, which they could understand, after losing a baby.

'I will help with little Olive,' Tish said to Mary, when they were in the kitchen. 'I'll be only too pleased.'

'I know you will,' Mary said. 'I expect that's what she meant, only she couldn't think straight.'

'It's not like Kitty, not to think straight, no matter how poorly she is. Where's that letter she talked about?'

Tish leaned on the sitting-room table, the letter from Kitty's father in her hand. Mary had returned upstairs to attend to a hungry baby. Tish found it hard to believe that a father could write these cruel words; she knew how much Kitty loved him, too. To sling her out like this! It was nothing short of wicked – just like Mary's mam and dad. This must be what Protestants did; they couldn't get forgiveness, and they couldn't give it. Her own dad would never write a letter like that, even if he could write. There was a row in the Kelly house, once, when Biddy had got caught out that first time, but it was what you might call a good-tempered row, with their mam bawling what sort of a flaming-fool daughter had she got, to be three months gone before she as much as let on – then lots of hugs and crying all round, as Mother Kelly called in a friendly lady of the parish to fix it. Ah, religion was a tremendous thing, and the longer Tish lived, the more she saw the beauty of the one True Faith.

They had to wait until Kitty had been some weeks on her feet to learn if her mind had really been wandering. It had, but merely in one well-ordered circle.

When finally she revealed her meaning to Tish and Mary, they heard her in silence. There was so much in it that was attractive to all concerned, yet so much that could go wrong, that neither girl dared venture an opinion. Against all bounds of possibility, here they were installed in this lovely house with Kitty, and they were afraid to push their luck further. However, when Kitty explained things in that tough way of hers, it was often impossible to hold out against her. Mary admitted that the plan was very much in her child's favour, if Tish didn't mind being dragged into it. Tish could see no great burden for herself in that, but felt driven to ask once more what would happen if Henry Bonham found out.

Kitty dismissed that. 'He's only interested in keeping

his name out of it,' she said bitterly, 'and in paying me to play ball, so I can't see him making any enquiries, ever.'

'She's in for a nasty eye-opener one day, when she's asked for her birth certificate,' Mary said, stroking Olive Mary's soft blonde hair.

'Can't we just lose it?' Tish asked. 'Perhaps we could get a different one with Kitty's name on it.'

'We could not,' said Kitty. 'No mucking about with things like that. We'll *say* she's Olive Mary Catchpole, and that'll have to be it. There's nothing against that. Schools don't want birth certificates, do they? I thought they only wanted the fees.'

'She'll be all right at St Joseph's,' Tish said with confidence. 'You'll get all the understanding you want from the Sisters. They're always women of the world.'

'It's a good while off, anyway,' said Mary, finding comfort in distance. 'Right. I'm her auntie, Kitty's her mum, and we'll tell her when we've got to.'

'When she's old enough to know what's what,' Kitty agreed.

Tish handed the baby's photograph to Kitty; she had been trying to erase all trace of pencil-writing off the back. 'You can still read it.'

'It wasn't half hard, this pencil,' Kitty sighed. 'Rub it with the handle of a knife.'

Tish went to work with the breadknife. 'Now it's all shiny,' she said. 'Look at it.'

'Give it another do with the rubber,' Mary suggested. 'Yes, that's better.'

'I'm leaving the number on it.'

'Of course,' said Kitty. 'That can stay. Let's have it, then.' She inspected the erasure closely. 'I don't know. . . . You can see it's rubbed out. I'm not sending it like that. Where's the scissors?' She cut neatly round the oval portrait; shorn of its outer mount, it was very small, but at least it bore no sign of Mary's inscription. With care, Kitty wrote the new legend on the back: *Olive Mary Catchpole, ten weeks old*.

'Twelve weeks,' Mary corrected.

'Ten. I must send if off soon. What's two weeks? If I'd put ten days, he wouldn't question it. Men notice nothing.'

'It's the gear, Kitty,' said Tish at last, 'if you can get away with it.'

'I'm not getting away with anything,' Kitty told her sharply. 'I feel it's my right, and it's Mary's right. Henry Bonham's got the money; he can pay his own debt and Bunny Harris's. Little Olive will have a start in life, which is more than we had, any of us.'

'You don't mind about St Joseph's, either of you?' said Tish, still uncertain.

'Not now,' Kitty replied. 'I don't, if Mary doesn't.'

Mary smiled. 'If he says it's a good school. . . . I'm getting more worried about what he'll say when he hears the house is full of lodgers.'

If Kitty had private qualms about Olive Mary's future, should Henry discover the truth, then she kept them gamely to herself. For the other girls, her short argument had carried authority. They, too, were prepared to meet the worst if and when it arrived. Not one of the three felt the slightest diffidence in accepting for the baby, and for themselves, a chance made possible by someone who thought himself a cut above their kind. Olive Mary Catchpole was to prove the answer to him. Their theory of education being splendidly vague, they all believed that a child in attendance at a 'good' school, over a decent period of years, must ultimately emerge brimful of information and crammed with culture; never did it occur to them that Olive

Mary might turn out to be rebellious, lazy or downright slow. She was destined to become a paragon of the virtues, educational or otherwise, and in the full glory of this remarkable state she might one day stand on the domestic threshold of Henry Bonham and confound him with a refined shout of 'Father!'

Kitty's letter caught up with Henry in Singapore. Eric had sent it on from Cassis. He was in no hurry to open it, as he sat with his whisky in the greeny shade of the Palm Court. He was in the hotel he loved best; palm fronds and the frail bougainvillaea trembled in the slight breeze; he was not reminded of those other palm fronds, in a different setting. A letter from Eric lay in his pocket. He took it out and read it again. At last his friend's health was improving. Henry studied the pages with pleasure, smiling at the sly wit, and at the affection they contained. Eric was still resenting the sea's claim on Henry, and would certainly never rest until this had been rejected positively, in favour of his own.

The captain had appeared at a far table. They waved to each other. A young stranger joined the Old Man. Henry had not seen this handsome specimen before. He picked Kitty's letter off the table, and opened it.

His reaction showed so clearly in his face that the hovering waiter made himself scarce. How could he have been such a blasted idiot? He had no copy of the agreement with him, but needed none; he realized too well that no veto on lodgers had been included. Damn Miss Catchpole and her smart ruses to get Mary Gibson nicely established in his house! In all probability, she had Tish Kelly on the premises, to boot. And yet — this hint that his allowance was insufficient might have some point; it was not much for Kitty and her child, even if most of their class would consider it a fortune. Her parents had apparently washed their hands of her; he could do nothing about that. But if she wished to earn a living, why should he prevent her? It would certainly save too great a drain on his purse. He emptied his glass and went in search of pen and paper.

Dear Kitty,

Your letter has reached me in Singapore. I am glad that you and your baby are well. You do not mention the child's name!

I was rather disconcerted when I read that you propose going into business. I trust the number of lodgers will be kept to a minimum, so that the private nature of the property can be preserved. It goes without saying that only men of officer class, or their equivalent in the professions, may be admitted to my house.

I shall be interested to hear, from time to time, of both the child's progress and your own.

Yours sincerely,
Henry Bonham.

He ran cursorily through Kitty's letter with much the same displeasure as before. He folded it and tried to return it to the envelope. It refused to fit because of a small obstruction; shaking this out, he saw it was an oval of grey pasteboard, bearing Kitty's handwriting: *Olive Mary Catchpole, ten weeks old*. With some curiosity, he turned the scrap over; the fat Gibson baby stared back at him. Henry's laughter was so unrestrained, and went on for such a time, that the skipper came to investigate.

'I thought it could only be you! You can't sit there, Henry, laughing your head off! Come back, and have a drink with us. We can all share the joke.'

'In a minute, sir,' Henry said, sobering down. 'I'll be

there, but it's a very secret joke. I shan't be telling it to anyone – ever.'

'Mean boy! Hurry up!'

Henry took up his pen once more. The exit door was open to him; he could wreck her little game with two or three nicely turned lines and that would be the end of the episode. The best liar in Skinners' Place had failed again. For one brief moment, he was retying the tulle scarf about that bent brim. Wiping an inky wisp off the end of his Waverley nib, and picking up an irritating blob of blotting paper in the process, he wrestled with his conflicting feelings, and cursed the captain's attempt to hustle him.

Finally, with the nib in better trim, Henry Bonham added his postscript:

P.S. I have just discovered the little portrait. Your Olive Mary seems a thriving infant for her age. As a mere man, I would have thought her at least a couple of weeks older.
H.B.

HESTER DARK

Emma Blair

Even to a girl from the slums of Bristol, the streets of Glasgow were inhospitable and grey; the wealth and splendour of its mansions cold and heartless. But for Hester there could be no turning back – she would make this cruel city the home of her dreams.

Everyone said that Hester was lucky. Lucky to have a wealthy uncle in Scotland who was willing to take her in. Lucky to have all the advantages that his money could buy. But Hester's new, bright world held dark secrets, jealousies and fears. And no one had spoken of the woman who would despise her for her beauty and her independence – and the men who would buy her soul and call it love.

THE RUNNING YEARS

Claire Rayner

She was born in 1893, in the slums of London. The daughter of immigrants, the descendants of exiles, she was part of a people doomed to wander, forever strangers in the lands they had chosen as home.

But Hannah Lazar was different. She was born and bred a Londoner, and London was where she belonged. As Strong-willed as she was beautiful, Hannah would uproot herself from the gloomy poverty of her parents' lives to enter a world of elegance and wealth. As her ancestors had journeyed from land to land, with only their own resilience and determination to help them survive, Hannah would move from the slums of the East End to the salons of Mayfair, to a life that she could call her own.

The Running Years is Claire Rayner's most powerful and spectacular novel to date, a breathtaking testament to the human spirit – a richly dramatic and intricately woven story that traces the fortunes of two Jewish families from the razing of Jerusalem in 70 AD through two thousand years of violence, love and change.

'A huge canvas, this, with powerful characters and a gripping story' *Woman's own*

'A feast' *Yorkshire Post*

BESTSELLING FICTION FROM ARROW

All these books are available from your bookshop or news-agent or you can order them direct. Just tick the titles you want and complete the form below.

☐	THE COMPANY OF SAINTS	Evelyn Anthony	£1.95
☐	HESTER DARK	Emma Blair	£1.95
☐	1985	Anthony Burgess	£1.75
☐	2001: A SPACE ODYSSEY	Arthur C. Clarke	£1.75
☐	NILE	Laurie Devine	£2.75
☐	THE BILLION DOLLAR KILLING	Paul Erdman	£1.75
☐	THE YEAR OF THE FRENCH	Thomas Flanagan	£2.50
☐	LISA LOGAN	Marie Joseph	£1.95
☐	SCORPION	Andrew Kaplan	£2.50
☐	SUCCESS TO THE BRAVE	Alexander Kent	£1.95
☐	STRUMPET CITY	James Plunkett	£2.95
☐	FAMILY CHORUS	Claire Rayner	£2.50
☐	BADGE OF GLORY	Douglas Reeman	£1.95
☐	THE KILLING DOLL	Ruth Rendell	£1.95
☐	SCENT OF FEAR	Margaret Yorke	£1.75

Postage _____

Total _____

ARROW BOOKS, BOOKSERVICE BY POST, PO BOX 29, DOUGLAS, ISLE OF MAN, BRITISH ISLES

Please enclose a cheque or postal order made out to Arrow Books Limited for the amount due including 15p per book for postage and packing both for orders within the UK and for overseas orders.

Please print clearly

NAME ....

ADDRESS ....

....

Whilst every effort is made to keep prices down and to keep popular books in print, Arrow Books cannot guarantee that prices will be the same as those advertised here or that the books will be available.